D1825320

A HOLIDAY CHRISTMAS ROMANCE

A SEASON OF DESIRE BOXSET

MICHELLE LOVE

HOT AND STEAMY ROMANCE

CONTENTS

❀ Created with Vellum

SECRETS & DESIRES

A CHRISTMAS ROMANCE (SEASON OF DESIRE 1)

Rule number one in my job: Don't fall in love with a customer. Never.

But, of course, That's what I did. Nox Renaud is perhaps the richest entrepreneur in New Orleans.

But he's also the most stunning, attractive and seductive man I've ever met. And he wants me.

Every time he touches me and is in me, it feels heavenly.

It's pure ecstasy.

Our love is so pure, so real, so animalistic ...

Nothing will divide us, not even the dark forces that threaten us.

Nothing and no one will be able to stop me from loving this man forever ...

CHAPTER ONE

Amber Duplas squinted at her oldest and dearest friend as he handed her a plate of perfectly-cooked eggs. "Nox Renaud, you are a pain in my ass."

Nox, his green eyes amused, grinned at her. "Well then, my work here is done. But why?"

Amber sighed and bunched her auburn hair up into a ponytail. "You're one of the wealthiest land owners in New Orleans, an incredibly successful businessman, *and*—according to Forbes —one of the world's most eligible bachelors. And yet you stand in your own palatial kitchen ..." she gestured around the vast room, "cooking me eggs for brunch *yourself*. Haven't you heard of chefs?"

Nox shook his head. He was used to this line of questioning from Amber. "You know I don't like a lot of people around me, Ambs."

Amber forked some egg into her mouth, almost swooning at the taste. "Which is why you're a pain. I'm worried that you'll become a hermit."

"I think hermithood arrived a while ago," Nox said mildly. "Look, I know you mean well, but I'm nearly forty, and I'm set in my ways. I like being alone." He dumped a panful of eggs onto his own plate and sat down. "And anyway, in a few days, the best and brightest will be here to drink my champagne and bother me all night. God, why do I do this every year?" He groaned and Amber laughed.

"Such a Grinch." She ruffled his dark curls and he grinned, though he was sighing on the inside. The Renaud family had given a Halloween charity benefit since way before Nox's birth—it had been a special project of his beloved mother's. Before the tragedy, of course. Despite his solitary nature, Nox could not bear to dishonor his mother's legacy.

His eyes flicked over to the framed picture of her and Teague, his adored elder brother, on the kitchen counter. Both of them dark and beautiful, laughing and hugging. Both of them gone so senselessly.

The tragedy of the Renaud family was known throughout Louisiana and beyond. Tynan Renaud, a respected business-man, adoring husband to the Italian-born Gabriella, and heroic father to his sons Teague and Nox, had suffered a psychotic break and gunned down his wife and eldest son one night before turning the gun on himself. Nox, away at college at the time, had been destroyed. After dropping out of school and coming home to the huge plantation mansion out on the Bayou, he had struggled for years to understand what his father had done.

Amber and his other friends had tried to persuade him to sell the place where his mother and brother had been murdered, but Nox refused. He took over his brother's business with his friend Sandor, and together, they had made a success of it. The company, RenCar, quickly became an outlet to forget his pain, with Nox pouring twenty hours a day into the work. Luxury food importing had never been his dream—was it anyone's?—but he had found something he was good at, and that was enough for him. His boyhood dreams of becoming a musician were pushed aside for something that would utterly distract him. The studio his mother had set aside for both of them to work in had stood empty for almost twenty years now ... as had Nox's heart.

He realized he wasn't listening to Amber now and apologized. She rolled her blue eyes. "Nox, I'm used to you spacing out on me, but listen, this is your party. I'm just saying, why don't you try to be more gregarious for a change? These people pay a lot of money to come here."

"Mostly to see the murder house," he mumbled, and Amber made an annoyed click with her tongue.

"Maybe so, but the money we raise goes to a good cause, doesn't it? Something good to come out of—damn it, Nox, you're not the only one who lost someone." To his horror, he saw tears in her eyes. He reached over and took her hand.

"Ambs, I'm sorry, I know. I miss Ariel too, every day." He sighed. *So much pain, so much death.* Amber was right; he needed to get out of this self-pitying funk.

"All I ask is for you to do your part on the night. Mingle and talk to your guests." Amber's tone was calmer now and she smiled at him, her face soft and her eyes on his, holding them for a beat too long. Nox nodded, looking away finally.

"I promise."

After Amber had gone, he wandered into his living room and flicked on the television. Local news station WDSU was doing a feature on Halloween New Orleans, the magical, manic mayhem of the festival the city threw every October. Nox sighed and waited for the inevitable mention of his party. "Wait for it," he muttered to himself. "Will it be the *Renaud Family Curse* or the *Mansion with the Dark Secrets*, first?"

The anchor looked serious. "Of course, before the festivities kick off on Halloween night, the New Orleans elite will gather at the Renaud mansion out on the Bayou. Regular viewers will know that the annual *Creepy Cocktails Gala Benefit* is held every year at the place some locals call 'the mansion with a dark history.' More on that after these messages."

Nox clicked off the television with an annoyed flick of his hand. Same story every year, and now his guests who watched the news would be all the more curious about the only remaining Renaud. *Damn it.*

His cellphone rang and he answered it gratefully. "Sandor, man, you have impeccable timing."

His friend laughed. "Any time. Listen, we may have a deal on the Laurent restaurant chain."

Nox sat up. "Really?" The Laurent business was worth twice what they had offered, but had been on the market for two years with no interest. Nox knew if they got it at a cheap price and refurbished it, it could make them a fortune. He and Sandor had decided to branch out into buying restaurants to serve their luxury foods as a new income stream—not that either of them needed it, but they both were bored with their business. They wanted to get their hands dirty and *do* something—something physical rather than just importing food for, well, people like them.

"Yep. Gustav Laurent is getting a divorce and he wants to get rid of the property quickly."

Nox was astonished. "*Gus* is divorcing *Kathryn*?"

"Seems so. Seems like she was sleeping around on him."

Nox made a half-amused, half-scornful noise. "Like Gustav hasn't been fucking around on her for years."

"You know Gus."

"Sadly, yes. Listen, I can be there in a half hour."

"Good," Sandor replied. "And, afterward, I'll spot you lunch. Deal?"

Nox smiled down the phone. "Deal. See you then."

. . .

LIVIA CHATELAINE BALANCED three plates expertly along her left arm and carried them to the table. The two women and the child seated at the table smiled gratefully at her as she laid their food in front of them and returned their grins. "Enjoy, folks. Let me know if you need anything else."

She skirted back to another table that was waiting for their check and settled up with them quickly and with her innate friendliness. She had been working at Le Chat Noir café in the French Quarter for three months now, ever since she had packed her whole life into her battered old Gremlin and driven across the country from San Diego.

Moriko, her best friend from college, had been in New Orleans for a year and had gotten her the job at the café—it didn't hurt that the owner, a handsome, dark-haired Frenchman called Marcel, had a huge crush on Moriko and would have hired *anyone* she recommended. Thankfully, though, Livia and Marcel had become good friends, and Livia showed up early, stayed late, and worked her ass off for him. In return, he gave her the shifts that fit best with her studies and paid her enough that she could afford the tiny apartment she shared with Moriko.

Livia had decided as she left San Diego that she wouldn't return to her hometown again. It held no interest for her now, and there wasn't any family left there that she cared about. An only child, her mother had died when she was young, and Livia had brought herself up. She'd worked hard at school and at various jobs to put food on the table, while her father drank himself into a stupor every night and screamed at her if she disturbed him. Livia had stopped caring years ago about the man. As far as she was concerned, he was merely the sperm donor. What she remembered of her mother were warm, happy memories. Cancer was a fucker and it had stolen her happiness away when she was five. Livia's last memory of her mother was of the beautiful woman kissing her goodbye one day before school, and that was the last time she had seen her. Her father hadn't let her see her after she died.

Livia had put herself through college on a scholarship and by working three jobs, and it had become second nature to always fight and scrape for everything. It gave her energy and reason, and when she had graduated top of her class, it had all been worth it. Her tutors had been loath to let her go and had championed her to apply for post-graduate research scholarships, but it had taken Livia four years to finally secure an offer from the University of New Orleans.

"Hey, dreamer." Moriko nudged Livia out of her reverie and her friend smiled at her. Moriko, a tiny Japanese-American of exquisite beauty— and she knew it—hoisted herself up onto the counter. "Marcel needs a favor."

Livia hid a grin. When Marcel sent Moriko to do his dirty work it meant that, whatever the favor was, it would be a big— and probably inconvenient—one. "What is it?"

"Well, he's been asked to cater the Renaud party on Saturday. You know which one I mean?"

Livia shook her head. "Nope."

Moriko rolled her eyes. "It's an annual thing Nox Renaud does. He throws a Halloween gala party and gives a ton of money to charity."

"Never heard of him, or it. So, what's the favor?" Livia thought she could guess—Marcel needed waitstaff. A moment later, Moriko confirmed her suspicions.

"He was going to hire in silver service staff, but apparently they don't want anything but canapés and cocktails. Silver service staff would cost him more than he's making so ..."

Livia smiled at her. "It's no problem. Usual uniform?" She

pulled down on her too-tight white shirt and tucked it back into the black mini she wore to serve. It barely contained her lush curves—her full breasts and softly curved belly. Her legs, long and slender, were encased in black tights and she wore flat pumps, absolutely refusing to wear heels to wait tables. Livia wasn't the tallest girl, but her long legs made her look taller than her five-five height, and her long tawny waves were her crowning glory. She had pulled her almost waist-length hair into a bun, but it was forever escaping the clips. Moriko grabbed it now and twisted it up for her. Livia shot her a grateful smile. "Thanks, boo. I really should cut it all off."

"No way," Moriko said, her own shiny black hair falling in a straight curtain down her back. "I'd kill for your curls."

"So, Saturday night, waitressing for the rich muckety-mucks?"

"I'll be there too. Hey, at least we get to snoop around the rich guy's house."

Livia sighed to herself. She honestly didn't mind helping Marcel out, but she had very little time for rich boys with too much money. She'd had to wait on them enough in her time.

She went back out to the café and grimaced. Two regulars had just come into the restaurant. *Speaking of rich muckety-mucks,* she thought, plastering a fake smile on her face. The woman, an icy-looking blonde with bright red lipstick and cold blue eyes, looked at her dismissively. "Egg white omelet with spinach and a mangotini." She didn't look at the menu once. Her companion, a suave-looking man who at least smiled at Livia and said please and thank you whenever he was in, nodded.

"Same for me please, Liv. Good to see you again."

Livia smiled at him. She judged him for the company he kept, but if she was fair, he was always polite to her. She knew his companion was called Odelle, and her father was one of the richest men in the state. It didn't impress Livia. "You too, sir. Sure

I can't interest either of you in some French fries to go with your salad?"

Odelle looked horrified, but her companion grinned. "Why not?"

Livia grinned and disappeared into the kitchen. Marcel slunk in and smiled at her. "Thanks for Saturday, Livvy. I'll pay you double."

She kissed his cheek. "No problem, pal."

Marcel, his eyes so dark you couldn't see the pupils, nodded to the restaurant. "I see Elsa and Lumiere are in the restaurant."

Livia laughed. "You're getting your Disney all mixed up, and anyway, he's okay. But, yeah, she is the Ice Queen."

"Don't let their wealth get to you. It was all inherited, not earned."

"Oh, I know, and it doesn't bother me. Money can't buy breeding," Livia shrugged off the woman's rudeness. "I can honestly say these people and their ways don't keep me up at night, Marcel."

"I'm just saying because I know the man, Roan Saintmarc, is Nox Renaud's best friend. It's more than likely they'll be at the party on Saturday." Marcel grinned at Livia, who rolled her eyes. "Just promise me you won't tip their meals into their laps."

Livia snorted. "I promise, honey."

"Good girl."

LIVIA FINISHED OUT HER SHIFT, then walked home through the busy streets of the French Quarter. She had fallen in love with this city—the slow, sensual heat, the sultry, laidback nature of the people. Strangely, for a city known for its voodoo and black magic, she had never felt uneasy walking the streets at night here.

Moriko was still at work when Livia got back to their apartment, so Livia took a long hot shower, then made herself a bowl of soup, grabbing some saltines from the pack in the kitchen. As she ate, she flicked through the television channels, but soon got bored. Dumping her bowl in the sink, she washed it out, then decided to go to bed to read. She had a piano recital coming up and she wanted to go through the score again, miming her key strokes in the air. She fell asleep with Moriko's cat cuddling in next to her and didn't hear her roommate come home.

OUT ON THE BAYOU, Nox too had fallen into a deep sleep, but his was not so peaceful. Almost instantly the nightmares came. A woman, a beautiful young woman he knew but one whose face he could not see, was calling to him, begging him to save her. There was blood, so much blood, and he ran through the darkened mansion, wading through something—blood?—to get to her. A dark, malevolent force overcame everything, stopping Nox from reaching the girl. He heard her screams cut off abruptly and knew he was too late. He sank to his knees.

He felt a hand on his shoulder and looked up. His mother was smiling at him. "Don't you know you'll never save them?" she said softly. "Everyone you love will die, my beloved son. I died, your father, your brother ... Ariel. You'll always be alone."

Nox awoke, gasping for air in a pool of his own sweat, the certainty of his dream mother's words screaming around his mind.

Don't fall in love. Don't risk it. Don't let anyone else get hurt.

CHAPTER TWO

Odelle Griffongy lit another cigarette and stood out on the balcony of her bedroom. She hated this holiday and hated this party. And yet Roan, of course, wanted to support his best friend, Nox, and so now they were getting dressed to attend. Thank *fuck* Nox never had a dress code for the cocktail party—Odelle would have feigned a headache otherwise.

She looked back into the bedroom where Roan was dressing, his dark gray suit spectacular with his coloring—medium brown hair and bright blue eyes. Ripped to the max, his hard body and his huge cock made him a machine in bed. Roan Saintmarc was, with the exception of Nox, the handsomest man in New Orleans—probably the state, even—and he was *hers.*

Odelle might have been brought up in the upper echelons of New Orleans society, but she knew her brittle beauty would only last so long and that her cool, aloof nature wouldn't make her many friends. That's why she was staggered when Roan, known as the fun-loving one in his group of Harvard grad friends, made a play for *her.* He could have had anyone.

Odelle turned back to see the crowds on the streets of the

city. New Orleans went crazy for Halloween—parties everywhere, people haunting the streets, and the locals playing up the myths and legends to sell more drink, food, and tourist crap. The normally serene street where Odelle and her cohorts lived were no different: pumpkins and jack o' lanterns, trees bedecked with twinkle lights and fake cobwebs, and Odelle's least favorite thing: kids trick or treating at every house.

Her doorbell rang, and although Odelle knew her staff would answer it, she couldn't help an irritated, "Oh, fuck off." Her voice carried down to the street, and she heard Roan's throaty laugh from behind her.

"Don't be a bitch, Delly. It's a rite of passage, trick or treating."

Odelle made a disgusted noise. "I never did that."

Roan smiled at her, sliding his arms around her waist. "No, you were too busy casting spells and mixing potions."

Odelle studied him coolly. "You think I'm a witch?"

"Cue cheesy line from me about you casting a spell on me. No, baby, I don't think you're a witch, and—mostly—not even a bitch. You just have a warmth deficiency." He said it with a grin, and although Odelle knew he meant it as a joke, it still stung.

Because it's true, she told herself. *What is wrong with me? Why can't I be more like Roan?* Or Nox, whose heart was so big it actually scared Odelle. Or even Amber, her frenemy, who had once had a thing with Roan. *No,* Odelle told herself. *Don't go there. Not tonight.* She attempted a smile as Roan brushed his lips against hers.

"You're right. It's just one night."

"That's my girl." Roan looked her up and down in her tight black dress and when his gaze met hers, Odelle saw the desire in his eyes. "Nox won't mind if we're a little late."

Odelle smiled and, turning, she bent over the balcony and hitched her skirt up to her waist. She heard Roan chuckle.

"Out here? What *will* the neighbors think?" But then, with a grunt, she felt him thrust into her from behind, his massive cock reaming her cunt as he gripped the metal balustrade with both hands.

Odelle closed her eyes, reveling in the feeling of him filling her so completely. Her hand drifted down to stroke her clit as he fucked her, and soon she was moaning and shivering through one orgasm after another, not caring who heard her. Roan was a brutal lover, especially when he came, and Odelle winced as he thrust harder and harder until he blew his load inside of her and withdrew, panting for air and cursing softly with release. He spun her around and ground his mouth down on hers. "God, woman, you drive me fucking crazy."

Odelle smiled and squeezed his diminishing cock in her hands. "Do that to me once more and then we can go to the party."

And they began again.

LIVIA AND MORIKO helped Marcel and his sous-chef Caterina— Cat—load the trays of canapés into the restaurant's van before Liv and Moriko hopped in the back for the drive to the Renaud Mansion. Livia was trying to keep the trays from tipping and tying her thick mane up into a chignon at the same time, but the weight of it would not stay clipped. Moriko grinned at her.

"Just pull it back. You'll never get it all up."

"I refuse to be beaten," Livia muttered. Eventually, Moriko pushed Livia's hands out of the way.

"Let me."

As Livia held the trays of food, Moriko deftly worked Liv's hair into a messy bun at the nape of her neck. "That's the best you're going to get, girl, so live with it."

Livia tentatively patted it. "You're a miracle worker. From now on, I'll pay you to be my hair wrangler."

Moriko laughed. "You couldn't afford me."

When they arrived at the mansion, they were stunned into silence. The old plantation home had been modernized to some extent—a plaque on the door detailed its history and its passage to the Renaud family in the 1800s, wherein all slaves were freed and the plantation became a family homestead rather than a working freehold.

The imposing white building with shuttered windows and soft light radiating from within was decorated with high-quality Halloween trimmings. Moriko grinned at Livia as they passed a batch of expertly carved pumpkins. "You think they got Michelangelo to do them?"

Livia rolled her eyes. The place screamed money and opulence, but Livia wasn't impressed. As they moved into the kitchen, she saw Marcel talking to a young man who was dressed in a dark navy sweater and jeans, and who Livia guessed was the owner's assistant. He had dark curls and the most intense—and beautiful—green eyes she had ever seen.

The stranger sensed her scrutiny and looked up. Their eyes met and Livia felt a shudder of desire ripple through her. God, if even the *staff* looked like supermodels here ...

She nudged Moriko. "Does Marcel want us to change now or after we've set up?"

"After. Apparently, there's a dedicated room for us."

"Fancy."

"I know, right? Usually we have to squat in the back of the van to get ready."

Livia snorted and, between them, they quickly arranged the canapés on the silver trays. When they had finished, Livia saw the handsome assistant had gone and Marcel was nodding at them. "Lovely job. The food looks great. So, this thing kicks off in an hour, but guests are starting to arrive, so we'll start with the welcome pumpkin-spice sidecars first up. Think you can cope?"

"No worries, boss," Moriko hugged Marcel, who turned red with pleasure. "We'll show these rich kids a good time ... wait, that sounded dirtier than I meant it to."

Livia snorted with laughter as Moriko shrugged. "Come on then. Let's get dressed."

A HALF HOUR LATER, Livia was regretting the tightness of her skirt. It had been her go-to throughout college—short, black, and figure-hugging even back then when she was ten pounds lighter. She'd dragged it out of her closet this morning—it had been the cleanest, most professional skirt she could find. *I need to go shopping,* she told herself as she plastered a smile on her face and made the rounds with a tray of drinks.

The mansion's main ballroom ("*Main* ballroom," she'd muttered to an amused Moriko. "Because the other ballrooms are too *small.*") was decorated beautifully, even the cynical Livia had to admit. Twinkle lights draped the walls and soft music was playing as the guests milled around, talked, and drank. Moriko was making the first pass with a canapé tray, and Livia could tell her friend was gritting her teeth, fending off unwanted remarks and come-ons.

"Hey, Livvy." She heard Roan Saintmarc's voice behind her and turned. She was actually relieved to see a friendly face; if the guests weren't turning their noses up at her presence or trying to talk her into bed, they looked through her as if she were invisible. Roan's smile was friendly. He indicated the man he was talking with, a tall, dark-haired man with a neatly-trimmed beard and dark brown eyes.

"San, this is my friend from my favorite restaurant. Livia, this is Sandor Carpentier, a good friend of mine."

Sandor Carpentier had a warm, open smile as he shook Livia's hand. She grinned at them both, happy to see friendly faces at last. "Can I get you fellas a refill?" She waved the bottle of Krug she was holding and topped up their glasses. "Boss tells me the good bourbon will be out soon," she said with a wink.

"If I know Nox, it will be," Roan said, and looked around. "Speaking of whom, have you met our lord and master yet, Liv?"

She shook her head. "But he would probably tell me to get back to work. Nice seeing you, Mr. Saintmarc, Mr. Carpentier."

"Sandor, please," the man said, and Livia decided she liked his merry, twinkling eyes. He didn't seem as aloof as the others. "And if you knew Nox, you'd know that's unlikely. He'd probably insist you join us for a drink."

Livia smiled and made her excuses. Despite what they said, she didn't want Marcel to get into trouble if she was caught fraternizing with the guests. She made her way back to the kitchen to refill her tray. Moriko was just coming in from the garden.

"Hey, boo, I just finished up my break, and Marcel told me to let you grab one now that I'm done. There are a couple of good places to hide and take your shoes off out there."

Livia smiled at her friend gratefully and headed out of the kitchen door into the lush gardens. It was darker down here than at the front of the mansion, and she could see a fog coming in off the bayou at the end of the property. Livia thought it was much spookier, befitting the Halloween vibe of the party, and yet more beautiful than any of the decorations inside.

With a soft moan, she eased off her heels and wondered why she hadn't worn her usual flats. No, she knew why—she had wanted to make a good impression for Marcel. She knew she could pull off the cool professional vibe with her heels on, and at least it gave her a few extra inches when she needed to be seen. Still, her feet pulsed with pain, and when she put her hot soles on cool ground, she sighed with relief.

She crept barefoot into a little grove, and seeing the edge of a stone seat, headed for it. She stopped, seeing the other end was already occupied. "Sorry," she said, then saw it was the assistant she'd shared a moment with earlier.

He had changed out of his sweater and jeans and was now wearing what looked to be a very expensive black suit. *Perks of the job*, she suspected, but her attention was drawn by the way it fit his broad shoulders and slim figure so well. She meant to turn and go, but the sheer sadness in his eyes took her breath away. "Are you okay?" Her voice was soft, and the man stared at her, his eyes intense, before he half nodded, then shook his head.

"Not really, but common manners dictate I say I am. So ..." His voice was deep—a beautiful deep baritone that sent a shiver through her. Livia hesitated for a moment, then sat down next to him.

"Escaping from the melee? Me too. Just for a minute." She smiled at him, noticing again how gorgeous he was, except for that pain in his eyes. She wished she could take it away for him. "Are you hiding from the muckety-mucks?"

His mouth hitched up in a half-smile. "Kind of."

She leaned forward conspiratorially. "I won't tell," she whispered, and he laughed. It changed his whole face, turning it from brooding and slightly dangerous into a boyish, joyful thing.

"Right back at you." He looked at her name tag. "Livia. Not O-livia?"

She shook her head. "No, just Livia." She shivered at the cool air coming up from the water. "It really is beautiful here."

He nodded, and seeing her trembling, he shrugged out of his jacket and put it around her shoulders. She felt her face get hot. "Thank you."

They gazed at each other for a long moment, and Livia felt tongue tied. He smelled wonderful too, all clean linen and woodsy spice, and for a moment she found herself having to resist the urge to run her fingertips over his long, thick lashes. They were so black, they looked like he had eyeliner on.

She swallowed hard, the desire to kiss this stranger overwhelming and bewildering. She cast around for something to say. "I was thinking, that mist from the bayou must have known there was a Halloween party here tonight." *God, could she have sounded any dumber?* She cursed herself, but he smiled at her.   .

"I guess it must have known. I find it ... romantic. Dark and malevolent, perhaps. But also sensual."

Livia could feel a pulse beating furiously between her legs and was amazed. She hadn't had this reaction to a man in forever ... or *ever*, if she was being honest. Electricity hung in the air between them. She had to dispel it before she did something reckless. She had Marcel and Moriko to think about here.

She nudged him with her shoulder. "Hey, you better get in there before all the food is gone. Honestly, they're like sharks, these people. Fins and everything. The food is really good, too. I hope your boss agrees."

Another smile, amused and sweet. "I'm sure he does." He stood and offered his hand. "Shall we sneak into the kitchen and grab something, then?"

Trembling, she took his hand—the skin surprisingly soft and dry—and stood. "Okay. But afterward, you have to tell me your name."

Their bodies were really close now, and Livia could feel his body heat through her clothes. He trailed a finger across her cheekbone, and Livia shivered. She smiled, but stepped away from him. "I think we'd better get inside." *As much as I'd like to fuck you right here, right now.*

His smile didn't change and he squeezed her hand. "Of course."

"Nox!" They both heard the female's voice from across the garden. "Nox, where the hell are you?"

A thrill of panic went through Livia as her companion called out. "Right here, Ambs. Keep your shirt on."

I should have known ...

Livia was frozen. *Shit, shit, shit.* This was *Nox Renaud.* He smiled down at her and put his finger over his lips for a second before his smile widened into a conspiratorial grin. "I have to go."

She nodded and shrugged out of his jacket. "Here, you better have this back. I'm going inside now, anyway."

He thanked her, taking the coat, and with a last regretful look towards her, disappeared back towards the direction of the shouting woman.

"Oh fuck," Livia hissed to herself. "Way to be unprofessional. Catering one-oh-one, don't almost *kiss* the client. *Jesus.*"

Her face flaming with embarrassment, she went back into the kitchen and managed to work the rest of the party while avoiding any contact with Nox Renaud or his friends ... difficult, but not impossible. When it became clear the party was winding down, Livia hid out in the kitchen and dealt with the clean-up.

Marcel was all smiles when he came to thank them both. "Liv, you didn't need to do this," he said, looking in amazement at the stack of empty, clean trays she was loading into the van. She grinned at him.

"No problem, boss." She made herself busy untying her apron. "Did you get good feedback?"

"*Very* good feedback. And a somewhat unexpected bonus, which you'll find in your paychecks. No, don't argue. Say what you want about the Renaud family, but Nox is a very generous man. He also told me that I was his go-to caterer for the future, which isn't saying a lot because he rarely entertains guests, but it's still something."

"It *is* something. It's a *big* something." Moriko kissed Marcel's cheek and he gave her a hug.

"Thanks, Morry. He also said he'd be recommending me to his friends and clients. Good guy. Jeez, look at the time. Come on, kids, let's get out of here. I'll buy you both a late dinner."

LATER, at home in bed, Livia could not help but look up Nox Renaud on the internet. She flicked through pages of photos of him, drinking in the shape of his face, the green eyes that looked just as sad in his childhood pictures as in every photo of him as an adult. She traced his face with her finger. In some pictures he had a beard, which made him look even more handsome, she thought. When she began to read about his history—the murder/suicide of his parents and brother, the mysterious death of his teenage sweetheart, the years of suspicion aimed at Nox himself—she learned he'd been thoroughly investigated after the death of Ariel Duplas. Nox was only eighteen at the time and was the only suspect, but the police had completely exonerated him. The piece Livia was reading made it clear that his family's deaths had broken the handsome young man.

SINCE HIS FAMILY tragedy and the subsequent investigation, Renaud has kept a low profile. His luxury food importing business with friend Sandor Carpentier has made him a billionaire, but this has just served to draw more attention and comparisons to other tragic figures. Many locals refer to him as New Orlean's own Howard Hughes—a reclusive man with a myriad of secrets. Only once a year do we really get to see the man, at his annual benefit on Halloween, but it doesn't stop gossip magazines the world over wondering about the romantic life of this devastatingly—and some say, dangerously—handsome young man. As he approaches forty, will Nox Renaud ever break free of his past?

GOD, *I hope so.* The thought came unbidden to Livia as she slid her finger over his photograph. Not that it would have anything to do with her, but she had sensed something special in the man she had met—that he was more than just another handsome rich boy. There were hidden depths there, she was sure of it.

When she went to sleep that night, she dreamed of Nox Renaud and his beautiful green eyes, and of the moment his lips would press against hers.

CHAPTER THREE

Amber rolled her eyes as Nox sat down at the table. It was the French Quarter, with busy streets and lunchtime crowds, and the restaurant Amber had chosen was almost full. "You're late again, Renaud. Where's the Rolex I bought you last year?"

Nox sighed, kissing her cheek. "You know I don't like to wear it out in public. It looks too ostentatious. Not that I'm not grateful for it," he added, seeing Amber's frown, "it was a lovely gift. I just don't know if it's really *me*."

Amber opened her mouth to argue, then gave up. Nox looked different and had seemed different—lighter—since the party. Amber had wondered if it was just the relief of getting it over and done with for another year, but it had been a week since the party and every time she had seen him, Nox had been *happy*.

"What's going on with you?" she asked him now, and Nox, who was reading the menu, glanced up and smiled at her.

"What do you mean?"

"I mean ... you look different. You look ... lighter."

"I haven't lost weight, far from it."

Amber rolled her eyes again. Nox was nowhere in the vicinity of overweight. "I mean *emotionally*. You seem to be carrying yourself more cheerfully than usual."

Nox laughed, his green eyes twinkling. "Do I?"

"Fine, don't tell me then." Amber snatched the menu from him grumpily and sulked behind it. Nox smothered a grin.

"Ambs ... you ever have one of those moments in life, however fleeting, where someone or something just reminds you why you're alive? Someone who sets off a thought process that makes you reevaluate your entire existence?"

"Is this your fancy way of saying you got laid?" Amber felt a twinge of jealousy go through her and brushed it away. *He doesn't belong to you ... he never did.*

Nox shook his head. "No, I haven't ... no. I just had a moment with someone, a woman, at the party. I'd like to see her again, is all."

"Really?" Amber ran through all of the party guests in her head, and Nox just smiled and shook his head. "Who?"

Nox hesitated and smiled ruefully at her. "Can I just have this secret for a little bit? I swear, the moment it becomes more than a ... *moment* ... you'll be the first to know."

Amber relaxed. "Of course, honey." She reached over and squeezed his hand. "I'm very happy for you. It's about time you got your pickle tickled."

Nox burst out laughing and Amber joined in, her blue eyes amused. As they ordered their food, she studied her friend. They had known each other for more than half their lives. They'd been drawn together by Amber's twin, Ariel, who had come home from school one day and told her family that she had met the most beautiful boy in the world.

She hadn't been wrong. Nox Renaud was the kind of boy that sculptors made statues of. That strong jaw, those perfectly symmetrical features. Big green eyes. Sensual mouth. *God.* More than once since Ariel's death, Amber had wondered if she and Nox would end up together—mostly out of convenience—but he'd never made an advance and she had never found the courage.

She had to admit, it hurt a little that Nox had finally shown interest in someone and it wasn't *her*, but she could not begrudge her friend his happiness. Amber's own love life was ... complicated. She always kept two lovers at a time, but never let either near her heart. Her beauty, her wealth, her position in society—she didn't need a husband, which made her lethal to the women of New Orleans, who kept their husbands away from her. Little did they know, Amber wasn't interested in any of them. What she wanted was far more complex. *Far more Nox-like,* she told herself, then pushed the thought away. He would never be hers, and she would have to accept that.

"So, when are you going to make your move?" she asked Nox, who blinked with nervousness. To her amazement, two spots of pink appeared on Nox's cheeks as he shrugged.

"I don't know. I've been working on getting the courage up to approach her."

Amber almost spat her water out. Nox Renaud—billionaire, drop-dead-gorgeous businessman—was *nervous* about asking a girl on a date. "Wow. I haven't seen you like this since ..."

She trailed off and looked away. Ariel was always there, always between them. Amber swallowed the lump in her throat. Nox's smile had faded and he nodded. "I *never* thought this day would come, Ambs ... and look, no one, *no one* will ever replace her."

"I know that, sweetie, but hopefully someone will mean just as much to you some day."

His eyes danced in a way she hadn't seen for years. "I hope so too, Ambs. I really hope so too."

. . .

LIVIA TRIED to stop thinking about Nox Renaud as she practiced her scales up and down, using the plain rhythm to distract herself. In the week since she'd met him, her body had felt wired, her brain whirling. To have that much chemistry with someone she probably would never see again … it didn't seem right. She faltered in her playing and then crashed her fingers down on the keyboard.

"Unless you're going for some kind of weird Stockhausen thing," a voice behind her said, "I'm guessing you're having an off day."

Livia turned to smile at her tutor. In the few months she had been at the college, her tutor, Charvi Sood, had become more than just a teacher to her. The two women had bonded over their love of jazz, of Monk, Parker, Davis, and to Charvi's delight, their mutual admiration for Judy Carmichael, the reason Livia had fallen in love with the genre. Listening to Carmichael's radio shows when she was living at home with her father, her headphones plugged in to dull the sound of her father shouting drunkenly at the television, she had used the genre as her way to transport herself out of the San Diego heat and here to New Orleans.

Charvi put down the stack of scores she had in her hand and peered over her glasses at her young student. "You okay? You've been in here practicing all week. You *can* rest, you know. It may be your master's degree, but rest is vital for brainpower."

Livia smiled at her. "I know. I'm trying to distract myself from thinking about a boy. It's very annoying."

Charvi laughed, shaking her head. "It happens to the best of us. Want to share?"

Livia picked out a tune with her forefinger. "It's embarrassing. He's way out of my league and—"

"Let me stop you there, young lady. *No one* is out of your league."

Livia sighed. "It's Nox Renaud."

That stopped Charvi. "Ah. Well, I would say the problem there isn't that you're out of his league, it's that he's Nox Renaud."

Livia looked at her friend curiously. "You know him?"

"I knew his mother. I've met Nox a few times. He's ... an enigma. At least if you believe the gossip."

"He has the saddest eyes I've ever seen, and he seemed so sweet. Lonely, but sweet. Nice. God, nice is such a bland thing to say, but he was friendly and warm and ..."

"You have an enormous crush on him."

Livia shrugged. "Yes, but it doesn't matter. It's not like we run in the same circles. Forget I said anything."

Charvi smiled. "Well now, let's channel that desire into your playing. Give me something slow and sensual. And make it up as you go along. Think about Mr. Renaud and let your fingers move across the keyboard."

At first Livia was embarrassed, feeling exposed, but as her fingers stroked the keys she began to find a melody. She closed her eyes and thought about the feeling of him trailing his finger across her cheek, the scent of his skin, the ocean-green color of his eyes. She played a melody so sweet she wanted to cry, and when she finished and opened her eyes, she felt her face burn red.

"Wow, you have it bad," Charvi teased her and held up her phone. "It needs work, but there's something there. I've recorded it and I'll email it to you. Your homework is to score it and mold it into a piece you can perform at the end of semester recital."

Livia gaped at her. "Are you kidding me?" She felt panicky at revealing something so personal to an audience. But Charvi nodded.

"I'm deadly serious. That was the most connected I've ever seen you with your piano, Liv." She checked her watch. "And I have a seminar. Work on it, Liv, and I swear you'll see what I mean."

Left alone, Livia checked her laptop. Charvi had indeed emailed her the MP3 and as Liv played it back, she realized there *was* something there. She grabbed some blank score paper and began to write.

NOX LOOKED up as Sandor knocked on the door jamb. "Hey."

Sandor grinned. "You still working? Dude, it's Friday night. Let's go out and have drinks."

Nox chuckled. "I would, but I'm waiting on a call from Italy. Haven't you got a date?"

Sandor shrugged. "She blew me off. I'm kind of relieved, to be honest. I'm getting too old to be dating a different pretty girl each week."

"My heart bleeds for you. So, I'm your consolation prize?"

Sandor grinned. "Yup. Grab your cell phone and take the call on that. We're going drinking."

Nox hesitated. "All right, but let's go to the French Quarter."

"Wanna mix with the tourists? Come on then."

AN HOUR and two shots of bourbon later, Nox relaxed back into his seat and glanced around the bar. He hadn't told Sandor that the bar he'd chosen was across the street from Marcel Pessou's restaurant—or that ever since they'd gotten here, Nox had been looking for any sign of Livia. He hadn't had one night of peace since he'd met her.

The feel of her soft skin, her huge chocolate brown eyes, the way her tawny hair fell in messy waves over her shoulders; it all haunted him. The faint flush of pink when he'd touched her face. He'd been so close to kissing her—which would have been *entirely* inappropriate. But, God, the feelings he had thought he'd never feel again were whirling and thrashing through him like a storm.

He had to see her again—to see if the connection between them hadn't been just *that* moment in time. To see if it was real, tangible, and something they could build on. Also he really, *really* needed to kiss her gorgeous pink mouth—it was driving him crazy.

"Nox? Buddy?"

Nox blinked back into the present. "Sorry, what?"

"I was saying, I was talking to Roan at the party. He seems pretty keen on working with us on the Feldman project."

Nox snorted and sipped his bourbon. "What does *Roan* know about the luxury food trade?"

"Nothing, but he does know about the *shipping* trade," Sandor gave Nox a reproachful look. "Look, I know you think he's a playboy, but he's got a good head on his shoulders. Besides ... he wants to buy his way in."

"What?"

"He told me he wants us three to go into business together. He wants in on the company."

For the first time that night, Nox stopped thinking about Livia, leaning forward to study his friend. "How come he hasn't said anything to me?"

Sandor chuckled. "Because he *knows* you think he's a playboy. He's your best friend, but there's always been the joker in the pack, and it's always been Roan. He was feeling me out in the hope I'd do the approach. So, I am. I think it's something we should talk about. He wants to impress you, buddy, is all."

Nox considered. "I'm open to talking about it, certainly."

Sandor smiled. "So, I can tell him yes?"

"*Talking* about it, San. Nothing more at this stage."

"I love it when you get masterful. Another drink?"

"Go for it."

Nox leaned back, his eyes flicking automatically to the restaurant on the other side of the street. He could see the pretty Asian girl who was working with Livia at his party waiting on tables, but there was no sign of Livia. He thought about what Sandor had said. Roan was Nox's oldest friend but he was also someone who acted on impulse—he would best be described as reckless. Nox had worked too hard on the business, and not even his love for his friend could override the fact that Roan was not a good bet. Nox rubbed his eyes. Maybe he should loosen up, take a risk.

Take a risk ... His mind went back to the lovely girl he'd met at his party. Yes, he would take a risk. Enough of skulking like a creep across the street. Tomorrow, he would go the restaurant and ask for her. If she wasn't there, *he'd* leave his number. If she *was* there ...

He was still smiling when Sandor returned with the drinks.

IT WAS after midnight when Livia left the practice rooms, and as she didn't have enough cash on her for a cab, she decided to walk home. When she got back to the French Quarter, she decided to go the restaurant and see if Moriko wanted company on her walk home.

As she turned into an alley leading to Bourbon Street, she suddenly felt herself being jerked back, and a heavy arm locked around her throat. Shocked into action, she threw her elbows back with all her strength, cussing and screaming at her attacker. "*Get off me, motherfucker!*" She slammed her fist back into the man's groin and he groaned, releasing her.

Her anger at full flood and the adrenaline spiking in her system, Livia punched and kicked the mugger until, still groaning, he took off. Yelling "*Bitch!*" at her as he ran, she unleashed a litany of curse words at him, beyond caring who heard her. Finally, she caught her breath and picked up her bag, turning to go to the restaurant.

She stopped. Nox Renaud was looking at her, astonished admiration in his eyes. Livia's breath caught in her throat.

"Well," he said finally, a grin slowly spreading across his face. "Hello again."

CHAPTER FOUR

"I'm absolutely *fine*," Livia complained as Marcel fussed over her, making her drink the bourbon he offered. Nox Renaud sat across from her, a small smile playing around his lips. It was as if they shared a secret now, and Livia couldn't help but grin.

"I heard you holler," Nox told her, "and came to help, but you'd pretty much wrecked the guy by the time I got there. Pretty badass, if you ask me."

"A girl's got to look after herself," Livia said. She couldn't stop looking at him—she *hadn't* imagined how gorgeous he was. Those green eyes, that dark hair and messy curls, they were all as beautiful as she remembered. The way he was looking at her sent thrills through her entire body.

Marcel and Moriko seemed to notice the charged atmosphere and, after making sure Livia really was okay after the shock of her mugging, they discreetly disappeared. The restaurant was closed now, only a couple of lamps still on, and in the gloom, Nox took her hands in his.

"I haven't been able to stop thinking about you," he said honestly. "I admit, my friend and I came to the Quarter for drinks and I deliberately chose the bar across the street from here ... I hoped to see you."

"Which friend?"

"Sandor? You might have met him at the party."

Livia nodded. "I did. He seemed lovely."

Nox smiled. "He is. But as lovely as he is, I don't want to talk about Sandor. Liv, those few moments we spent together in the garden ... I don't want to presume, but to me, there was something there."

"I felt it too." She began to tremble as he got out of his seat and stepped closer to her. He was so tall, she felt tiny next to him. He pulled her out of her chair and slid his hands onto her waist—tentative, a question in his eyes.

"Is this okay?"

Livia nodded and Nox smiled. He bent his head and Livia felt —at last—his lips against hers. The first kiss was brief, hesitant. But it didn't stop at one, and went on, becoming more passionate, his fingers tangling in her long hair, pulling her closer. Livia could feel his heart beating in his chest as her own arms snaked around him, her hands feeling the taut muscles of his back.

Kissing him was like taking a shot of pure heroin, she imagined. Heady, overwhelming, electric. His lips shaped themselves perfectly to hers, his tongue caressing, massaging hers, his breathing ragged. Finally, desperate for air, they broke apart.

"Wow." Livia breathed. "*Wow.*"

Nox brushed his fingertips across her face. "Livia, may I please take you on a date?"

His words seemed so formal after that breathtaking kiss that she giggled. Nox grinned. "I'm sorry, I'm out of practice. What I mean is, I would like to see you again. And again. And *again.*"

His words made her melt, and she leaned into his embrace. She gazed up at him. "I would like that too, Nox, very much. But

... what will your family, your friends think? I'm just a waitress. Well, a grad student, but I'm clearly not of your social circle. Won't they think badly of me?"

"I really don't care. There is no 'just' a waitress or a student. Both of those things are honorable, genuine things. But who cares what our jobs are? You're Livia, I'm Nox. The rest is just window dressing."

Livia gave a soft moan of desire and he tightened his arms around her. "I'd just like to get to know you, Liv. We can work anything else out together. Let's just try, that's all I ask."

HE WALKED her back to her apartment, but didn't ask to come in. He kissed her again and it was just as spine-tingling as their earlier kiss. She could feel the tension in his body, the way his huge erection pressed against her belly when he held her tightly, but Nox Renaud was clearly a gentleman. "May I see you tomorrow?"

So proper, so polite. She nodded, grinning. "Tomorrow is my day off, so yes."

"Then would you spend the day with me?"

"I'd like that very much."

Nox brushed his lips against hers, his hands gently cradling her face. "Then shall we say ten a.m.?"

"Perfect."

The kiss deepened, once again leaving Livia breathless. Nox smiled at her. "Goodnight, lovely Liv."

"Goodnight, Nox."

SHE FELT bereft as she saw him walk away, turning to look at her once more before he turned the corner. His grin made her heart swell. For a moment or two, she stood out in the cool night, blinking. "Did that actually just happen?"

She chuckled and went inside. As she opened the door to the apartment, Moriko, dressed in Hello Kitty pajamas, held up a bag of potato chips and said, "You, on the couch, *now*. You're not going to bed until you've told me *everything*."

HE HAD WATCHED Nox and the girl, Livia, walk back to her apartment, following at a safe distance. They were obviously smitten with each other, and he guessed they must have met at the party. The party where she was a *waitress*, and Nox was the billionaire party host. He couldn't fault Nox on his taste. Livia was beautiful, all sumptuous curves and softness. But still, a waitress ... The scandal would be great indeed, especially amongst their cohorts, but that wasn't what was making him smile. No, it was the thought of Nox and Livia possibly falling deeply in love, so deeply in love that when she was taken from him, Nox would finally be destroyed.

And that was all he had ever dreamed of ...

CHAPTER FIVE

Moriko was sitting on the bathroom cabinet, watching Livia apply her makeup. "I cannot believe you didn't sleep with him."

Livia rolled her eyes. "Dude, we haven't even been on a date yet."

"Prude."

Livia grinned. Moriko was a seize-the-moment kind of girl; Livia preferred the slow-burn. "Besides, if we'd had sex in the restaurant, Health and Human Services would have been outraged." God, just thinking about sex with Nox was making her hot, but she brushed the thought aside before Moriko could pick up on it. "Look, we're going on *one* date. Don't jump the gun."

"Where's he taking you?"

Livia sighed. "*We're* taking *each other* ... I don't know. We haven't discussed that yet."

"Too busy sucking face."

Livia laughed aloud. "Well, do you blame me? Have you seen him? Now, go away, I need to finish up here and you're distracting me."

Moriko hopped down, grinning, and tapped a closed drawer. "Plenty of condoms in there. Take a handful. Better safe than sorry."

Livia pointed out at the door and, grumbling but grinning, Moriko left her alone. Livia shut the door behind her and sighed, leaning against it. Her whole body felt as if she were wired up to the National Grid. If Nox even touched her once, she would jump him. "Calm the fuck down," she muttered to herself. Still, when she'd finished getting ready, she grabbed some condoms from the drawer and shoved them deep into her purse.

Nox was five minutes early. "Sorry, couldn't wait."

Livia saw Moriko make a crude gesture behind Nox's back and glared at her. "Do excuse Moriko; she was raised by wolves."

"All the best people are," Nox grinned at Livia's friend, who smiled back at him.

"Look after her," she said. "Later, lovers." She disappeared back into her bedroom while Livia's face burned red.

"So," she said, trying not to look flustered in his presence, "what's the plan?"

"Well, last night your roommate told me you hadn't been in New Orleans for long, so I thought maybe we could take a steamboat trip. We could see the city and talk at the same time. What do you think?"

Livia smiled at him. "I think that sounds perfect."

THE STEAMBOAT NATCHEZ was full of tourists as it began to float down the Mississippi River, but neither Nox nor Livia cared. They sat out on the deck, the weather still very warm despite it being November, breathing in the fresh air. Nox asked Livia about where she had come from.

"Southern California, so I'm used to hot weather," she

grinned. "It is different heat here, more humidity. Sultrier. New Orleans is a very sexy city."

Nox laughed. "If you say so. I'm NOLA born and bred, but I have to admit, sometimes the heat during the day gets to me. So why did you leave SoCal?"

Livia looked away from his gaze. "No family to speak of, and Moriko was here. I managed to get a scholarship to the University, so that made it official. I haven't regretted it once. Especially now."

They smiled at each other and Nox leaned in to kiss her again. "Livia, that night at the party ... I haven't felt a connection like that in years."

"Really?" She was delighted, then frowned. "No, I mean, really? Look at you, you could have anyone."

"I'm fussy," he said lightly with a grin, but she could see something behind his eyes.

"You don't give away a lot, do you? I mean, I could see the sadness in your eyes when we met ... You can talk to me, you know?"

Nox's expression changed for a split second—fear?—but he shook his head. "I'm a firm believer in the past staying in the past. What I want now is for us to get to know each other. Is that something you'd like, Livvy?"

She studied him, leaning on the railing of the steamboat. "Charvi was right about you. You *are* an enigma."

"Charvi? Charvi Sood?" Nox's eyes lit up and Livia nodded.

"Yes, she knew your mother?"

"I'll say. Charvi was my mom's best friend." He looked so excited, like a little boy. "I had no idea she was back in New Orleans."

"She is. She's my tutor, my mentor, really. I'm sure she'd love to see you."

Nox gave a short laugh. "Why wouldn't she come to see me

herself?" He frowned to himself, obviously deep in thought, and Livia wondered if she had made a mistake mentioning Charvi to him.

Nox shook himself. "Well, yes, I'd love to see her." He smiled at Livia. "So, you're a master pianist?"

She laughed. "Oh, no, I'm really just a beginner, at least when you consider the scope of the craft. My focus is on jazz piano, for this program at least. But, really, I love all classical music. And rock, and blues, and on and on ..."

"I'm afraid my music knowledge extends as far as Pearl Jam and Tom Petty. That kind of music."

"I adore *both*," Livia encouraged him. "For my undergraduate thesis, for the recital, I did a slowed down piano version of "Rearviewmirror.""

"I gather speed, from you fucking with me ..." Nox quoted and their gazes locked. Livia felt breathless.

"Anticipation is a marvelous thing," she said softly and Nox nodded.

"Oh, I agree." He grinned and swept her hair back over her shoulder, stroking the back of his finger down her neck. "Your skin is so soft."

Tingling sensations were racing through her body at his touch. *God, I want you,* she thought. But as she'd said, the anticipation of making love with this man was electrifying. Her eyes dropped to his groin, his erection obvious in his denim jeans. She looked up at him from underneath her lashes. "I wonder how long we can hold out."

Nox grinned. "Personally speaking, and to be blunt, I think it would be amazing to be inside you right now ... But yes, let's keep this going until we don't have a choice. Why bow to society's pressure to rush into anything?"

Livia suddenly crushed her lips to his, sliding her hand over his groin and squeezing. God, he was *huge*. Nox gave a moan. "God, Livvy, try to make it easy on me, why don't you?"

She chuckled, loving that he'd used her nickname so soon. "Listen, you have all the cards here, Mr. Billionaire. This, at least, is on *my* terms."

Nox laughed, burying his face in her neck. "You smell so good, it's intoxicating."

She stroked his dark curls. "How is it I feel like I've known you forever?"

Nox sat up and studied her. She stroked the thick dark eyelashes she had been dreaming about, and he leaned into her touch. "I know, I feel that too."

She grinned at him. "Nox Renaud, we're going to have a lot of fun together."

And she meant it. She wanted to erase the haunted look in his eyes forever, even if this thing between them was only fleeting. The thought caused an unexpected shock of pain—already she felt so comfortable with him, they were so in tune with each other. A small voice inside her whispered, *you don't know him yet*, but she pushed it away. For now, they would have fun, and that was enough.

THEY SPENT a blissful two hours on the riverboat, and then took a cab back to the French Quarter to an upscale burger joint that Livia suggested. Nox didn't seem the type to turn his nose up at everyday fare and she was right, he practically swooned over the juicy burger, which was smothered in sautéed mushrooms and melted cheese. Livia grinned at him.

"It's good, right?"

"Damn good." He took a swig from his bottle of beer and she grinned, picking a stray mushroom from his cheek.

"I like a man who enjoys his burgers."

Nox muffled a belch in his fist and apologized. Livia chuckled. "Excuse me," he said and she kissed his cheek. There was already such a change in him now from when they had met. He was relaxed and laidback, and even the sadness in his eyes was less apparent. She couldn't believe it was because of *her*.

"Tell me more about yourself, Nox." Her smile faded a little and she looked at him steadily. "I'm so sorry about your family."

There it was, the wariness in his eyes, and he looked away from her for a moment. "I'm sorry," she said. "I shouldn't have said anything."

"No, it's okay," he said. He wound his fingers through hers. "I can't pretend it didn't happen and I want to be honest with you from the start. Yeah, it was rough. That doesn't begin to cover it, but for now I'll just say ... it took some getting over."

"Can you get over something like that?"

He shrugged. "I don't know."

Livia stroked the back of his hand with her finger. "I think society places too much pressure on someone to 'get over' things. Why? Why *should* we get over things? Can't we just acknowledge that the pain will always hurt like hell, no matter how much time has passed? We just go on, live our lives, pretending we're okay when we're not." She cupped his face in her hand, her eyes locked on his. "That night in the garden, you were so honest with me. I asked you if you were okay and you said you weren't. Let's always be that honest with each other, whatever happens, wherever this goes. Deal?"

Nox's eyes were intense on hers. "How old are you, Livia Chatelaine? Because you have the wisdom of someone much, much older. Yes, of *course*, deal." He leaned over and kissed her. "We have so much to learn about each other, and I can't wait. One question ... I'll be forty in two years and you're what, twenty-three, twenty-four?"

"Twenty-seven."

"Does the age gap bother you?"

Livia shifted around and sat on his lap, not caring if the other diners were watching them. She hooked her arms around his neck and nuzzled his nose. "You just said I was much older," she whispered to him. "So ... *what* age gap?"

Nox slid his hand under her shirt and stroked her belly as she kissed him. The feel of his big fingers against her skin made her weak. "God, I want you." She gave a small moan.

Nox grinned wickedly. "Anticipation, remember?"

She wriggled against his groin, feeling his cock harden almost instantly, and he groaned.

"You are a very bad girl, Livia Chatelaine. The moment I'm inside you can't come—excuse the pun—soon enough."

She hopped off his lap and smirked. "Anticipation ..."

"Devil woman." And they both laughed.

AMBER SIGHED as she saw Odelle approaching her. It was late afternoon at the salon and Amber had just had a blissful massage. The last thing she wanted was for Odelle to ruin her buzz. The blonde woman smiled tentatively at her but it didn't reach her eyes. That wasn't anything new with Odelle

"Always good to see you, Odelle," Amber said smoothly, and indicated the tea tray in front of her. "Won't you join me?"

Odelle nodded. "Thank you." She sat and Amber poured her some herbal tea.

"Did you enjoy Nox's party this year?" Amber was being facetious—she knew Odelle hated public gatherings. Odelle, despite her beauty, didn't mingle well with people and Amber had always wondered why. Odelle's famed iciness aside, she rarely made the effort to get to know other people, almost as if she were protecting herself from something. Odelle, Amber, Nox, and Roan had known each other since they were teenagers, but still Amber felt as if she had never really known Odelle. All she knew was that Roan had pursued the blonde woman, and that Odelle had only ever opened up to Nox, who she regarded as an older brother.

She studied Odelle now. The other woman looked tired. "Is everything okay with you, Odelle?"

"Of course. Roan and I are thinking of getting engaged."

Amber tried not to spit out her tea. "Really?" She couldn't help the tone of cynicism that crept into her voice, but she regretted it when Odelle flushed red with annoyance.

"Is it so hard to believe?"

"No, of course not, I'm sorry. It's just Roan never mentioned it. Are you sure you want to be tied to, let's just say, to a man who …"

"Can't keep it in his trousers?" Odelle's smile was bitter. "You think I don't know about his other women, Amber? Of course, I do. Maybe not *all* of them, but I have my suspicions." She looked hard at Amber, who met her gaze steadily.

"Then why would you marry him? Why not set your sights on someone else? Nox, for example. You adore him, and he thinks very highly of you."

"You think of our group as a revolving door of bedhopping and casual hookups, Amber. Nox is my *family*. Roan may have his peccadillos but I assure you, it's me who he comes home to."

Suddenly Amber realized why Odelle had sought her out. She was warning her off. She wanted to marry Roan—*Roan,* of all people—and was making sure that his friends knew he belonged to her. Amber gave a sad smile. Poor deluded Odelle.

"I believe you." Amber casually sipped her tea and they sat in silence for a while. When Odelle left, Amber pulled out her cellphone. She listened to the buzz at the other end of the line and when he answered, she didn't let him speak. "Roan, just how long has Odelle known about you and me? When did she find out we were fucking?"

R OAN HUNG up the phone and rubbed his eyes. *Fuck.* He and Amber had been so careful, but now Odelle knew he'd broken her one rule. *Don't shit where you sleep.* "I don't care about random hookups," she'd told him the night he'd first mentioned marriage. "I do care about you fucking around in our social circle."

And he had been careless. *Shit.* Marrying Odelle would secure his future—her father was richer than even Nox—and besides, he liked fucking her. He liked seeing behind the icy façade.

Fuck it. Now he would have to lose all his other girls and make nice with Odelle. He should never have started up with Amber again—Amber, who had nothing to lose by admitting their affair. And that was the allure of the redhead—she simply didn't give a crap about anyone. Except Nox, of course. Roan couldn't help the jealousy he felt towards his friend sometimes; Nox was just so damned *good*, it was infuriating.

Roan sighed and grabbed his cellphone. He would forget the crap with the women in his life and just focus on getting his shot together for the meeting with Nox and Sandor. He wanted in on their company. He was ready to grow up and he needed to focus, because there was one glaring problem in Roan's otherwise perfect life.

He was stone-cold broke.

CHAPTER SIX

After eating, they had wandered the streets, enjoying the atmosphere. Later in the evening, they found themselves at The Spotted Cat, a jazz venue that was jumping with music and crammed with people. Livia and Nox found standing room by the bar and ordered drinks. Livia looked excited. "I keep meaning to come here but never found the time."

Nox grinned at her. "Out of interest, how do you manage? I mean, I know you have the scholarship, but working at the café can't pay for everything. Actually, scratch that, it's none of my business."

She laughed. "It's okay. I get by. I've always had to fight for the basics so it's become second nature. Sharing with Morry helps, and I don't need a lot. Thank God for the scholarship, though."

Nox smiled at her openness. She really didn't care about money, and that was refreshing. He could imagine her happy with just a book and a sandwich—this wasn't a woman who needed diamonds and pearls. Of all the things he could give her, what she seemed to want was his time. He swept his hand into her hair and pulled her lips to his. "You're gorgeous," he murmured against her lips, "and I adore you."

Livia chuckled. "You barely know me, but I'll take that. You're not so bad yourself, rich boy."

Her words were totally without reproach and he felt her mouth curve up in a smile as he kissed her. A band was just setting up and when they began to play, Nox slid his arms around Livia's waist and pulled her back against his chest. Livia leaned back into him, comfortable with the intimacy already.

The band was wild, fun, and Nox lost track of time in the sweltering heat, the drink, the heady feeling of this beautiful woman in his arms. More and more people were cramming into the space and his arms tightened around Livia. She turned her head to smile at him and something shifted in both of them as their eyes caught. He pressed his lips to hers and she turned in his arms, her own wrapping around him. They forgot about the club, the music, the other people.

He gazed down at her and mouthed the words "come home with me." Livia's smile grew wide and she nodded. *Enough anticipation ...*

TWENTY MINUTES later and they were in a cab back to his mansion. Nox couldn't stop kissing her, tasting her lips, sweet from the liquor, his fingers tangling in her glorious mane.

He hardly remembered how they got to his bedroom but then he was sliding her dress straps down her shoulders and taking one pink nipple into his mouth. He heard her soft moan as she pulled his t-shirt over his head and he tumbled her onto the bed. Livia giggled as he blew a raspberry on her belly then proceeded to tug the rest of her dress and her underwear off. Her fingers went to his zipper as he returned to kiss her mouth, and he felt a wave of pleasure as she freed his cock from his pants.

Livia stroked him until his cock was so hard it was painful, but he resisted the temptation to plunge into her and instead made his way down the bed until he could bury his face in her sex. His tongue lashed around her clit and she shuddered and trembled as she became even more aroused.

"Nox ..." she whispered as her sex became swollen and sensitive, then he was back, kissing her mouth again.

She looked up at him with huge brown eyes that were shining and sleepy with desire. "Do you have a ...?"

He grinned. "Of course, sweetheart." He reached over and opened the drawer in his nightstand and pulled out a condom. "Want to help me with it?"

She grinned and helped him roll it down over his cock. "Big boy." She chuckled and yelped as he tickled her, but as he hitched her legs around his waist, she suddenly looked nervous.

"Are you okay?" Nox was concerned, but she nodded.

"I'm so good, Nox. I just want to savor this moment ..."

He grinned and slowly, his grin growing at her impatience, slid into her. Livia moaned softly. "You feel so good," she whispered and smiled up at him as they began to find their rhythm.

Nox kissed her throat then found her lips again. Her body was so soft, her breasts pillowy, and he admired the way her body undulated beneath him as they made love. As the intensity grew, their gazes locked and Nox began to thrust harder, faster, deeper, until Livia's back arched up and she cried out his name as she came. The sound of it tipped Nox over into his own climax and he came hard, groaning her name.

They collapsed back on the bed, laughing, panting for air. "I guess we didn't hold out for so long," Livia laughed and rolled onto her side. Nox enjoyed the feel of her breasts pressed up against him and looped an arm around her.

"Listen, I wanted to do that for at least a week, so we held out just fine." He laughed as she rolled her eyes.

"Okay, I'll let you have that one." She pressed her lips to his. "God, Nox, that was incredible."

"And only the start." He smoothed a hand down her side. "You have the body of a goddess."

She giggled. "Thank you. Speaking of incredible bodies ..." She bit down on his nipple gently. "I've been dreaming about this one nonstop all week. I even wrote some piano porn about you."

Nox laughed loudly. "Piano porn? I think I'm flattered, even if I'm not too sure what you mean."

Livia grinned. "It doesn't matter, I was just being silly." She kissed his chest then rested her chin on it. "Nice digs you have here." She looked around the palatial bedroom for the first time, and Nox watched for her reaction. "Actually, really nice."

Nox watched her check out the navy-painted walls, the fireplace stacked with wood—his bedroom could have come out of a Tommy Hilfiger ad.

Livia sat up and nodded. "I like your room. Classy, elegant—just like you." She grinned and ran her hand through his dark, messy curls. "Usually elegant." She looked at him for a long moment, and he was surprised to see her color.

"What is it, Liv?"

She bit her lower lip, hesitant. "Can I tell you something?"

"Of course." He stroked his finger down her cheek. "Anything."

"I've never ...I'm mean, I'm not a virgin, but I never knew it could be like that. Sex, I mean. So exhilarating, so ... overwhelming."

Nox was silent for a moment. "Baby, are you telling me you've never ...?"

"Had an orgasm? Yup," she was blushing furiously now. "I've

never let myself go like that. I honestly couldn't have cared less whether I lived or died at that moment, I felt so utterly blissed out. My whole body was ... *God*, I can't even describe it."

Nox chuckled. "Then I'm honored your first was with me. I promise to do my best to see you come like that every time."

Livia smiled. "I know it sounds ridiculous, but it means a lot to me. And it doesn't hurt, Mr. Renaud, that you are *gorgeous*. Seriously, look at you—who wouldn't come?"

"Ha, ha," he brushed off her compliment, embarrassed. "Liv, you know how you said you wanted honesty? That goes for when we're in bed too. If I do anything you don't like, tell me."

"And the same to you."

"Deal."

She snuggled into his arms. "So, what do you want to do now?"

Nox kissed her. "I'm starving, actually. Want something to eat, and I'll give you a tour of the rest of the house?"

Livia stuck her tongue in her cheek. "As long as you promise to show me every single ballroom in the place, I mean I've only seen the *main* ballroom and ... oww ... *oww*! Stop, you maniac!"

Nox TICKLED her until she couldn't breathe from laughing, then they showered together and wandered down to his kitchen.

"This looks familiar." Livia grinned at him as she hopped up onto a seat at the breakfast bar. "Is this your main kitchen or do you have eleven smaller ones for each meal?"

"Funny girl," Nick leaned over to kiss her. "No, just the one. It's big enough to feed all seventeen ballrooms though."

Livia laughed. "Can I help?"

"Nope, let me feed you, woman. Grilled cheese?"

"Perfection."

They chatted easily while he cooked, Livia admiring the way

the muscles on his back flexed as he moved. He really was glorious. She adored the way his shaggy black curls fell around his head, the way his green eyes crinkled at the edges. She still couldn't quite believe she was there, that they had just made love, and that it had been even better than she had dreamed. It seemed somehow surreal, and yet to be with Nox was so natural. Livia studied him with unashamed lust, and when he caught her eye, he pushed the pan to the back of the stove and came to her.

"How," he murmured, brushing his lips against hers, "am I supposed to concentrate on cooking while you look at me like that?" He stepped closer and pulled her legs around him.

She was wearing his dress shirt—way too big for her, obviously—and he began to unbutton it, letting the fabric fall apart. He drew the pad of his thumb from her lips, down to her throat, between her breasts and down to her navel, making her shiver with desire. "You're so beautiful, Livvy."

God, this man ... She pulled his lips back to hers then, as they kissed, freed his cock from his jeans. Nox, grinning, produced a condom from the back pocket. "Always be prepared."

She laughed and rolled it onto him before guiding him inside her, moaning as he filled her entirely. "God, Nox ..."

He thrust hard into her, supporting her with his strong arms as they fucked. Livia bit his chest, kissing his neck and throat, before Nox ground his mouth down on hers. "Livia ..."

His cock reamed into her cunt so hard she thought she might slip from her position, and a second later they tumbled to the floor. Livia straddled him as they took each other to the edge of ecstasy all over again. Nox's fingers gripped her hips, pressing into the soft flesh as she rocked above him, taking him as deep as she could.

Livia came once then Nox flipped her onto her back and began to ram his hips as hard as he could, his cock growing harder and thicker, his hands pinning hers to the cool tile floor. Livia urged him on, coming again and again as he neared his peak. Finally, with a long moan, he came, shuddering and trembling, gasping for air. "God, Livia ...can we just do that all the time?"

"No complaints here." She grinned at him as he laughed, kissing her tenderly.

THE GRILLED cheese was unsalvageable so Nox made fresh sandwiches and they both ate as if they were starving. "It's all the energy we used up," Livia said, nodding her head wisely and making him laugh. "Don't mock. It's fact that sex uses up four-point-six megatons of kilojoule energy for every orgasm."

"You *just* made that up."

"All right I did, but still."

"Lunatic."

She stroked his face. "You're gorgeous."

He smirked. "Oh, I know." And he strutted around like a peacock, making her giggle.

"What was *that*? Mick Jagger crossed with a chicken?"

Nox gave up his comic strut. "Buzzkill."

Livia giggled. Gorgeous *and* funny. "Nox Renaud ... how on earth haven't you been snatched up by some woman already? I mean, apart from that face of yours, you're the full package, aren't you? I don't get why you would ever be single."

The smile cracked a little, faded, and Livia cursed herself. "Shit. I'm sorry. Did I put my foot in it again?"

Nox was silent for a moment, gathering his thoughts. He played with her fingers as he tried to decide what to say. "Liv ... when I was a teenager, there was someone. Ariel. We were inseparable, and we both knew it was inevitable that we would end up together. One night, I was getting ready to go pick her up for our senior prom. Amber—that's her twin sister—called the house in hysterics. Ariel was missing." A cloud passed over his handsome features and Livia took his hand, holding it tightly. He smiled at her gratefully before clearing his throat. "They found her body the next day, laid on one of the tombstones in the cemetery. She'd been st—" his voice broke and he looked away from her. Livia was horrified to see tears in his eyes. "Stabbed to death. And not quickly either. Whoever murdered her took his time."

"Oh, God, no." Livia felt cold. Poor, poor Ariel. The heartbreak on Nox's face was still obvious even though two decades had passed.

Nox looked at Livia now, his green eyes filled with pain. "I never thought anyone could ever ... not replace, I hate that word —and it's not true when you're talking about another human— but that I would meet someone who made my heart soar. I was wrong."

Livia touched his face. "I want to make you happy again, Nox Renaud."

He wrapped his arms around her. "You already have, Livia."

She kissed him, her heart pounding with sorrow for him. "What will your friends think about me? I mean, I know you're still friends with Amber ... will she think I'm just a gold-digging interloper?"

"No. Amber has always told me that she wants me to be happy. I think, for both of us, we had no closure over Ariel's death because whoever killed her is still out there. I think you and Amber would be good friends. I certainly hope so."

"On my part, I have no qualms ... except perhaps the total chasm in our social situations."

Nox shook his head. "You shouldn't fixate on that. Really."

"I promise," she smiled up at him, but then her face turned

solemn. "I'm so sorry about Ariel. That's horrific. The police really had no clues?"

"None. Ariel was the sweetest person. No one could have had a reason to harm her."

Livia sighed. "Sadly, there doesn't seem to be much reason to kill a woman. Some do it just for the thrill."

Nox was silent for a while, but Livia felt his arms tighten around her. "When I heard you scream that night," he said softly, "when I saw it was you ..."

"That was just some dude trying to mug me, Nox. I dealt with it."

"Badass."

"You betcha."

He kissed the top of her head. "Okay, my little warrior woman. Let's go back to bed and keep each other up all night."

CHAPTER SEVEN

L ivia's head was bent over her piano when she heard the commotion outside the practice room. She looked up as Charvi, followed by a couple of excited students, came into the room. Charvi looked stunned, overwhelmed, and shocked all at once. She nodded at Livia and then the piano.

"You might want to sit down and play that old wreck one last time."

Livia blinked, completely discombobulated. She had been working on her composition, *Night*—her 'piano porn,' as she had told Nox—and had been so into it that the sudden interruption made her shake her head. "What?"

Charvi smiled. "Your boyfriend is a *very* generous man." She turned as the wide doors of the music room were opened and a gang of workmen, huffing and puffing, wheeled in a vast trailer. Livia stood as they maneuvered the covered item onto the floor.

"You can take this one out," Charvi ordered them, tapping the piano Livia was working from, "save us the trouble."

The foreman shrugged. "Sure, no problem."

Livia quickly grabbed her stuff from the rather battered, but much-loved piano, even more confused. Charvi and her students grabbed the dust cloth on the new piano and pulled it off with a flourish. Livia couldn't help but gasp. Underneath the cloth sat the most beautiful instrument she'd ever seen. Charvi looked gleeful. "You know what this is?"

Livia nodded her head weakly. "It's a Steinway, a Model D Concert Grand Steinway." Her legs were shaking. Nox had done this? "It's Judy Carmichael's piano. Not hers personally, but her piano of choice."

Charvi was watching her. "That's right. And Nox donated not just one of these, but *four*. He's donated four of these babies to the university, plus countless other new instruments and a huge endowment."

Livia was shocked to her core and also conflicted. She and Nox had only been dating for two weeks ... and this was beyond generous.

One of the other students was looking at her enviously. "Damn, you must be good in bed."

"Tony." Charvi glared at the student. "That's enough."

"Sorry."

Livia shook her head. "It's okay. Four Steinways, though?"

Charvi looked at the other students. "Give us the room, will you?" After they had gone, Charvi sat Livia down on the new piano stool. "You look like you're about to collapse. Sit, breathe."

"I just ... I mean, what? What does this mean?"

Charvi nodded, but she didn't smile. "I think it means he's smitten."

"This is too much, Charvi. I mean, God ... it's been *two* weeks. Not that I'm not happy for the university, but ..." She opened the lid of the piano and began to press down on the keys. "God, listen to that tone ..." She began to play her composition, listening to the deep bass of Swedish steel and copper wire, the treble so sweet and pure. She played through all she had written so far—twice—forgetting Charvi was in the room.

Closing her eyes and moving her fingers over the smooth spruce keys, she lost herself in the composition. Livia thought not of the notes she had to play, but of Nox, and of making love with him, the fun and laughter they had shared over the last few days. They had become almost inseparable in such a short time ...

She sighed and finished playing, opening her eyes. Charvi gave her a round of applause. "That, sister, is coming along nicely."

Livia grinned. "My piano porn?"

Charvi laughed. "I don't think we'll call it that in the program. Do you have another title?"

Livia flushed. "*Night*."

Charvi sighed. "I guess it's no use now to ask you to be cautious with this man."

Livia felt stung. "Charvi ...what is it? Why are you so nervous about my relationship with Nox Renaud?"

Charvi rubbed her eyes. "It's not Nox himself so much as it is the people who surround him. I worry about them affecting you."

Livia snorted. "Charvi, I can look after myself in that respect. Why is it I think you're keeping something from me? Tell me straight ... is Nox dangerous? Tell me now before I fall in love with him, because that is a very real possibility."

Charvi looked upset, and as if she were about to say something, but then relented. "Just be cautious around his friends. If Nox is anything like Gabriella, then I wish you two nothing but happiness. She was the best person I ever knew."

"Then he is like his mother," Livia said softly, trying to keep the tone of reproach out of her voice and Charvi smiled apologetically.

"In that case ..." Charvi patted her shoulder. "He might have donated the instruments, but you had already started to write that beautiful piece about him, and now you've given it his name. Have you invited him to the recital?"

"Not yet, but I will. I just have to make sure it's perfect."

"You will."

Livia looked at her watch. "I have to go thank him."

"Thank him for all of us, would you? Obviously, the dean will be writing to him to express his gratitude, but from me, from the music department and faculty, say thank you."

Livia hugged her teacher. "I will. And you know, I think he'd love to see you again."

Charvi's smile faded. "I'm not sure I'm ready. Gabriella was like a sister to me. Her death still hurts and I ..." She sighed. "I'm scared that if Nox has grown to look like his father too much, I might flip out on him and say all the terrible things I wanted to say to Tynan. So, not yet, please. Let me work my way up to it."

Livia nodded, sadness making her chest hurt. One moment in time and so many lives had been wrecked. "Of course. Let me just say ... Nox is a wonderful man. You won't find a more generous or kind and open man."

"I believe you. I just need time is all."

ROAN STARED AT NOX, who looked back steadily. "After all that, just 'no?'"

"Roan, you knew this was a long shot coming in here. If you need money, just ask, but we both know you're not cut out to be in this business."

"It's food importing!" Roan threw his hands up in the air and stood up. Nox could see he was agitated and shot a glance at a silent Sandor. Sandor cleared his throat.

"Roan, it's purely from a business standpoint. We've made our reputation on no drama and no gossip, by being above board and transparent on everything. And while you're a fantastic salesman, that's not who we are." He tried to lighten the mood. "It would be like Freddie Mercury joining ... Coldplay."

"Or the Allman brothers."

"Sigur Rós."

"Snoop Dogg joining the Spice Girls."

"You're Scary Spice."

"Am not."

Roan's mouth hitched up at one side as he tried not to smile. "Don't make me laugh. I'm mad at you guys."

"We're just saying we're too *staid* for you, buddy. Rather, this *company* is. Look, you want to talk about setting up a new company doing something entirely different, something that will suit you and that we could invest in, go for it."

Roan, mollified, sat back down. "You'd consider a new company?"

"Sure thing. Something where you'd be the lead and we would be silent partners."

Roan chewed on his lip, and Nox shot Sandor a meaningful look. Sandor nodded. "Look, I have to make some calls. How about I come back for you in twenty minutes and we'll grab some lunch?"

"Sure thing."

When they were alone, Nox looked at his friend. Roan seemed diminished somehow, stressed, not his usual ebullient self. "What is it, Roan? There's something going on with you, something more than wanting a new career."

Roan sighed and rubbed his face. "Don't worry about it."

"I *do* worry about it." Nox frowned. "Do you need money?"

Roan stayed silent. "You just have to ask," Nox said in a quiet, calm voice. Roan shook his head.

"Thank you, man, but I have to find my own way out of this."

"Surely Odelle's family ..." Nox trailed off as Roan laughed.

"Man, if I could keep it my pants maybe she wouldn't hate me right now."

"*Fuck,* Roan."

"That's what I do. Maybe I should start a male escort business."

Nox ignored that remark. "Odelle knows?"

"Yup."

"Who?"

Roan hesitated before looking at his friend. "Amber."

Nox rocked back. "You're kidding?"

"Nope."

"Jesus, Roan, don't you know not to sh—"

"Shit where you sleep? Yup. I'm that much of an idiot."

"Jeez."

Roan sighed. "Look, I'll work on Odelle, apologize, make it up to her. Marry her."

"Odelle may be a strange fish, but she won't fall for any fake sentiments or actions. If you marry her, you had better damn mean it. Or you'll have me to answer to, as well as Odie." Nox was irritated, but Roan held up his hands.

"I hear you." He studied his friend. "What about you? You made a move on the lovely Livia yet?"

Nox couldn't help his smile. "That is going very, very well, thanks. She's adorable."

"You bringing her to Thanksgiving? You can, you know. She can meet the gang."

Nox smiled, but didn't answer. "Look, get together an idea for the kind of business you'd like to run and we'll talk more, make a business plan. There's a couple of empty offices here you can use as a base. Don't harass the female staff, is all I ask."

"Would I?"

"*Yes.*"

Roan laughed. "I promise to be good. Thanks, man. I appreciate this."

"Just take it seriously. This could be a turning point."

Roan smiled at his friend. "You know, you're an excellent big brother."

Nox ignored the pain that shot through him—an excellent big brother, just like Teague had been—and hid it with a smile. "Damn straight. And I *will* kick your ass if you screw this up."

Roan stood and shook Nox's hand. "I swear to you, Nox, I won't let you down."

"Go tell that to Odelle."

"I will. Thanks, brother."

LIVIA WAITED as the receptionist tried not to stare at her. She smiled at the young woman, who flushed slightly. "Sorry."

Livia shrugged. "It's okay. What's your name?"

"Pia."

"Hey, Pia, I'm Liv. I'm kind of seeing your boss."

Pia smiled. She was young, early twenties, Livia guessed, with big blue eyes and jet-black hair. Gorgeous. "I know. He's such a great guy, great boss, too."

Livia smiled and wondered if Pia had a crush on her boss. She couldn't blame her. The next minute, Livia realized Nox *wasn't* the object of Pia's affection when Sandor came into the reception and handed her some notes. Pia flushed a deep scarlet and Livia hid a smile.

Sandor grinned at her. "Hey, Livvy, great to see you. Does Nox know you're here?"

She shook her head. "I told Pia I'd wait until he was free."

Sandor threw a smile at Pia, which made the young woman light up. "Nah, come on, it's only Roan who's in with him."

Sandor led her back to Nox's office. As she walked with him, she nudged his shoulder. "That girl has a king-sized crush on you."

Sandor rolled his eyes. "I'm old enough to be her father, Liv."

"So?"

Sandor laughed. "I'm not a cradle snatcher."

Livia felt a little sting—after all, there were twelve years between her and Nox. Sandor saw her smile falter and guessed what she was thinking. "*Totally* different situation," he said hurriedly. "I'm forty-five, Pia is *nineteen*."

"Ugh, okay, I get it. Don't tell Pia I told you."

Sandor knocked at Nox's door, grinning. "I won't. She's young, she'll find some young boy to fall in love with next week." He opened the door. "Hey, Renaud, found this little treasure in reception."

Nox looked delighted to see her. "Hey, beautiful, what a nice surprise." He came to greet her, kissing her on the mouth, lingering over it.

Roan snickered. "Get a room."

Livia, blushing, giggled. "Hey, Roan."

"I was just telling Nox here that we look forward to meeting you formally at Thanksgiving."

Livia rocked back a little. "*Formally*?"

Nox rolled his eyes. "He means *properly*, all of us. We'll talk about it over lunch. Guys, do you mind if I take a raincheck?"

"Nope."

"Not at all."

LIVIA TOOK him back to her apartment. He walked around the tiny kitchen/living space and nodded. "I like it. It suits you. Yeah, this is welcoming, warm. And even better, it smells like you—all soft flowers and fresh air."

Flushing, Livia was pleased. Her and Moriko's home was

small but they both loved it, decorating it with colored scarves and art pieces and books. The couch was big and squashy and Livia pushed Nox down on it before straddling him. "So, Mr. Renaud, before I feed you, there's a little matter of a huge 'thank you' to be discussed. Nox, I cannot believe your generosity. Thank you, on behalf of the university, the faculty, the students, and the music department. I'm overwhelmed."

"I thought you might appreciate practicing on the same instrument as your heroine," he said shyly, and Livia kissed him, crushing her lips against his.

"You're perfect," she whispered and sat up, unbuttoning her dress one button at a time, slowing peeling it off. She was naked underneath and Nox groaned, fixing his mouth on her nipple, sucking and teasing them both until they were unbearably sensitive. Livia opened his shirt and his fly, running her hands over his taut muscles, his flat belly. "God, I want you so badly."

With a growl, Nox tipped her to the floor, pressing her knees to her chest and taking her clit into his mouth. Livia gasped at the sensations he sent flooding through her.

"I'm supposed to be thanking *you*," she gasped and felt the vibration from his laugh rumble through her sex.

"You are," he said, his voice muffled. As he brought her to orgasm, she trembled and cried out his name. He moved up to kiss her mouth.

"When you call my name like that ... God, Livvy." He kissed her deeply, passionately. Livia pulled away from his kiss and made her way down his body, trailing her tongue down his chest, his belly, and then took his cock into her mouth, licking the salty pre-cum from the tip and running her tongue down the thick shaft. His fingers tangled in her hair as she worked on him, feeling his cock harden even more and quiver under her touch.

"Jesus, Livvy ..." She felt him jerk underneath her, and then his hands were under her shoulders, pulling her on top of him.

He slid a condom on and she spread her legs wide for him as he thrust into her. She moaned softly as they began to move together—really, there was nothing like the way he felt inside her, his cock so thick and long, harder than steel, yet the skin silky and soft.

They made love slowly, taking their time, their eyes never leaving the other's face. Livia had never felt a connection like this, had never experienced this intimacy so quickly with someone. She already knew the planes of his face, his mannerisms, the way his eyes would become more intense as they made love —as if she was the only thing he could see, or wanted to see. When they were this close, she wished she could sink into him, become one with him. Her fingernails dug into his firm, rounded buttocks now as he plunged into her again and again. *I could die right now and be happy,* she thought, and then pulled herself up. *Really? Oh shit.* She was falling in love with him.

No, no, no. It was too quick, too soon. *Calm down,* she told herself, burying her face in his neck and kissing his throat. *Just let it happen. Nox is the man for you and you know it ...*

"I'm crazy about you," he whispered suddenly and she nodded.

"And I, *you,* you gorgeous man." She kissed him, feeling a surge of certainty before all other thoughts were swept away and she was coming, riding her orgasm like a wave as Nox climaxed with her. She wondered if she should tell him she was already on birth control. Something in her wanted to feel his seed deep inside her, to feel his cock inside without any barrier. She was sensible though—they weren't yet at the stage where they could discuss that and she knew it. But God, to feel his skin against her ... would that be something he would go for? Her brain was too endorphin-soaked to think straight right then.

Nox's lips were against hers. "God, you're beautiful." He smoothed the hair away from her face. "Chocolate eyes."

She grinned. "Ocean eyes." He laughed and kissed her.

"So ... what were we talking about?"

"Your incredible generosity. Nox, you didn't need to do that."

Nox smiled good-naturedly. "I know, and it wasn't a 'thank you for screwing me' gift, so don't think that. It was time I did something for the university, and now I had a focus. Was Charvi pleased?"

Livia nodded. "She was."

"Good, I'm glad. I hope that we can meet soon."

Livia wriggled into his arms. "I did speak to her about that. Nox ... she's not ready. She told me she still has so much anger towards your father that if she saw you, saw that you looked like him, she might have some kind of left-brain-hip-check and freak out on you."

Nox was silent for a while. Livia studied him, her brow furrowed. "I hope I haven't upset you."

"No." But he sat up and rubbed his face. He picked his shirt up and started to put it on. "I guess, well ..."

"What?"

"I guess I should tell you. Charvi and my mom ... way before she was married to my dad, they were close. *Very* close."

"Lovers?"

Nox nodded. "I was the only one who knew. My mom used to confide in me and she always told me, although she never regretted marrying my dad and having Teague and me, that she hated being estranged from Charvi. That she had loved her entirely."

"Why did your mom leave her?"

Nox gave her a sad smile. "Family."

"Enough said. God, the tragedy of it all." She stroked his face. "Do you think that's why your father went crazy? He found out?"

"I don't know, Liv, I honestly don't. Dad was pretty open-minded, pretty progressive. I can't imagine he would freak out over something like that. Then again, I never imagined he could kill my mother and brother in cold blood."

Livia shivered. "My father was, or is, a drunk asshole, but he never laid a hand on me. I can't imagine what it must have been like for you."

He kissed her forehead. "That's the thing. He was a great dad. *Really* great. None of that machismo you-are-boys-so-you-must-be-tough and women-belong-in-the-kitchen crap. I guess I'll never understand."

Livia was quiet for a while. "Why did the police believe he was guilty so easily, then? Why didn't they look into it further?"

He looked surprised. "It was pretty cut and dried, sweetheart. They found Dad with the gun in his mouth, gunshot residue all over him."

"He could have been framed."

"Unlikely, according to the forensic team, but I appreciate you thinking well of him." He kissed her again. "What about you? You don't talk about your family that much."

She shrugged. "Not much to tell. Only child; Mom was amazing, but cancer doesn't discriminate. If the world was fair, it would have taken Dad."

"Do you think you'll ever see him again?"

"I doubt it. It's no loss, really. My family is here. Moriko and I met first semester in college and have been roommates ever since." She checked her watch. "Speaking of which, she's due home any minute so you might want to get dressed."

"Too late." The door was opening as Livia was speaking and a grinning Moriko strode in. "Hey, kids. *Nice* cock," she added admiringly to Nox, who was trying to cover himself with his jeans and laughing. Livia burst into giggles as she covered his groin with her body. Moriko's high laughter rang out as she disappeared into her room. "Let me know when you're somewhat decent and I'll come out."

A few minutes passed and Moriko stuck her head out of the door. She looked disappointed. "Oh. You're dressed. Give a girl a treat, why don't you?" She winked at Nox, who grinned back.

Livia shook her head. "You are terrible. Look, we're going to order pizza and beer—want in?"

"Hell, yes, if I'm not disturbing anything."

"Not at all."

When the pizza arrived, Livia passed out cold beers and they sat out on the tiny balcony that looked over the city. "If you squint," Moriko told Nox, "you can see Bourbon Street from here."

Nox looked in the direction of the famous street. "Really?"

"Squint harder ... harder ... now close your eyes and imagine Bourbon Street." Moriko cackled at her joke and Livia giggled, throwing a piece of pizza crust at her friend.

"Don't tease."

"No, no," Nox said, grinning, "that's what best friends are supposed to do to the paramour. It is the law."

Moriko nodded wisely. "You are wise, Young Padawan."

Livia coughed and it sounded suspiciously like 'geek.' Moriko smiled, cat-like. "You may mock, Liv, but me and *Wondercock* here are bonding."

Nox choked on his pizza, laughing, and Liv threw an apologetic look at him. "Sorry, she's not housetrained yet."

The three of them were having so much fun that Nox decided not to go back to work, and they spent the late afternoon and evening drinking and laughing. At ten p.m., Moriko got up. "Well, it's been swell, guys. I'm outtie."

"Hot date?"

"Tepid, but doable." Moriko threw her denim jacket on. She winked at Nox. "Good to meet you properly. Look after each other, kids." And she disappeared into the apartment. "And keep those windows open ... it *reeks* of sex in here."

"Yeah, it *does*," mumbled a decidedly drunk Livia, with a satisfied grin. Nox laughed and hoisted her onto his lap.

"You're drunk."

"Yep." She kissed him. "And you're beautiful. Take me to bed, Renaud, and fuck the brains right out of me." She shrieked as he stood and threw her over his shoulder, carried her into her bedroom, and proceeded to do exactly as she asked.

CHAPTER EIGHT

"The lavender one ... no, not that one ... does that look lavender to you? *That* one, yes."

Moriko was barking orders at Livia as she dressed for the Thanksgiving meal at Nox's home. The dinner with all his closest friends. All of them. And their girlfriends and boyfriends and *oh God* ... Livia felt sick with nerves. She stepped into the dress Moriko had directed her to, then shook her head. "No. I don't feel right in it."

"What about the white one?"

"I don't want to come off as a vestal virgin. And anyways, gravy stains. Thanksgiving dinner, remember?"

Moriko sighed. "Fair enough. So, we're looking for something that says 'Hey, don't mind me, I'm the good-to-go-but-not-slutty-girlfriend from the wrong side of the tracks ...' I've got it. Let's go find some knocked-up-from-the-thrift-store pink dress and Duckie can take you to the dance."

"What the *hell* are you talking about?" Livia was feeling irritated now. She'd tried on several of her dresses and was getting down to the last few she owned. Moriko rolled her eyes.

"*Pretty in Pink*, Doofus."

"Moriko, this is serious. Nox is picking me up in fifteen minutes and I have nothing. *Nothing.*"

"Jeez, don't have a cow. Hang on."

She disappeared and Livia heard her rifling through her wardrobe and frowned. "Dude, there isn't a chance in hell I'll fit into anything of yours." While Livia was curvy, Moriko was a size-zero, so stealing each other's clothes had never been an option. *Which probably saved many roommate arguments,* Livia thought now.

"Quiet, woman." Moriko came back bearing a large box. "I was saving this for your Christmas present, but I think you need it now. Open it."

Livia's eyes widened when she saw the label on the box. "Oh, no, Morry, you can't afford this."

"Shut up and open it."

Livia lifted the box lid and shifted the tissue paper. She gave a little gasp. She pulled out the mauve dress and held it up against her.

"Put it on, moron."

Livia slid into it and turned to look at herself in the mirror. The neck came down in a vee-shape—not too low, but low enough to show off her long neck and décolletage. The color picked out all the gold highlights in her golden-brown hair and complemented her large eyes and creamy skin. It hugged her curves and fell to just above her knee. Classy and elegant. "Oh, Morry, I can't believe this. Thank you so much."

Moriko's eyes were soft. "I knew as soon as I saw it, it was made for you. Wear your gold locket with it. Here, let me." She hooked the necklace over her friend's head. "Lovely. And wear your hair up. Here ..." Once again, she took charge and a moment later, Livia's thick, dark golden hair was swept up into a chignon, with a few strands falling down to soften it. Some subtle gold eyeshadow and a slick rose pink lipstick and Livia couldn't believe the reflection in the mirror. Was that really her?

"You look incredible," said Moriko with a self-satisfied grin. "Who's your momma?"

"You are." Livia laughed and hugged her. "Thank you, boo."

"Now, I hear a car door which means Nox is early as always. Probably wants to get in a pre-dinner fuck. Have a lovely time and don't let anyone look down at you, you know. Do this for the Sisterhood."

Livia grinned. "Looking like this? They wouldn't dare." She high fived her friend as the doorbell rang.

Livia was flattered by the expression on Nox's face. "Wow," he said, his voice cracking. "*Wow*, Liv."

She flushed and kissed him, but seconds later Morry came out and stuck a Post-it note just above his groin. Nox laughed as he read it.

"*Livia Chatelaine, do not touch/squeeze/suck/bounce on this until* after *the dinner party and you no longer need to look perfect. Do not ruin my masterpiece.*"

Livia choked out a shocked snort as Nox howled with laughter. Moriko grinned and closed the door behind her. Nox offered Liv his arm.

"Ready, beautiful?"

HE WATCHED the couples as they walked into Nox's huge, welcoming home, already dressed for the meal. The silver service staff moved silently around them with trays of champagne cocktails and amuse-bouche. There were going to be twenty guests in all, mostly couples, but a few were flying solo. But all he was really interested in was his host and his beautiful, wrong-side-of-the-tracks girlfriend.

He shot an amused glance at some of the other women and

wondered just how bitchy they were, how much they would look down their nose at her. That would be fun, at least. All the while he would be watching the girl, seeing just how smitten Nox was with her. Gauging how devastated he would be by her inevitable demise.

It would all come down to timing. Murder her too soon, and maybe Nox wouldn't be as crucified as he needed him to be. He gave another laugh. No, that sap Nox would always take these things hard, no matter how long he'd been fucking her. But he didn't want to rush this. He'd waited over twenty years to do this to his old friend again. Ariel had been easy—no one's guard had been up. He still remembered the look of shock, of horror on her lovely face as he'd plunged the knife into her. The look of confusion, of abject horror. He itched to see that again.

The door opened and Nox led Livia into the room. The beautiful couple immediately took the attention of the guests, and as Nox began to introduce Livia to his friends, the man who would soon be her killer watched her—the way she moved, the curve of her body, her full breasts, the sweet smile on her lush pink lips. He smiled. He would enjoy her murder as much as he would enjoy Nox's pain. And by the look on Nox's face, he was already in deep.

"Nox Renaud is in love again. Who knew?" he murmured to himself, and went to join the party.

CHAPTER NINE

"Rules of society mean we shouldn't be sitting next to each other at dinner," Nox said to her and grinned at her stricken face. "Luckily, I've never been one for rules."

She pinched his buttock hard and he laughed. "You'll pay for that later, Renaud."

"I do hope so. At last, Amber's here. Come on, you're guaranteed a warm welcome with her."

Livia followed him over to where a stunning redhead stood talking to Sandor. Sandor winked at Livia and she gave him a grateful look. Amber, too, smiled at them both.

"Well, at damn last. Hi, Livia, it's great to meet you finally."

"You too." Livia cursed the fact that her voice shook with nerves, but this was Nox's best female friend, and she wanted to make a good impression.

Amber was *sensational*. There wasn't another word for it. Tall, at least five-eleven, her long cherry red hair fell in waves down her back, her makeup was perfect, and her hourglass figure was poured into a red dress that should have clashed with her hair but worked perfectly on Amber. Amber watched Livia size her up with a grin on her face.

"It's all artifice, darling. At the end of the night I'm in sweats, shoveling French fries down my throat and watching Netflix. I look like the Swamp Thing."

Livia choked out a laugh. "Somehow I don't think so."

Amber grinned. "Let's leave these dudes and go have some girl talk somewhere."

Uh-oh. Was this the 'you hurt my friend, and I'll hurt you' talk? Well, Amber was entitled, Livia thought, but she couldn't help throwing a nervous glance back at Nox. He winked at her and mouthed, 'Don't worry.'

Whatever she expected Amber to start out with, it wasn't, "Thank you."

Livia's eyes widened. "For what?"

"For putting a smile back on my friend's face. It's been a long time coming. Here," she snagged two glasses of champagne and handed one to Livia, "drink up. Let me give you some tips on how to survive this party. Believe me, it's nothing to be nervous about, just a crash course in who to avoid."

Livia had just spotted Odelle Griffongy walk in with Roan. "Well, there's one I *do* know to avoid."

Amber followed her gaze. "Odelle? Well, she's not the friend-liest, but neither is she malevolent. Unlike Mavis Creek over there." She nodded to a squirrelly-looking, rail-thin blonde who was making puppy eyes at Nox. "Now, she has always had a thing for your man. Little does she know, we all call her Mavis Creep."

Livia smothered a snort of laughter as the woman shot daggers at them both. Amber pointed out everyone to avoid, which thankfully wasn't too many. "Nox invites them out of politeness. I would have kicked them to the curb a while ago, but then I'm not as nice as Nox."

Livia grinned at her. "Is anyone?"

Amber grinned. "Oh, he has his dark side, the same as all of us. But," she said in a stage whisper as Nox approached them, "his weird fetishes are something we should discuss another time. Remind me to tell you about the thing he had for—oh, *damn,* Nox, you're here and it was just about to get interesting. Sorry, Liv, we'll have to talk about his peccadillos another time."

Nox was grinning, clearly having heard her. "Liv, don't listen to this one. Just go on pretending I'm perfect."

"Oh, I will." Livia winked at Amber, who grinned and excused herself.

Nox kissed Livia, his lips soft against hers. "You okay, sweetheart?"

She smiled up at him as he slid his arms around her waist. "I really am. I love Amber already."

"Good. Seriously, there's nothing to worry about. It may look elite, but really, it is just Thanksgiving dinner."

NOX'S IDEA OF 'JUST' Thanksgiving dinner was a lot different than most people's, Livia thought a half hour later as they sat down to eat. Three huge turkeys, perfectly roasted and ready to be carved by the waitstaff, sat on the sideboard. On the tables were huge silver platters of mashed potatoes, yams, bowls of cranberry sauce—sure, Livia thought, all the same food, but you could tell how rich the food was. How it was expertly made by the best chefs money could buy, and when Livia put the first piece of moist, beautifully seasoned turkey in her mouth, she almost groaned with how delicious it was. The meal had its luxurious touches—shaved truffle on the turkey, a sharp sorbet between each course as a palate cleanser—but the whole atmosphere was just as Livia, who had never had a family

Thanksgiving, had always imagined. There was love between these people, and she reveled in it.

Halfway through the meal, which she had to admit she was enjoying with Nox on her left and Sandor on her right, she felt someone staring at her. She looked up and saw Odelle gazing at her. "Have we met?" Odelle's voice cut through the entire table's conversation and Livia flushed red as everyone went silent and looked at her.

"Yes, we have."

"Where?"

"Livia was at my Halloween party," Nox said smoothly, but Livia heard an undercurrent in his voice. Was he embarrassed, or was he angry with Odelle? She couldn't tell.

Odelle studied Livia. "No, that's not it."

Livia sighed. *Just get it over with.* "I work at *Le Chat Noir.*"

Of course, there was a silence. "The chef?" This was from Mavis Creep ... *Creek,* corrected Livia in her head. Amber was right, the woman was obsequious—she clearly knew Livia *wasn't* the chef. "No, I wait tables. I bring you your egg white omelet, Odelle."

She couldn't read Odelle's expression—the other woman simply nodded and turned back to her meal. Mavis Creek was sniggering to herself, nudging her partner, who rolled his eyes and tried to ignore her.

"Livia is a grad student at the university. She's earning her master's degree, Mavis, and working to pay her dues. The stuff of good character, wouldn't you say?" Nox's voice was like ice and Mavis's smirk disappeared.

"I worked the graveyard shift at Home Depot during my college experience. My father wouldn't pay for my tuition unless I worked too," Sandor piped up. "I had to pay my own rent. Nothing wrong with working your way through."

"What are you studying, Liv?" Amber jumped in now and Livia told her. Amber looked impressed. "That's fantastic."

"We need to hear you play, I think." Roan joined in and she smiled at them all gratefully. Nox had good taste in friends. They had deftly diffused the situation she had been most wary of, and with class and good humor. Nox took her hand and squeezed it and Livia felt tears well up in her eyes. God, she *loved* this man. Who cared if they'd known each other less than a month? She adored him.

Sandor nudged her and she turned to smile at him. Sandor nodded at Nox. "He's very smitten. It's truly great to see."

"Thank you, Sandor. I'm crazy about him. Really, truly crazy."

"I'm glad. He deserves happiness."

Livia studied him. Sandor, with his dark brown hair cut short and neatly trimmed beard, was handsome, his eyes merry, his manner calm and friendly. "What about you, Sandor? Anyone special?"

He grinned. "Confirmed bachelor, Liv. I was married about ten years ago but it didn't stick. Shame. She was a nice girl, but I'm not good at sharing my life, I'm afraid."

"I get it. Before I met Nox, I was all set for a life of singledom."

Sandor looked skeptical and grinned. "Have you *seen* yourself, Liv? That would never happen."

She blushed, but laughed. "Because I can't take a compliment, I'm going to swiftly change the subject." Sandor laughed as she grinned. "What about your family?"

Sandor nodded. "Only child, mom died of cancer, Dad has Alzheimer's. Some days he has full recall, but mostly he's lost in time."

"God, I'm sorry."

Sandor nodded. "It's okay. It's harder on me than him, but I can take it. He's usually locked back in a world where my mom is alive. Your parents?"

"My mom had cancer too. She died when I was young and my dad, well, I think of him more as just the sperm donor. He's a mean-ass drunk and if I never see him again, it'll be too soon." Livia didn't know why she was sharing such intimate details with this man, she only knew that she had liked him from the first. He had a warm manner, open and friendly, and she could see why he was Nox's friend and business partner. "You know how I met Nox. How about you?"

Sandor grinned. "I was actually his brother Teague's college roommate. But here's the weird thing, my dad and Nox's dad were actually old friends, although they'd drifted apart. When Teague and I became friends, they reconnected for a while. Until the tragedy, of course."

Livia nodded. "Heartbreaking."

"Indeed. Still, I have to say, Nox looks happier than I've seen him in years, thanks to you."

AFTER DINNER, some of the guests began to drift away until only Amber, Sandor, Roan, and Odelle were left. Odelle was looking antsy to leave, but Roan showed no sign of leaving. Amber sat sprawled across an armchair, her long legs crossed over the side of it; Sandor sat with Odelle, his arm around her shoulders, friendly, comforting. Livia sat on Nox's lap, shoes kicked off now that the formal dinner was over with. She ruffled Nox's curls and he grinned at her. She tickled his beard and rubbed her nose against his.

"Did you have a good time, baby?"

She nodded. "I really did." She lowered her voice. "I love your friends. I mean, *most* of them." She grinned as he laughed. "I have to say, I had preconceived opinions and I was wrong."

"For the most part." Nox nodded subtly at Odelle. "She means no harm, really."

"I get it."

He stroked her cheek with his finger. "Will you stay tonight?"

She leaned into him. "You know I will."

As THE OTHERS left after midnight, all vaguely drunk except Odelle, Roan hugged Nox and swung a giggling Livia around. "You, my little pocket rocket, have made my friend smile. Adore you."

She was still giggling when she and Nox walked back into the mansion. It was so quiet, and Livia looked back out of the window. "The spooky fog is back." Nox joined her at the window, running a hand down her back. They stared out at the mist coming off the bayou.

"It's late November." Nox turned and trailed his lips down her neck. "Do you think it's too late for a little ... alfresco?"

Livia began to smile, turning to pull his lips to hers. "If I ruin this dress, Moriko will actually kill me. Literally, not figuratively."

"Then you'd better take it off in here, woman, because there's no way we're not going out into that garden and making love in five ... four ..."

Livia shrieked with laughter as he advanced and she quickly peeled the dress over her head. Nox tugged his own shirt off and then hauled her over his shoulder.

Livia beat a drumbeat on his buttocks as he carried her out into the garden, and when he laid her in the damp grass, she grinned up at him. "You are a doofus."

"A doofus that's going to make you come again ... and again ... and again."

Soon they were naked and clawing at each other as they

fucked with abandon. The mist drifting up from the bayou was chilly and they both shivered, their skin damp with sweat, as they made love. Afterwards, they lay wrapped around each other. Livia kissed his mouth. "You make everything so magical, baby. You know what I'd love to do?"

"What's that?"

"Remember that little grove where we met?"

They walked slowly, holding their clothes until they slipped into the secluded little grove. Livia walked to the stone seat and patted it. "Come sit with me."

Nox sat, his face confused, and Livia smiled, placing her palm on his cheek. "When I first saw you here, I thought you were the saddest person I had ever seen. And something in me wanted to take that pain away."

Nox leaned his forehead against hers. "You have."

"I hope at least I've begun to. You deserve every happiness, Nox. Every single moment of your life should be full of joy."

"It is when I'm with you."

She kissed him. "Remember that night? I was so sure you were going to kiss me, and when Amber called your name ... God, I was so disappointed. I've always wondered if I imagined that moment."

Nox shook his head. "You didn't." He grinned slightly. "I wanted to do a lot more than kiss you."

She laughed. "Well, I wanted that too. So ... let's make good on that wish right now."

She had barely finished her sentence when he crushed his lips against hers. "God help me, Livia Chatelaine," he said when they were both breathless, "but I think I'm falling in love with you."

Livia felt a surge of joy. "I love you, Nox Renaud. I don't give a shit if it's only been a few weeks. I *love* you."

They were so wrapped up in each other as they began to

make love again, that they never saw the man slip quietly from the corner of the grove into the darkness.

HE WATCHED THEM MAKE LOVE, their love for each other obvious and palpable. They made a beautiful, ethereal couple, pale skin in the moonlight, their gasps and sighs and moans of pleasure the only sound in the night.

Enjoy her, Nox. Enjoy her for as long as you can.

He couldn't tear his eyes away from Livia's lush body. At dinner, he had studied her, those huge, warm brown eyes, the way she had dealt with the sniping of Mavis Creek. Those pink full lips curving up in a smile. Yes, he imagined it would be very easy to fall in love with Livia Chatelaine. He would pay more attention to her, her life, her friends ... it would be interesting to mess with her head too, before she became his victim.

In the meantime, Nox ... He would make his old friend think he might be losing his mind. That was next, and he knew just how to do it ...

He looked back at the couple, crying out as they came, and smiled. *Yes, enjoy the beautiful Livia while you can, Nox. Because sooner rather than later, before the winter is out, before the last of the pine needles has fallen from the Christmas trees ... she'll be dead.*

And you, Nox, you will be rotting away in a jail cell, charged with the depraved, brutal, bloody murder of the woman you love.

CHAPTER TEN

Odelle stared at Roan for a long moment, and then reached into her purse for a cigarette. Roan waited, his heart thumping against his ribs. Odelle lit her cigarette and studied him.

"Why?"

Roan's mouth hitched up in a smile. "Why else do people get married? I want to be your husband, of course."

Odelle didn't smile. "Roan, I think we both know this isn't a love match. Why else would you be fucking other women if it was?"

She had a point and Roan nodded. "I admit, I have been. I'm immature, Odelle, and that's not an excuse. I can change."

Odelle gave a snort of laughter. "Be honest, Roan. I marry you, you get my father's money, and you'll be back to your old ways within a year." She sighed. "I deserve better. I deserve what your friend and that waitress have. Did you see the way they were looking at each other?"

"We used to look at each other like that."

"No, we *never* looked at each like that."

Roan sat back in his chair. "So, you're saying no."

Odelle half smiled. "I didn't say that. I'm saying I'll think about it. Prove to me you can stay faithful. Do this. I'll give you one week to finish whatever you've started with your whores. One week's grace. Fuck them and tell them goodbye. Do that, and I'll agree to an engagement."

Roan nodded. "Fine." He got up and went to her, trailing the back of his fingers down her porcelain cheek. "Odelle, we can make this work. I'm sorry I've made you feel ..."

She looked at him steadily. "Second best."

He shook his head. "You were never that."

"Then never make me feel that way again, Roan, or you won't know what's hit you. Agreed?"

He nodded, his blue eyes serious for once. "Agreed."

LIVIA GRINNED at Nox's text message as she pushed her way into her music room.

Good to know you're on your way to practice your 'fingering.' I hope to do the same later. I love you, x.

She giggled. Since Thanksgiving and their declaration of love, their relationship had become even more fun, and *definitely* dirtier. They'd fucked in practically every room of his mansion —except for those two rooms he kept locked. She never mentioned them, guessing it was where his family had died. She did wonder why he had continued living there after the deaths. She would ask Sandor or Amber if she could—both of them had quickly become her confidantes and Livia was delighted that Nox's friends had accepted her so readily. Tonight, it was her friends' turn to meet Nox—Marcel and Moriko, plus another couple of staff from the restaurant—and now Livia was hoping to persuade Charvi to come too.

The music room was empty as she dumped her stuff on the floor and sat down at the Steinway. She ran her hand over the smooth surface of the piano, wondering again at Nox's generosity. She closed her eyes and thought back to this morning, to waking up in his bed, his mouth on her nipple, then her belly, and finally his tongue lashing around her clit until she came. Livia sighed. Her body still ached from the night before; they'd made love all evening and most of the night until they were exhausted, and now her vagina ached from the pounding of Nox's huge cock. He owned her body when they made love, and she loved it.

"Hey ..." Livia opened her eyes to see Charvi frowning at her. "Do you feel better?"

Livia was confused. "Huh?"

"You said you were sick and wouldn't be in today."

Livia shook her head. "Not me."

"You didn't call the admin office?"

"No."

Charvi shrugged. "They must have gotten the names mixed up. Damn it, then the room is double booked."

"Oh." Livia was disappointed. "No matter, I'll come back later ... Shoot, no, scratch that. I promised Marcel a couple of hours at the restaurant. Well, it doesn't matter."

"Sorry, honey."

"Can't be helped." Livia started to pick her things back up. Charvi smiled apologetically at her.

"Hasn't Nox bought you a Steinway for home use yet?"

Livia grinned. "Where the hell would I put it? And no. It's one thing for him to spend that money on the music department, quite another to spend it on a personal gift."

"He doesn't have a piano at the mansion?"

Livia shook his head. "You know, I never even considered that, but no."

"Huh."

Livia's eyebrows shot up. "Why?"

"You don't know?" Charvi pulled out her iPad and flicked to a page on the Internet. She handed it to Livia.

It was a page from the archives of *The Advocate*, the newspaper of New Orleans, Baton Rouge, and Lafayette. The story was dated twenty-five years previously.

Local Boy Wins Prestigious Music Award.

THE SON *of New Orleans society maven Gabriella Renaud has been awarded top prize for his solo composition,* Lux, *at the New Orleans Children's Music awards. Twelve-year-old Nox Renaud wrote and performed the piece on the cello to an audience of local luminaries at the Lafayette Emporium Music Theatre. Also rumored to be listening to the young prodigy were members of the illustrious Peabody Institute. Sources close to the Renaud family, whose patriarch, Tynan Renaud, is one of Louisiana's richest philanthropists, say that the family is encouraging the young man to seek a future in music. Nox's elder brother, Teague, is currently being feted by Harvard and Brown, and the family has a long history of academic excellence.*

LIVIA LOOKED UP AT CHARVI. "I had no idea. Why wouldn't he mention it?"

"I don't know. But I'm guessing, since he and his mother—she was a pianist like you—used to play together, it's too painful."

"Oh." Livia felt a little sick. "And here I am, rattling on about ... *God.*"

"Hey, *no*, don't do that. If I know Nox, this is like ... a lifeline. Not that he's using you to remember his mother, but through you, he can get something of her back, you know? I'm sure it's entirely separate from how he feels about you."

Livia half smiled. "We're having dinner with Moriko and

Marcel and a couple of others tonight. Come. He'd love to see you."

Charvi hesitated but Livia could see there was a small desire in her to see her lover's son. "Please," Livia said softly.

Charvi smiled. "All right. Just tell me where and when."

Livia grinned and hugged her. "It will be wonderful, I promise."

Charvi nodded. "Look, the next student isn't due for ten minutes. Have a quick practice before you go."

"I will, thanks."

When she was alone, Livia couldn't stop thinking about Nox. He was a cello player? She wondered what his composition had been like. She could picture him, his dark curls messy, hanging in his face as he bent over his cello, the intensity of his green eyes as he played. She could see him as an adult, taking the applause of his audience, looking devastatingly handsome in a suit as he played. She had to get him to open up to her.

She was still smiling as she opened the lid of the piano. An envelope slid out and to the floor, and as she bent to pick it up, she realized it was addressed to her. She didn't recognize the handwriting and assumed it was some college communication. She ripped open the envelope.

Ice shot through her.

Break it off with Nox, or I'll make your life hell, whore.

Livia couldn't help the gasp of hurt that escaped her lips. What the fuck? She glanced at the envelope and then shook herself. *Are you really looking for a return address?* It was so vile, so hurtful for a moment, that she couldn't breathe. Then, adrenaline shot through her, a flash of anger. Who the hell would send such a spiteful note?

"Whoever you are," she said to herself grimly, "you can just go *fuck* yourself." She crumpled the note and shoved it into her coat pocket. She had a pretty good idea of the one person it might be. *Mavis Creep.* Livia grabbed her stuff and began to walk from the college to the local bus stop. She smiled grimly to herself.

Well, Mavis, just for that, I'm going to ride Nox longer and harder than I ever have tonight. What do you think of that, bitch? She wished she could say it to the other woman's face.

SHE WAS SO WRAPPED up in her thoughts that Livia never saw the man following her. He rode the bus with her back to the French Quarter and followed her to *Le Chat Noir*. He watched her interact with her friends—the cute Asian girl, the darkly-handsome Frenchman who clearly owned the restaurant. Close friends of hers, obviously. Good, that was good. It meant she was vulnerable.

When her shift finished, he followed her home. Was she alone now? He imagined the fun he could have if he surprised her alone.

But a quick thrill kill wasn't his plan for her. This was the long game. The note would have unsettled her but not scared her. Probably just made her angry.

It begins ...

He was going to enjoy this.

CHAPTER ELEVEN

Nox felt something shift inside him as he saw Charvi arrive at the restaurant. His hand tightened reflexively on Livia's and she smiled up at him. "It's okay, baby," she whispered, and kissed his cheek.

He stood to greet his mother's old lover. Charvi looked nervous too as he kissed her cheek. "You look just like her," Charvi said, her voice trembling. For a moment, they stared at each other. Then, as a tear dropped down Charvi's cheek, they fell into each other's arms.

"I miss her," was all she said and Nox, overcome with emotion, nodded.

"I know. I know."

They sat down, Nox noticing Livia quickly brushing a tear away from her eyes. He kissed her. "Thank you," he murmured into her ear and she smiled.

"I love you," she said, sweeping a loose curl away from his forehead.

After that, the tension had all but gone from the small party. Marcel and Nox chatted about business, Charvi, Moriko, and Livia about nothing in particular. Easy, fun. The restaurant they had chosen was spectacular. Nox liked Livia's small group of friends; they were funny, erudite, down to earth—just like Liv. She was sitting in the curve of his arm, her body next to his as she ate and laughed with them all. He buried his face in her hair and breathed her in as she talked to her friends, but he felt her hand on his thigh. God, he loved this woman.

His cell phone bleeped and he glanced at it. His throat constricted and he stiffened. Ariel. A photograph of her, laughing and smiling, her dark hair backlit by the sun. He frowned. Who the hell was sending him this *now?*

There was no return phone number. Another text came through. This time, it was a crime scene photo, one he had seen so many times it was seared through his brain. Ariel, dressed in a gray gown, lying on top of one of the tombs in the Lafayette Cemetery, her blood soaking both her gown and the white marble tomb she was laid upon. She looked like she had been sacrificed to some dark God. The blade of the dagger was still buried deep in her belly, her eyes were open and her mouth locked forever in a scream of terror and pain. Nox felt a wave of nausea.

"Excuse me," he muttered and got up to go to the restroom. He made it just before he threw up. Someone was playing a sick game sending him those photographs.

But this wasn't the first time. After his family had died, friends of Ariel's had sent him the photographs then, taunting him, making it clear they thought he was a killer. It had gotten so bad that in his lowest points, he had even asked himself if he had done it ...even though, rationally, he knew it was impossible. The police had questioned him for hours—days—after both tragedies and had released him without any charge, or any caution. Nox knew he was innocent, but it didn't stop him from feeling the weight of responsibility.

He went back out to the group. Livia looked at him, concern in her warm brown eyes. "You okay?"

He smiled at her. "Perfectly, baby. Sorry, just felt a little queasy for a second. Probably just a kickback from being nervous earlier."

Livia slid her arm around his waist and kissed him tenderly. "I think it went very well," she said in a low voice, a subtle nod to Charvi. Nox nodded.

"Thanks to you."

Livia shook her head. "You would have found each other again, with or without me."

Nox brushed his lips against hers. "I never want to be without you again."

"You never will."

AFTER DINNER they said their goodbyes. Nox and Charvi had a moment alone together. "Your mother would have been so proud of the man you've become, Nox. And she would have adored Livia. You two are made for each other."

Nox smiled at her. "I think so too."

"You promise you'll take care of my girl?"

"With all my heart."

Livia came back to stay with Nox again. As they walked into his bedroom, he smiled at her. "Liv ... you know, you could move in here with me."

Livia was silent for a while, and then she sat on the bed. "Is it too soon?"

Nox felt a little stung, but he could see where she was coming from. "I honestly don't know. But I do know I'd like it— very much."

She half-smiled at him. "I would too, but I don't want to leave Moriko in a difficult position. We can barely afford our apartment between the two us—and before you make any grand gestures, hear me out. We both needed to do it. We both needed to prove we could—can—make it on our own. Nox, you know that that fact that you're rich has never bothered me—I'm not interested in your money, it's you I want. But neither am I naïve. I still stay here with you, eat your food, travel with you ... But it is important to me that I keep in touch with my base. I make my own money, I pay my own way. I have no earthly idea if I'll ever be on the same financial footing as you—as a musician, probably not," she laughed. "But I have to have a balance. I won't be *that* woman, you know."

Nox crushed his lips against hers. "Do you know you're my heroine?"

"With an 'e' or without?" She grinned and he laughed.

"Both. Definitely both. And yeah, I get it. Can we compromise?"

"How so?"

"At least bring some stuff over here, take space in my closet so that when you're not here—"

"You can dress up as me?" Livia was grinning widely now and Nox burst out laughing.

"Dang it, woman, you see right through me."

"I can see it now. I get a text message *'I'm at home, dressed as you. Bring chocolate syrup and a riding crop.'* Kinky."

Nox wrestled her back onto the bed. "You want kinky, I can *get* kinky, woman." He noticed her breath quicken, excitement in her eyes. "Oh, you like the idea of that, huh?"

She nodded, her pink lips parted, and he felt his cock get hard. "So, what is your kink, Ms. Chatelaine?"

He pushed up her dress and buried his face in her soft belly and Livia chuckled. "Well, that's nice for a start."

"Nice, but not very kinky," Nox mumbled, rimming her navel with his tongue. He felt her shiver with pleasure.

"You know, I honestly never thought about it ... but there's very little I won't try with you, Mr. Renaud."

Nox groaned. "God, Liv ..." He unbuttoned her dress and shimmied her panties down her long legs. "Every inch of you is heaven."

"What do you like, Nox? Tell me and I'll do it."

"All I can think about right now is your creamy skin and the fact that my cock needs to be inside you."

She giggled and he moved up her body. Livia unbuttoned his shirt and fly as he kissed her, then she waved his tie at him. "Want to tie me up, bad boy?"

Nox's eyes lit up. "Good idea." He wrapped the tie around her wrists, pulling them above her head. "Ha, now you're really at my mercy." He nibbled at her ear as she giggled and writhed beneath him.

"What do you like, Nox, really? I'll do it, whatever it is ... you can spank me, whip me ... anything. I'm yours."

She felt his enormous cock swell even more and he groaned, burying his face in her neck. "What you do to me, Ms. Chatelaine ..." He looked into her eyes. "May I please lay you on her belly and take you from behind?"

He turned her over and Livia felt him part her legs gently, and when his cock—so rigid, so massive—pushed into her cunt, she felt it in every cell of her body. The added friction on her clit was heaven, and Nox bunched her hair up in his fist as he thrust, pulling her head back and up so he could kiss her mouth.

"Take me, Nox, harder ... harder ..." She was gasping as he fucked her, thrusting deeper with his hips, his cock reaming her cunt until they both came, Nox coming inside her for the first time, his seed shooting deep into her belly.

Livia sighed happily as she basked in her own climax. "Nox?"

Nox's mouth was on the back of her neck, kissing, biting her skin in his frenzy for her. "Yes, my darling?"

She turned to look him in the eye. "Fuck me in the ass, Nox. Fuck me hard."

He gave a growl of desire and, sliding a condom onto his cock, took her just as she'd asked. Easing into her perfect round ass, they made love again. Livia gave a long cry as she came; it was a mellower orgasm, but just as thrilling.

Tearing the condom off, Nox rolled off of her, flipping her onto her back and freeing her hands. She grabbed his curls and pulled hard, making him grin. "God, woman, you are a little animal."

Livia kissed him, biting his lower lip, wanting to absorb him into her soul. "Fuck me again, and again, and again ..."

Nox gathered her to him, rolling them both to the floor, where he pressed her legs up to her chest and sat back, admiring her body. "You have the most perfect little cunt, Ms. Chatelaine. Why don't you feel for yourself while I watch?"

He began to stroke his cock back into rigidity as Livia stroked her own sex, slipping her fingers inside herself, feeling his cum deep inside her. When Nox could stand it no more, he pushed her hand aside and plunged his cock back inside her. "I want to fill you with my cum, baby."

"Do it," she urged, her eyes almost feral with desire. "Fuck me like you want to hurt me."

And he did, slamming his hips into her, pinning her hands to the floor, kissing her, tasting blood until they were both exhausted.

Afterward, they showered together. Livia sucked Nox's cock as the water pulsed down on them. He carried her to the bed after they'd dried and lay down, their naked bodies entwined.

Livia stroked his face. "I don't know a lot about bondage," she said, "but I think it's exciting to find out. Have you ever done that with someone before?"

Nox shook his head. "I haven't, but like you said, I'm excited about the thought of doing it with you. We can take it slowly, find out what we like. We can even get some toys if you'd like."

"I *would* like." Livia grinned at him. "I like the thought of wearing the leather gear for you, you restraining me as you fuck me. Dominating me."

"Damn, woman." Nox nodded down to his cock, which was getting hard again. "You're not going to let me have any sleep tonight, are you?"

Livia laughed, rolling him onto his back and straddling him, guiding him inside of her. She gave a shuddering moan as she impaled herself on him. "I honestly could stay like this forever," she said as she began to ride him. "Talk dirty to me, Nox. Tell me what you like."

He cupped her breasts as they jiggled with her motion. "I like your beautiful tits," he said, "so pillowy and plump. I sometimes think of them when I'm at work, just imagining putting my mouth on each pink nipple and sucking them until you scream. I think of your hot, tight cunt, my tongue, my fingers, my cock exploring it as you clench your muscles."

He pinched her clit as she began to moan, her speed picking up. "God, Nox, yes ... that's the stuff ..."

"I imagine pressing you up against a cold stone wall someplace public and just fucking you until people wonder what the screaming is. Or clearing off a table in the restaurant and ripping that cute little waitress dress off you, fucking you in front of all those people. Watching them admire your perfect body ..."

Livia cried out as she came, so turned on by his talk, but Nox was enjoying himself. "I want to fuck you like an animal, Livia. I always dream that you've forgotten your panties just so that I can take you at anytime, anywhere I want ..."

"I'm yours, Nox, for always, for always ..."

Her cry brought him to climax and he shot his load deep into her belly, her vaginal muscles clenching him, milking him as she gazed down at him, looking so ethereally beautiful that his heart seemed to grow. "God, I love you, Livia Chatelaine."

And she bent down to kiss him again, and there was no more talking for the rest of the night.

ROAN LOOKED at the girl sitting in the passenger seat of his car and tried to smile. "I'm sorry about this."

God, why had he picked such a young one? Someone who didn't know the game. Instead, there were tears in her big blue eyes, and he hated that it was he who had put them there.

"Pia, I'm sorry. It's my fault; I should never have picked you up that day." He tipped her chin to his. "Listen, you're beautiful. There's probably already a queue of people who would love to be with you, and I guarantee they'll all be a lot better for you than me. I'm broken, Pia. I'm not a good person."

"But I was falling—"

"No. Don't say that. You're too young to know what love is."

She suddenly opened the door of his car and got out. *Uh-oh.* This wasn't a good idea. It was past midnight and the city was no place for a girl like Pia at night. He got out and called to her. "Pia, get in the car."

"Screw you."

He sighed. Would it be easier to let her walk away? Yes. It wasn't like she could threaten to tell Odelle—she would just shrug and say, "What else is new?" And, after all, he was doing what Odelle had asked him to do. Saying goodbye to all his side pieces. *Probably stop referring to women as side pieces too,* he thought to himself reproachfully. He definitely shouldn't have started up with Pia. "Just let me drive you home."

"No. *Go.* I only live two blocks from here, anyway." She stopped and looked back at him, and her expression was resigned. "Go, Roan. It's okay. I won't tell anyone about us."

She stalked off and disappeared around the corner. Roan stood arguing with himself then followed her. By the time he got to the corner, she was gone.

"Shit."

Too late. He couldn't exactly blame her if she ran to Odelle, or even Nox. Nox would be more problematic—he would not approve of Roan seeing his nineteen-year-old assistant. Roan wanted to convince Nox he was responsible? This *wasn't* the way to do it.

"*Shit,*" he said again, and got back into his car.

PIA WAITED until she heard his car start up and go before she ducked out of the doorway. She didn't want him to know that her home wasn't two blocks away, but a few miles. Still, she could walk it. Maybe it would get some of her humiliation out. She stalked along, her long legs carrying her easily. The night was cool, and she tugged her coat around herself tightly.

God, what the hell had she been thinking, sleeping with Roan Saintmarc? The dude was a walking man whore, everyone knew it. But, Pia had to admit, it had bought her some cachet in her peer group. Sandor wasn't showing any signs of interest, unless you counted paternally—*ugh*—so when Roan had put the moves on her, she'd gone along with it. And he had been a spectacular lay, she had to admit. She did wonder if he guessed she had been a virgin, but he'd never said. At least she could finally say she'd gotten rid of her v-card.

She sniggered to herself. Telling him she'd been falling in love with him ... *no way*. She'd just wanted to make him feel bad for dumping her. And it had worked. *Good.*

As she turned into the next street, she heard the step behind her. Turning, she realized a man's head was blocking the streetlight and was in shadow. He grabbed her throat and thrust her back hard against the wall, his other hand covering her scream of fright.

He's going to rape me ...

But the attacker made no attempt to lift her skirt, or grope her. For a millisecond she didn't know what the hell he wanted, then she felt it. The pain. A knife being brutally and repeatedly thrust into her stomach. *Oh God, please, no ... no ...*

She felt her legs give way and she slumped to the ground. Her killer crouched next to her, ripping open the tattered dress and stabbing her again. As Pia bled out, she managed to croak out, "*Why?*"

Her murderer slid the knife between her ribs into her heart and she never knew the answer.

CHAPTER TWELVE

Livia woke in the dark hours before dawn to an empty bed. She shivered—the window was open and a cold breeze blew into the room. She got up, snagging Nox's shirt and pulling it around her as she went to close the window.

"Nox?"

The house was silent. Livia padded into the hall and listened. Something—water?—was making a sound somewhere in the house and she followed the noise to the far end of the house, to where the two locked rooms stood. Hesitating, Livia reached out and turned the handle of one of the rooms. It opened, and she now heard the definite sound of water running —someone was in the shower in the en-suite.

She took a deep breath in and walked silently to the door of the bathroom. She tried not to look at the room itself but as she reached the bathroom door, she glanced to her left—and saw the huge, dark bloodstains on the floor. *Oh, God. Why, Nox? Why leave it like this?* It was like some sort of macabre torture chamber for his psyche.

Livia had no doubt who she would see when she pushed open the bathroom door. Nox was in the shower, naked, scrubbing at his skin furiously. He looked up, but Livia could see he wasn't really seeing her. He was sleepwalking. He raised his arms to her. "I can't get the blood out. I can't get the blood out."

As Livia looked on in horror, Nox began to sob. "I can't get the blood out, Ariel. God help me, what have I done? *What have I done?*"

CHAPTER THIRTEEN

Amber got out of the car and saw a pale, shaken Livia waiting for her at the door of the mansion. She came out to meet her and hugged Amber, and Amber could feel her trembling. "Thank you for coming, Amber. I got him back into bed but I didn't know what else to do."

Amber hugged her tightly. "You did the right thing, Livia. Is he asleep?"

Livia nodded, her brown eyes large and frightened. Amber took her hand and they went inside. Nox was asleep in their bed, his handsome face wracked with pain. Amber studied him for a moment, and then nodded for Livia to follow her out.

They sat in the kitchen and Amber made Livia drink some hot, strong coffee. It was a little after dawn. Amber, her face make-up free, her red hair tucked up in a bun, tried to smile at Livia. "First up, don't be too scared. He's done this before. Sleepwalked, I mean. Twice that I know of. Once when Ariel died, once after his family. Tell me, what did you two do last night?"

Livia told her about the dinner, and the reunion between Nox and Charvi. Amber nodded. "Ah."

Livia looked at her unhappily. "I blame myself. I encouraged them to reconnect."

"You know what, you shouldn't feel bad. At least we were able to control it, this way. What if he'd run into her unexpectedly? No, this is good. Maybe Nox will start to deal with all of it now. He never did, you see? He stuck his gorgeous head in the sand and just got on with the grief. He never processed what happened."

Livia's eyes filled with tears. "God."

Amber patted her hand. "You're good for him, you know? This is a good time for him to start processing. He has you. I suspect he's never felt stronger."

Livia smiled at her. "You are so kind."

Amber sipped her coffee. "Anything else happen last night you can think of? Was it just seeing Charvi?"

"There was something ... He got a text message and afterward, he went to the bathroom and got sick. He said it was just the release of nerves, but I don't know."

"Where's his phone?"

"Upstairs, I think. I'll go get it."

Amber waited while Livia went to get Nox's phone and when she came back, her face was stricken. "Amber ..."

"What is it?"

Livia looked down at the phone. "It's Ariel. There's photos."

Amber swallowed and held out her hand. "Livia, please."

Livia hesitated, then handed over the phone. Amber knew what she'd see before she clicked on the message but she couldn't help the small sob that escaped her when she saw the brutalized body of her twin sister. Livia's arms went around her then and held her tightly while she cried. Livia smoothed her hair, murmuring, "I'm sorry. I'm so sorry."

Amber pulled herself together, but leaned her head against Liv's. "Sorry, boo. Always a shock."

Livia smiled at her, handing her a tissue. "I can't imagine what it must be like for you. Who would send this?"

Amber sighed. "Hard to say. Someone fucking with his head. The killer. No, he or she would have sent personal photos, surely? These are the photos the press used of Ari when she was alive, and a crime scene photo. Anyone could have gotten hold of them."

"But why? Why now?"

Amber gave her a crooked grin. "If it's someone being malicious—someone *jealous*, maybe—I would say it's because of you. Not you, Livia, but you and Nox. Anyone can see how in love you are."

"You know what? I forgot this ..." Livia went out into the hall and came back with her coat. "This was left for me at the college yesterday."

She handed Amber a crumpled-up piece of paper. Amber read it aloud. "*Break it off with Nox, or I'll make your life hell, whore.* Delightful. Well, then, I think we can guess who would be so spiteful."

"Mavis Creep." Livia's tone was icy. "Fucking bitch. I'll rip her to pieces with my bare hands."

Amber grinned at her. "At least we can rule out any *actual* threat."

Livia frowned. "Threat?"

"Don't you get why these pictures were sent to Nox, honey? They're implying the same will happen to *you* if you two don't break up."

Livia snorted. "Then *come at me*, bro. I don't scare easy."

"You're a feisty one," Amber grinned at her.

"You have no idea."

They both turned towards the sound of Nox's voice. He smiled at them both, his eyes exhausted, and he slipped his arms around Liv. "Sorry I scared you, baby. Just a little nutty."

"No problem, big guy. I haven't even begun to show you *my* crazy yet." She grinned up at him and Amber smiled.

"Now, if you two are going to get mushy ..."

"Seriously, Ambs, thank you for coming. I don't know what I would have done." Livia's expression was earnest. "You're a real friend."

Amber reached for her hand. "Listen, you two are good for each other. Which doesn't mean you're not going to go through crap like this, but I'll always be there. You," she fixed Nox with a steely look, "I've played softball with you for twenty years now. Now that you have Livia, it's hardball from now on. You need to see a shrink, you need grief counseling. It'll hurt, it'll really fucking hurt, but it needs to be done."

Nox nodded. "I agree. It's time." She saw his arms tighten around Livia, and she smiled.

"Good. Now, I'm going to leave you alone, but I'm a call away."

Livia shook her head. "Stay. Have breakfast."

"I would but I left a rather attractive Australian in my bed and I think I need to go deal with that."

Livia groaned. "God, Amber, I'm sorry."

"I'm not. He woke up and wanted to *talk*, of all things." She grinned as they laughed. "Bye, peeps. I'll see you later."

AS THEY WATCHED HER GO, Livia looked up at Nox. "She's good people."

"She is. Come inside, Livia, there's something I have to show you."

Hand in hand, they walked upstairs to the room where Livia had found him earlier. "This was my mom's room. Dad killed her and Teague in here." He sat down heavily on the bed. The heavy counterpane puffed up with dust. "The police told me

Teague died instantly, a shot to the heart, but Mom was shot in the stomach and bled out slowly. My father killed himself in the next room."

Livia sat down next to him and took his hand. Nox stared at the bloodstain on the rug. "I had to identify their bodies. Dad ... he shot himself in the head, so you can imagine ... but Mom and Teague. They just looked so ... peaceful. Asleep. It didn't make sense that they were gone. I was waiting for Teague to open his eyes and grin at me and shout 'Psyche!' Fuck." He rubbed his eyes.

Livia pressed her lips to his cheek. "I've never seen a photograph of Teague." She tried to say it lightly, so that if he needed to break down he could without thinking she was trying to jog him out of his melancholy. Nox stood and went to the dresser, picking up a frame. He handed it to her.

Livia looked at the photograph of a happy family. Teague and Nox, both tall, were handsome and smiling. Nox had his mother's green eyes, Teague, his father's dark brown. Tynan Renaud looked so proud of his family. His wife, Gabriella, was beautiful, her arm around her youngest son. Livia traced her finger over Nox's teenage face. He looked so young, like a Greek youth, so gorgeous and free of hurt. She looked up at him.

"I wish I could take your pain away, Nox."

He took her hand and pulled her into his arms. "You do, Livia. You *do*."

She touched his face. "Come back to bed, Nox. I'll show you happiness." And she led him back to their bedroom.

CHAPTER FOURTEEN

"So," Livia began awkwardly as she sat in the kitchen of *Le Chat Noir* with Moriko. Their shift had just ended, just after the lunch rush, and Marcel was talking to an attractive young woman out front. His sous-chef Cat was having a sneak cigarette outside and Liv and Moriko had the kitchen to themselves.

"So?" A small smile was playing around Moriko's lips, like she knew what Livia was going to say. She wasn't going to let Liv off the hook though, clearly, and so Livia took a deep breath.

"So ... Nox has asked me to move in with him. Now, I want you to know, I gave him a big long speech yesterday about being independent and all that ... but fuck it, Morry. Life is short. I want to be with him."

Moriko smiled. "It's not the biggest surprise, Liv."

"But," Liv went on, "I'm still going to be paying half the rent on our place, the utilities, everything I'm paying now."

Moriko sighed. "I wish I could tell you that was silly, but the truth is ..."

"Exactly. Look, please let me do this. I love Nox, but I hate to abandon you."

"You're not abandoning me, Liv; this is life, and I'm beyond happy for you. Also, however perfect he seems, he'll still get on your nerves eventually and this way you'll have somewhere to come to cool off and have girls' nights in."

Liv grinned. "You got it, sweetie."

"When are you moving out?"

"Not clear, yet, but it won't be too long. Next couple of weeks."

Moriko nodded. "Has Nox any idea of the tsunami of paperback books that's about to hit his beautifully appointed home?"

Liv grinned. "He sort of knows ... just not the extent."

"Well, I'm happy for you, sweetheart, I really am."

"Will you be okay?"

Moriko rolled her eyes. "Doofus."

Livia hopped off the countertop and hugged her friend. "Love you, Morry. Come on, I'll treat you to lunch."

Nox spent the morning trying to find a good counselor. Overjoyed that Livia had agreed to move in with him, he was determined he would repay her trust by getting the help he had known he'd needed for years. He contacted his family's old doctor and asked for his recommendation, then made an appointment with a psychiatrist in the city. He had just hung up the phone when Sandor knocked at his door, a frown on his face.

"'Sup, dude?"

"Have you seen Pia this morning? She's usually at her desk before any of us, but there's no sign. Shannon from Human Resources called her home, but her mother says her bed wasn't slept in."

Nox sat back. "Really? Well ... she's an adult, so I think the police will ask us to wait twenty-four hours. She could have hooked up with someone. I'll call her mother and see what she wants us to do."

"I'll get Shannon to give you the number." Sandor disappeared and Nox frowned. It was out of character for Pia to not show up. Nox had always been impressed with her work ethic, even at her young age.

Shit. He hated this sort of thing—the uneasiness creeping over his skin, the same way it had all those years ago. He still remembered the police showing up at Ariel's parent's home to tell them a body had been found. He'd known, even then, that she was dead.

He called Pia's mother, who tearfully asked him to keep her informed if Pia showed up. Then, needing to hear her voice, he called Livia.

"Hey, gorgeous." Her warm greeting made the tension in his body ease. He told her about Pia and she expressed her concern, but told him not to stress unless something concrete was known.

"I know it seems bad, baby, but she could just be around a girlfriend's house—or a boyfriend's—and overslept, or so hungover that she forgot to call. She's nineteen."

"I know. I'm not trying to make unnecessary drama either. It's just that I worry."

There was a small silence on the end of the phone. "Did you make the appointment?" Her voice was wary, like she didn't want to nag him, and Nox's heart warmed. This girl really did love him.

"I did, sweetheart. I promised I would and I did. Dr. Feldstein will see me next week."

"Proud of you," Livia said, her voice catching. "I love you so much, Nox."

"I love you too, funny face."

"Old man."

"Saddlebags."

Livia giggled. "That's so mean, but I love it. Listen, I have a tutorial ... I'll call you afterwards, okay? I hope there's news on Pia soon."

ROAN WALKED into the RenCar offices, his portfolio and draft business plan under his arm, and asked to see Nox. Nox himself came to get him. "Come on in, buddy."

Roan smiled at his friend as he sat opposite him. "Now, I know this is quick, and it's only a preliminary idea, but I wanted to run this by you."

"Awesome, Roan, let's get Sandor in here too."

When the other man had joined them, Roan cleared his throat. "The other day, when we were talking, I was joking around and said I should start an escort service."

He saw the alarmed looks on his friend's faces and, grinning, held up his hands. "No, hear me out. I'm seriously not talking about a traditional escort slash undercover prostitution service. In fact, penalties would be severe if any sexual activities were discovered. What I'm talking about is a kind of reverse Ashley Madison. Say there was a congressman who needed a dinner partner, but his wife was sick or just didn't like the spotlight. That's where I'd come in. I'd arrange for an escort. Now, here's the rub. Say I have a female scientist who needed an escort for the same function. I'd partner them up for an introduction fee. Now, admittedly, this is all a bit hazy at the moment."

Nox looked unconvinced. "I'm just thinking, Roan, that despite your best intentions, it will operate *exactly* like a traditional escort service. People are people, no matter their social standing. If they want to fuck, they'll fuck. Seems to me, you're doing exactly what Ashley Madison does, but putting a different spin on it. Sorry, dude."

Roan's shoulders slumped. "What about if I put safeguards in place? Like contracts?"

"Contracts don't mean a thing if two people want to break it. Who's going to sue them?"

"Me."

Nox shook his head. "You'll lose. I can't think that there'll be one judge who'll rule in your favor on this—and your reputation, no matter how well-intentioned, will take a hit. Look at that guy who was the arranger for Berlusconi ... what was his name?"

"Tarantini," said Sandor, brushing down his trousers. "He got eight years, I think."

"In *Italy*." Roan rolled his eyes. "Look, you said to focus on my passion. I like fucking."

"Exactly. You like fucking, and you're doing what you do without charging for it, perfectly legal. Dude, look, you have to take this seriously. You're more than just a cock, Roan, grow up. You let it rule your life and screw up everything. You got through Harvard, for crissakes; you have a business degree."

Roan stared out of the window for a long time. "Maybe this is a bad idea, friends going into business together. Maybe I should just find a job myself." He felt irritated that his idea, no matter how vague, had been pooh-poohed. Surely he should be allowed to see where it went. It still hurt when Nox nodded.

"Maybe you should."

Roan got up. "Well, thanks for your time." He didn't wait around, just walked out of the building and got into his car. "Well ... *fuck*." He let out a long breath and started the car.

SANDOR AND NOX sat in silence for a long moment. "Well, that could have gone better."

Sandor shook his head. "What was he thinking?"

Nox looked unhappy. "He wasn't. That's the whole problem with Roan."

Sando studied his friend. "You notice something else?"

"No, what?"

"He didn't mention Pia. He always mentions Pia, always stops to talk to her. He didn't even glance at her desk as he came in."

Nox paled a little but then waved his hand, dismissing Sandor's observation. "He was too full of his damn fool idea. It isn't anything more."

LATER, as he was enjoying a light supper with Livia at his home—soon-to-be *their* home—Nox couldn't help but think of what Sandor had said.

Livia smoothed her hand over his face. "What's up? What's going on in that mind of yours?"

He told her about Roan's plan—she rolled her eyes as he'd expected—then related what Sandor had said. Livia agreed with Nox—it was nothing. "Does Sandor not like Roan? I would never have guessed."

"He likes him just fine, I think. He's never said anything to the contrary."

"It's just a little strange he would say that. I mean, does Roan even know Pia?"

Nox considered. "Well, he talks to her whenever he comes into the office. I don't think Sandor meant any malice."

"Hmm." Livia thought about it for a moment more, then shrugged. "Probably not. So, no news?"

"None."

"God. I hope she's okay."

"Me too, darling. Let's change the subject. How did Moriko take your news?"

Livia grinned. "Surprisingly well. I told her I'd still be paying for half the rent so it takes a little pressure off of her, and she was grateful."

"You could let me take care of that."

"I could *not.*" She chucked his chin and he grinned. "Actually, she was more worried that you have no clue what you're letting yourself in for. I have so many books and art supplies, and all sorts of music crap."

"Is that right?" He put down his fork and took her hand. "Come with me."

He led her across the house to a room she hadn't even known was there. "Just how many secret rooms does this place *have*?" Livia grinned as Nox laughed.

"You haven't even scratched the surface, baby. Anyways, come on in." He said it lightly but he felt his heart beating hard against his ribs. He opened the door, and Livia stepped inside.

It was his and his mother's music studio. His old cello stood in its stand, his mother's piano covered in a dust sheet. Other, less played, less beloved instruments, dotted the room. Livia looked at him with wide eyes. "I'm sorry I didn't tell you about this room earlier," he said softly. "I didn't know whether I was quite ready. But, after last night, I think it's important."

Livia took his hand. "How much does it hurt?"

Nox considered, then smiled ruefully. "It's excruciating."

Livia cupped her face in her palm. "And it's okay to feel that. Acknowledge it. Speak it. We can go, if you like—I think this is a huge step."

Nox took a deep breath. "No, I brought you here for a reason. My mother's piano. I think it should be heard again, and it just seems right it should be you. Would you play for me?"

Livia, trembling, nodded. "Will you play *with* me?" She nodded to his cello and Nox hesitated. "You don't have to, but I think it would be good for you."

Nox touched his cello, dislodging a thick smear of dust. "Do you know Sonata no. 3?"

"Bach? I sure do. Let's see." Livia shifted the dust sheets from the piano and opened the lid. She pressed a few of the keys. "Good, it's still in tune."

"I hope I can say the same for this thing." Nox rested the cello between his legs and took up the bow. "Ready? First few bars."

They played slowly at first, the music tentative but sweet; then as they both settled into the rhythm, they played through the first act, both making minor mistakes but smiling encouragingly at the other as they did.

Nox lowered his bow. "Wow."

"How do you feel?" Livia was watching him and he smiled at her.

"Conflicted."

Livia closed the piano lid and went to him. She lifted the cello back into its stand and held out her hand. "Associations. Let's start to change your association with this room and this instrument. Let's turn your memories into pleasant ones." He took her hand and let her lead him to their bedroom.

Inside, she dropped the straps of her dress down her shoulders and wiggled out of it as Nox sat on the edge of the bed and watched her. She turned around slowly in her underwear and looked back over her shoulder at him. "You want this, baby?"

Nox grinned. "You know I do. Strip for me, gorgeous."

Livia chuckled and slowly began to take her underwear off, unclasping her bra, and sliding her panties down her legs. When she was naked she came to him, kissing him, then nuzzling his neck. "Fuck me, Nox, but keep your clothes on."

Nox grinned and laid her back on the bed, standing to unzip his fly and take out his cock. Fisting the root of it, he gazed down at her as she spread her legs wide for him. "God, you're so fucking beautiful, Livia Chatelaine."

His cock, huge and throbbing, stood proud against his belly as he tugged her legs around him waist. Livia arched her back up as he plunged into her, moaning at the feel of him. They made love fast and furiously, primal in their desire for each other. As they came, Livia pulled him onto the bed and tore at his clothes, biting at his chest and his nipples before straddling him and taking him deep inside her. He cupped her breasts, his thumbs strumming a beat over her nipples until they hardened. They made each other come again and again until, exhausted, they fell asleep in each other's arms.

IT WAS dawn when Sandor arrived with the police, looking pale and shaken. They had found Pia's body. A shocked and horrified Nox and Livia listened as he told them she had been found laid upon Ariel's grave with a message scrawled in her blood across the cold marble.

"What did it say?" Nox's voice sounded tight. Sandor winced and put his hand on his friend's shoulder.

"I'm sorry, Nox. It said, '*Everyone You Love.*'"

"*Jesus.*"

A worried Livia hugged Nox as he dropped his head into his hands. The lead homicide detective cleared his throat. "I'm sorry to do this at what is obviously a very distressing time, but Mr. Renaud, I do have to ask. Where were you the night before last?"

CHAPTER FIFTEEN

Moriko listened as Livia filled her in on what had been happening. "God, how awful. So they arrested Nox?"

Livia shook her head. "No, they just wanted to ask him questions. He offered to go with them to the station for a formal interview but they said he didn't need to ... yet. God, what a mess. Poor Pia."

"Were you close?"

"No, but we met a few times. She was only nineteen."

"Jesus."

Livia nodded, miserable. "Horrific."

Marcel came into the kitchen. "Hey, you okay?" He frowned at Livia. "You're really pale. Are you sure you're okay to work?"

"I am, thanks, Marcel. I'd rather be here; it will take my mind off the other stuff."

The restaurant was busy in the run up to Christmas. Although the weather outside was still mild, people were wearing coats and trying to get into a winter mindset. Livia wondered aloud if it ever snowed in New Orleans.

"Sure, it does," Marcel told her. "Last time was Christmas

Day, appropriately enough, back in '04, before that in '89. It doesn't happen often, but we're lucky sometimes. We're due some this year, I believe, some weather phenomenon to do with global warming. I don't know, but yeah, you might have a white Christmas if you're lucky. Just don't count on it being several feet deep."

Livia was daydreaming about sharing a white Christmas with Nox at his mansion when Moriko nudged her. "One of your rich friends is in."

Livia saw Odelle Griffongy seated in her section, her back ramrod straight, and groaned inwardly. The woman creeped her out a little, she had to admit. She went over to her. "Hey, Odelle."

Odelle blinked at her as if she had only just remembered Livia worked there. "Oh, hello. It's …"

"Livia."

"Of course. Hello again, Livia."

There was a small smile playing around Odelle's lips and Livia couldn't work out if Odelle was mocking her or not. She decided to give her the benefit of the doubt. "What can I get for you today?"

Odelle was studying her. "An egg white and spinach omelet, please." The smile was back and Livia realized Odelle was attempting to make a joke with her.

She smiled back tentatively. "Of course."

"And your company, if that's possible. Just for a few minutes."

Livia's eyebrows shot up and she looked around. "Well, um …"

"If you can't, that's okay."

Livia glanced at Marcel. "I guess I'm due a break but I'll have to run it past my boss."

"Of course."

Livia spoke to Marcel who seemed surprised but shrugged. "Go for it. We're slowing down now anyway."

"It's just for ten minutes at the most."

Livia sat down with Odelle, feeling oddly out of place. The blonde woman smiled at her, but her eyes were searching Livia's face. Finally, she spoke. "Nox is very taken with you."

Livia nodded. "And I with him," she said carefully, having no idea where Odelle was going. Was she about to give Livia the full-on 'gold-digger' warning?

Odelle picked at her omelet. "Nox is very important to me. You may have noticed that I don't make friends easily. I have a tendency to speak my mind and people tell me I have no tact, so forgive me if I say anything out of turn."

"Sure."

"I like seeing him happy. He deserves it."

Livia held up her hands. "Odelle, let me preempt you. I'm not interested in his money."

"But he does *have* money."

"It's his, not mine."

Odelle nodded. "For what it's worth, I actually never considered you to be that kind of woman. You genuinely do seem to care about him."

Livia lifted her chin. "I do care. I love him, Odelle."

"I believe you. What I wanted to say was this—be careful which of his friends you trust. They are not always who they seem to be."

"Like ... Roan?"

Odelle smiled. "Roan, God bless him, is not blessed with brains or cunning. No, I mean ... Amber Duplas."

Livia felt awkward. "She has been nothing but kind to me, Odelle."

"And I'm sure she means it. But she's also been fucking Roan behind my back."

Livia was shocked. "Odelle, I'm so sorry."

"It's okay. I'm not naïve. I know who Roan is; I know who Amber is. I'm going to marry Roan; did you know that?"

Livia shook her head. "I didn't ... Odelle, are you sure you should?"

Odelle smiled. "You see things as very black and white, don't you? I'm marrying Roan because, despite his infidelities—and yes, there have been more than one—he needs me. And I need him. You might have seen I don't do well in social situations. He is my anchor, and I am his. Where he puts his dick ... I gave him an ultimatum. Get rid of the other women. Do I think he'll be faithful forever? No, of course not. But he's trying. For me. Mostly for my money, to be fair, but also for me."

"Why are you telling me all of this, Odelle?" Livia felt uncomfortable.

Odelle smiled. "Because I like you. I don't often feel that towards other women, but you, Livia, seem like the genuine article. No bullshit. Despite your relative low background ..." She stopped and held her hands up. "There goes that sledgehammer tack again. What I mean is, despite the difference in our social standing ...that's no better ..."

Livia chuckled suddenly. "It's okay, Odelle, I get it."

"Sorry. But what I mean is ... you are completely guileless. It's refreshing to me."

"Fair enough. Look, I really do have to get back to work but ..." Livia pulled her notepad from her apron and scribbled her cell phone number down. She gave it to Odelle. "If you ever need to talk."

"Thank you, Livia."

"Take care, Odelle."

.   .   .

LIVIA TOLD Nox about Odelle's visit and he seemed pleased. "Despite her manner, she has a good heart."

"I'm just getting that." Livia had decided not to tell him about Odelle's warning regarding Amber. Nox looked exhausted and drawn and she stroked his face. "Did the police have any other information?"

Nox shook his head. "Only that Pia was killed in an identical manner to Ariel. I went to see Pia's parents. They're broken."

"God, poor things."

Nox held her hand to his face. "When I think of how you used to run around the streets alone ..."

Livia frowned. "Nox ... I won't let this stop me from living my life, you know. I don't want to be stuck in an ivory tower. I have work, I have college."

"*Everyone you love*. That's what the killer wrote."

"Are you sure he means you?"

"Why else would he put Pia on Ariel's grave? No, I'm sorry, Liv, until he's caught, you get a protective detail."

Livia was annoyed. "How about you *talk* to me about it, rather than tell me, Nox? I don't want some hulking guy with me all the time. I can look after myself." She pushed back her chair and took her plate to the sink, flicking on the water and rinsing it. She felt Nox's arms slide around her waist but she was too pissed to let it go.

"Sorry," he mumbled into her hair. "I'm just terrified something will take you away from me."

She turned in his arms. "I get it, but don't ever dictate how I run my life, okay? That's not going to be how this works between us."

He nodded, his eyes sad. "I know. Forgive me." He bent his head and brushed her lips with his. Despite herself, Liv responded to his touch, kissing him back. She really couldn't get enough of him, his taste, his scent, his hard body and beautiful face. She smoothed his curls back from his face.

"Take me to bed, Renaud, and show me how sorry you are."

Nox's cell phone rang and they both sighed. "Raincheck for a few? It might be about Pia's case."

"Go ahead," she said and let him go. She cleared their dinner things as he answered the call, once again glad Nox wasn't someone with a huge staff. It would make these intimate dinners difficult. She listened to him speaking.

"Thanks, Detective ... are you sure you don't want me to make an official statement? Yes, anything, anything to help. I'd like to pay for the funeral but I also don't want to upset the family ... yes ... yes, of course."

He hung up and sighed, rubbing his eyes. Livia could see the strain on his face and went to him, pulling him into her arms. "I'm so sorry, baby."

He held her tightly, burying his face in her neck, and she could feel his tears. "Just promise me, Livia ... don't ever leave me."

"I promise," she whispered, and knew the truth of her words.

CHAPTER SIXTEEN

Livia was worried about Nox's state of mind for the next few days and although he told her he was making good progress with Dr. Feldstein, he looked drawn and tired. Livia comforted him the best way she could, spending all her spare time with him talking, making love, and hanging out.

Soon though, she felt unable to cheer him and asked him if he would like Amber to come see him.

"Amber's out of town."

It was Livia's turn to look surprised. "She is?"

"Yeah, why?"

She shrugged. "It's just, you never said."

"Should I have?" Nox smiled at her, his expression a little confused.

"No, I guess not." Livia brushed it off but she wondered why Nox knew exactly where Amber was at any one time and why it bothered her so much.

Nox was studying her. "She wanted to get away because Pia's murder dragged up bad memories, sweetheart. Nothing insidious. I thought you liked Amber?"

"I do, very much," she reassured him, but something felt off to her. Why would Amber desert her best friend at a time like this? Even if it did bring up memories of her sister's murder, why wouldn't she want to be around the people she was closest to? Livia felt her skin prickle with unease. What did she really know about these people and how they operated?

"Are you okay?"

She nodded. "Actually, I'm pretty bushed, but I have to practice for the recital. Do you mind if I use your mother's studio?"

"It's your studio now, baby, and of course. Would you like some alone time?"

"If you don't mind," she smiled to soften the blow, "otherwise I'll be distracted by your gorgeous body. I'll make it up to you later."

Nox grinned, his whole face lighting up, and Liv felt a frisson of desire go through her. "I'll hold you to that."

At the piano, she ran through her composition again and again, concentrating on the finer details of it. She wondered if it even counted as jazz now, it was so slow and almost classical in its melody. Charvi had assured her that it still had its roots in her favorite genre.

"It's very New Orleans jazz," she had told Livia at their last tutorial. "Slow, sensual, laissez-faire. It's almost listless in its sexuality, as if, yes, you desire this man, but just being with him, being *still* with him, is enough."

And it was true, Livia did love just being with Nox, even if they were napping on his couch or reading together, his head on her stomach. Or just *being*. Being in the moment with Nox felt so natural.

Maybe that's why this thing is freaking you out, she told herself. *It's all a bit* too *easy, as if I'm waiting for the other shoe to drop.*

She moved her fingers over the keys again and again, and when after an hour or two, she heard the music room door open, she smiled to herself. She had her eyes closed, practicing the chords as she felt his fingers sweep her hair back from her shoulder and his lips against her neck. She continued to play as he unbuttoned her dress slowly, stroking the skin of her back, then trailing his lips down her spine. Livia shivered, closing her eyes as Nox chuckled, a deep sound from the back of his throat.

"Keep playing, beautiful."

Livia giggled softly as he lifted her and slid underneath her, perching her on his lap as he began to peel her dress away from her shoulders. Livia managed to keep playing the melody as he stripped her to the waist. She wiggled against his groin, feeling his cock long and hard against her buttocks. Nox nibbled at her earlobe as he caressed her bare breasts. "You want me inside?"

She nodded, turning her head to kiss his mouth. Nox gently closed the piano lid and set her on top of the piano, removing the rest of her clothes. Livia kissed him as he stripped.

With him seated on the piano stool, he lifted her on top of him. Livia took his cock in her hand, marveling at the thick, hot length of it, and then guided him inside of her, moaning softly as he filled her. They rocked together, eyes locked on the other's, their mouths hungry as they kissed.

"God, I love you," Nox growled as their lovemaking became more intense. He swept her onto the floor and began to thrust hard as she wrapped her legs around him. The sensations he was sending through her body were intoxicating and she forgot all of her earlier irritation and misgivings, giving herself to him entirely.

Nox, knowing he had command of her body, smiled down at her as he drove her towards orgasm. "You and me forever, Livvy. Promise me."

"I promise, *God*, yes. *I promise ... Nox ...*" Her back arched up and she felt him climax as she gasped through her own ecstasy, pumping thick, creamy cum deep inside her. Livia panted for air, laughing and telling him how much she loved him as they collapsed to the floor.

Nox smothered her in kisses, making her giggle, and then started to blow raspberries on her stomach, tickling her sides. Livia shrieked with laughter, twisting and turning to escape him. She turned on her side—then gasped as she saw it. At the window of the mansion, a figure.

Someone was watching them.

CHAPTER SEVENTEEN

At Livia's scream of fright, Nox took off, immediately grabbing his pants and shoving his legs into them even as he began to run to the door. Livia followed him down the long hallway of the mansion, but she stopped as he yelled at her, "Stay inside, baby. Call 911."

Adrenaline was spiking in her veins as she grabbed her cell phone and called, cursing for once the fact that Nox refused a security team. She got through to the emergency services, who assured her someone was on their way.

"Keep calm, ma'am, and stay on the line. Is your partner back?"

"No," Livia tried to stop her voice from trembling, "he's still out there." She went to the door, peering out into the cold night, shivering from terror and from the cold. She had only managed to grab Nox's shirt to cover herself. She couldn't see Nox, couldn't hear him. "Nox!"

"Stay inside!" His voice was far away but she felt a little relief that he was still within earshot.

"He's still looking for whoever it was," she told the dispatcher. "Please hurry."

"We are, sweetheart, just stay calm."

A gunshot rang out in the night and Livia screamed, dropping the cell phone. "Nox!" Her terror made tears pour down her face as she ran out into the night, not caring about her own safety as long as she got to him. She heard shouting, and another gunshot. She ran towards the sound, screaming his name, and it was a huge relief when he came into view.

Nox looked at her, a strange expression in his eyes, and Livia stopped. "Baby?"

"I told you to stay inside," he said softly, and to her horror, blood began to drip from his hairline down his perfect face. He reached for her as his knees gave way, and Nox Renaud collapsed to the ground.

Livia didn't know how she had managed to stop screaming. After the police arrived, followed a few minutes later by a medical team, she watched Nox being loaded, unconscious, into the ambulance. A policewoman wrapped a blanket around her and when they got to the hospital, a kindly nurse gave her some scrubs to put on. They wheeled Nox straight into the emergency room and it wasn't long before the doctor came to look for her.

"Mr. Renaud was shot in the head but, thankfully, it's a relatively minor wound. I say *relatively* because, obviously, any head-shot will have its complications. What's encouraging is that the bullet took out a chunk of skull bone but didn't penetrate his brain. We're going to go in now and see how much damage was done, and I'll come update you as soon as we know more."

"Doc? Will he be okay?"

"We're going to do everything we can. Keep the faith."

The police officer with Livia thanked the doctor. When they were alone, she asked Livia to go over what had happened again and Livia told her again.

"Could you make out whether the intruder was male or female?"

"I saw them for maybe a split second before whoever it was stepped away from the window." Livia was calm, knowing the police had to ask these questions, but desperately worried about Nox. "Nox went out after them and I called you. The next thing I know, Nox is on the ground, bleeding." Her voice broke as the shock hit her full-force. "Oh God ... *oh God* ..."

She dropped her head into her hands and began to cry. The police officer rubbed her back, and shortly afterward, Livia heard a familiar voice as someone sat down next to her and pulled her into his arms.

"Shh, it's okay." Sandor held her tightly as she leaned against him. She cried herself out then looked up. Sandor, drawn and shocked, tried to smile at her. He handed her a tissue and rubbed her back. "He's going to be okay, sweetheart."

"You bet your ass, he is," Amber stated determinedly as she walked into the room, nodding at the police officer. "Hey there. Amber Duplas."

"I know who you are, Ms. Duplas, and thanks for coming."

"You called them?" Livia, wiping her eyes, looked surprised.

The police officer nodded. "You were in no condition, and we know Mr. Renaud's contacts. We thought it would be best to call them."

"Thank you. You're very kind."

"I'm going to step out now, but I'll be back to ask more questions."

"Of course."

When she was alone with Sandor and Amber, she told them what had happened. "They *shot* him," she said incredulously. "They actually shot Nox."

Amber put her arm around her. "Listen, the docs say he'll be fine ... most likely."

"They told you that?"

Amber smiled. "I'm legally Nox's next of kin. We're each other's, actually—comes of having no living relatives."

"I see." Liv felt a wave of exhaustion and Sandor seemed to notice.

"Livvy, they may be hours. We can get the nurse to bring a cot in for you so you can rest."

"Thank you, San, but I couldn't. I just need some coffee."

Amber stood. "I'll go find some."

Sandor kept his arm around Livia. "At least lean on me and try to relax some. They may be operating for a while."

In the end, the doctor came back after a couple of hours. He was smiling, and Livia felt some of the terror lift. "Mr. Renaud will be fine. The bullet didn't enter the brain cavity at all. As we thought, he lost a bit of skull bone but he was incredibly lucky. The bullet glanced off of him. He'll be missing a chunk of skin and hair for a while but we were able to close the wound. He won't even need to see the plastics team. He's in recovery now, and then we just need to wait for the anesthetic to wear off. He might have a concussion—in fact, I'd say that's a given, so we'll keep him in for a couple of days."

Livia felt the tears pouring down her face. "Thank you, doctor, thank you so much."

He patted her hand. "Get some rest. You can see him in an hour or so."

Alone with Sandor, Livia finally broke down and sobbed, a mix of relief and terror. Sandor held her tightly and let her cry herself out before she finally fell asleep in his arms.

WAKING AN HOUR LATER, Livia felt her eyes were swollen and heavy with salt and tried to smile at Sandor. "I know I look like the Swamp Thing, but I need to see Nox."

"Doc said we could go through to his room when you awoke."

Livia stood, then felt a blood rush and wobbled. Sandor caught her and she leaned against his solid body. "Liv, have you eaten anything?"

"Not since last night."

"We need to get some food inside you."

"I want to see him first."

Sandor didn't look happy, but he also looked resigned. "Come on then, hold onto me."

WHEN LIVIA SAW NOX, the tears came again. His head was bandaged and Livia could see dried blood and the beginnings of a huge bruise, red, purple, black, and blue, angry and vicious, on the right side of his head. "God."

"Remember what the doc said. It looks worse than it is."

Livia bent over her lover and kissed his lips, glad to feel that they were warm. "I love you so much," she whispered and then smiled as Nox opened his eyes and focused on her.

"Hey, beautiful." He gazed up at her for a few moments, a smile on his face, then his eyes closed and he fell asleep again.

Livia gave a sigh of relief and leaned her forehead gently against his. "Thank God, Nox."

Sandor rubbed her back. "Come sit down before you fall down, Liv. I'll grab you some hot food."

IT WAS nighttime and Nox was still asleep. Livia stroked his curls back from his pale face and sighed. She had sent Sandor and Amber away, but she was exhausted. She got up, bending over Nox to kiss his cold lips. "Gonna go find some coffee, baby. I'll be right back."

She went to find a vending machine but the one on Nox's floor was out of service. She walked down the stairs, hoping the exercise would wake her up. Now that she knew Nox was out of danger, her adrenaline had disappeared and her body felt heavy and listless. Who the hell would shoot her beloved Nox? Who had been watching them? Her flesh crawled at the thought of it. How had the evening gone from one of sensuality and love, to horror?

She tried the door to the floor below and went into the corridor. It was silent, and Livia could see that some sort of remodeling was being carried out. No one was around. To her relief, the vending machines were working and she quickly purchased a strong black coffee and a Power Bar. She snagged some fresh cold water from the cooler and drained the plastic cup.

A breeze blew cool against her back and she heard a door slam. Turning, the breath caught in her throat as she saw a figure in shadow standing at the end of the corridor, watching her. Livia took a shaky breath in. "Sorry if I'm not supposed to be down here, but the coffee machine on ..."

She trailed off as the figure started to walk towards her without speaking, and that's when she saw it. The knife in his hand.

Jesus, no ...

She dropped the hot coffee and turned and ran. The intruder was between her and the staircase, so she darted deeper into the corridors, looking for any other way out. She heard him behind her, could hear his breathing as he ran after her. She weaved and slammed through any open door she found until, as she opened a final door, she realized she had run out of luck.

In a second, she felt him grab her shoulders and pull her back towards him. Livia screamed, kicked, and struggled with her attacker, determined to fight until either she escaped or he killed her.

He was strong, too strong, and when he slammed his fist into her temple, Livia crumpled to the ground, dazed, terrified, and knowing she could do no more.

She lay on her back and felt her attacker pushing her top up, exposing her abdomen. She saw the flash of the blade once before she passed out.

CHAPTER EIGHTEEN

"Livia? Livvy, sweetheart, wake up."

She could hear Sandor's voice but was confused. Why was he telling her to wake up? Wasn't she dead? Her murder had been surprisingly painless, she had to admit, but now her head screeched with agony. She opened her eyes. White light. Blinding.

"Ouch," she said, and heard Sandor's relieved chuckle.

"Hello again, beauty. You had us scared."

"Livia? I'm Dr. Ford. We found you unconscious on the floor below. What happened, my dear?"

Livia blinked and immediately reached down and ran her hand over her stomach. There were no stab wounds. She reached up and touched her temple. Her hand came away bloody. "He chased me and hit me. I think he wanted to kill me ... why didn't he?"

She saw the doctor and Sandor exchange a skeptical glance and felt idiotic. She pushed herself up into a seated position. "Who's with Nox? If someone tried to kill me, then he's not safe either."

"Amber's with him, sweetheart. Now, the doc's going to fix your head right up and the police want to talk to you, okay?"

"Sure." Livia felt as if they were humoring her. "Maybe *they'll* believe me." She couldn't help the snippiness that flooded her tone. The doctor said nothing but Sandor smiled at her.

"It's not that we don't believe you. It's that when I found you downstairs, it clearly looked like you'd fallen and hit your head, is all. There were no signs of a struggle. Are you sure you didn't just panic? You're very tired, honey. It's been a long night."

When he put it like that ... could she have imagined it? Livia closed her eyes and felt her head spinning. The doctor was cleaning up her head wound. "You won't even need stitches."

Livia thanked him. When she and Sandor were alone, she felt tears in her eyes. "I don't know what to think, San. I was so sure ... he had a knife. I saw it."

Sandor sat on the edge of the gurney and put his arm around her. "Why were you down there?"

"Coffee. The vending machine on this floor isn't working. Hey, I remember dropping the cup of coffee when I was being chased." She looked at him hopefully but he shook his head.

"We didn't find any spilled liquid, honey."

Fuck. Was she going crazy? "I want to go see Nox."

"Of course."

LIVIA WALKED a little unsteadily back to Nox's room. When she pushed open the door, a shot of jealousy flooded through her when she saw Amber stroking Nox's forehead. He was awake, and when he saw her, he smiled such a sweet smile that her heart lifted.

"Hey, you. They told me you had a fall."

Livia smiled at him cautiously, shooting a glance at Amber, who gave up her bedside seat for Livia. "We'll give you two some space," she said and took Sandor out of the room, closing the door behind them. Livia leaned over and kissed Nox's mouth.

"You gave me such a scare, baby."

"I'm sorry, honey. You didn't answer my question—you had a fall?"

Livia hesitated, not knowing what to tell him, but then nodded. They had more important things to talk about right now. "I'm fine ... but, Nox, do you remember what happened before you were shot?"

She couldn't help touching the bandage on his head. He caught her hand and pressed it to his face. "I can. We were making love; some creep was watching us. When I was outside, I heard something and went towards it. I saw ... something—a figure—and went after them." He sighed, closing his eyes as she stroked his face. "When you called out, I saw the figure turn towards the sound of your voice and I was so scared he'd come after you. I almost caught up with him, then he—or she —shot me. I remember not knowing if I was a dead man walking—I just wanted to see you one last time, so I came back for you."

He opened his eyes and met her gaze. "Sweetheart, I was dazed and concussed, but in the moment before I passed out ... I saw someone behind you. God ..." His expression was guilt-ridden and Livia felt her throat close.

"He followed us here," she said softly, "and he attacked me. I didn't *fall*. San and the doctor don't believe me. Who the hell is coming after us, Nox?"

Nox shook his head grimly, and he reached for her. She crawled into the bed with him and he wrapped his arms around her. "I don't know, sweetheart, but I can tell you this. He won't get near us again." He kissed her forehead. "I know you hate the idea, but first thing in the morning I'm arranging an entire security detail. Agreed?"

And Livia could not argue with him. "Fine. Whatever you think, honey."

Nox kissed her forehead. "Does it hurt?"

She shook her head and smiled. "Not as much as yours, I'll bet."

"They've got me hopped up on morphine."

Livia chuckled. "Things are about to get wild."

Nox laughed. "Actually, I'm beat. I could do with some more sleep and by the looks of it, so could you."

Livia slept in the bed with Nox, despite the disapproving glance of the nurses who came in to check his vitals. When they awoke, it was evening again. Livia kissed his mouth tenderly.

"Thank God you're okay, Nox. I don't know what I would have done."

He stroked her face. "Now you know how I feel. Whatever is going down, we'll beat it, Liv. I want my happily ever after with you."

They heard raised voices outside in the hallway. Nox and Livia looked at each other as Roan and Odelle, both looking angry and scared, came in. Odelle gave a huge sigh of relief. "Thank God."

Roan, who looked worse for wear, clutched his friend's hand. "Jesus, Nox, when they said on the news you'd been shot ..."

"It's on the news?"

Odelle nodded. "That's how we found out."

Livia got up. "I'm sorry, that's my fault. I should have called you." She wobbled and Odelle stepped forward to steady her.

"No, *Amber* and *Sandor* should have called us. You had this to deal with ... what happened to your head? They didn't mention you being hurt, too."

"This happened in the hospital. I'll tell you about it later." Livia glanced at Roan, who looked distraught. "Is he okay?" She lowered her voice and Odelle shook her head.

"No, he isn't. Look, we have to talk you, and I ... let me just have a moment with Nox and we'll go for some coffee and some hot food. You look like you could do with some."

Livia nodded, and turned to kiss Nox. "I'm going to give you a moment with your friends, darling. I'll be right back."

She looked back and saw Nox open his arms and hug Odelle. Livia was astonished to hear the other woman crying. Odelle was so emotionless most of the time that it came as a shock to hear her upset. Livia realized how much Nox meant to Odelle then, and it warmed her even more to the other woman.

And Roan ... there was something going on with him, something that made him look like a man who was barely hanging on. It was beyond being upset about his friend being shot.

Livia went to the restroom to freshen up, using one of the disposable toothbrushes to brush her teeth. She felt dirty and itchy; the scrubs she had been given were spotted with dried blood. A bruise was forming over her temple and she could now see the outline of knuckles in the wound. She gritted her teeth. She hadn't been hallucinating or imagining the intruder coming after her.

So why hadn't he killed her? She pulled her top up and examined her abdomen. Nothing, not even a scratch. She was about to drop the top when something caught her eye. A small cut on the inside of her navel. A speck of dried blood. What the hell? Was it a warning, or had the man intended to carve her up slowly but got interrupted? Maybe by Sandor looking for her? It made her flesh crawl and her breath quicken to realize that if Sandor hadn't looked for her, she could be dead right now. Lying disemboweled, her blood pooled around her, forgotten on the floor below until Nox asked where she was. The assailant had shot Nox in the head then come for her—so why didn't he finish the job? She had been utterly vulnerable.

Everyone you love ... The warning from Pia's murder scene hit her again. Who was he talking to? Nox? But why? What on Earth had triggered this vendetta twenty years after his family and his lover had all died?

Livia stared into the mirror. What the hell was going on? And why did she feel so sure—overwhelmingly sure—that Amber had something to do with it all? Amber and Roan ... both of them, she felt sure, knew more than they were saying. Was Amber looking for revenge for Ariel's death now that Nox had finally moved on and fallen in love with another woman? Or was it just that she wanted Nox for herself?

What about Roan? He looked like a man destroyed. She couldn't quite believe it had been Roan stalking and attacking her ... but then again, Roan was a passionate man. Would he have hesitated to kill her quickly and brutally, no matter who was coming? She didn't think so.

Livia shook herself. "And it could be just some random psycho who killed Pia, and no more than an intruder staking out Nox's mansion to rob it." She spoke the words aloud to try and reassure herself, but faltered. No, it was something more insidious. She knew it in her bones.

She jumped as the restroom door slammed behind her and turned. No one. Which meant someone had been watching her. She darted to the door and looked out. Whoever it was, they were long gone. Livia gritted her teeth, but as she looked down, she saw it. A long red hair on the linoleum floor. *Amber.*

Livia went back to Nox's room, hearing him speaking in a loving, tender tone. "It's okay, Odelle, I'm fine. I'll be out of here in a couple of days."

"I can't bear the thought of anything happening to you or Livia. You're my family."

Livia was unbelievably touched. Who would have thought she meant so much to the ice queen? She knocked gently at the door and poked her head in, smiling at them both. Roan had disappeared. "I hope I'm not intruding."

"Not at all, baby."

Odelle came to her and hugged her, and Livia returned the embrace. "We're okay, Odelle, really."

Odelle sniffed and Livia realized she was crying again. The other woman drew away finally, wiping her eyes. "Sorry."

"Don't worry about it." Livia smiled at her then went to Nox, taking his hand.

Odelle gathered herself. "Look, I can get on the phone right now and have protection set up here, at the home, at the restaurant, and your office, Nox."

Nox nodded. "That would be a weight off. Thanks, Odie."

Odelle got straight on her cell phone, stepping out into the hallway. Livia nudged Nox. "Odie?"

He grinned. "I'm the only one she lets call her that. And even then, only on special occasions."

"Like being shot in the head?"

"Like that." They both laughed, the tension lifted by the joke. Nox kissed her. "By the way, I'm liking the hot scrubs look."

Livia rolled her eyes. "I'm filthy."

"Look, baby, I'll get Sandor to take you home. Eat proper food, grab a shower, and some sleep. I'm not going anywhere."

It did sound tempting and after a while, Livia agreed. "As long as someone is with you."

"I don't think Odelle is going anywhere."

"Where did Roan go?"

Nox shook his head. "He got choke up, mumbled something about being sorry, and left. Odelle is annoyed with him about something."

They sat in silence for a while, holding hands. Livia cleared her throat. "Nox ... I have this feeling. A feeling that whoever is behind all this ... is close to us. To you."

"I agree."

She studied him. "Do you think ... Roan?"

Nox sighed. "I hate saying this, but I can't imagine anyone else. He's been drinking, he's broke ..."

"Isn't he marrying Odelle?"

Nox's mouth set in a straight line. "He is. And he should think himself lucky. But it still doesn't guarantee him any money. Odelle's father won't permit it."

Livia looked at him askance. "Odelle's father realizes this is the twenty-first century, right?"

"I don't mean he won't consent to the marriage, but Odelle is an heiress. She doesn't have money of her own—it's all tied up in her trust fund, which her father can withdraw at any time."

"So, why is Odelle marrying him anyway?"

Nox gave her a strange, half-sad smile. "Because she loves him."

"Nox, would Roan shoot you?"

"I can only tell you that Roan is a superb marksman. If it *was* him, then he didn't intend to kill me." Nox looked sick at having to say the words. "When I get out of here, beautiful ... we need to talk about a lot of things. Your safety is paramount. Our future, too. Odelle tells me they have your name in the press. They'll be hounding you at the college and at the restaurant too."

"I can cope with that."

Nox studied her. "You have no idea what they're like. Vultures. They'll dig up anything on you."

Livia shrugged. "I have no skeletons."

"Then I have to warn you," Nox said, his handsome face serious, "they'll make some up, just for you. Things really are about to get crazy."

. . .

ODELLE THANKED the doorman as she made her way into her apartment building. He called her back. "Mr. Saintmarc is waiting upstairs for you."

Odelle nodded, her face impassive. "Thank you, Glen."

She took the elevator up to her penthouse and stepped out into the atrium. Roan was slumped against the wall. He looked up at her, desperation in his eyes, and Odelle's plan to send him away evaporated. She had never seen him look so desolate. She crouched next him. "What is it, Roan? What's the matter?"

Roan began to sob as he blurted out the words. "They're going to say it was me, Odelle ... they're going to say it was me ... that girl, Pia ... I was with her the night she was killed ... and they're going to say it was me ..."

THE POLICE INVESTIGATION brought up nothing, and as it drew nearer to Christmas and the weather finally turned cold, Livia and Nox holed up in his mansion. Livia only left for work or school, and Nox for any business meetings he couldn't do from home. Neither of them said it, but the self-imposed nearness seemed to have opened up a new element to their relationship, a new intimacy—a closeness they had not known was missing.

Of course, their more adventurous sexual exploits had now been restricted to their bedroom. Odelle had hired what appeared to be an army of protection for Nox and Livia, and even they were a little stunned by how much of their lives was restricted now.

"I can't send them away. Odelle would kill me ... and I like to restrict being murdered to just once a year." Nox grinned at Livia, who laughed.

"It does get in the way of stuff, doesn't it? I mean, I was just murdered the other day, and I had a whole bunch of laundry to do."

"How inconvenient."

"Isn't it?"

They had been joking with each other like this since Odelle had told them about Roan. He had been sleeping with Pia and had been with her the night she was killed. Odelle had persuaded him to go to the police and speak to them. He had been questioned and then charged on suspicion of murder. Odelle had paid the two-million-dollar bail money, and now Roan was locked away in her apartment until the trial.

Neither Nox nor Livia could believe the turn of events. Worse, when Roan was questioned about the night Nox and Livia had been attacked, he couldn't provide an alibi. The police, desperate to find someone guilty for Pia's murder, had used Nox's rejection of Roan's business proposition as motive.

"Their case is weak," Roan's lawyer, William Corcoran, told them when they met at Nox and Sandor's offices, "but at the moment, he is the only person with motive and we know he was with the girl. I understand you have arranged a twenty-four-hour guard on him, Ms. Griffongy?"

Odelle, pale and drawn, nodded. "He's not going anywhere, Mr. Corcoran. He wants to be proved innocent."

Livia took Odelle's hand and squeezed it. "We're here for you, Odelle." She couldn't bring herself to say that she was there for Roan too—she could well believe that he would hurt Nox, and Pia, to keep her from telling Odelle about their affair. Odelle looked shattered, and Livia's heart went out to her.

"We never did get our girl talk, did we?" she said in a low voice to Odelle as Nox and Sandor were talking to the lawyer. "We should do that. Soon."

Odelle nodded. "I'll come by your restaurant around lunchtime tomorrow, if that's okay?"

"Sure."

. . .

THE NEXT DAY, Moriko and Marcel gave her a hard time and she couldn't blame them. She had called them from the hospital, but wouldn't allow them to visit. She told them it was because Nox had too many visitors already, but truthfully, she didn't want Moriko and Marcel on the killer's radar anymore than they already were by associating with her. Pia had barely been a part of the circle, and now she was dead. No one was safe.

Moriko took one look at the cut on Livia's head and her mouth set in an angry line. "And you didn't mention *that*, either."

"I slipped on some water at the hospital. No biggie." She hadn't told them about being attacked.

Marcel shook his head at her. "This is serious, Liv. I don't want you hurt."

Livia nodded back at the two huge bodyguards sitting in the restaurant. "It's okay. Those two are always with me—unfortunately."

She dumped her bag in the backroom and went into the kitchen to wash her hands. She felt tired and drained, but at least she was back to doing something familiar. Nox had been reluctant to see her back at work, but couldn't dissuade her. "I have responsibilities, baby."

Now she tied her apron around her dress and went out front. The restaurant was quiet, the lunchtime rush a way off yet, and Moriko and Livia polished wine glasses and chatted as they laid out the tables.

"So, I have news," Moriko said with a grin and Livia's eyebrows shot up. She glanced at Marcel, which made Moriko roll her eyes.

"Will you stop with that? I adore Marcel, but I also *work* for him. No, it's not Marcel, but I did meet someone."

"Who?"

"Not ready to say yet. But I am giving up the apartment. I thought you should know."

"You're moving in with whoever it is?" Livia was shocked but Moriko just stuck her tongue in her cheek and gave her friend a defiant stare. Livia grinned sheepishly. Yep, she had *no* right to be scandalized. "Sorry. Where are you moving to?"

Moriko told her and Livia whistled. It was an upscale apartment building in the city, a block or two from where Odelle lived. "Very nice."

"It has one of those old-fashioned elevators, like you see in French movies. All wrought iron and fancy schmancy." Moriko sounded so proud that Livia couldn't help but giggle.

"Fancy."

"You bet your ass it's fancy. Hey, maybe we'll have to do soirees like you do with all your fancy new friends."

Livia grinned. "Shut up. Well, I'm happy for you, boo. When do we get to meet Captain Elevator?"

"Ha ha. And soon, hopefully."

"At least tell me his first name."

"Nope. Live with it."

"Spoilsport."

ODELLE ARRIVED JUST after one p.m. and Livia took her break. They sat two tables away from Livia's conspicuous bodyguards. Odelle looked amused. "It must be strange for you to have them around."

Livia nodded. "It is, but don't think I'm not grateful, Odelle."

"You can call me Odie, if you like."

Livia smiled at her. "You've been a true friend to me and Nox, Odie."

The other woman flushed a little. "I'm not good at making friends," she said, "especially with women. They don't trust me, for some reason. I don't know why; it's not like I'm sleeping around with their men. Unlike Amber."

Livia sighed. "I've been having doubts about her, tracing back to what you said. But at the same time, she hasn't done anything wrong—I don't think. Certainly, Nox doesn't see anything amiss, and I'm hesitant to say anything negative. They're so close."

"Understandable. Look, maybe I'm biased. I've never liked the woman, and now that I know she was sleeping with Roan ..."

"Was?"

Odelle smiled. "As soon as she knew I found out, she dumped him. Amber has no use for men after the wife or girlfriend finds out." She looked at Livia. "Does that upset you?"

Livia nodded. "I wanted to believe she was a good one. I thought that she was."

"Livvy, you're your own woman. Do I think Amber is malicious? Not where Nox is concerned, certainly, and to be fair, she's seemed to take to you too."

"So, if we rule out Amber and Roan, who else would have a grudge against Nox?" Even saying the words made Livia tremble.

"I honestly don't know. We both know Sandor is straight as a die."

"He's a teddy bear."

Odelle smiled. "He is. He's a good one. If only I'd fallen for him instead."

Livia chuckled. "I would pay to see that. So, anyone else?"

"Well, there is someone. An ex-girlfriend of Nox's. Well, not really a girlfriend, but a fling. At least for Nox. Janine Dupois. Has Nox mentioned her?"

Livia shook her head. "No, but we've never actually had the 'ex' talk, so I don't blame him for not doing so. Who is she?"

"Fashion editor and socialite. I heard she moved to New York but made the mistake of trying to break into the scene up there without proving herself."

Livia rolled her eyes and Odelle laughed. "It's the way it works, I'm afraid."

"If Nox and I are going to be long-term—and I hope so—I do hope I won't be expected to become ..."

"Like me?" But Odelle was smiling and Livia squeezed her hand.

"You know what I mean. I'm not a socialite. I don't know anything about that world."

Odelle studied her. "You know, Nox is a pretty down-to-earth guy. He wouldn't—*couldn't*—have fallen for someone who wasn't suited to him. Don't ever be afraid you won't fit in, Livvy."

When Livia arrived home later, she was feeling more optimistic than she had in weeks. Nox arrived a little after her and she went to greet him at the door. She kissed him tenderly. "I missed you."

She took his hand and immediately led him up the stairs. Nox was grinning. "Well, if this is how you miss me ..."

In their bedroom, Livia pulled his tie from his neck, kissing his chest as she unbuttoned his shirt. Nox slowly unzipped her dress, his fingertips trailing up and down her spine. As she pushed his shirt aside, her tongue found his nipple as her fingers unzipped his fly and reached into his pants. His cock was already hard as she freed it from his pants and she chuckled as she heard his sharp intake of breath. She pushed him down on the bed and tugged his pants off.

"Just lay back, baby. I'm in charge." She wiggled out of her dress and Nox wolf-whistled at her. Livia grinned but then knelt between his legs and took him in her mouth. Tracing the veins along the silky, thick shaft, she tasted the salty pre-cum then flicked her tongue on the sensitive tip to drive him crazy. She heard his long groan of desire as she sucked, tasted, and teased him, and when he was close and tried to pull away, she shook her head. He came in her mouth, groaning her name over and over.

Livia swallowed his seed down, and then shrieked with laughter as he swept her onto the floor and started to kiss her furiously, as if an animal had been unleashed inside him. He sucked at her nipples until they were rock hard and she was writhing beneath him, so turned on she thought she might pass out. Then, as he moved down her body, licking, tasting, biting at her breasts, her belly, she moaned as his mouth found her sex. "God, Nox ..."

He pleasured her until she was begging him to fuck her, and then he launched his diamond-hard cock into her, pressing her knees to her chest and slamming his hips against hers. Livia screamed her pleasure, not caring if every security guard in the place heard her. She lost herself in this heady delirium, kissing him, telling him again and again how much she loved him.

Finally, exhausted, they climbed into bed and wrapped themselves around the other. They kissed and chatted quietly, enjoying the time together.

"Odelle called me 'Livvy' and I get to call her 'Odie,'" Liv said with wide eyes, making Nox laugh.

"She told me she adores you. You don't bullshit—she likes that."

"You are a lot closer to her than I first thought," Liv observed, "which makes me think we—you and I, that is—should spend more time getting to know each other, in addition to fucking each other's brain out."

Nox laughed. "As long as we can keep doing that too."

"Hell, yes. So ..."

"So, what do you want to know?"

"More about Ariel, if it's not too painful."

Nox was silent for a while then nodded. "Okay."

Livia stroked his face. "In your own time, baby."

"It's all right, Livvy, I'm not going to break down. The psychiatrist I've been seeing has helped me immeasurably." He paused for a moment, taking a deep breath. "Here goes. We met when we were kids, when Ariel and Amber's family moved here. Their parents were nice people, moderately wealthy like us, and Amber's father was a business associate of my dad's. Ariel and I hit it off straight away. You know she and Amber were twins? Non-identical. Ariel had dark brown hair and dark eyes like yours. She always thought she was the plain one, which was a joke."

Livia remembered seeing the photographs of Ariel. "She was lovely. I know you've told me how she died ... maybe it would help to talk through what happened in the days leading up to her death."

Nox looked at her for a long time then nodded. "Okay. Okay then, let's talk."

CHAPTER NINETEEN

T*wenty years ago ...*

ARIEL FIXED Nox with a determined stare, trying not to giggle. "I've thought long and hard about it, and I think I know the perfect outfit for prom for both of us."

Nox grinned at her, knowing well the look of mischief in her eyes. "Oh, yeah? Hit me with it."

Ariel stood, and proceeded to shuffle sideways then back again rapidly on her carpeted floor. Nox burst out laughing. "What the hell?"

"I'm giving you a clue," she said breathlessly, then started to do the Running Man, moving her arms and legs energetically.

"You are quite insane, Miss Duplas—and I have no earthly idea what's going on here."

"Imagine baggy pants." Ariel moved up and down her bedroom, flailing her arms and urging him to guess. "Maybe if I sing ..."

She began to intone 'oh-uh' repeatedly as she moved, then came to an abrupt halt, shouting, "Stop!"

Nox finally got it. "*Hammertime!*" He collapsed with laughter as Ariel cheered, then collapsed on the bed beside him, panting for air.

"So, what do you think? We both go in Hammer pants and fuck the patriarchy. Why should I wear a dress?"

"You could wear anything and still be the Queen of the Ball."

Ariel pretended to puke and Nox laughed. "You really can't take a compliment, Ari, you know that?"

"You know me, Noxxy. I leave the cotillions and debutante stuff to Amber. It's her thing."

Nox sensed an undercurrent in her voice. "What's up?"

Ariel shrugged. "Nothing, really. We're just having one of our time-outs. We're not getting along particularly well at the moment."

"Any reason?"

Ariel hesitated, then shrugged. "Just reasons."

Nox wound a long lock of her hair around his fingers. "You don't want to talk about it?"

"Not really. So, now that you know what I've planned for prom ..."

Nox grinned. "You think I don't know you by now? You say that, then I turn up in Hammer pants, and you'll look like some ethereal goddess in a perfect gown. I still remember junior prom. Remember?"

"That was hilarious."

"For *you*. My mom spent weeks on my sailor costume."

Ariel giggled. "So, so gullible, Mr. Renaud." She bent her head and kissed him, lingering over his lips. "Now, seriously ... do you want to see my dress? I ask because ... it has some complicated fastening, and you may need to practice if you want to get it off me."

Nox's smile widened. Like most couples, they had planned for prom night to be the first time they slept together ... even though they'd done practically everything else already. Neither of them could wait. "You know, it might be a good idea."

Ariel sent him out of the room while she changed and when she was ready, called him back.

Nox pushed the door open and his breath caught in his throat. The pale gray chiffon draped beautifully over her body, clinging to her curves and setting off the pink tones in her creamy white skin.

"Wow. Wow." Nox walked to her, cupping her face in his. "You look insanely gorgeous."

Ariel blushed, but laughed. "That is the correct answer. You may kiss me now."

The kiss went on for so long that Ariel, laughing, had to push him away. "One more day, Nox, and we'll finish that kiss and then some."

Nox nodded. "Then I'd better get out of here before you make it impossible for me."

"And your blue balls."

"*And* my blue balls." He grinned as she squeezed his groin. "Damn, woman, you're impossible."

"You know it." She stood on her toes to kiss him. "Tomorrow, Nox Renaud."

PROM NIGHT. Ariel and Amber got ready separately—each in their own rooms, not communicating at all. As she finished her makeup and slipped into the gray dress, Ariel considered going to see her sister, trying to bridge the strange chasm that had opened up between them lately. She had lied to Nox yesterday about what was causing the void—it was Nox himself. Ariel knew Amber was in love with him, and did not blame her sister

—or Nox—for it. Nox was easy to love. Amber knew she would never be with him, and to her credit, she didn't even try to take him from her sister, but ... her way of dealing with it was to keep her distance from both of them.

Ariel tapped cautiously on her sister's door. "Ambs?"

"Still changing." Flat tone, no invitation in it. Ariel sighed.

"Okay ... well, I'm just going to grab a smoke outside. Distract Mom if she comes to look for me?"

"I will."

ARIEL STEPPED out into the sultry Louisiana evening. Sweat popped up on her skin immediately and she cursed, hoping she wouldn't end up with pit stains—this chiffon was too good for that kind of treatment. *Not that Nox would give a crap*, she smiled to herself fondly, shaking a cigarette from her pack. Her mother probably knew she smoked, but it was a strict don't-ask-don't-tell policy in her house.

She walked around the main house to where she sneaked her smokes, out of sight of the house. Hidden by the trees draped with Spanish moss, she breathed in the night air. The bayou was extra smelly on nights like this, the stench of rot creeping across the night. Ariel flicked her butt to the ground and, using the toe of her shoe to stub it out, she turned to go back in.

The first thing she registered was a stinging in her neck, then a wave of breathlessness as whatever had been injected into her flooded her veins. She barely had time to acknowledge that someone had grabbed her before everything went dark and she passed out.

. . .

COLD. She was lying down and whatever it was, it was cold against her back. She shivered despite the heat of the night, and then opened her eyes. Her head whirled, her eyes were blurry, and her chest felt heavy. Focusing, she saw him ... she assumed it was a him. He was sitting on her legs, straddling her. He was so still that it frightened her, as if he had been waiting for her to wake. Ariel looked around and felt a wave of panic. They were in a graveyard.

"What the hell is going on?" Her voice trembled as the black-hooded figure seemed to look right at her. She couldn't see any features, and the stranger's silence was making her panic even more. "Please ... whatever you want ..." Her voice trailed off when she saw the knife in his hand, and she knew. "Oh, God, please ... please *don't* ..."

He didn't listen. Before Ariel could scream, he clamped a gloved hand over her mouth and plunged the knife into her belly over and over. Ariel's back arched up as she moaned in agony as he murdered her. His hand fell away from her mouth when he saw she was struggling to breath.

"Why?" Ariel gasped as her killer sat back to watch her bleed out. A tear ran down her cheek. "Please tell me ... *why?*"

But he never answered her.

NOX WAS GETTING into his car when his mother called him back. Her face was tense. "Amber's on the telephone. She's hysterical, and I can't understand what she's saying." It took Nox a few moments to realize Amber was telling her Ariel was missing.

THEY FOUND her body the next morning and a devastated, distraught Nox drove straight to the cemetery. He fought with a police officer who wouldn't let him near her, so much so that they had to cuff him to calm him down. "Please, please let me see her."

In the end, to appease him—he was the son of a powerful New Orleans scion, after all—and possibly to gauge his reaction, they let him see her.

The sight of Ariel, gutted and broken, her gray chiffon soaked in blood, lying pale and dead on the grave, brought Nox to his knees. Something inside him died.

The funeral was hell for Nox. He barely acknowledged anyone else, not even Amber or Teague when they tried to reach him. Amber was destroyed by her sister's death—she was changed forever by it.

Eventually, the society around them got back to normal, but Nox and Amber spent more time together, feeling disenfranchised from everyone. The police had no leads. Nox had an airtight alibi, and so the police quickly ran out of clues. The case got put on the backburner, much to the rage of the Duplas and Renaud families. Then almost exactly a year later, Tynan Renaud murdered his wife and son and shot himself, and Ariel's case was pushed even further to the background.

Now

Livia stroked Nox's face as he told her everything. "I always felt guilty because when my family died, Ariel was almost forgotten by our circle, by the press, by the police." He sighed, leaning his forehead against hers. "I swore I would never let that happen and yet I was so utterly destroyed by what my father had done ... It was almost as if Ariel had been relegated to a place where young, beautiful women are viewed as 'probable targets' just by being young, beautiful, and female."

Livia kissed his eyelids. "Sadly, though, it does seem to be a truth. We women always have to be careful. Don't go out alone at night, because a man might rape or kill you. Don't dress a certain way, we're told, as if we're the ones responsible for not 'making' a man rape or kill us. It's sick and disgusting, but it is how we live in this world."

Nox shook his head. "Christ. What a messed-up way to live."

"And yet normal for every woman on the planet." She sighed, thinking about the terror of her recent assault. How close she had come to death.

"Can I just apologize for my gender?"

Livia laughed. "No, you cannot. You're one of the good ones, Nox, and don't forget it. Don't take the responsibility of others on your shoulders. Just promise me we'll raise our sons not to think of women solely as sexual beings."

Nox kissed the tips of her fingers. "Absolutely promise ... and, our sons?"

Livia flushed. "I'm not presuming anything, just ...if it happens."

"God, I hope so." He pressed his lips to hers, pulling her close. "I want a bunch of them with you, Livia. But you're young, and you have your career in front of you."

"Waitressing? Yeah, I'll get right on that."

Nox laughed. "I meant your music career."

"Oh, that. Nox, I love music. It is my passion. But I never envisioned a career in music as such. I want to be good enough to teach it, like Charvi. I would love that. Maybe play some small concerts here and there, but as far as a fully-fledged career as a musician—I think that's a pipe dream."

"You don't want to be famous?"

"Good God, no. No, *ugh*, can you imagine? The press every-where ... Wait. Yeah, you *can* imagine. God, I'm dense. Sorry."

Nox laughed. "It's okay. You know, once they get hold of the fact we're dating, you have them to look forward to."

Livia groaned and rolled on top of him. "Let's not worry about that at the moment. I'm hoping to put that off for as long as we can. Agreed?"

"Promise."

Nox didn't realize just how soon that promise would be broken.

CHAPTER TWENTY

At work the next day, the restaurant was so full of customers that Livia and Moriko didn't have time to catch their breath, let alone catch up. Livia had mentioned to Nox that she wanted to see more of Moriko. "I feel since I moved out that we've been drifting apart, and I would hate that. Morry's my girl, you know?"

She said as much to Moriko when they were finally relieved of duty by the evening staff. Moriko asked Livia to come back to her new apartment, wanting to show off, she said with a grin. Shadowed discreetly by Livia's bodyguard, they went to Moriko's new apartment building, traveling up to the seventh floor in the wrought iron old-fashioned elevator.

"Fancy," Livia said with a wink at Moriko, who grinned.

"Jealous? Not that you need to be, living in a freaking mansion."

"Ha. Listen to us, we're both kept women. What happened to the Sisterhood?" Livia sat down on a vast dark blue couch. "God, this is heavenly."

Moriko laughed. "I know, right? And speak for yourself—I pay Lucas rent."

"Lucas, is it? Tell me more, girl. You've been keeping this Lucas secret for too long."

Moriko handed Livia a bottle of beer and sat down next to her. "Well, if I saw more of you ..."

Livia punched her shoulder lightly. "I know, I'm sorry. I always swore I wouldn't be one of those women who deserted her friends when she fell in love, but I seem to be doing just that. I am sorry, Morry. I'll do better."

"How are things out on the bayou?"

Livia talked to Moriko about her life with Nox, about how close they had become, and her friend listened with a frown on her face. "Sure you two aren't becoming co-dependent?"

Livia was stung. "What do you mean?"

Moriko sighed. "I mean, how long have you actually known each other? Not even two months, right? You moved in with him —less than a day after giving him the whole 'I'm an independent woman' speech, I might add—and now you're practically imprisoned in that place. The place where your boyfriend got shot, for crissakes ..." Moriko stopped, dragging a shaky breath into her lungs. Livia had never seen her so riled up before.

"Morry? Where's this coming from? I mean, I—"

"No, let me finish. I'm scared, Liv, I'm terrified. I feel like something bad is going to happen to you, like you might die. Like Nox is a dangerous person to be around, and something— someone—could hurt you and then his circle of friends will close ranks and we'll never really find out what happened."

Livia was stunned for a long moment. "I know the thing with Pia is horrific, and yeah, we got assaulted but—"

"And his girlfriend was murdered and his family got killed. Jesus. Death follows him around, Livia. Look, I like Nox, I do ... I just don't think he's good for you."

Livia felt her eyes fill with tears. Having Morry's blessing for her relationship was important to her, and she hadn't seen this coming. "So, what? You want me to leave him?"

"Yes."

"Are you kidding me?" Livia blinked at the sudden change in the atmosphere between them, and looking closely at her friend, she could see the strain on her face, the dark circles under her eyes. "Morry, is something else going on? Are you okay?"

"No, I'm not okay," Morry yelled suddenly, making Livia jump. "Jesus, every time I get a phone call, I think it's the police telling me you're dead."

"Dude, you are *way* overreacting."

"No, I'm not. Someone shot your boyfriend, attacked you in a freaking hospital, butchered a young girl to send Nox a message. '*Everyone you love*'? Jesus. *Liv* ..."

Morry was trembling, but she backed away when Livia tried to hug her. "I had no idea you felt this way."

"You are my family," Moriko said fiercely, "My sister. I'm scared, Liv."

This time she let Livia hug her. "It's okay, Morry, really. Look at the hulking slab of beef I have outside the door. Actually, that's mean. Jason is very nice and he's protecting me."

"Don't you see how messed up it is that you have a body-guard?" Morry clearly wasn't going to let this go, Livia thought in dismay.

"Look, I get it, I do. But it's only until they catch the guy, Morry. Nox is a powerful man; he's bound to attract weirdos." Even to Livia's ears that sounded like a feeble way to describe what they were going through.

Moriko looked at her with cold eyes for a long minute, then stood and went into her bedroom. Livia heard her moving around, then she re-emerged carrying a stuffed manila folder. She flung it at Livia. "Just a weirdo, huh?"

Livia caught the folder, papers scattering everywhere. She slid down to the carpet to spread them out. Old police reports, clippings from newspapers. Livia saw the photographs of a young Nox, dressed in an exquisite suit, being comforted by his mother as a medical examiner and his team removed Ariel's body from the cemetery. The photos of the funeral, the intrusion even into this most private of days, was jarring and sickening. All of the photos were accompanied by sensationalist press, condemning the young man before Ariel's body was even cold. The blood on the gravestone.

Then later, Nox alone at a funeral service, standing in front of the caskets of his mother and his brother. The look in his eyes was searing, and Livia couldn't help the sob that escaped her. Moriko didn't attempt to comfort her. Again, the press eviscerated Nox, the only survivor. Had he been in it with his father? He was the only heir now, after all ...

"Moriko, if you believe any of these lies about Nox ... I don't see how we can continue to be friends."

She looked up to see Morry's eyes soften. "Of course, I don't. The press is, and were, scum. I want to kill them for what they did to that poor boy. But, Liv, you have to see ... Darkness follows Nox. He couldn't have a more appropriate name, could he?"

"I can't leave him. I love him so much. He really is a good man. What kind of person would I be to leave him now?"

"A person who stays alive." The coldness was back.

Livia closed her eyes and rubbed her face with her hands. To say she felt as if her equilibrium was smashed was an understatement. Moriko was the balls-out one of them, the ride-or-die girl, and now she was telling Livia to cut and run.

No. Livia stood, gathering the folder to her. "Can I keep this for a while?"

"Sure."

A long silence, then Livia sighed. "I better go."

"Okay."

Moriko didn't follow her to the door, and Livia felt her heart falter as she turned to look at her friend. "Soon?"

Moriko gave a stiff nod. "Stay safe, babe."

Livia made it back into Nox's town car before she burst into tears.

Nox was actually finding success in putting everything to the back of his mind, although not for the greatest reason. Sandor had come to him that morning and said two words that made him sit up and take notice.

"Hostile takeover."

Nox looked up sharply as Sandor came into the room. "What did you say?"

"You heard, Nox." Sandor sat down heavily. "I can't believe we didn't see this."

"Whoa, back up. What are you talking about?"

"I'm talking about Roderick LeFevre and his gang of merry men."

"So? They only have thirty percent share in the company."

"Not anymore. Seems Rod has been quietly buying up every last share that you and I don't own."

"What the actual fuck?" Nox's adrenaline pumped through his veins. "How do you know?"

Sandor smiled without humor. "Rod had one holdout. Zeke Manners. Zeke called me and told me Rod was offering him three times market price. Zeke told him to drop dead." He sighed. "I blame myself. If I hadn't urged you to float the company, we would still retain overall control."

"Wait," Nox looked aghast, "you're saying we don't?"

"Do the math, Nox. We gave up fifty-one percent." Sandor sighed and leaned forward. "Look, whatever Rod's planning, we've still got, with Zeke's shares, a majority. It just means we have to bring Rod in as partner due to the deal we made. It's not the end of the world."

WHEN NOX GOT HOME that night, he heard Livia playing piano and went to the music room to find her. He stood at the door watching her, her fingers moving lightly over the keyboard, her body swaying to the melody. He went to her, bending to kiss the soft skin of her shoulder.

"Don't stop," he said as she started slightly, so Livia continued to play while he sat down beside her. He put his arms around her waist and buried his face in her hair. *Fuck work, fuck everything else,* he thought. *This is all I want, this woman. She and I —us. Nothing else matters.*

"Come away with me for Christmas," he murmured. "We'll go somewhere where no one can find us, nothing can bother us. You and me and a log cabin in the mountains. A white Christmas."

His lips were at her ear, then they trailed down her neck and he felt her shiver. She stopped playing and turned to kiss him. "That sounds perfect. Just perfect."

"I'm just so sick of everyone interfering in our relationship, in our lives, our work. All I want is you, Livia ... for all time."

She wound her arms around his neck. "And I, you. Just you."

He kissed her deeply, pouring all the love he felt for her into the kiss, leaving them both breathless. "I love you," Livia whispered, brushing her lips back and forth against his. Nox smiled and, standing, pulled her to her feet.

"Come with me." He led her into his study and to the huge globe he kept in there. "Pick somewhere, anywhere in the world, and that's where we'll go. Anywhere. I know you won't let me splurge on you often ..."

"Unless it's to buy freakin' Steinways for my college," she interrupted, grinning, and Nox inclined his head with a grin.

"*Touché*, but please, let me do this. Let me give you the most romantic, over-the-top Christmas. It's our first one together. Let this be my gift to you."

Livia studied him for a long moment then smiled. "I guess, for our first one, it would be Grinchy of me to decline. Okay then, Nox Renaud, this one's on you ... with two conditions."

By the grin on her face, he knew she was about to make a joke. "Go ahead."

"One ... next year, it's my choice, my budget."

"As long as you promise there will be a next year, and a year after that, and after that, and so on."

She kissed him tenderly. "God, yes, I promise."

His arms tightened around her and he gazed down at her lovely face. "And the second one?" He deliberately pressed his erection against her, making her sigh happily.

"That you never, ever make me listen to that God-awful Mariah Carey song."

Nox laughed. "What? 'We Belong Together?'"

"Ha ha, no, I actually *love* that one. And we do."

Nox kissed her again. "Yes, we do. Now, stop prevaricating and choose somewhere to go on vacation."

Livia hummed over the globe, spinning it gently. "What about you? Where do you want to go for Christmas?"

"All I want for Christmas is you," Nox said innocently, then laughed as she punched his arm. "Ouch, devil woman. Have you made up your mind?"

"Okay," Livia said, closing her eyes and spinning the globe. "Wherever I put my finger, we go there."

"Deal."

She let the globe spin a couple of times before pushing her finger against it.

"That's the middle of the Pacific Ocean, doofus, spin again."

"Darn it." She repeated her process, but before she could open her eyes to see where she had landed this time, Nox turned her and spun the globe around. "I didn't see where I landed," she complained to him but he just smiled.

"I know ... I'm going to leave it as a surprise until the day. Can you get the time off work?"

She nodded. "Marcel closes for five days over Christmas, but he'll need me back for New Year's Eve."

"Understandable. I'll be partying at your place that night too." They wandered slowly to the kitchen, hand in hand, and Nox pulled open the refrigerator. "Pasta?"

"That's good." Livia sat on the tallest stool and watched him prepare their meal. "So, yeah ... you're really not going to tell me where we're going?"

"For as long as I can keep it secret. We'll use my private jet ... yes, we will, just this once," he shot her a glare. "I know, the environment, yadda, yadda, but this will be the last time. I'm selling it afterward, so allow me this one last play with my boy toy."

Livia grinned. "I like playing with your boy toy."

"Rude girl."

"You're really selling it?" Livia was impressed.

Nox grinned ruefully. "Your guilt-tripping worked, Enviro-Woman."

Livia snorted with laughter. "Seriously the dullest sounding superhero name."

"Isn't it?" Nox dumped some onion and garlic into a pan, and chopped some herbs.

"Where did you learn to cook, Renaud?" Livia reached over to steal a piece of Parmesan cheese, grinning when Nox batted her hand away.

"Mom. Italian, you see?"

"Did you ever spend a lot of time in Italy?"

Nox nodded as he expertly skinned some tomatoes. "Long summer vacations. The heat is intense, drier than here, but still. Dad owned some olive groves and vineyards which we spent hours in, picking fruit. We stayed in rustic villas and drank wine with every meal, and it was heaven. Simple life."

Livia tugged on a lock of his hair gently. "You sound as if you want to go back."

"I haven't been since my parents died. I was waiting for you to come along. I can see us spending summers like that, making love and walking around the hills of Tuscany. Florence is beautiful. Or watching our kids run and play." He stopped and gave a little laugh. "Doesn't it seem surreal to you that we've only known each other this short time and yet, we're talking about kids and the future?"

Livia successfully stole another piece of cheese. Popping it into her mouth, she grinned. "I think it's what happens in all relationships. Right now, I can't imagine doing that with anyone else."

He kissed her, brushing her lips with his. "Me either."

THEY ATE TOGETHER THEN SHARED a long soak in the tub. Livia leaned back against his chest as he traced patterns with the soap bubbles along her body. "Nox?"

"Yeah, babe?"

"Do you think we're co-dependent?"

Nox looked askance. "No. What the hell?"

"Just something Moriko said."

Nox was silent for a while. "She doesn't like me."

"She does," Livia sat up and turned to face him. "She does,

she just thinks ... with all that's going on, that ... God, I don't know."

He cupped her face in his hand. "This is really worrying you, right?"

She nodded. "We didn't leave things in the best place, but I don't know how to fix it. She wants me to break up with you and there's no way that's happening."

"She actually said that?" Nox rocked back a little, hurt.

Livia nodded, her face miserable. "She's worried someone's going to kill me because of our relationship."

Nox sighed. "Well, I can't blame her for thinking that. It's something I wrestle with every day. Why should I force all this shit on you?"

Livia shook her head. "Don't go falling into the trap of thinking you have any responsibility for this. I just wish that we knew who and why this was happening. Nox ... I think we should look into things ourselves. I just have this feeling, and I don't know where it comes from, that there are things from Ariel's murder and your family's deaths that are right in front of us and yet we can't see. Everyone said they couldn't believe your dad would turn on his family ... well, I believe that too. Even though I never met him, anyone who could bring a man like you into the world couldn't be bad."

Nox's eyes were soft. "I love you for saying that."

"But do you feel it too?"

Slowly he began to nod. "I do. I always have, it's just I've never had someone in my corner. I never had you. I think we were destined to meet, Livvy, not just because we fell in love, but because we were meant to heal each other. Dang," he added with a grin, "that was cheesy. Maybe we are co-dependent."

Livia laughed and kissed him. "Yep, let's not get too intense here. All I'm saying is ... let's be proactive and look at everything

—and everyone—who could be behind this. Because one thing is for sure ..."

"What's that?"

Her smile faded, but she looked at him steadily. "It's someone we know."

And with a sinking heart, Nox nodded. "I know. I know it is."

CHAPTER TWENTY-ONE

Two days before they were due to fly out to wherever Nox was taking Livia for Christmas, Livia had to perform at her end-of-semester concert. She sat in the dressing room now, surrounded by her fellow students as they got ready. She felt sick to her stomach. Charvi had decided that Livia would finish the show with her new composition, and worse, every single one of her friends would be there to watch ... except Moriko.

"I have to work, sweetie," Moriko had apologized to her over the phone. "Both Marcel and I wanted to come but one of us has to be here. He won. I'm sorry, boo."

Livia had reassured her that it was okay, but she knew Moriko had probably volunteered to stay behind at the restaurant. Things hadn't been the same since they had last seen each other.

Livia took a deep breath in, listening to the music from the concert hall as it was piped back through the speakers into the dressing room. As each performer was called, the room got emptier until Liv was left alone. Because she was in college, she had asked Jason to stay outside, not wanting the extra attention of a bodyguard around her. She needed to breathe, to get herself into a space where she could perform.

She went to splash her face in the small restroom. Looking in the vanity mirror, she saw how pale she was—she hadn't slept well the night before. She rubbed her cheeks to get some color into them, hearing the dressing room door open. Expecting the stagehand coming to call her, she was surprised when there was silence. She walked back into the dressing room.

A hand was clamped over her face, an arm hooked around her waist, and she was thrown to the floor. Not having time to scream, Livia kicked out at her attacker. *Not again, no way.* But this time, he was so much stronger, pressing his forearm against her throat, choking off her air supply.

In horror, Livia felt him push up her dress, tug at her panties. *Oh, God, please no ...*

She kicked out again, her head whirling from lack of oxygen, but desperate to keep him away. He slammed his clenched fist into her stomach and she gasped, doubling up in pain. He ripped her panties from her and forced her legs apart.

"No, please, please, don't ..." Her voice was cracked, barely a whisper despite the fact that she was screaming inside her head. She felt him touch her, but to her great relief, he didn't try to rape her. She felt him pulling and jerking at his penis and realized he was masturbating. He gave a grunt and she groaned in horror as she felt his semen cover her skin. The knife was in his hand then, pressing against her throat.

"Tell anyone, and I'll kill all of them. Nox, Amber, Sandor, and your pretty little Asian friend. I will be back for you, Livia, don't forget it. The next time you see me ... *this,*" he brandished the knife, "will be buried deep inside you, like it was inside of that whore Ariel."

Then he was gone. The whole attack had taken less than three minutes. Livia lay for a few moments, deeply in shock, before dragging herself up and tidying her clothing. She felt numb. She sat down on the chair again, smoothing the skirt of her dress. She couldn't even cry.

A knock at the door and the stagehand, Jim, stuck his head in and beamed at her. "Hey, Livvy, two minutes and you're on."

"Thanks, Jim."

He didn't notice her voice was faint and cracking. Livia blinked a couple of times, and then moved like an automaton through the hallways to the wings. Her ears rang, her body trembled and she felt colder than she ever had in her life. She barely registered when she was announced, and she walked onto the stage to applause and whoops of delight from her friends.

Automatically her eyes searched the room until she saw Nox —and immediately wished she hadn't. She wanted to scream, to cry, to run into his arms. He was smiling and cheering her, but as she stood still, she saw his expression change to one of concern. The audience had stopped applauding and were now murmuring, wondering what was going on.

Nox started to stand up but Livia shook her head and went to sit at the piano. She closed her eyes and took a deep breath in. She began to play, her fingers moving across the keyboard, a slowed down version of her piece, channeling all her shock, her fear, her pain into the recital. She had no awareness of the audience or anyone else as she played, only wanting to reach one person, wanting him to know just how much she loved and needed him.

She played for nearly an hour, cycling through every section easily. Her fingers ached, her back was sore as she finished and sat, numb and still.

The audience broke out into rapturous applause, which broke Livia out of her reverie. Shakily, she stood and moved to the microphone at the front of the stage, opened her mouth to speak ... and passed out cold.

CHAPTER TWENTY-TWO

Nox looked over at Livia as they flew across the Atlantic Ocean towards Europe. Livia had hardly said a word since the attack at the concert. After she'd collapsed, he'd been the first to reach her, clambering over the seats to get to her. Charvi, Amber, and Sandor had looked on in shock as he'd carried Livia off stage and to the dressing room. She awoke in his arms, then screamed when she saw where they were. He'd looked around and noticed signs of a struggle, her torn panties, and his weeping love, and he knew what had happened.

At the hospital, they did a rape kit, even though she told them her attacker did not penetrate her. "This is still a serious sexual assault, Ms. Chatelaine. Let us care for you."

Nox insisted she let them tend to her, and then the police came. A kind female police officer took her statement. "The rape kit shows he did ejaculate on you, I'm sorry to tell you, so we'll need to ask you for a DNA sample. And Mr. Renaud, too."

"Of course," Nox told her calmly, "anything to help."

Livia didn't want to stay in the hospital overnight and so Nox brought her home, putting her to bed and lying down next to her. He stroked her face. "If you want me to go sleep somewhere else tonight," he said gently, "I won't be offended. Anything you need, baby, just ask."

Livia gazed at him. "Just hold me, please, Nox. I'm so cold."

And so, he did, wrapping his arms around her. Neither of them slept. "Do you want me to cancel our vacation plans? We can always reschedule."

"No," she said quickly, "I want to go far away. Far, far away, Nox."

"Is Europe far enough?"

She half smiled. "Europe, is it?" He felt her body relax. "Yes, that's perfect."

He pressed his lips to her forehead. "You want me to tell you where?"

"No, keep it a surprise."

He studied her face. Her eyes were haunted. "I'm so sorry this happened to you, baby. I would do anything to turn back time and prevent it. I swear, the day we find out who it is ..."

Livia shook her head. "Please, don't. Don't stoop to his level."

She hadn't yet told him everything she'd told the police. "What aren't you telling me? What did he say to you?"

Livia hesitated for a long moment. "That he was going to kill me the next time he saw me. Like Ariel."

"*Jesus*." Nox closed his eyes and drew in a deep breath. "That's it. No more sending Jason away. No more late shifts at the restaurant. Liv, please ... won't you consider taking a leave of absence? We could stay in Europe as long as it takes to get the asshole. I want you safe."

"I'll quit my job at the restaurant. I'm no good to Marcel if I'm behaving like a scared rabbit every time a stranger comes in. I think he's kind of expecting it anyway. But after New Year's—I don't want to abandon him at his busiest time."

Nox's mouth had set in a thin line. "Deal—if you agree to extra protection. I'll make sure Marcel is compensated for the lost business. I'll have obvious guards and plainclothesmen there. No one will get to you. But afterward, please, I know it's a lot to ask, but I just want you safe."

Livia tried to smile. "After all my independent woman rants, I'm agreeing to be a kept woman."

"A safe woman. An *alive* woman. After we catch this guy, you can have at the world. Until then, I don't think it's wise to be that exposed."

So NOW, two days later, they were finally on their way to Europe. Livia looked healthier, at least there was that, but she was subdued. He went to sit next to her and took her hand. She turned and smiled at him. "Hey, you."

He leaned in to kiss her, felt her lips move against his. "I love you."

She tangled her fingers in his curls. "Let's make this vacation a time where we forget the horrors of the past, recent and otherwise, and just make this about *us*. Romance, making love."

Nox looked vaguely surprised. "Honey, if you're uncomfortable with sex at the moment, we don't have to."

She kissed him fiercely. "Nox Renaud, you better fuck me good on this vacation, because that's what I intend to do to you."

He laughed with a little shocked surprise. "Well, then, you have a deal." If that was what she wanted—or what she thought she might want—who was he to argue? But Nox knew, if it came down to it and she panicked, he'd be there for her any way she needed him. Hell, if she just wanted to get mad and pummel someone, he'd let her.

HE WAS able to distract her from brooding even more as they crossed into Europe. They flew over France and Germany before he finally relented and told her. "Vienna. Or rather, a small ski lodge just outside of it. I thought you would love the musical heritage of the city."

Livia looked delighted. "Seriously? My God, Nox, you couldn't have chosen better."

"Actually, *you* chose it, remember?"

Livia squinted at him. "Are you sure?"

"I swear. Your finger landed on Austria ... or near enough."

Livia started to giggle at the mischievous expression on his face. "What does near enough mean? Where did I really point?"

Nox shrugged. "Somewhere in Kashmir."

Livia started to laugh and she slid over and perched on his knee. "You are a bad man." She giggled as he blew raspberries on her shoulders. "Crazy boy."

Nox grinned up at her. "Your boy. Are you mine?"

"I'm your girl always, baby."

THE SKI LODGE, located halfway up a mountain, was secluded and private, and warmly lit for their arrival. Livia walked around it, her mouth open. "This is gorgeous, Nox. Just beautiful." She shrugged out of her coat—a log fire was already burning in the grate. She grinned at Nox. "Did you have your Christmas elves come in before we arrived?"

"Something like that," he laughed and held out his hand. "Come with me. I have some more surprises for you."

In the kitchen, he showed a refrigerator stuffed with every kind of food, ready for their Christmas. "And a pantry filled of things made entirely of sugar, butter, and chemicals," Nox said this with a mock serious expression on his face, knowing Livia would laugh.

She grinned. "Good job."

"And now the bedroom." He led her along the hallway and

pushed open the door to reveal a bedroom, fittingly all in white, with a huge bed in the middle and a glass window overlooking the mountains, the pines heavy with snow outside. "From the living room, at night, you can see the city lit up."

"This is heavenly," Livia enthused, then nodded at a box on the bed. "What's that?"

Nox grinned a little sheepishly. "I was in two minds about this after what's happened, but I think you'll enjoy it. Open it."

Livia pulled off the lid of the box and the layer of tissue paper. She began to laugh. "Oh, you *dirty* boy."

Inside lay a supple leather harness, with creamy brown straps that would lie against her pale skin, crisscrossing her body. A riding crop, dildos, lube, and velvet ties were amongst the array of sex toys Nox had gathered.

He grinned. "I went shopping."

"You certainly did." Livia picked up the leather harness and held it against her body. She could tell it would fit perfectly. "God, Nox, even looking at this stuff is making me horny."

Nox laughed. "Can you imagine what shopping for it was like? I did it online, of course, because I'm—"

"Chicken." They both laughed, and Nox curled a lock of her hair around his finger and pulled her toward him.

"You bet. But, also, in the city, there's a very well-known and very well-stocked adult shop. One of Europe's best. I was thinking if we need anything else ..."

Livia wound her arms around his neck, feeling absurdly happy for the first time in a while. Here she could pretend nothing bad was happening to them back home, that the rest of the world was just an illusion. "Nox Renaud, you make this woman very happy." She pressed her lips to his. "Now, what say we grab a shower and something to eat, and then plan our vacation? You want me to slip into this gorgeous harness tonight?"

Nox grinned. "Actually, I was thinking we save it for Christmas day."

"As that's tomorrow, I'm okay with that. Just regular old fucking tonight, then?"

"Oh, dang it," he said, rolling in his eyes, "if we *must*." He tickled her until she cried with laughter, then they took a long bath together.

Livia worked shampoo into Nox's dark curls, which had grown even wilder of late, studying his handsome face. "You know, when I look at us as a couple, you wouldn't know there's twelve years between us. You look so much younger than your age."

Nox immediately screwed up his face and she laughed. "Now, that's hot."

She poured water over his head to rinse his hair. "You know, no one's done that for me since I was a kid and my mom used to sing to me while she was washing my hair."

"That's sweet. Every time I see photos of her, I can see you in her features. Not so much your dad."

"Yeah, that's what everyone said."

THEY ATE A SMALL SUPPER, sitting at the large picture windows of the cabin, overlooking the lit-up city. "It's so peaceful here, so serene."

"As long as there isn't an avalanche," Nox grinned as she squeaked in alarm. "Relax, I'm kidding." He took her hand. "I love you, Livia Chatelaine."

She beamed at him. "Love you too, rich boy."

He laughed. "You know, if you married me, it would be your money too."

Livia stopped. "What?"

Nox half-grinned. "Just something to think about."

Livia swallowed hard. "I wouldn't marry you for your money, Nox."

"I know that, silly."

There was a long silence. "Nox ... it's only been three months."

"Which is why I'm not asking the question *yet*," he said lightly, but she could see the depth of his emotion in his eyes. "But make no mistake, I *will* be asking the question. This is it for me. You are the love of my life, Livia Chatelaine."

Tears dropped from her eyes then. "And you are mine, Nox Renaud."

He lifted her left hand and kissed her ring finger. "One day. Soon."

LATER, after they'd made love, Nox lay with his head resting on her stomach, his hands under her hips. Livia tangled her fingers in his hair and brushed her thumbs gently over his face.

"You handsome," she sang at him. He pulled a face and blew a raspberry on her navel. She giggled. On all fours, he climbed up the bed until their faces were level. He gently bit her bottom lip and then kissed her. She pulled him down so his whole weight was on her and sighed happily.

"What are you thinking?" he asked, kissing her neck all the way down to her shoulders.

"I'm thinking I wish I could erase the past twenty years for you and make this last forever."

"Well," he rolled to one side. "I can't erase the last twenty years. But I can promise this will last forever." He grinned at her and ran his hand down her body, splaying his long fingers over her belly. Livia wriggled with pleasure and looked at him, seeing his expression fall.

"What is it?"

He looked away. "I wish ... I wish my family could have met you. My mom, Teague ... even my dad. Liv, I've been thinking and thinking and I'm *damned* if I believe he killed my mom and brother. I want the case reopened. I knew my father, *knew* him. There's no way he would have done that. I think he was murdered and set up."

Liv sat up, nodding, energized by what he said. "Good. Good, Nox, I'm glad you're thinking like that because I agree. Let's find out the truth. Something tells me that it's linked to what is going on now. I'm glad, sweetheart, and I'll be with you all the way."

"He was a good man," Nox said finally and Livia nodded.

She pressed her mouth against his. "So are you. The very best."

Nox started to shake his head. "No, I screw up too often ..."

She didn't let him finish. "Everyone makes mistakes; everyone has their demons. You're not perfect. I'm certainly not. No one is. But you and me together, well, I like those odds."

She straddled him and he grinned up at her.

"Oh, you the boss now?"

She laughed. "I am chief now. You may call me Chief ... Always Ready for Action."

"A fine Native American name."

"I thank you."

"Chief?"

"Yes?"

"I think that's *my* night stick you've got hold of."

"Uh-huh."

"Okay then ..."

IT WAS late evening when the residential home called Sandor to tell him his father had passed. Sandor listened in silence then thanked the nurse. "I'll make the funeral arrangements," he told her, stoic as ever, but when he hung up the phone, he felt a shift inside him. *Damn it, Dad, couldn't you have waited until after Christmas?*

He felt bad then. He had known this was coming, that his father was spiraling downwards, but it was still a shock. His last remaining family. *Shit.*

His cell phone rang again and he saw it was Odelle calling. "Hi, Odie, what's up?"

"It's Roan. The police just called me because Nox and Livia are out of town. The semen Livvy's attacker left matched Roan's DNA. Goddamn that man, Sandor. I'm sorry to call and interrupt you, but I didn't know what to do."

"It's okay, sweetheart. Where's Roan now?"

"I don't know. He's been gone all day. I almost called Amber to see if she was with him, but then I thought I might go off on her, so ..."

"I get it. Look, let's meet and talk. Are you at home?"

"I am."

"I'll come to you and we'll figure out what to do."

He hung up and sighed, knowing he wasn't at all surprised that Roan's DNA had been found on Livia. He wondered how he should break the news to them, but didn't want to interrupt their vacation. Instead, he called Amber and got her voice mail. "If you know where Roan is, Amber, tell me now. This has gone too far now. Call me back."

IT WAS Christmas morning and Nox was cooking eggs for their breakfast, sipping his coffee as he gazed out over the snowy landscape. He heard the shower running and then, a few minutes later, Livia emerged, dressed in a thin white robe, her long hair damp. Nox smiled at her.

"God, what a beautiful sight. Merry Christmas, baby."

She stood on her tip toes to kiss his mouth. "Merry Christmas, gorgeous."

"Hungry?"

"God, yes."

They ate breakfast, then as they were brushing their teeth, he saw her grinning to herself. "What are you up to with that cheeky smile?"

She turned to him. "Want to open your Christmas present?" She nodded down at the belt of her robe and, grinning, he hooked a finger into it and pulled it open, leaving her robe to fall open.

Underneath, she was wearing the harness he had bought her, the leather crisscrossing her body, her breasts, and her belly, before sweeping between her legs. Nox felt his cock harden immediately.

"My God ..." His voice shook and Livia grinned, slipping the robe from her shoulders and taking his hand.

"Let's go play, baby."

As he followed her into the bedroom, he admired her perfectly rounded buttocks, the dimples of Venus, the smooth, flawless skin. His cock strained painfully against his linen pants and Livia cupped it in her hand. "Is that all for me?" She looked up at him from beneath her long eyelashes, her mouth parted slightly, and Nox gave a growl of desire.

"Every inch. I'm going to fuck you so hard, pretty girl."

Livia giggled as he swept her up into his arms and onto the bed. He kissed from her neck down to her breasts, sucking on each nipple until it was rock hard, then rimming her belly-button with his tongue. Livia squirmed beneath him, her pleasure obvious, and when—finally—his tongue found her clit, Nox saw her sex become red and swollen, ready for him to fuck her in any way he saw fit. It made him feel like the most powerful man on Earth. To prolong their pleasure, he brought her to near orgasm then stepped back to strip.

Livia watched him, lust in her eyes, a small smile playing around her lips. Nox stripped slowly, then, reaching into the box, he slipped a cock ring around the base of his already engorged penis. "You want this?" he said to her, fisting the root of it and she nodded.

"I want to taste you."

Nox grinned. "In time, beautiful. First ... let's tie you up, and see how you like the whip."

Livia moaned softly. She was beyond turned on. She spread her legs so he could see how much she wanted him. "I want you so badly."

Nox smiled. "Remember our first date? When we talked about anticipation? Well ..."

He tied her hands and feet to the bedposts, then, grabbing a tube of warming lube, he slicked some into her sex. "Can you feel the tingle?"

Livia nodded. "God, that feels so good."

He took the riding crop out of the box. "Shall we try this? Where would you like it?"

"Breasts and belly," she said breathlessly, then cried out both in pain and excitement as he brought the crop down across her belly, leaving a red welt.

"You like?"

"More, please, baby, more ..." Her back arched up as he struck her again, the crop marking a cross on her soft skin. It turned him on so much but he held back, even though his cock was straining and pulsing and aching to be inside her. He grabbed a dildo, slathered it in lube, and plunged it into her cunt, making her squeal. He kissed her passionately as he fucked her with the dildo, then when he couldn't wait any longer, he plunged his cock deep inside her, lifting her hips with one strong arm as he reamed her into ecstasy.

"Are you mine?" he said, gazing into her eyes, and Livia nodded, her face adorably flushed pink.

"For all time," she gasped then gave a cry as she came, her body shuddering and trembling. Nox buried his face in her neck as he pumped thick creamy semen deep into her belly.

"God, I love you, Livia ... so much, so, so much ..."

They collapsed, breathless and sated, Nox freeing her from her bonds. "Wow," Livia breathed, "that's definitely the way to celebrate Christmas."

Nox laughed. "That's probably quite tame compared to what we could do."

"We have plenty of time." Livia rolled onto her side, hooking her leg over his body and snuggling into his chest. They lay in companionable silence as they caught their breath, kissing softly now and then. Nox gazed down at her.

"I cannot imagine my life without you now, Liv. It just wouldn't make any sense."

"I feel the same. Weird, when you think of the coincidences that got us here. I keep thinking, what if you had never decided on Marcel to cater your Halloween party? Or what if I had moved to Seattle instead of New Orleans?"

Nox looked surprised. "You never mentioned Seattle before."

Livia smiled. "It was the other option. Moriko and I had another roommate, Juno, and she's a Washington girl. You'd like her and her family, actually. It was a toss-up between there and New Orleans. NOLA won out."

"Any reason?"

Livia gave a small laugh. "It was further away from my father."

"Understood." His arms tightened around her. "You don't talk about him a lot."

"Nothing to say. He's an asshole who never gave a crap about me or Mom, so as soon as I could get away from him, I did. Worked multiple jobs at one time to get through my undergrad degree, but I tell you, it was worth every lost hour of sleep."

Nox smoothed his hands over her face. "Have I ever told you you're my heroine?"

Liv smirked. "Dude, it's not an unusual story, truth be told. So many people don't have access to college when they show so much potential. We had a couple of people in our class who could have, and I'm not exaggerating, gone on to become world-class musicians. They had to drop out after not being able to afford to eat, even working two or three jobs. It was tragic."

An idea was forming in Nox's head as she spoke. "You know ... we could do something about that."

Liv grinned at him. "You have that 'I want to save the world' look in your eyes again. What's the idea?"

"A charitable foundation—in your name—to help support students with musical ability but who have no means to fund their education or future."

Nox saw Liv's eyes fill with tears. "Nox ... I'm speechless. Could we make it work?"

"With your help? Definitely. Maybe we could get Charvi and some of the music department faculty to help. Would that be something you'd be interested in?"

"Hell, yes! But I do have one suggestion."

"What's that?"

She touched his face. "We should do it in your mother's name. The *Gabriella Renaud Foundation*."

Nox felt his throat close. "She would have loved that. And I love you for suggesting it."

Livia smiled, kissing him softly. "But first, Nox, we need to get this thing at home dealt with. Then we can truly move on to better things."

"I agree."

Liv sat up. "We should start to make a plan of how we're going to approach this."

Nox laughed and pulled her back into his arms. "After this vacation," he said firmly. "Until then ... this is all that matters."

Roan Saintmarc buried his head in his hands. He had heard Odelle take the call that had damned him, and he knew the police would haul him in and arrest him for assaulting Livia as well as killing Pia. He was a dead man. He walked out of Odelle's house with nothing in his hands, nothing in the world.

He withdrew as much cash from his checking account as he could and, after debating, he went to Nox's mansion, breaking into the basement. He knew Nox and Livia were away and that the mansion was empty. He also knew he could live down in Nox's wine cellar, that at least he would have food, drink, and shelter. It didn't take him long to find his way down there; he and Nox had found the hidden entrance from the garden when they were kids. He had dumped his cellphone in the city and purchased a bus ticket with his credit card to throw the police off his trail. Hopefully, they would think he was long gone.

He found his way into the wine cellar and dumped his bag. Jeez, he'd forgotten how goddamn cold it was down here in the winter. Cold and dark ... he grabbed an extra flashlight but just as he lit it, he heard the step behind him. Whirling around, he only caught the shape of another human as something heavy connected with his head and everything went dark.

CHAPTER TWENTY-THREE

On the last night of their vacation—their blissful, relaxing, sensual vacation—Nox and Livia shared a bath in the huge tub. The window overlooked the snow, and they'd lit a bunch of candles to make the room softer, more romantic. Livia didn't know how this vacation, this place, this man, could be any more romantic, but the candles were a nice touch. She kissed Nox's temple. "Can we stay here forever?"

Nox laughed. "It would be nice, huh? But I think eventually, you'd get bored. Besides, it'll be nice to have somewhere we can always guarantee to be stress-free, a safe haven to go when things get bad."

Livia stroked her hands down his chest as he laid his head back against her breasts. "Speaking of which ..."

"Yeah."

"Back to the real world tomorrow."

"Ugh."

Livia laughed. "But, we have a purpose now, baby. We're finally going to lay every single ghost to rest, however painful it is. I got your back."

Nox wound his fingers through hers. "Couldn't do it without you."

"You know what surprises me?"

"What's that?"

"That none of your friends have ever suggested doing it. Really looking into the case, seeing if there's a link between Ariel's murder and what happened to your family. It seems to me that if they are linked, then you are at the heart of it. How come Sandor or Roan or Amber never said to you, 'Come on, let's find out what's really going on here'?" She sighed and leaned her head against his. "Maybe they thought they were protecting you."

"Maybe."

"It's a pity Sandor's dad couldn't throw some light on what was going on with your dad. I know they were close."

Nox looked surprised. "They were business associates, but I wouldn't say they were close. Dad was weirdly protective of Sandor, and it seemed to me that he was shielding him from things Sandor's father did. What, I don't know."

"This is getting complicated."

"Well, that's kind of why we left things so long. Too many questions, not enough answers."

"Was Sandor's dad a bad man? I should say, is he a bad man, sorry?"

Nox considered. "He's not someone I would have chosen to hang out with."

"I guess the apple fell far from that tree."

Nox nodded. "Very far. Sandor is one of the best men I've ever known."

She smiled fondly and pulled him back against her, kissing the top of his head, running her hands down his chest.

"You like everybody."

He laughed. "Yeah." He lifted himself off her and, with much splashing, turned to face her.

"I like you best." He pulled her to him, His hand gathered up the damp hair from her neck, the other slipped between her legs. She sighed at his touch as he buried his face in her neck. He pulled the plug out and as the water drained away, they wrapped themselves around each other, tangled limbs, making love until they were both exhausted, laughing, and sweating on the bathroom floor.

LATER, as Livia slept, Nox went over what she had said. *Yeah, this was going to be complicated.* Back in the day when his family had died, DNA profiling wasn't such a big thing, but now, he wondered if it would help in any way. Could he have his family exhumed and their skeletons tested? What would it prove? God, this was so confusing, but he knew in his bones that something was wrong about the accepted storyline. It was only now that he had found the courage to acknowledge that he believed his father hadn't killed his mother and brother. It just wasn't the man he had grown up with. Not even a psychotic break was believable. Tynan Renaud wasn't a man who got depressed—he worked the problem and found a fix. *No.* There was no way he would kill Gabriella ... Nox's mother had been the love of Tynan's life, just as Livia was Nox's. For a horrible moment, he pictured himself shooting Livia in the stomach and watching her die a slow, agonizing death.

"God, stop," he muttered to himself, rubbing his eyes to scratch the image from his brain. Focus on the beginning. His father, mother, and brother had been shot dead. Who would have wanted to kill his family? Jesus, he knew why the police had questioned him for hours; he still remembered the incessant jabs.

Who did you hire to do it, Nox?

Did you want your inheritance that much?

Why'd you did you do it, Noxxy boy?

It dawned on him then that even the police didn't buy Tynan Renaud as a murderer. Why hadn't they pursued that line of thinking even after they'd cleared Nox of all blame?

Someone must have asked them to drop it. A shock ran through him. God, yes. That must be it. Someone had paid the police off. It wouldn't be unheard of. But why?

He could rule Sandor out then, to his relief. Sandor might be rich now because of his own hard work, but there was no way he would have been able to afford the payoff the cops would expect. Which left Roan, Amber, and Odelle. Odelle he ruled out immediately—the woman might be an odd ball but she truly loved Nox and his family.

He winced when he thought of Amber and Roan. They had the money, certainly, and the influence ... but why would ...

God. Had Amber blamed him for Ariel's death and had his family killed because of it? He shook his head. *No way.* No way could Amber have kept that secret for twenty years. But the thought kept nagging at him.

"Nox?"

Livia looked up sleepily from the bed and he went to her, lying down beside her. She stroked his face. "Are you okay?"

"I am. Just thinking about what we're about to do."

Livia smiled, her cheek adorably crumpled from the pillow. "Sexy times?"

Nox chuckled softly. "I actually meant our little sleuthing adventure, but I like your thinking."

He moved on top of her as she rolled onto her back and wrapped her legs around him. "We're going to make everything okay again," she said softly, "I promise we will."

And Nox believed her.

CHAPTER TWENTY-FOUR

Back in New Orleans, Nox and Livia made a plan. Nox would go to the police and ask them to reopen his family's case; Livia would research as much as she could about the family and his father's business connections.

At first the police were hesitant to even listen to Nox, but finally, a younger detective, Brian Jones, called him back. "Mr. Renaud, I want to help. I've been working cold cases for a couple of years and although the official record is murder/suicide, something has always struck me as off. Let's talk."

Nox called Liv. "That's fantastic," she enthused, "a real step forward. Haven't found anything online yet, but I'll keep digging. I do have to go into work tonight."

"I'll try and be back to take you, but if not, make sure you take Jason with you."

"My pet bodyguard," she sighed, but agreed to his request.

Livia searched the Internet and looked at every news story, feature, article, and blog post she could find on the Renaud family tragedy. More than one linked it to Ariel's death, calling Nox cursed, which just made Liv angry. By the end of the afternoon, her eyes were sore and she went upstairs to change for work. As she walked into their bedroom, she froze. On the bed was an envelope, which she knew for certain hadn't been there that morning. She felt her chest cramp up with unease. The envelope looked like the same heavy paper brand as the one that had been left for her at the college. Expensive paper. Careful not to touch it too much, she eased the note out of it. She couldn't help the gasp that escaped her.

I TOLD *you to leave him. Now everyone will have to die before I kill you, beautiful Livia.*

"Jason!"

Her bodyguard came running, flanked by another couple of Nox's security men. She showed Jason the letter. Grim-faced, he told the men to search the house.

"And you're sure it wasn't here before this morning?"

"Positive."

Jason nodded and got on his phone. One of the security guards came back, his face ashen, and visibly shaken. "Boss, the wine cellar. You need to see this."

Livia insisted on going with them, but immediately wished she hadn't. "Oh, Jesus ..."

Blood. Lots of it smeared across the whole room, stinking, rotting. The corpse was leaning up against the wall, belly sliced open, entrails hanging out.

All of them retched. Jason kicked the corpse with his toe. "Who the hell brings a *cow* down here to gut it?"

Livia, covering her mouth and nose, nodded at it. "Someone sending a message. It's what he's going to do to me."

"Get the police down here now," Jason barked at his men, then turned to Livia was trembling. "Ms. Chatelaine, we need to get you someplace safe. I'm taking you to Mr. Renaud's offices. I don't think it's a good idea for you to be out in public."

"No, I need to go to work," Livia insisted. "Marcel is always shorthanded near New Year's."

Jason wasn't happy and called Nox. When he spoke to Livia, Nox listened to her. "I don't want to be the one to tell you what to do, even if I think this is beyond worrying."

"I want to go to work," she insisted. "It was a *cow*. Someone's idea of trying to scare me. Fuck them, Nox."

He gave a low chuckle. "Fuck them. Okay, but I'm taking you to work, and there will be a fleet of security with you all night long."

"Deal."

MARCEL GREETED her with a warm hug, but Livia noticed the strain in his eyes. "You okay?"

Marcel shook his head. "Liv, I don't want to pile on but ... have you seen or heard from Moriko? She didn't come in last night, and it's not like her. I tried to call her but there was no answer."

Livia looked at Nox, and there was terror in her eyes. Nox nodded to Marcel. "We'll go to her place."

In the cab, Livia held Nox's hand tightly. "Please be okay, please be okay," she kept whispering as she tried in vain to reach her friend on the phone. In the elevator to Moriko's apartment, she grew almost angry.

"Why the hell isn't she answering?"

As she spoke, something hit her shoulder. Liquid. They both looked at it. Blood. It had dropped from above. They both turned to look as they approached Moriko's floor and with mounting horror, they realized that the floor was covered with blood and that it was definitely pooling out from Moriko's apartment.

"No, no, no ..." Livia fought with the elevator doors and

finally wrenched them open. Nox tried to stop her, his instinct telling him what she'd find, but his outstretched hand missed her. Instead, he kept close as she burst through the door to her friend's apartment. They both saw her at the same time. Moriko, beautiful, sweet Moriko, half sat, half lay against the wall of her apartment, ripped open by a knife that still protruded from her body. Her clothes were soaked in blood, her eyes were closed, her face deathly pale.

"*Oh, my God. God, no please ...*" Livia sank to her knees and crawled to her dead friend, willing life back into her, but they both knew she was gone. Butchered. Stabbed to death. Livia let out a howl of agony that Nox would never forget and gathered Moriko's body to her, willing her to breathe, to please, please come back to her. She clutched her to her, not caring that Moriko's blood was soaking her, her sobs heart wrenching. Nox, his voice shaking, quietly called for backup and the paramedics, but she could see from the amount of blood that there was nothing they could do. Moriko was dead. Murdered.

ALL LIVIA COULD SEE or smell was blood, even after Nox put her into the shower at the hotel. He had told her the mansion was too dangerous now and she had nodded numbly, not really taking anything in. She felt detached from everything and everyone, even Nox. Moriko was dead.

Now she lay in a strange bed, listening as Nox and the police spoke in the other room. She tried to shut out their voices but also wanted to know what the hell was going on.

There was a knock at the door and Odelle came in, shutting the door behind her. She didn't say anything but sat on the edge of the bed and held Livia's hand.

For a long time neither of them said anything. Then Livia, her voice trembling, spoke. "Moriko's dead."

"I know. I'm so sorry, Livvy."

"He killed her because Nox and I are together."

Odelle shook her head. "Whoever it was killed her because they are psychopathic, Liv. This is not your fault."

Livia closed her eyes, letting out a sob. "Why is this happening?"

"I wish I could tell you, lovely, I do." Odelle stroked Livvy's hair awkwardly. "They're looking for Roan."

"Do you really think Roan is behind this?"

Odelle looked so sad that Livvy sat up and hugged her. "I used to think *no way*, but now ... I just don't know. I still think Amber knows more than she's telling, but that just might be my bias. Have you seen her lately?"

"Not since before Christmas."

Odelle sighed and let Liv go. "Well, I guess the police will question her too."

"Nox said she went out of town."

"I think she did. She's been acting strangely ever since she broke things off with Roan."

Liv studied her friend. "Odie ... would Roan have hurt Amber? Or vice versa?"

"I don't know. I got the feeling their relationship was about sex and that was it. Roan doesn't do deep."

"Unless he's with you."

Odelle half-smiled. "I was going to argue that but I think you're right, actually. He does confide in me. Share his dreams and hopes."

"I really want to believe that this isn't Roan's doing, Odelle. For your sake as much as his, and ours."

Odelle nodded sadly. "Me too, Livvy, me too."

. . .

BUT A WEEK LATER, as Livia was arranging Moriko's funeral, the police came back to them with devastating news. Roan's semen had been found on Moriko's body and the slaughtered cow's body. A countryside alert was sent out for him.

Nox, Livia, Sandor, Odelle, and Amber sat together in a low-key bar in the French Quarter. All of them looked shattered, but Livia couldn't help studying Amber, who seemed to be on the edge of something else—hysteria? Grief? The other woman, her red hair dirty and unkempt, was biting her nails down to the quick.

"What is it, Amber?" Livia asked her gently but Amber ignored her.

Nox fixed his friend with a stare. "God, are you high? *Jesus*, Amber, at a time like this?"

She shook her head, but now that Nox had mentioned it, they could all see Amber was tweaking. Odelle rolled her eyes and instead spoke to Livia. "How are you doing, Livvy?"

Livia shrugged. "I keep seeing her lying there, Odie."

"It's not your fault, Liv. The medical examiner said she'd been dead for hours."

"I should have gone to find her sooner. Days sooner. She always looked out for me; I should have done the same for her." Livia smiled through her tears. "One time, at college, she shouted at me for opening my dorm room door to her without checking who it was. It was *her* room too, the doofus. Anyway, she made me promise to always check who was at the door, and if I didn't know who it was, then I didn't open the door." Her face clouded over. "What kind of friend am I that I was—"

"Too busy fucking Nox in various European cities," Amber suddenly said, her tone harsh. "Poor little Livvy, precious little Livvy, spreading her legs for the nearest billionaire ..."

It was Odelle, moving quickly, who slapped Amber hard across the face, making them all jump. Amber rocked back, then lunged for Odelle, who side-stepped her, leaving Amber to sprawl on the floor. Sandor picked Amber up as Nox stepped between the two women. Livia was too shocked to move.

"Amber, go home and get cleaned up. And don't ever, ever talk to Livia like that again. *Ever.*" Nox was furious.

Amber spat at him. "You think that little piece of trash can replace my sister? My sister who loved you? Was devoted to you?"

"Get out of here!" Livia jumped up to stop Nox from going after Amber, and Sandor stepped in between them.

"I'll take her home, Nox."

Everyone was staring at them, some people even taking photographs. Nox put his arms around Livia. "It's okay, love. She's gone."

"What the *fuck* was that?" Livia said in an incredulous voice. Nox shook his head, holding her tightly.

"I don't know, baby."

"It's Amber's birthday," Odelle said quietly, and Nox groaned.

"Oh, God, I forgot. It's Ariel's birthday too."

"I've never seen Amber so high on something though. She usually keeps it to pot. *That* wasn't pot."

"No."

Livia said nothing. Amber's attack had been so out of the blue. Livia could feel the foundations of her composure crumbling, but she leaned into Nox's embrace. "Maybe you should go see her. I'm not trying to replace Ariel."

"I know that. Amber knows that. I apologize on her behalf … she's not herself."

Livia looked up at him. "Go see her. Make amends. See if she needs help."

Nox smiled down at her, stroking her face. "This is why I love you."

. . .

Nox went to meet Amber the next day, and it was a contrite Amber who sat with him. "I didn't mean what I said," she began, "please, *please*, tell Livvy I love her. I didn't mean any of it. I was just ... God, Nox, I miss Ariel so much."

Nox nodded. "I do too, Amber, you know that. But neither of us could have stopped what happened."

Amber was silent and Nox was surprised to see something else in her eyes. "What? What is it, Ambs?"

She shook her head. "I can't ... I can't tell you, Nox. It's too ... it's something I did. Something I have to live with, except ... I don't know how to live with it anymore."

Nox was really worried now. "Amber ... please tell me you didn't have anything to do with the threats to Liv?"

Amber gave a mirthless snort. "No, Nox. Not the threats."

"Then what?"

She mumbled something and Nox couldn't clearly make out the words. "What? Did you say 'scare her?'"

Amber stared at him with endless sorrow in her eyes then suddenly got up. "I can't ... I can't ... I'm sorry, Nox."

It wasn't until he was in bed with Livia later that it dawned on him what Amber had said. When he realized, it sent a cold arrow right through his heart. He said the words over and over to himself, hoping beyond hope that they didn't mean what he thought they did.

"He was only supposed to scare her."

Amber wasn't talking about Livia ... she was talking about Ariel.

Amber knew Ariel's killer.

CHAPTER TWENTY-FIVE

"Are you sure?" Livia was looking at him with shocked eyes. Nox had related his entire theory to her as they sat eating breakfast the next day, and now Livia sat back, her distress obvious. "You think she hired someone to scare her sister and he went too far and killed her?"

"That's exactly what I think," Nox said, grim-faced. "I always knew Amber was jealous of Ariel, but I never thought she would have done this."

Liv shook her head. "Maybe it was a prank gone wrong."

"Pranks gone wrong don't end with a woman being stabbed to death, Livia. Whoever killed Ariel meant it. He gutted her ... he enjoyed doing it."

"So, Amber got in with the wrong crowd. Maybe she wanted someone to scare her sister, but she picked a psycho who killed Ariel instead and has been blackmailing Amber ever since."

"Wow, you really ran with that theory." Nox was impressed.

Liv half smiled. "It just came to me. It's not hard to figure out Amber's motive."

"It isn't?"

"*You*, numbnuts. Amber's in love with you."

"No."

Livia rolled her eyes. "Dude, wake up. *Of course,* she is. She always has been, but once the plan with Ariel went awry and Ariel died, she knew she could never be with you, that it would make her look guilty and sooner or later she would give herself away. Problem is, what do you do now? Do you go to the police?"

Nox sighed. "I think I'd better talk to her again first. If the killer is the same guy and she knows it, then maybe we get it out of her in return for not bringing her into it."

"But how will we tell the police how we figured it out?"

Nox's green eyes were dangerous. "We don't. I'll deal with whoever it is."

Livia swallowed hard. "Nox."

"No one threatens the woman I love. *No one.* And for Moriko, for Pia, for Ariel ... I'll deal with it."

Livia was both scared and turned on by the menace in his tone. She leaned over and crushed her lips to his. "I love you," she whispered, "please take care."

"I promise." His kiss was sweet and tender and went on for a lot longer than expected before they were interrupted by his cell-phone buzzing. Looking regretful, he broke away from her and glanced down at the screen.

"It's Detective Jones." He answered the call and Livia listened as he spoke, his face clouding over.

What now? She thought wearily, and got up to go take a shower. Nox caught her hand and she saw his distress. "Okay, thanks, Detective. I'll be right down." He hung up the phone.

"What is it, baby?"

"Amber's going to have to wait. They're digging up my family today."

.   .   .

NOX INSISTED on watching as his family members were exhumed from their family mausoleum. Livia stayed with him, holding his hand as his expression changed from determination to sorrow as the coffins were raised. He turned away as the medical examiner opened his brother's casket.

Nox gagged and threw up while Livia, not knowing what else to do, rubbed his back and tried to console him. "I'm so sorry, baby."

Nox wiped his mouth. "It's okay. I know we're doing the right thing."

His family's caskets were loaded into the ME's van and taken away. Left alone, Nox and Livia gazed down at the empty graves. "Promise me," Nox said, "that when we die, we won't be buried like this. Let's both get cremated and fly in the wind for eternity."

"Agreed, baby. Mausoleums creep me out."

Nox half smiled at her attempt to cheer him up. "Our family will be a happy one."

"Certainly will." Livia said firmly. "All this crap we're dealing with right now will be behind us, and we'll have a bunch of kids and we'll be happy. Summer vacations in Italy, Christmases in Vienna."

"I can't wait." He splayed his fingers out over her belly. "Is it wrong that I kind of want you to be pregnant right now?"

"Ha," she said. "Let's wait until psychopaths aren't threatening to kill me, shall we?"

His smile faded and she nudged him. "Sorry, bad joke."

"I won't let anything happen to you."

"Right back at ya," she said. "Come on. Let's go see Detective Jones."

· · ·

HE WATCHED them from the farthest end of the cemetery. They had no idea that whatever they were doing was only going to make his plan to kill Livia better. He had almost brought them to their knees ... but what he would do next would destroy Nox Renaud forever. There was just that one loose end to tie up, and he would do that in spectacular style.

Amber.

AMBER WAS pale but sober when Nox met her in a small café in the city. To her credit, she didn't attempt to speak before Nox sat down and said simply, "*He was only supposed to scare her.*"

Amber lifted her head from where she had been staring at her coffee and nodded. "It was supposed to be a prank. I knew she would go outside for a smoke before you picked her up. He was supposed to take her for a ride around the block and then bring her back immediately. I knew something was wrong after a while when he didn't call me like he was supposed to."

"Who is he, Amber?"

She shook her head. "Please, let me finish the story. He had agreed to do it because ... he was mad at you. Something to do with your family, I don't know exactly. When he didn't bring her back, I knew. I'd always suspected he was a little off, but nothing like this. When I saw what he did to my sister ..." She covered her mouth and choked back a sob. "He told me if I ever told anyone, he would let them all know that I planned it, that I wanted her dead. I *never* wanted her dead, Nox, you have to believe me."

Nox, a vortex of emotions swirling inside him, stared at her coldly. "The sad thing is, I loved you. You and your shiny cap of red hair and your thousand-watt smile. And you loved me too— as long as I stayed in the box you made for me. Lonely, bereaved —*less*. While I still grieved for Ariel, you knew you controlled me. I scared you, I know. Once I crept out from the box and began to stretch and crack my limbs out to their full extent, once I stopped letting myself tamp down this fire—this life. This love. This love for Livia. I didn't want to think you were one of those women who only see other women as a threat. One of those friends who kept me around just to make them look better—I've had a lifetime of those. Leeches. I never thought you would turn out to be one of them. But you were the worst of them, because I loved you like a sister, Amber."

He fell silent then, swirling his glass, watching the ice melt in the green liquor. Melon. The door blew open, and a cackle of noise rushed in with the rain. Rain on wooden floorboards. Two elderly women, huddled in woolen coats, trying to warm up from the cold.

Tears dropped silently down Amber's face. Nox shook his head. "You killed her. Your own sister. Why?"

Amber looked at him, her eyes not angry, just sad. "I loved you. I *love* you."

Nox tried not to lose his temper but his voice shook as he asked her the questions he need to. "Did you have anything to do with the attacks on Livia? On me? Did you murder Pia? Moriko?"

"No, no, I swear," Amber seemed almost desperate. "It wasn't me. Look, I really like Livia, and I can see she is perfect for you. God ... no. I swear. But ... I did do one thing, and I can't believe I did it."

Nox wasn't convinced. "What?"

"Roan would ... He would leave his used condoms tied up in my trash can."

Nox made a disgusted noise. "What the hell does that have to do with anything?" He leaned forward to make her look at him. "Who did you hire to kill Ariel, Amber?"

She closed her eyes. "I didn't *hire* ..."

There was a sharp crack and, for a second, everybody in the café froze. Amber's eyes widened, then a thin stream of blood began to stream from her temple.

In utter shock, Nox saw the bullet hole in the window in the seconds before it smashed. And then Amber slumped forward, her eyes open and staring but very, very dead.

Bedlam. People screaming. Nox was up and running, out into the street to see where the gunman was—*who* the gunman was. But, of course, the killer was in the wind. Nox slumped to the ground, deeply shocked, and waited for the police to arrive.

LIVIA RAN straight into his arms. "God, Nox, thank God you're all right." She held him tightly as he buried his face in her hair.

"Enough," he said, his voice muffled, "*enough* people have died. We need to find him, right now."

"Who, darling?" Livia stared up at him with scared eyes. "Who?"

Nox looked shattered beyond belief as he said the words. "Roan. We need to find Roan."

JANUARY SLUNK onwards as the surviving friends worked with the police to find Roan. More convinced than ever that Roan was the killer, Nox asked the police to compare any old DNA that didn't belong to his family to Roan's.

Detective Jones agreed. "We've issued a countrywide search for Saintmarc, but if he is the one who shot Ms. Duplas, he's obviously around New Orleans, waiting to finish the job. Do you have adequate protection?"

Nox nodded. Sandor looked at Livia and Nox now. "Look, being at the hotel doesn't work. Come stay with me. It's no mansion, but there's a hell of a lot less dark places for a stalker to hide. Odelle, you too. We need to stick together until Roan is found."

SANDOR'S HOME was large but comfortable, and Livia felt safer there than she had anywhere else for a while. She worried about her friends though, knowing one of their own was responsible for so much of the mayhem and murder. She had hatred in her heart for Roan Saintmarc, and although she wouldn't say it aloud, she almost wanted him to come for her so she could avenge her friends. Avenge Moriko, avenge herself. Even if it killed her.

She could feel Odelle keeping an eye on her, though, and knew that if she needed to break down, Odelle would be the one to help her. She didn't want to add to Nox's pain. Of all of them, he was the most affected, she thought, having seen Amber killed in front of him. He looked shell-shocked still, even after a few weeks, and it was hard to tell if it was from Amber's murder or Amber's admissions.

"What I don't understand," she said to him, "is how Roan knew to shoot her at the moment she was about to tell you about him. He couldn't have been bugging her, for crissakes; he didn't have the resources."

"It may be that he *doesn't* know she didn't reveal him," Nox said, "in which case, he knows we know and will hopefully trip himself up out of desperation."

"Or do something reckless that takes someone else's life." Livia sighed. "God, what a fucking mess ... but what the hell is his motive? I don't get it."

"I can't help you there. I honestly have no idea."

Livia chewed her lip. "And what did Amber mean about Roan's discarded condoms? That makes no sense ... Unless ..."

Nox was studying her closely. "Unless what?"

Livia was sickened. "Unless she was telling us someone was using Roan's semen to frame him. And Amber *knew*."

DETECTIVE JONES CAME to see them one afternoon at Nox's office. Having given up her job at *Le Chat Noir,* Livia now worked on her college projects at Nox's office during the day. She found, to her surprise, that they didn't get tired of seeing each other all day and all night.

"This bodes well," Nox grinned as she said as much one night, and she laughed. It was a relief to laugh and be happy, and they made love often, clinging to each other.

They also talked more about their charitable foundation ideas, asking Charvi to be involved. Charvi—who, much to her disgust, also had a protective detail—was enthusiastic. "For a rich dude, Nox Renaud, you're quite the guy." But she looked at him with proud eyes and Livia knew her approval meant the world to him. Charvi got tearful when Nox told her they were naming the foundation after her former lover, and she hugged Gabriella's son.

"I always thought you might resent me," she told him, wiping her tears, "for being with your mother before she met your father. But she loved me truly, and she loved Tynan truly. There was not a bad bone in that woman's body."

Nox got choked up then, and nodded. Livia smiled at them both. "Family isn't just blood. I know that. I'm looking at mine right here."

WHEN DETECTIVE JONES came to see them, family was on their minds again. "Something strange, Mr. Renaud. When we went to compare your father's DNA to your friends, we found a match. A familial match. The thing is, the lab messed up the labeling. So, we need to take your DNA again to test against the sample, in case, for some reason, we've made a mistake."

The detective was being cagey, and Nox and Livia shared a look. "What aren't you telling us?"

Detective Jones drew in a deep breath. "Look, if the lab is right then one of your two closest friends is also your half-brother."

Nox's eyes widened. "You're fucking kidding me?"

"No, sir."

WHEN THE DETECTIVE HAD LEFT, Nox and Livia stared at each other. "My brother ..."

"This is just bizarre. I'm sure they must have gotten Teague and someone else's DNA mixed up."

"It must be. My parents did *not* cheat on each other." Nox was fierce in his denial, but Livia could see the doubt in his eyes.

"Look, it can only be Roan or Sandor, if it's anyone. I can't see any physical similarity between any of you."

"It's a mistake," Sandor was at the door then, obviously having heard the conversation. "The police fucked up. Dude, as much as I think of you as my brother, it's not possible. Dad had a vasectomy after they had me, and Mom died before even Teague was born."

"It doesn't explain how it can be a *half*-brother, if Teague's DNA got mixed up. Teague *was* my brother; you can see the likeness between us." Nox sighed. "Okay, so maybe my dad wasn't a killer, but—"

"What?" Sandor looked surprised at that comment, and Nox and Livia exchanged a look.

Nox cleared his throat. "I've been passive for too long, Sandor. I do not believe my father killed my mom and Teague. I do not. Someone else killed them, and I want to know who."

Sandor nodded slowly, and Livia studied him. Was there something behind that closed expression, or was it just shock? "Well, good. I think you need to look into it. It's been haunting you too long. I got your back, dude."

"Thanks, man."

Sandor smiled at them before disappearing back out of the room. Livia chewed her lip. Unease settled over her—Sandor's reaction to the news that they were looking into Nox's family tragedy had got her thinking. However, she stayed silent—Nox didn't need more complications.

"You look tired, baby." Nox pressed his lips to her forehead and she wrapped her arms around his waist.

"I am. Let's go home."

"I'll see if Sandor needs a ride home."

Livia hesitated. "I meant ... *our* home. I want privacy."

Nox sighed. "It isn't safe, baby. There are too many ways to get into it, and believe me, Roan knows all of them."

"And we can't get them secured?"

Nox was the one to hesitate now. "Baby ... it's more that I'm scared. Bad things happened there—more than once—and I'm terrified I'll lose concentration for a second and someone will get to you. Seriously, Sandor's place is safer."

Within a week of Nox making that statement, he would realize just how horribly wrong he was.

CHAPTER TWENTY-SIX

Sandor didn't come home with them. "I've got some paperwork to catch up on, then I think I'm going to meet a girl."

Nox grinned. "Oh yeah?"

Sandor shrugged. "It's nothing. But enjoy the privacy and I'll see you later."

In the car on the way home, Livia was pensive. "Huh."

"What?"

"Sandor said *enjoy the privacy*. How does he know Odelle won't be home?"

Nox shrugged. "Probably forgot. She does tend to keep to herself—except when you and she are plotting something." His cell phone buzzed. "It's the detective. Hey there."

He listened and paled. "You're sure? God. Okay, yeah, we'll be right there."

He ended the call and looked at Livia. "They've pulled a body out of the bayou near the mansion. They think it might be Roan. They want me to go down there and identify the body."

. . .

LIVIA WAITED in the medical examiner's office while Nox went with the doctor. Soon he was back. He shook his head, looking shaken. "Impossible to say. The body's been in the swamp."

He didn't have to say anymore. Detective Jones followed Nox out of the morgue.

"Look, we'll do the DNA work then see where we go from here."

Livia cleared her throat. "Detective Jones? Has Sandor Carpentier submitted his DNA sample?"

"I'll check, but I think so. Why?"

"Just curious. No reason."

Detective Jones smiled at her. "Well then, I'll leave you. Thanks for coming in—and sorry to put you through that, Mr. Renaud."

"Anything to help."

In the car, Nox let out a long breath and Livia looked at him sympathetically. "Was it bad?"

Nox nodded. "The body was mutilated and barely looked human. As much as I blame him, I hope to God it wasn't Roan. That body's been in the swamp a while."

WHEN THEY GOT HOME, Odelle was there, and Nox told her gently about the discovery. Odelle nodded calmly. "It's him," she said, "I know it in my bones. Nox ... I think we need to start looking for somewhere else to stay."

Nox's eyebrows shot up. "Why?"

"I don't feel safe here. Do you feel it, Liv?" Odelle looked at her and Livia nodded.

"I do, but I don't know why. Maybe it's the confusion over the DNA, or that the body—if it's Roan's, it means he didn't kill Amber ... But until we have confirmation that Sandor's DNA is in the all-clear ..."

Nox stared at them both. "You honestly think Sandor might have something to do with this?"

"Let me be clear," Odelle said, "it's just a feeling I have. I have no proof of anything, just my gut instinct."

Nox turned to Livia. "And you?"

"The same. There's just been something off lately about Sandor—or, to be fair, it could be paranoia on my part, given what's been happening. The only people I trust right now are in this room."

Nox sighed and Livia could see him struggling with the idea that his friend might not be who he thought he was. She put her hand on his arm. "Look, we're not saying Sandor has done *anything* wrong. Just be cautious."

"That's fair enough." Nox thought it over for a while. "Okay, look, we'll tell him we're going to move out because ... God, I don't know, to give him his privacy back. I'll look into renting something short term."

In the end, it was Livia who told Sandor they were moving out. He came to find her one morning while Nox was at work. Livia was packing a bag when she heard a step behind her. She spun around, startled to see Sandor there. He smiled at her. "Sorry, I didn't mean to scare you."

Livia, her hand on her chest, tried to smile. "It's okay. I just didn't expect to see you. I thought you were at work with Nox." Her heart was beating uncomfortably against her ribs. Sandor sat down on the edge of the bed without being invited and nodded at her bag.

"Going somewhere?"

Livia felt awkward. "Has Nox spoken to you?"

"About what?"

"About us moving out? We just feel that we're giving into the killer by huddling together." A thought occurred to her and she half-smiled. "Nox and I don't want to put you and Odie in the line of fire anymore than you already are. I couldn't bear it if anything happened to either of you." *That's it, lay it on thick.*

Sandor touched her face. "You're very sweet, Livvy." He stood and, to Livia's surprise and unease, took her face in his hands. "Every day," he said softly, "I see more and more why Nox fell in love with you. You are beautiful, inside and out, Livia Chatelaine. Is it inappropriate to say that I wish I had met you before Nox did?"

Livia was about to brush off the compliment, but then Sandor gently, quickly, brushed his lips against hers. He immediately dropped his hands and stepped back, making a good show of looking horrified. "Gosh, I'm sorry, Liv. That was so inappropriate. I'm sorry."

There was a curl of fear in Livvy's stomach. What the hell was going on here? "It's okay."

"I'll leave you alone. I will miss all of you, but I understand why you're moving out."

He left her alone, stunned, and feeling weirdly tearful. She sat down on the bed heavily and wondered why she felt so upset. The kiss had been *wildly* inappropriate, but it wasn't even that which upset her. It was the expression in Sandor's eyes the whole time he was speaking. Cold. Dead. Not the eyes of the man she had hoped—had assumed—he was.

Her gut instincts were kicking in again as she closed the bedroom door and called Nox. When he answered, she burst into tears and it took her a minute to calm herself before she said what she wanted to say. "Please, Nox. Come get me out of here."

.   .   .

THEY MOVED into a hotel to begin with, although Odelle simply went home. "I've hired extra protection," she assured them, "and I don't want to play the third wheel, as much as I love you both."

At the hotel, Nox and Livia ordered room service, took a long hot shower together, then made love. Livia hadn't felt comfortable having sex at Sandor's place, so now, reveling in their privacy, Livia clung to him as he fucked her slowly and tenderly. She smoothed his dark eyebrows as he moved above her. "I love you so much, Nox."

He grinned as his pace quickened and she gave a little cry of pleasure. "As I love you, pretty girl."

Livia tightened her legs around his hips, squeezing her vaginal muscles on his diamond-hard cock. Nox groaned. "God, yes, just like that, baby." He slammed his hips against hers, and Livia took him in deeper each time, tilting her pelvis so his huge cock could drill ever harder into her. "God, I love fucking you, Livia Chatelaine ... your body was made for fucking."

Livia grinned then arched her back as her orgasm hit, pressing her belly against his. "Nox?" She was gaping as his pace grew rougher and quicker. "Come on my belly."

Nox, panting for air, drove himself to the peak then withdrew, shooting thick, creamy white cum onto her belly, fingering her clit as he did and making her come again.

Afterward they caught their breath as Nox massaged his cum into her skin. He circled her navel with his finger. Livia gazed up at him. "I'm thinking about our Christmas getaway and all those dirty games we played."

"You enjoyed them?"

"You know I did. When all this is over, I'd like to do that again. Maybe even try some new stuff."

Nox slid his finger into her cunt and moved it gently in and out, while his thumb stroked her clit. Livia could feel the excitement build again in her body. "That's it, Livvy, just lie back and let me do the work." Nox nipped her nipple with his teeth before taking it into his mouth as he stroked her. Livia tangled her fingers in his dark curls as he sucked at her breasts, making her nipples rock hard. Then he moved down to tongue-fuck her navel.

"God, that's so good."

"Sensitive belly."

"You know it." Livia sighed as he moved further down to take her clit in his mouth, while his fingers moved up to stroke her belly. Livia spread her legs wider and Nox, his tongue dipping in and out of her cunt, began to finger-fuck her navel with his thumb, finding a rhythm that drove her crazy. He made her come again and again, before plunging his straining cock back into her. Livia cried out as she came hard, breathless and sweating, clawing at his buttocks, urging him deeper.

At moments like these, she could pretend everything was okay, that everything was happy. Nox knew how to command her body entirely, and he was relentless in making her come every single time. God, she loved this man. She would do anything, try anything he wanted to, but in the end, it came down to their animal selves, almost feral in their carnal desire for each other.

They fucked until they were exhausted. Then, his head resting on her breasts and her arms around him, Nox fell asleep, but Livia's mind was whirling with questions.

This whole thing was so confusing, with a myriad of suspects. But in her mind, Livia felt sure she knew who was behind all of this, and tomorrow she would start to find out more about the man she was certain was trying to kill her.

Sandor.

CHAPTER TWENTY-SEVEN

Charvi Sood was surprised to find Livia not in the music room, but at one of the computers in the college's library. "Hey there, kiddo."

"Hey, Charvi."

"What are you doing?"

Livia smiled at her. "Research. Charvi, you might be able to help me out." She looked around the library then lowered her voice. "What do you know about Florian Carpentier, Sandor's father?"

Charvi felt cold inside. "Why do you ask?"

Livia just looked at her and Charvi nodded. "Okay, but not *here*."

They went to Charvi's office and the older woman locked the door behind her. She offered Livia a cup of coffee and when they had their drinks, they sat on her old comfortable couch. Charvi sighed. "What I'm about to tell you, I've never told anybody, mostly out of respect for Gabriella's wishes. When she died, I thought about going to the police about it, but they seemed so certain that Tynan had killed her and Teague that I didn't want to cause Nox any more pain. That was the real reason I stayed away from him." She sipped her coffee, collecting her thoughts.

"Before Gabriella met Tynan, and after we had decided to split up—she was worried what our relationship could mean for my career, can you believe it? —she worked a little for the Carpentiers as a consultant. Eleanor Carpentier was a lovely woman and she and Gabriella became good friends. Then one day, Gabriella called me, hysterical. I went to her apartment to find it in disarray, and Gabriella bleeding and bruised. She had been raped."

"Oh, God." Livia felt sick.

"At first, she wouldn't tell me by whom, she just said she couldn't go out in New Orleans anymore for fear of seeing him. Eventually I got it out of her. Florian Carpentier was not a good man. He beat Eleanor, raped her too, I believe, and Florian didn't even bother to hide it. I tried to make Gabriella go to the police but she swore he would kill her if she did. She swore me to secrecy and for a time it seemed like things would go back to normal. Then, about a month later, Gabriella left town unexpectedly and didn't return for a year."

Livia's eyes were full of understanding. "She was pregnant."

Charvi nodded. "She had the child and Florian and Eleanor brought him up as their own."

"Sandor. Sandor is Nox's half-brother."

Charvi nodded. "When Eleanor died, and when Florian got Alzheimer's, Sandor took over the business with Teague. Then, when Nox was at college, they all died. Over the years, I've tried to find reasons why Tynan would have done it, but there are still none. He loved Gabriella, and those two boys were his life. I truly believe they were all murdered."

Livia swallowed. "By?"

"I think Florian got confused and thought his secret might be revealed. He went mad and shot them all."

"But how the hell would he have had the brainpower to frame Tynan then?"

"He was a vicious man, no doubt about it, and thought himself above the law. But I believe he had help."

Livia closed her eyes. "Sandor."

Charvi nodded. "Over the years, I've become more convinced. I don't know Sandor at all, so I can't speak to whether he takes after his mother or his father. Wouldn't any loyal son help his father, even after his father committed such a heinous act?"

Livia was silent for a time. "But to frame Tynan? And do that to his supposed best friend? Did Sandor know he was Gabriella's son?"

"I don't know."

"What if he found out? Got angry? Sandor does a good job of appearing friendly and warm, but there's something else there. An anger. What if it wasn't Florian who killed Gabriella? What if Sandor, on finding out the truth about his parentage, got angry and went to confront her? He took a gun, and when she tried to deny him, he killed her. Tynan and Teague were collateral damage."

Livia looked sick, but Charvi nodded. "It could have easily happened that way."

"And Ariel ... what if Amber and Sandor had planned the prank together, then Sandor went way, way off script. Got off on killing women. He could have been ..."

"Livia, darling, let's work one problem at a time. But I think you should stay well away from this if your theory is correct."

"I have to talk to Nox," Livia said, "but Sandor is his business partner as well as his best friend, and I know that they're having enough trouble. Someone's been buying up all the shares."

"Sandor, perhaps? Trying to oust Nox?"

Livia shook her head. "He mentioned someone called Roderick LeFevre."

"Rod?" Charvi looked surprised. "I'm surprised. It doesn't seem like his m.o. The Rod I know is a straight shooter."

"If you know him, could you get me in to see him?"

"I'm sure that can be arranged."

AN HOUR LATER, Livia was waiting nervously in the reception of Roderick LeFevre's company. His opulent offices and sleek staff made Nox's building look shabby and old-fashioned. Why on Earth would Roderick be interested in it?

"Ms. Chatelaine?" A tall, blonde, classically handsome man smiled at her. "Rod LeFevre. Please, we'll meet in my office."

Liv followed him. "So, you're the lady who's won Nox's heart?"

She smiled hesitantly at him. "I am. And you're the man who's been buying all the shares in his company."

Rod laughed. "I am. I like you already. Straight to the point." In his office, he invited her to sit. Livia studied him. He was a little older than Nox, mid-forties, short hair, dark green eyes. His face could go from friendly to dangerous in a moment, she guessed, but he exuded warmth and honesty. She drew in a deep breath.

"You seem like you like honesty, so here goes. Was it your idea to buy all the shares you could in RenCar, or did Sandor Carpentier come to you and ask you to do it?"

Rod's eyebrows shot up. "My, my. Okay, well, Ms. Chatelaine—"

"Livia."

"Livia. I could, of course, tell you to mind your own business."

"You could, and I would respect that." Livia met his gaze steadily.

Rod smiled. "Yes, I *do* like you. Well, to answer your question, yes, he did. He told me he wanted to buy the company from underneath Nox, that he thought Nox's heart wasn't in it anymore and he wanted to give him the push to try something new. Sandor told me that if I bought the shares, he would pay me double for them."

Livia scoffed. "And you believe him about him wanting to help Nox?"

"Of course not, but that's none of my concern. I'm a businessman, Livia, and what Sandor was suggesting would have made me in the region of seven hundred million dollars."

Livia whistled and shook her head. "You people deal in figures I can't even comprehend."

"What is it you do, Livia?"

She lifted her chin proudly. "I'm a grad student and until recently, a waitress."

Rod smiled. "Both admirable vocations. I had heard you were one of the finest students ever to study at the university."

Livia looked surprised and Rod laughed. "I do my research too, Livia. And because I am who I am, if women were my type, I'd be fighting Nox Renaud for a woman like you." He grinned. "Thankfully for all of us, my husband would object."

Livia giggled at his teasing and decided she liked this man very much. "Could I ask you not to reveal our conversation to Sandor, please?"

"You have my word."

He walked her to the door, but then stopped her. "Livia ... I won't share this conversation, but I can't speak for anyone who might have seen you come here. New Orleans is a relatively small town when it comes to who knows who in certain circles.

Please, tell Nox you came here and make sure you have adequate protection in place."

Livia studied him. "You think Sandor's dangerous?"

"I have no evidence of it, just—"

"Gut instinct."

Rod nodded, half-smiling. "Exactly."

Livia nodded. "Did you know Sandor's father? Florian Carpentier?"

Rod's smile faded. "I did, unfortunately."

"Why 'unfortunately?'"

"He was a vicious *fuck*." There was that honesty again, and Liv half smiled.

"Understood. Thank you again, Mr. LeFevre."

"Rod, please. Goodbye, Livia."

LIVIA, being driven back to the hotel by Jason, called Nox. She didn't want to tell him what she had discovered over the phone, just in case Sandor was listening in, but merely said she'd come to his office later that day. "I love you."

"Love you too, babe."

After she ended the call, she looked over at Jason. "Jason, could we stop somewhere else, before home?" She gave him the address and he turned the car around without comment.

At the residential home, she asked if she could see Florian Carpenter. "I'm his niece from out of town and I just got here," she lied smoothly. "I haven't seen him in years."

The receptionist looked at her for a long moment, then turned away. "Just a moment please, ma'am."

Nervous, her hands clenched with fingernails digging into her palms, Livia waited. Soon enough a smartly dressed administrator came to collect her. "If we could just step into my office."

Shit, they didn't believe her 'niece' story. "If I could just see my uncle."

The administrator, whose named tag said Susan, ushered her into the office. Her expression softened. "I'm so sorry, Ms. Carpentier. We assumed all the family knew. Did Mr. Carpentier's son not inform you?"

"Inform me of what?"

"I'm sorry to tell you that Mr. Carpentier Sr. passed away last month."

Livia stared at her, not needing to pretend her shock now. "What?"

"I'm so sorry, my dear. He passed peacefully."

God, no. I didn't want him to pass peacefully, I wanted him to fucking suffer after what he did to Gabriella. Livia tried hard to keep the hatred off her face. Susan, reading her, mistook her anger. "You weren't down as his next of kin, you see."

"I haven't spoken to Sandor yet," Livia said by way of explanation. She sighed, closing her eyes. "May I see his room?"

"I'm afraid it's occupied, dear. Unfortunately, we can't keep the rooms open for long. Too much demand."

"Of course, I'm sorry." Another idea came to her. "Did Sandor, I'm sorry, I mean, Mr. Carpentier Jr., take possession of Florian's personal items?"

Susan nodded. "He did. He didn't want to linger. He arranged the cremation quickly, and took the small amount of personal possessions that were left."

Livia thanked the woman and left the residential home. She sat in silence in the car as Jason turned the car. "Where to, Ms. Chatelaine?"

She chewed her lip for a moment. "You know, I think I left some personal items at Mr. Carpentier's mansion. Do you think we could swing by there?"

CHAPTER TWENTY-EIGHT

Nox looked up as Sandor poked his head around his office door. "Skipping out for some lunch. Want to join?"

Nox shook his head. "Not for me, thanks. I'm meeting Liv in a while."

"Cool. See you around."

Nox got back to his paperwork but found he couldn't concentrate. Livia was right, there was something off about Sandor. Oh, he gave the impression of just being your friendly everyman, but behind his eyes ... *fuck,* Nox shook his head. Were they both just paranoid? Instead he called Livia. He was surprised when she seemed cagey. "Where are you?"

"Um ... I left something at Sandor's place and we're just about to go pick it up."

Nox frowned. Livia had been so adamant that she didn't feel safe there. "Why not just get Sandor to bring it to the office?"

"I don't want to bother him; it's only a hairbrush."

She was lying, he knew it in his bones. "Liv ... what are you up to? Tell me."

"Nothing, honestly. I spent the morning with Charvi and

then remembered I'd left my hairbrush at Sandor's—random, I know. But it was a present from Moriko."

"Ah. Well, is Jason with you?"

"Of course, darling. It won't take long."

A FEW MINUTES LATER, Harriet, the new receptionist, called him. "I have a Roderick LeFevre on the phone for you."

Nox was surprised. "Calling to buy my shares too, Rod?"

Rod gave a chuckle but then his voice turned serious. "No, actually, it's about your lovely lady."

"Livia?" Nox was astonished.

"Unless you have more than one."

Nox shook himself. "What about Livia?"

"She came to see me this morning. Asked me point blank if Sandor Carpentier was the one who was really buying all the shares in your company."

"And what did you tell her?" Ice was creeping through Nox's veins. What the hell was going on?

"I told her he was."

The shock hit Nox full-force in the chest. "What?"

Rod LeFevre explained the same thing to Nox as he had to Livia. "Sandor Carpentier is not your friend," he concluded, "and goddamn it if I can't stop worrying about your lovely lady. If Sandor finds out she was asking questions ..."

"Thanks, Rod. Listen, I have to call her."

"Stay safe, Renaud ... and I'm sorry."

Nox tried to call Livia, and then Jason, but to his distress, could not reach either of them. As he hung up, his phone rang again and it was Detective Jones.

"The body *is* Roan Saintmarc," the detective told him, "and he's been dead a good couple of months. Multiple skull fractures; he was beaten to death. He couldn't have killed Amber Duplas or Moriko Lee."

Nox closed his eyes. "What about the DNA? Sandor?"

"It's confirmed. Sandor Carpentier is your half-brother. We have men on the way to your office and to his mansion right now."

"He's not in the office ... and Livia is at his home."

"Gotcha. We're on our way."

He got up and raced out of the office, ignoring Harriet's startled yell as he pushed past her and out to his car. "Answer your phone, goddammit!"

He called Charvi in desperation. "Charvi, I know Livia came to see you this morning. I need you to tell me everything. *Everything.* Right *now* ..."

CHAPTER TWENTY-NINE

As Livia moved through the hallways of Sandor's mansion, her heart thumping, she looked for his security team but there was no one. "Where the hell is everybody?"

Jason was looking tense. "I think we should get you out of here, Ms. Chatelaine."

Livia shook her head, heading for Sandor's study. "Keep a lookout for me. I'll be quick, I promise."

Inside, she rummaged through every drawer in Sandor's desk, every file she could get her hands on from his cabinet. Nothing. Finally, she found a box shoved on the window sill behind the curtain. She opened it and saw various personal items—toothbrush, toiletries, old postcards, and photos. At the bottom, a stack of letters. She flipped through them and saw they were all addressed to Gabriella. She stuck them in the back pocket of her jeans and returned the box to where it came from.

"Ms. Chatelaine, I think we should go." Jason had stepped into the room, but before she could answer, he gave a strange gargling, noise, his eyes bulging, and, in horror, she saw blood spurt from his neck.

"Jason?"

He looked at her, his expression confused, pained. Blood spurted from the hole in his neck that Sandor's knife had made. Sandor grinned at her as he yanked the knife out of Jason, who slumped, dead, to the floor. "Hey there, Livia. Good to see you." He waved the knife. "Time to be gutted, pretty girl." And he went for her.

CHARVI TOLD HIM EVERYTHING AND, desperate, Nox drove like a madman towards Sandor's home, knowing he might be too late, that Sandor had a head start, and if he caught Livia snooping ... Images of Ariel dead, of Pia, all superimposed with Livia's face. Livia lying dead on the grave, her belly cut open, her blood soaking everything.

No. No. Not again.

And his family. Nox knew in his bones that Sandor and Florian had killed them, had framed his beloved dad, murdered his brother, shot the defenseless Gabriella and left her to die a slow, agonizing death. And all because Florian Carpentier was a jealous, psychopathic rapist. Fuckers.

But all he could think of now was getting to Livia, to save his love. *Please, please, let her be okay ...*

DESPITE BEING SHOCKED and terrified at Sandor's appearance, Livia was ready to fight.

"*Motherfucker!*" she yelled at him and launched herself at the man. Hitting him full force, they tumbled to the floor, the knife slicing through the air, precariously close to Livia's body. She pounded at his face, kicking him, totally enraged.

Sandor cuffed her across the face so hard her ears rang as she crashed to the floor. "I knew you suspected me, Livia, as soon as I saw your face yesterday. When the home called me this morning and told me you'd been snooping around ..." He straddled her and tried to bind her hands. Livia struggled, yelling at him, hoping that someone, *anyone* would come. He grabbed her head and bounced it viciously off the floor.

"Livia!"

Nox. Nox was coming. It gave her strength, and she brought her knee up, striking Sandor in the balls—but it wasn't enough. As she scrambled away from him, he jerked her back and slammed her back against the wall, ripping open her shirt. Livia struggled, but then he put his forearm across her throat, pressing down hard, and she couldn't breathe.

"Fuck you, asshole," she gasped, "you can kill me, but you won't get away with it."

Sandor merely smiled and drove his knife into her belly. Livia gasped at the agonizing pain that shot through her. "Shame I can't do this slowly, beautiful girl, but as you can tell, I'm in a hurry." Blood pumped from the wound and Livia could smell rust and salt. Sandor admired his work. "You bleed well, Livia. I'm going to enjoy this."

Dazed by the pain, Livia lost her breath as he stabbed her again, the knife driving through her navel and slicing deep into her. But then Nox was there, roaring, knocking Sandor off of Livia, who slumped to the floor. Livia rolled onto her side and crawled away, bleeding heavily, her hands clamped to the vicious wounds in her belly.

Seeing Nox and Sandor struggle, she crawled towards Jason's body. Grabbing the bodyguard's gun, she turned in time to see Sandor sink his knife into Nox's stomach. Nox yelled out in agony and Sandor laughed, yanking the knife free.

"No!" Livia screamed and aimed the gun at Sandor, pulling the trigger. The gun clicked. Livia cursed. Was the gun empty?

Sandor got in a vicious right hook to Nox's temple. Nox staggered away from Sandor and Sandor dived at Livia.

"Stupid bitch," he snarled, "you have to turn the safety *off*. Allow me to demonstrate."

As Nox, bleeding, came after him, Sandor turned the gun on Livia and shot her, the bullet tearing through her belly. It felt like fire ripping through her. Her body jerked with the impact and she could no longer feel her legs.

We're going to die here. We're both going to die here ... "Nox ..." Her voice was weak and she felt herself dying now. There was blood everywhere, and she could feel her body shutting down. Fighting with Sandor, Nox looked at her desperately.

"Hang on, baby girl. Hang on, please ... keep breathing, Livvy ..." He was struggling with Sandor now, trying to get control of the gun. Another shot rang out, the bullet burying itself in the wall, then another, and Nox jerked back, his shoulder gushing blood. Sandor laughed.

"Whatever you do to me now, Nox," Sandor snarled at Nox, "she's still a dead woman. Look at her, bleeding out. And I thought killing your Ariel was satisfying. You can watch while I empty the rest of this gun into your beautiful girl, Renaud." He aimed the gun at Livia again.

Nox, weakening from blood loss, nevertheless threw himself at Sandor again and the two men tussled once more. Livia was losing consciousness, but she was desperate to stay awake, desperate to help Nox. Somehow, she managed to crawl to where Sandor had discarded his knife. Grabbing it, she plunged it into the back of Sandor's knee, then yanked it out and sliced his Achilles tendon.

Sandor roared in pain, going down, and Nox grabbed the gun from him. Sandor laughed, knowing he was beaten. "I hope she suffers before she bleeds to death. My only regret is that I only got to kill her once." He spat out the words, looking up at

Nox in pure hatred. Without a moment's hesitation, Nox shot his half-brother in the face. Sandor went down, stone-cold dead. Nox staggered over to Livia, who was fading fast.

"Stay alive, baby, please ... we get our happy ending. I swear. We deserve our happy ending ..." He collapsed next to her, trying to stem the blood flowing from her body, ignoring his own savage wounds. "Please, Livvy, stay with me."

Livia stroked his face. "If I die, I want you to know, I loved you more than you will ever know. You are the reason I lived."

"If you die, *I* die. We go together or we live together, baby, that's the deal ... Liv? Liv, *please ... no* ..."

Livia heard his beautiful voice, begging her to live, hearing the love in his voice. But then the darkness took over, and she heard nothing more.

CHAPTER THIRTY

There was so much pain and Livia didn't want to open her eyes but she had to know if she was alive. *Please, please,* she begged, *let Nox be alive too. If he's dead ...*

"Livvy." She had never heard such a beautiful voice in her life. "Livvy, baby, you can open your eyes, sweetheart."

She opened her eyes and focused on his face. Nox was pale and needed a shave but he was there, alive and smiling at her. He stroked her hair back from her face. "We made it, Livvy."

"Kiss me." She said the words but no sound came out—her throat was so dry. Nox smiled and helped her sip some water.

"Kiss me," she said again and this time, her voice rang out, pure and strong. Nox pressed his lips to hers and she sighed happily. "We're alive."

"Yes, we are." Nox took her hand. "You, just barely. But you're a fighter, Livvy."

She touched his face as if she couldn't believe he was real. "Sandor."

Nox's expression hardened. "Dead. Good fucking riddance."

"Agreed. He was a hell of an actor though. Imagine holding

onto that anger, that jealousy, that rage, all those years, just waiting for when you fell in love again? All because his daddy couldn't keep it in his pants."

Nox nodded. "Sandor didn't intend to get arrested either. He left a suicide note and mailed it to the local news station. He intended to kill us, then himself. I saved him the bother. He'd killed Roan weeks before. That's how I knew it must have been Sandor; that's how I knew to get to you."

"My hero." She kissed him again then groaned. "God, I could kill him all over again for how much this hurts."

"I know. I'm sorry, honey. Press this if you need the morphine, but docs said you'd be in pain for a while."

Livia pressed the button and felt a warm rush of something in her veins. It took the edge off. "How about you? Why do you look so good?"

Nox grinned and pulled his shirt up. A heart-shaped scar was healing well, stark pink against his skin. Livia was confused. "Nox ... how long have I been out?"

Nox's smile faded. "Three weeks. You had a pulmonary embolism, plus the bullet damaged your liver. *God.* It was touch and go for a long time. You were in a coma, which, strange to say, was a blessing." He shook his head as if he couldn't believe what he was saying. Livia took all this in and then nodded.

"Nox?"

"Yes, baby?"

"Is it all over now?"

Nox nodded. "It is, honey. It was all in the letters Florian wrote to my mom. He didn't regret a thing, the bastard. He wrote such vile things, telling her the way he was going to kill her. He never mailed them, obviously. Florian raped my mom. She had the baby and gave it to them to raise. Then she met my dad. Florian held onto that jealousy for years, and one day, he just snapped. He killed them all, saving my mom for last. In his letters, he wrote that Florian wasn't even the one who pulled the trigger on my mom. It was Sandor."

Livia felt sick. "He murdered his own mother?"

Nox nodded. "He was a sick fuck."

"I don't get why he killed Pia or Moriko. I understand Roan, to frame him, and Amber to silence her, but why those two innocent girls?"

Nox hesitated. "Liv ... they think he killed a lot more than that. They think he'd been murdering women all over the country for years. He enjoyed it, darling. He got off on it. Sandor was quite the writer himself. They found diaries where he described his kills. He murdered Ariel and then blackmailed Amber into shutting up. Pia, Moriko ... there was an entire notebook on the myriad of ways he dreamed up to kill *you. God.*"

"Fucker."

"Quite."

Livia sighed. "How's Odelle? How is she taking the news of Roan's death?"

"She's doing okay. She's outside, if you want to see her."

"God, yes."

Nox grinned, kissed her forehead, and went to fetch his friend. Odelle walked in and her face was blank as she stared at Livia for a second.

"Well, look at you, lounging around doing nothing but costing my friend *more* money."

For a moment, Livia was shocked, but then Nox burst out laughing and Odelle cracked a smile. Livia giggled.

"Odie, did you just make a joke?"

"I think I may have. Hello, darling, it's good to see you awake." Odie bent down and kissed Livia's cheek then held her hand. Livia was surprised to see tears in her friend's eyes. "We nearly lost you."

"But I'm still here," Livia said, squeezing her hand. "And I'm not going anywhere."

"I'm so happy, honey, so glad you're okay. I love you so much."

Livia did cry then and Odelle hugged her—awkwardly, of course—but Livia clung to her friend. "Thank you, Odie. I love you too."

Odelle couldn't speak then, and soon after she left them alone, promising to come back—and bring some contraband food with her.

ALONE, Livia smiled at Nox. "Have I told you how much I love you?"

"Even though I got you into all this?"

She pulled his head down for another kiss. "I would take every minute of pain over and over again for you, Nox Renaud. This is us; this is our life."

Nox kissed her as if for the first time. "From now on," he promised, "I swear it will be a *good*, happy life."

"Nox?"

He pressed his lips to her forehead. "Yeah, baby?" His voice was soft and tender.

"Nox Renaud?"

He grinned at her formal tone. "That's me."

Livia gazed at him, her eyes shining. "Nox Renaud, would you do me the great honor of marrying me?"

Nox's eyes widened and he began to chuckle. "Well, damn, woman, you just stole my best line."

Livia grinned and pulled his face to hers, crushing her lips against his. "Is that a yes?"

Nox kissed her passionately and then nodded. "It's a *hell* yes, Ms. Chatelaine. It's a yes and a yes and a *yes* ..."

. . .

THE END

SECRETS & DESIRES EXTENDED EPILOGUE

The year after a tragic and deadly holiday season, Nox Renaud and Livia Chatelaine are finally able to move on with their romance. They marry in an opulent ceremony in New Orleans and then swap the sultry heat of Louisiana for the beautiful island paradise of Guadeloupe for their honeymoon.

Eager to enjoy their tropical Christmas, Nox, and Livia, now recovered from their terrible injuries, explore the kinkier side of their relationship in their luxurious private villa. They plan to come up with a way to free themselves of the past for good and move on with their happy life – especially when Livia discovers something that will change their lives forever...

Livia hid a grin as Odelle fussed around her. "You realize if it hadn't been for your passive-aggressive blackmail, Nox and I would have gone to City Hall by now?"

Odelle glared at her in the mirror. "Passive-aggressive is my thing, and you wouldn't have dared. You may think it's ridiculous, but you needed a society wedding. Despite everything, people are still side-eyeing you for marrying Nox."

Livia sighed. "The waitress gold-digger."

Odelle stopped, then put her hands on Livia's shoulders. "I didn't mean that, I'm sorry. You know me."

"No offense taken, and I do get your meaning. I see some of them looking suspiciously at me. Especially one."

Odelle leaned her cheek against Livia's, and they both hissed "Janine Dupois" before collapsing into laughter. Odelle brushed and twisted Livia's thick, tawny hair into an elegant up-do. "You know what she's like."

"I do. The way she kept coming to the hospital and fawning over Nox...yuck. She was lucky I was hooked up to those machines."

Odelle winced, and Livia smiled at her. "I have to joke about it, Odie, because if I don't, I'll scream."

Odelle nodded, understanding. Livia and Nox had almost died at the hands of Sandor Carpentier, Nox's business partner, supposed friend and half-brother, who had been obsessed with killing Livia and destroying Nox. Both of them were stabbed and shot, but Livia had gotten the worst of it, and after months of rehab, she only now began to feel like herself. She would always walk with a limp, the result of the bullet that slammed through her belly and buried itself in her spine, but now she had gotten to a place where she could function like her old self.

And today, she would prove it. She would walk down the aisle, with just Odelle and her old college friend Juno as brides-maids, no one giving her away – she didn't hold with that old-fashioned practice, she told Nox, who nodded in agreement. And that wasn't the only modern aspect of their wedding. Nox had asked her if she would like him to take her name after marriage. Livia had been stunned.

"You would really do that?"

"I would. It's your mother's maiden name, right?"

Livia felt tears fill her eyes. "It was. I never wanted my father's name."

"Then I would be honored to share it with you – if you'll permit me."

So, after their wedding, they would be *Mr. and Mrs. Chatelaine*. It touched Livia's heart beyond what she could express. Since then, she had been trying to find ways that she could incorporate Nox's family, slaughtered by Sandor and his father, into their wedding. She had already made up her mind that their own children could share his family's names, but she wanted Gabriella, Tynan, and Teague to be part of their day too. She'd finally come up with the perfect idea a week ago, and with Odelle's help, the wedding ring she would place on Nox's finger was inscribed with his family's names. She hoped he would like the idea.

"He will," Odelle told her now, "but he's going to have a hard time looking at anything else but you, Liv. I'm all done here. Take a look."

Livia got up and walked to the floor-length mirror. She hardly recognized herself. The word that came to her was elegance. She felt *elegant* for the first time in her life. The dress, ivory silk, was a slim column which clung to her curves. The top with its square neck and long, flowing bell sleeves made her look like an angel. Odelle had swept her hair up but left tendrils of brown hair to fall around her face. Livia's make up was light, just the way she liked it: pinky blush, a rosy lip and subtle gold eyeshadow to bring out the chocolate brown of her eyes. "Is that me?"

Odelle looked proud. "It certainly is."

Livia turned and hugged Odelle. "Thank you, Odie."

Odelle, never comfortable with physical contact, nevertheless hugged her tightly. "Congratulations, sweetheart. You made it."

THE LOOK on Nox's face as she walked down the aisle to marry him made her feel like crying with joy. The love in his eyes, his obvious admiration, the way his eyes smoldered with desire. He kissed her gently as she reached him. "You're glorious," he whispered, "I love you so much."

She grinned up at him. "I love you, and you have dirty in your eyes."

"You have no idea what I'm thinking about right now, but it's certainly not appropriate for church."

Livia covered a snort and Nox grinned as they turned to face the minister. In a few moments, they were pronounced husband and wife to the cheers of their friends. Odelle was openly weeping, much to Livia's shock, and her other bridesmaid, a grinning Juno, was comforting her. Livia made sure Nox saw the inscription on the inset of his wedding ring and Nox was moved beyond words. "That's perfect," he said, his voice breaking, and kissed her more passionately than was probably appropriate but neither of them cared.

After the wedding reception, Nox whisked her away to his private jet. As they settled in for the flight, Livia grinned at her new husband. "I thought you were going to sell this thing?"

Nox grinned sheepishly. "It's so convenient, though. I promised to have a thousand trees planted every time I use it. Which won't be much," he added, rolling his eyes at her disapproval. "Come here, wife."

Livia grinned, kicking off her shoes, and went to sit on his lap. She kissed him, her mouth curving up in a smile as he began to unbutton her dress. "Can I just say, Mrs. Chatelaine, that you looked like a goddess in this dress and that, despite my desperation to have you naked right now, I'm being very careful not to rip it?"

Livia laughed and helped him undo the dress. She stood and wriggled out of it, then unhooked her bra, letting her plump breasts fall into his waiting hands. She began to unbutton his shirt as he sucked her nipples. "Nox?"

"Yes, baby?" His voice was muffled as his mouth found her other breast. Livia sighed happily, pushed off his shirt.

"Take me to the bedroom back there and fuck me senseless. I need animal sex tonight."

Nox needed no more persuasion. He picked her up, wrapping her legs around his waist, and carried her to the small bedroom at the back of the plane, throwing her down on the bed and stripping the rest of his clothes off. As he stripped, Livia slipped out of her panties and spread her legs so he could watch her touch herself. Nox's cock was already ramrod hard against his belly, and he fisted the root of it as he approached her. "You have the most beautiful cunt in the world," he said, then thrust hard into her, finding her ready for him. "Christ, you're wet."

"I've been thinking about fucking you all day," she murmured, her lips against his, "Your cock deep inside me, reaming me into submission. I nearly came when you touched me at the top of the aisle, thinking about your body on mine, your mouth on mine. Fuck me hard, husband..."

He thrust harder and deeper with each stroke, Livia tilting her pelvis to take him in deeper. His mouth was rough on hers, tasting, caressing, nipping her lower lip with his teeth, drawing blood. Livia tightened her thighs around his waist, their eyes locked, as their pace quickened and, breathless, they drove each other to a shattering orgasm.

Livia felt his cum pump deep inside her, reveling in the feeling, her vagina contracting around his cock. "God, I wish you could be inside me for forever."

Panting, Nox chuckled. "Might make socializing a little awkward." He pulled out of her and collapsed by her side, kissing her mouth, tender now. "God, it just keeps getting better, huh?"

"You betcha." Livia grinned at him, tangling her fingers in his hair. "I'm looking forward to being thoroughly reamed by you in a tropical setting." Nox laughed with her.

"Such a lady. Well, I promise I'll make that particular wish come true."

Livia moved so she could lay on top of him. "I'm going to suck your cock until you beg me for mercy."

"Ha, I believe it. *Damn*, you're frisky today, wife," he said as she bit his nipple then moved down his body to take his cock in her mouth. She grinned up at him.

"I was denied your body for months. I'm just catching up."

Nox laughed and then sucked in a sharp breath as she sucked his cock, teasing the sensitive tip with her tongue, gently massaging his balls. "Wait," he said and turned his body around 180 degrees. "Wrap those gorgeous legs around my head, beautiful, I'm going to eat you out like never before."

He buried his face in her sex, his tongue lashing around her labia, seeking her clit as she continued to work his cock until they were both trembling and coming. Livia drank his seed down as he teased her clit, his tongue dipping deep into her cunt.

Afterwards, they lay in each other's arms, kissing, talking about their future, as the plane continued on its journey. Before the wedding, while they were recovering, Roderick LeFevre had come to Nox and offered to buy him out of his company.

"There's no pressure, but it would be a new start for both of you."

Roderick and Livia had formed a friendship – Rod sending her flowers in the hospital and visiting her. Livia brokered that kind of friendship between Nox – still mourning his friends Roan and Amber – and the other man, and now Rod had become a trusted friend of the couple. Nox had considered his offer ever since.

"I think I'm going to sell to Rod," he told Livia now. "My heart isn't in it anymore, and he's done a fantastic job of taking over the Asshole's side of the business."

'The Asshole' was how they referred to Sandor now, the man who had nearly murdered them both, and *had* murdered their friends, and worse, Nox's mother. Both Livia and Nox swore never to speak his name again after the police had finished their investigation.

Livia nodded. "I think it's the best idea. Will you concentrate on the Foundation?"

"Yes...with yours and Charvi's help. I also have some contacts, friends in Italy who might be able to help too. I think I was meant to start the Foundation, I really do, as much as I was meant to meet you."

"I do, too."

"So, are you going to finish your Master's? Charvi was concerned you might have lost the motivation."

"She was? No, I want to finish...and I think I'd like to get my Ph.D. too."

Nox looked impressed. "Sexy doctor? I'm all for that."

"Pervo." She giggled as he tickled her. "I'll wear my graduation cap to bed and bounce on top of your cock."

"That's a promise." Nox laughed then let out a long sigh of satisfaction. "After everything, we deserve this happiness."

"We certainly do." She kissed him and snuggled into his chest. Nox traced a circle around her navel, scarred by Sandor's knife.

"Maybe we can think about children too?"

Livia nodded. "I want a bunch, Nox, but you know what the

doc said. We have to be patient. It'll happen. He said I can still *get* pregnant, but with only one ovary..."

"I know. Damn that bullet."

"Damn it." Livia kissed him and smiled. "And yet, I'm still here, and we can still have our kids. It just might take a little longer. I stopped the birth control, but it takes a while to flush out of my system."

"I know." Nox kissed her. "And I enjoy practicing."

Livia laughed as he covered her body again. "Aren't men supposed to slow down after forty?"

"Hey, I have two years to go yet, and is this slowing down?" He thrust his cock into her again, and they made love, losing themselves in the other for the rest of the flight.

THE VILLA WAS SECLUDED but utterly luxurious, with large picture windows and white furnishings. It was night, and outside the bright moon shone on the ocean that lapped at the beach and Livia pushed open the doors and stepped out onto the sand. "Wow."

She breathed in the fresh ocean air. "How late is it?"

Nox slipped his arms around her, kissing her neck. "Nearly dawn. Are you tired?"

She turned in his arms and pressed her lips against his. "Would you hate me if I said yes?"

Nox grinned. "Not at all...I'm an old man, remember? I could do with a shower though."

They showered together and fell into the soft bed, Livia moaning at the comfort. "Now that we're an old couple, there'll be no more sex marathons, just missionary once a month."

Nox laughed. "Today, in *Most Unbelievable Claims*." He wrapped his arms around her as she snuggled into his chest.

"Sleep tight, baby, you're going to need your energy for what I'm going to do tomorrow."

"That sounds promising," Livia said then yawned widely, making Nox laugh. She closed her eyes and lay on his chest, breathing in his scent, her love, her husband.

THEY SLEPT until noon then made love slowly and tenderly before beginning their day. They explored the island and snorkeled in the clear blue ocean before finding a restaurant and enjoying. They walked hand-in-hand back along the beach as the sun set.

Livia leaned happily against Nox. "Could we be more cliché?"

"I don't care," he laughed. "We deserve some cheesy romance."

"Yes, we do." She looked up at him. "Nox...when we get back to the villa...*I'm* in charge for the night."

"You are, huh?"

"Oh, yes. I have quite the evening planned for you."

Nox raised an eyebrow at her, his mouth hitching up in a grin. "Mistress..."

"You bet your sweet ass." She looked him up and down as they reached the villa. "Wait here until I call you inside, boy. Lose the t-shirt, keep the linen pants on. I like the way they outline your cock."

Nox, already enjoying the game, saluted her. "Anything you desire, Ma'am."

Livia grinned at him as she disappeared inside. In the bedroom, she stripped quickly, slipping on the leather harness they had so enjoyed in the past, but hadn't used since before they'd been injured. She fastened the buttery soft straps around her body, outlining her breasts, framing her navel and slipping between her legs. She was shaven, loving the feeling of his cock on her bare skin, and now she slicked some flavored lube into her pussy – *not that I need it*, she thought with a grin. She slid her legs into knee-high leather boots. She had purchased some new sex toys before the wedding, hoping to keep them a surprise for their honeymoon, and gathered them now, walking back into the living area. She climbed into a wooden chair, then sat on the counter, opposite the French window where Nox was waiting.

"You may come in, boy."

Nox pushed aside the billowing voile drape and stepped into the room. Livia smiled at him, spreading her legs slowly and Nox sighed. "Wow...*wow, Liv...*"

"Ma'am."

"Yes, Ma'am."

Livia slid her finger into her cunt and Nox gave a moan. Liv grinned. "What would you like to do to me, boy?"

Nox grabbed his crotch and Liv could see his penis was already hardening just at the sight of her. "Lose the pants, let me see that magnificent cock."

He pulled at the draw-string, and his linen pants slipped to the floor. His cock stood proud against his belly. Liv smiled. "Tell me."

"I want to kiss your belly," he growled, "bite your ripe tits, fuck your perfect cunt until you scream. I want to eat your delicious pussy, finger fuck your deep, round navel, pull your hair and fucking taste every single goddess-like part of you."

Liv was so turned on, but she always wanted to control both herself and Nox to prolong their experience. She reached for a small vial of monoi oil and dripped it between her breasts, letting it trail down her stomach to form a pool in her navel before it dripped into her sex. "Put your fingers inside me, boy."

Nox slid his forefinger deep into her cunt, stroking her. "May I kiss you, ma'am?"

"You may."

Their mouths crushed against the other's, their tongues delving deep into the other's mouth, exploring, tasting as Nox slid another finger into her, then another, then another until only his thumb was free, stroking her clit. Livia gave a moan, but quickly controlled it, breaking away from his kiss, trying not to smile. "You may bite my breasts, boy."

Grinning. Nox took her nipple into his mouth, biting down, making her squeal. Livia tangled her fingers in his dark curls and pulled hard. "Do you like that, boy?"

"Yes, ma'am." Nox switched to her other breast. "Would ma'am like me to kiss her belly next?"

Livia nodded, her breath quickening as he moved lower, dipping his tongue into her navel, biting at the soft curve of her. Nox's hand slid down the leather boots, feeling the shape of her calves inside them.

"Boy."

Nox looked up. "Yes, ma'am?"

"Eat my cunt. Make me come."

And the moment his mouth touched her sex, Livia lost herself in the sensation of his tongue lashing around her clit. He was relentless, his mouth working on her senses until Livia came, shuddering and calling his name. Forgetting her role play, she grabbed his head, crushing her lips against his. "Fuck me, fuck me hard, Nox."

"Yes, ma'am." His grin was wide and triumphant as he thrust his hugely engorged cock deep into her swollen cunt, and Livia moaned. Nox picked her up and laid her on the floor, reaming her hard with his cock, pinning her hands above her head, kissing her so fiercely it made her head swim. "Madam is kind for letting me fuck her so hard, also for wearing those boots. Little Nox is very happy right now."

That did it. Breaking character, Livia started giggling furiously, and Nox lost his rhythm. They collapsed in fits of laughter before Nox managed to calm himself enough to begin again. Livia gazed up at him as he thrust slowly but harder each time, making her gasp with the force of him. Grinning, Nox pinched her clit hard between his fingers and Livia came with a jerk, gasping, panting for air. Nox pulled out and came on her belly, groaning and saying her name over and over. They collapsed together, limbs entangled.

"I love you," Livia whispered, and Nox nodded, kissing her tenderly. Livia grinned at him ruefully. "I guess I need to practice my Dom skills."

"You were perfect." He rubbed his nose against hers. "And the leather boots? Damn, woman."

"I thought you might like them. I bought us some new toys too."

"I like the oil, very sexy."

Livia kissed him. "The strawberry lube?"

"Nice, but I prefer your taste of cherries and honey." Nox stroked his hand down her belly. "And this belly, so soft." He splayed his fingers over it now, feeling the soft curve. He traced the scars that Sandor had left on her and a cloud crossed his face. Livia smoothed his brow.

"No frowning. What's past is past." That had been their rule during their long recovery. *No looking backward.*

"You're right." He drew his fingers up her body and cupped her face in his palm. "You're so beautiful, baby, inside and out. I'm the luckiest man in the world."

Livia kissed him, her fingernails trailing up and down his strongly muscled back. "Damn right you are."

She pushed him onto his back and straddled him. "Now, I'm going to ride you like a wild cat, then you're going to punish me for being such a slut with that lovely riding crop. Deal?"

"Deal?"

Their games lasted well into the night, finally ending when they fell into bed, sore, exhausted, but utterly blissed out.

"God, you have exhausted me, woman." Nox touched the welts from the crop on her breasts and belly. "Are you sure I wasn't too rough?" He frowned slightly.

"Perfectly sure," Livia said with a grin. "You know, you could get as rough as you like with me. No choking though. I'm not into asphyxiation stuff."

"Me either. You know, I bought some stuff too."

Livia grinned. "You did? What?"

"Oh no. You have to wait until tomorrow night. Tomorrow night, it's my turn to be in charge."

LIVIA HAD BEEN curious all day to see what Nox had planned, and when the evening came, he asked her to strip down for him while he watched. She did so, swaying to an imaginary beat as she slid out of her dress. She hadn't bothered with underwear; on one of their longs treks into the forests on the islands, she and Nox had fucked against more than one tree, once almost getting caught by passing tourists. She loved the way Nox looked at her naked body, how he touched her as if she was the most precious thing in the world, and the most carnal; that she was the most ethereal woman and the most animal.

He stood now and led her to their bedroom. He kissed her, stroking her clit gently. "Darling girl...I'd like to fuck you in your beautiful cunt, and in your perfect ass...but then..."

He went to the closet and pulled something else out. Livia gasped when she saw it. A strap-on. Nox grinned at her surprise. "I want our relationship to be totally equal."

"Like you taking my name wasn't enough," she laughed, but she took the strap-on from him and studied it. "Are you sure?"

"You have given your entire body to me, in every way. Your

generosity is beyond what I ever dreamed. So, this."

Livia kissed him, crushing her lips against his. "You are one unique guy, Nox Renaud."

"Nox *Chatelaine*," he reminded her with a grin. She touched his face.

"I love you beyond words, Nox."

They went to bed, enjoying making love until Nox strapped the dildo onto her pelvis. Livia grinned. "This feels weird, but kind of good."

"This part," he demonstrated," should rub against your clit and give you as much pleasure as you're giving me."

He said it with confidence, but she could see he was nervous. She grinned at him. "I promise I'll be gentle with you."

She made sure he was relaxed by straddling him and giving him a massage before they started, and when he was ready, she slicked some lube into the dildo and gently eased into his ass. Livia moved slowly, slightly unnerved by the feeling, but when she heard Nox's groan of pleasure, she felt more confident. They fucked slowly, building to a mellow but exquisite climax for both of them, then Livia took the strap-on off as Nox turned onto his back, his erection huge, and she lowered herself onto it and rode him hard. He massaged her breasts as she thrust onto him and when he came again, shooting thick cum deep into her belly, she cried out his name, throwing her head back.

Panting for air, she lay down on top of him, his arms tight around her. "Was that okay?"

"More than okay," Nox said, "Wow. I never thought I would enjoy that."

"And yet you agreed to it anyway."

"Like I said," he said, kissing her forehead, "this is a marriage of equals."

"Gosh."

"What?"

Livia looked at him and grinned. "We're *married*."

He laughed. "Has that only just sunk in?"

Livia chuckled. "You know what? I think it has, except, weirdly, I already felt married to you. Is that weird?"

"No, I get it. It felt like that for me very quickly into our relationship." He stroked his hands down her body. "God, you're intoxicating."

Livia smiled at him, stroking his damp curls away from his face. "Let's stay here, forever."

"Okay." They both laughed, and Nox kissed her. "We can live wherever you want, baby."

"I don't mind as long as I'm with you."

"I was thinking...we should sell the mansion, find somewhere that we both choose to live. Start afresh now. I don't want to bring our kids up in the place my family died."

Livia propped herself up on her elbow. "I think that's a terrific idea. I didn't want to say anything, because after all, it's your family home, but I was thinking...it's not exactly child friendly, either."

"Agreed." He curled a lock of her hair around her finger. "So, we'll contact some realtors when we get home. Still want to stay in New Orleans?"

Livia nodded. "I do. Odelle and Charvi are there, Marcel, Rod. They're all so important to me."

Nox smiled. "I'm still rocking back from the fact that you're so friendly with Rod LeFevre."

"*We're* friendly with him – and yes, he's become like my big brother. I love Simon too...talk about two people who were meant to be together."

"Agreed. And don't you love that Odelle hangs out with them all the time?"

Livia giggled. "Love it – and also afraid what they might unleash together. Rod has really brought out Odelle's fun side."

"Odelle is a totally different person from when I knew her before you. If anyone has brought her out, it's you." Nox smiled at her fondly, then sighed. Livia stroked his face.

"It's okay to mourn for Roan and Amber, you know. Roan was naïve and reckless, and Amber...well. She just got swept along with Sandor's psychopathy. Their faults cost them their lives, but we can still celebrate their gifts. We *should*."

Nox shook his head, smiling. "Your capacity for forgiveness blows my mind."

"Beats hanging onto resentment," she said, looking away from him. He read her mind.

"Your dad?"

"That's too much water under the bridge. He's not in my life, or our lives. That's all."

Nox was silent for a long time, then sat up, facing her. Livia frowned at his troubled expression. "What is it, baby?"

Nox drew in a deep breath. "Sweetheart...your father was in New Orleans before the wedding."

Livia felt a jolt of shock. "What?"

Nox nodded. "He contacted the office, wanted to speak to me. I declined his call, but I had someone tail him. They said he looked rough, real rough."

Livia chewed her lip. "He wanted to try and get money from you. He looked rough because he drinks a bottle of whiskey and smokes sixty cigarettes a day."

"Do you blame me for not taking his call?"

"Not at all. Did he leave New Orleans?"

Nox looked uncomfortable. "Liv...please don't be mad at me for not telling you this sooner."

Livia narrowed her eyes. "What?"

"Your father got into a bar fight, and lost. He got jumped out in the streets and was dumped in the Michoud Canal. The police pulled his body out the next day."

He waited for her reaction, but Livia merely nodded. "To be honest, I'm surprised he lasted this long. It's harsh, but I don't feel anything but relief. If you had taken his call, we would never have gotten rid of him. *Ever*. He deserved what he got." She smiled apologetically at Nox. "I know you would give anything to have your father in your life, but we grew up with very different men. I wish I had met Tynan, Gabriella, and Teague. I might not have known them, but I feel their presence in our lives every day and am so thankful for it."

Nox smiled at her, heavy emotion in his green eyes. "*You* gave them back to me, baby. Despite everything we went through, no matter what we lost, you gave them back to me."

Livia wound her arms around his neck. "We are a family, Nox, we have been since that first day in your garden."

He held her, pulling her tight against his chest. "You and me, now, Livvy. That's all that matters."

IT WAS the last day of their honeymoon when Livia had a dizzy spell. She was carrying their plates in from an outdoor supper when her legs wobbled, and she had to put the plates down on the counter quickly. Nox was at her side in an instant. "You okay, baby?"

She smiled, her head whirling. "Just a little dizzy, is all. I'll be okay."

"Maybe you should lie down."

Livia waited for a few minutes, but still feeling odd, she let Nox persuade her to lie down on their bed. She closed her eyes but her head still whirled, and after a few minutes, she felt a sickening wave of nausea and ran to the bathroom to throw up. Nox held her hair back and wiped her face with a cool cloth as Livia caught her breath. She looked up at him. "Do *you* feel sick? Was it something we ate?"

Nox shook his head, and then realization dawned on them both. "Do you think...?" He began, but trailed off. Livia's eyes were wide.

"It could be. Where's my bag? I have a couple of tests in there."

Their relationship was now so close that Livia felt no embarrassment about peeing in front of Nox. She washed off the plastic on the test strip and wiped it with some tissue. "Now we wait."

Pregnant or not-pregnant. Livia felt unbelievably nervous, and when she looked at Nox, she could see he was having the same thoughts. They began to count down together then picked up the test.

Positive. "Holy crap," Livia exclaimed as Nox whooped, gathering her up in his arms. "We made a freaking baby!"

Livia burst out laughing and crying at the same time, and a jubilant Nox twirled her around before remembering her nausea. "Sorry, honey." He splayed his hand out over her belly. "That's *our kid* in there."

Livia collapsed in sobs and Nox hugged her. "Why are you crying?"

"Because I'm so *relieved*, Nox, so happy that I can give you your children. For the last year, being stabbed, being shot, I was so afraid I couldn't have children and god, I was desperate for them, desperate to carry your child and now..." She sobbed harder, and Nox held her tightly.

"You are my heroine, my love, the mother of my children," he said, his voice breaking, "and I love you with every cell in my body. You have made me so happy, Livvy, so very happy."

They embraced, both crying now, both overwhelmed, both overjoyed.

. . .

EIGHT AND A HALF MONTHS LATER, Charlotte Gabriella Renaud Chatelaine was born, followed thirteen months later by Noah Tygue. Livia was a natural mother, filling her children's lives with fun and love. Nox doted on his offspring, the fun dad, the disciplinarian when needed, the teacher, the champion.

One night after the children were in bed, Livia and Nox sat on the balcony of their home, a modest Hacienda-style dwelling just outside the city, and pondered how lucky they were.

Nox held her hand, and they gazed up at the stars. "We got it good."

"We certainly do." Livia leaned over to kiss him. "Thank you, Nox."

He looked surprised. "For what?"

"For everything."

He smiled. "Then thank you too, wifey."

She laughed. "Still can't get used to that. It sounds so grown-up," she said incredulously, and Nox laughed aloud.

"We have two kids and being *married* is what's grown up?"

"Yup. About those *two* kids..."

Nox looked at her curiously. "Yes?"

Livia grinned at him. "If I said to you...*Supersperm*..."

Nox grinned. "Seriously?"

"Yup," Livia pretended to be resigned. "You done gone knocked me up ag'in, Mister."

Nox was delighted, and Livia laughed as he dropped to his knees and lay his head on her belly. "That noise you hear is gas. I'm only a month along, or so. I found out earlier."

And she laughed as Nox pulled her into his arms and kissed her until she couldn't breathe...

THE END

THE NAUGHTY ONE

A DOCTOR'S CHRISTMAS ROMANCE (SEASON OF DESIRE 2)

Romy Sasse, a young surgical resident, returns to her hometown Seattle and immediately meets her new boss, superstar surgeon, Blue Allende. The attraction between them is immediate and intense, and there's a twist ...

Romy's mom is about to marry Blue's father.
Soon, Blue and Romy are falling in love, and enjoying a steamy, sizzling relationship. Finally, Romy feels she has escaped her past and her violent ex.
As Christmas approaches, however, a series of horrific murders brings the past back to haunt the couple and they face the most serious test to their love yet ...
Will the Holiday Season bring resolution and a Happy Ever After?

CHAPTER ONE

S *eattle*

ROMY SHOVED her chestnut brown hair up into a ponytail as she jogged quickly along the hospital corridors. *Damn Seattle traffic.* She had been so organized right up until she'd hit the traffic accident on the Alaskan Way viaduct. Now she'd missed the first few minutes of rounds, and on the worst possible day. So not a good first impression to make. Still cursing herself, she hurried to catch up with her colleagues in the general surgery department.

Rounding the corner at a fast clip, she heard his voice before she saw him, a deep, mellifluous tone which she knew made woman weak. She might never have met the man, but his voice was as legendary as his surgical skills. Oh yeah. And his body. People talked about that in the same breath as his medical accomplishments.

He spoke again and she thrilled at the husky hint of an accent—Italian, maybe?—in it.

"If the infection worsens we'll consider a shunt, but in all likelihood, it will resolve rapidly since it was caught at the outset."

Romy blinked in surprise at the words. Blue Allende, he of the oh-so-sexy voice, was a superstar surgeon. Not even forty years old, he was at the top of his game, and also at the top of most hospital's wish-lists. With the reputed looks of a movie star and the serious, brooding intelligence of someone a lot older, Blue Allende's reputation preceded him. So why was he standing around with a motley crew of doctors, nurses, and interns, discussing something as mundane as a shunt?

It gave her pause and jumpstarted her liking for the man who, apparently, wasn't your average arrogant genius surgeon. But Romy was still late, and no doctor appreciated tardiness, particularly not one with such a packed schedule ...

Goddamn it.

Stopping outside the door she saw a bunch of other residents and slipped in among them, hoping she wouldn't be noticed and knowing she didn't stand a prayer.

Her friend Mac, an affable African American with a sweet face and a wicked sense of humor, grinned and nudged her. "Late for the rockstar, Sasse," he hissed, "*genius* move."

Romy poked him with her elbow, rolling her eyes. "What did I miss?"

Suddenly the crowd of doctors parted and she saw him where he'd been leaning over a sedated patient. Her breath caught in her throat as Blue Allende turned bright green eyes on her.

All the usual hospital noises faded into the background as she was caught in that fiercely intelligent gaze.

Jesus, Romy thought, *this man doesn't belong in an operating theater; he belongs on a cat walk or on the cover of* Vogue.

He was *gorgeous*. The bright green eyes were surrounded by thick, black eyelashes on a face carved from Italian marble. A shock of dark curls fell messily about his head … then she noticed his wide, sensual mouth set in a thin line.

Ah, shit. She'd like to have seen that mouth in something other than a scowl.

"Dr. Sasse, welcome."

That voice from up close. *Wowwowwow.* And … he knew her name? Romy prayed not to stutter. "Apologies for my tardiness, Dr. Allende; it won't happen again."

Was that a hint of amusement that flashed in those devastatingly beautiful eyes, and maybe a slight hitching up of the mouth? No sooner had Romy thought she'd seen it than it was gone. He turned back to his patient and Romy was grateful he hadn't shamed her in front of everyone else. One more point in his favor, bigtime.

"Got away with it," Mac muttered in her ear, and Romy sighed with relief.

As they moved through rounds, she was impressed by Allende's in-depth knowledge of his cases and the way he coaxed the residents to find answers to his questions, rather than merely lecturing. Even when they got a fact wrong, he didn't sneer or bark at them. Furthermore, he treated patients like friends, addressing them with as much candor as compassion, taking his time rather than rushing right along.

More than slightly blown away by the whole picture, Romy watched him carefully and was confused when she spotted him in an unguarded moment when the group was discussing a situation and he apparently thought no one was paying attention to him. Also not typical. Grandstanding surgeons believed the spotlight was always on them. In that brief second though, she saw something in his eyes that she recognized all too well.

Pain. Sorrow.

Romy was so distracted by the revelation that she didn't realize the focus had shifted and everyone was staring at her. Suddenly feeling the heat of their stares, she swallowed hard, flushing. "I'm sorry, Dr. Allende, could you repeat the question?"

The amused look was back, displacing sorrow. "I was asking if you could give me the ways we can use to diagnose *ankylosing spondylitis*?"

Romy cleared her throat. "Of course." She ran through the options and then concluded, "Of course, the disease is notoriously hard to diagnose, and once identified, it usually is a case of pain management. Opioids have little effect pain-wise, but we could try medical marijuana as a last resort."

"Hail Mary," said the patient, a young man in his twenties, and they all laughed.

"As a *last* resort, Billy." Blue smiled and Romy's entire body reacted to it. It lit up his handsome face and Romy could feel a beat pulsing between her legs. *Stop it,* she told herself, *do not get a crush on your boss.*

AFTER ROUNDS, Blue asked to see her in his office. He motioned to the chair opposite his desk and Romy sat down, trembling with nervousness. Was she about to be bawled out for being late?

"Don't look so scared," he said mildly, his tone neutral but somehow still warm. "It's just an introduction. I didn't get to meet you like the other residents."

From someone else that would have sounded passive aggressive. From him, it came across as oddly sincere.

"I'm sorry for being late, Dr. Allende," she apologized.

"Happens to us all."

Before she could blink at that, he picked up a file and opened it.

"Dr. Romy Sasse, age twenty-nine, graduated top of your class at Stamford, did your internship and part of your residency at Johns Hopkins ... why transfer here for your last year? Johns Hopkins was very reluctant to let you go; we had to fight for you."

Old memories made her cold inside. "I had to come home to Seattle. Personal reasons. Also, my mother is getting married, rather unexpectedly."

"And she needs you to be here?"

Romy hesitated. "No, it's not that, but ..."

"But what?"

Romy sighed. It was none of his business, but she owed him this much after being late. "My sisters, Juno and Artemis, asked me to come. I'm the middle sister, the peacemaker. They have some concerns about Mom's fiancé."

"Really?" Blue looked interested, even though Romy couldn't for the life of her figure out why. Or why she just kept talking.

"It's not that he's a bad person, though I still haven't officially met him yet. But he's so entirely not what we thought Mom would go for ..." Abruptly, she halted, catching herself in mid-ramble. "I'm sorry, you really don't need to know this."

"No, please go on."

Romy frowned. "Well, then, you should know, my mom is a free spirit, a rainbow child, a hippie. Look at our names."

Blue smiled. "Okay, so Juno and Artemis, I get, but Romy?"

"Short for Romulus. Yes, I know it's technically a boy's name but, you see, I was a twin. Fraternal. My brother, Remy—Remus—died when we were five years old." God, the pain of it still haunted Romy. "Mom thought I was a boy too when she was pregnant, hence the name."

"So your name is actually Romulus?"

She was grateful he didn't press her for more details about Remy. "No, she managed to change it at the last moment on the birth certificate. Romy is my legal name."

"And you don't like your future stepfather?"

"I don't know him."

Suddenly Blue grinned. "I think your mom and Stuart Eames will be just fine."

Romy gaped at him in astonishment. "How the hell ...?"

He laughed, and his face looked even more desperately handsome than ever. "Believe it or not, I wasn't interrogating you without an actual purpose. You see, Romy Sasse, Stuart Eames is my father. So, technically, we're about to be siblings. Welcome to the family, Romy."

CHAPTER TWO

Romy was still shell-shocked when she went to her mother's house that evening. Part of it was admittedly from the additional time she'd spent giddily talking in Blue's office—he'd insisted she call him that—and the rest was entirely due to his revelation.

"Why didn't you tell me Stuart was Blue Allende's father?"

Magda Sasse looked up from the cutting board and grinned at her middle daughter's abrupt greeting. "Hello to you, too. Because, dear one, Blue said he didn't want you to know right away. He wanted you to be on his service and thought you might not want to if you knew. Your reputation as a first-class doctor precedes you, honey, and I'm very proud."

Romy smiled and hugged her mother. "Thank you, Momma Bear. Anyway, Blue told me he will be with us for Thanksgiving?" Upon hearing that, she'd been hard-pressed to keep it together in the surgeon's office. Blue in her home, having dinner with her family ... why was that weirdly hot?

"Will it be awkward?" her mother asked in concern.

Romy hoisted herself up onto the kitchen counter and stole

a piece of bell pepper Magda was slicing for salad. "I don't think so. Well, at least I hope not. He's a pretty even-tempered guy."

Magda smiled. "You like him?"

God, yes. He's the sexiest man I've ever met.

"Yeah, he's nice."

Nice was an understatement.

"He's an incredible surgeon. Watching him is like watching a maestro at work."

"Speaking of maestros." Magda often changed the direction of conversations on a whim, so Romy wasn't fazed. "Your sister has a new job. She's going to work for Livia's foundation as a lecturer."

Romy's eyebrows shot up. "She is? Juno's moving out?"

Her youngest sister, Juno, was the sister who most resembled their free-spirited mother. Tall and willowy, with a shock of messy blonde hair, and a confirmed tomboy, Juno Sasse had made music her first love and passion from a young age. She was the cherished baby of the family and Romy had half-suspected she'd never leave.

"She is," Magda confirmed, a touch of melancholy in her voice. Eternally supportive of her daughters though she was, Romy knew her mother would struggle with empty nest syndrome. "Although I'm trying desperately not to think about that day. She's starting in the New Year, so at least we'll have Christmas as a family."

"With Stuart's family too?"

Magda shot her a nervous look. "Well, yes. If that's okay with you and Arti."

"Why wouldn't it be?" Romy asked.

Magda sighed. "There is some, how can I put it, some unpleasantness with Stuart's wife. Hopefully soon to be ex-wife, if she ever signs the damn papers. She keeps harassing Stuart, usually through her son."

Romy raised an eyebrow, not liking the sound of that. "What's the son's name again?"

"Gaius. I've only met him once, but he seems friendly enough. Hasn't Blue ever mentioned him?"

"We're careful to keep family stuff away from work, and I don't actually socialize with Blue Allende, remember? We'd never even met until today. He might be my brother soon, but he's still in a league of his own." Romy grinned as Magda rolled her eyes.

"You mean you don't socialize *at all*. Romy, you're beautiful, you're young ... don't let what happened in New York stop you from living your life."

Romy grimaced, feeling the familiar cold feeling at the memories. "Mom ... Dacre doesn't know I'm back home, and if he finds out, he'll come here and ... God, I don't want to imagine."

Her mother looked down at her hands as they continued to move swiftly, her knife skills in the kitchen as good as any surgeon's were in an operating theater. "I hate that you were with him. You're too young to have gone through a divorce or anything else he did to you."

Romy marshalled her emotions, reminding herself that those days were long past. She was safe now, however much Dacre Mortimer was an animal. Her leg still hurt from where he'd stamped on it and broken it the previous year at the same time that he'd almost beaten her to death.

"Look, at least I learned a lesson," Romy said to her mother now. "Don't go on first impressions. Dacre was Mr. Charm until he *wasn't*."

"Was that a dig at me?" Magda didn't sound upset, just sad. "Because I know Stuart and I haven't known each other that long."

Romy hopped down to kiss her mother's cheek and gave her a warm hug.

"Mom, no, it wasn't a dig at you, more one at myself."

Magda smiled in relief. "Romy, I have never felt like this. Not even with your father," she added apologetically.

"I figured, with Dad." Romy nodded, unsurprised.

Romy's father, a professor of Magda's back in the day, had never been present much in his daughters' lives. He supported them financially, but soon after Juno had been born, he and Magda had quietly and amicably divorced and James Sasse had remarried and moved to London. Being a single mother didn't faze Magda and she'd somehow kept her girls clothed and fed as they grew, bringing them all up to be independent young people who never depended on someone else.

The loss of Remy, Romy's brother, had shattered them all, but the four women were as close now as they had ever been. Artemis, Magda's eldest, had followed her father into the teaching profession and now taught physics at the University of Washington. Romy had headed for medical school as soon as she graduated from Harvard, and Juno was a musical prodigy. The one thing James had provided was money for their education, and Magda was grateful for that, she often told Romy.

Magda had been brought up in a hippie commune and she'd carried those values her whole life, finally having reached a point in her life where she could sculpt for a living.

Which was why Romy and her sisters had been astounded to hear that Magda was about to marry a multi-billionaire. Stuart Eames had made his fortune in tech and had such a large share of the tech market that no one could compete. Romy was looking forward to meeting the billionaire who had captured her mother's laidback heart.

A random thought occurred to her as she reached for the

salad bowl and started to assemble the various ingredients her mother had diced. "How come Blue has a different last name?"

Magda drained the pot of rice she was cooking. "He's Stuart's son from an affair."

Romy's eyebrows shot up.

"I think his mother was Italian," Magda went on, confirming at least that suspicion, though Romy was far more interested in the other revelation.

"So ... Stuart had an affair?"

Magda gave her a warning look. "Darling, if you had ever met his wife, you wouldn't blame him."

Though Magda was far from conservative, she was fiercely loyal and it was an unusual stance for her to take. Nevertheless, Romy decided to let it go, at least until she'd had a chance to cross-examine Eames and ensure that he wasn't about to cheat on her mother. Because if he did, she and her sisters would have plenty to say.

"Mom," she said, suddenly noticing how much food her mother was preparing, "you realize there's only four of us, right?"

"Five," Magda flushed bright red and ducked her head. "Stuart's joining us."

"Oh, getting in an introduction under the wire, huh?" Romy grinned. "I guess I should help you with the rest of dinner, then ..."

STUART EAMES HAD the same bright green eyes as his son, but his hair was close cropped and white. He had an easy smile that Romy liked, and a friendly manner which made the party all feel at ease. He greeted them all with utmost respect. "It's so good to finally meet you. Magda is so proud of you all."

Juno, curling herself into a chair, grinned at him. "I assure you, we don't deserve it."

Artemis, her blonde hair falling gracefully to her shoulders, shot her younger sister a warning look. "Don't tease, Juno."

Stuart laughed. "No, don't stop teasing. Blue and I are always busting each other's chops. It's what families are supposed to do. Speaking of which, do you mind if I just have a quiet word with your mom about something? I swear it'll take no more than five minutes."

"Sure thing."

Left alone, the sisters looked at one another.

"He's cute," Juno decided, and Artemis chuckled.

"Can you call a sixty-year-old cute?" Artemis smoothed her skirt down over her long legs, crossing them elegantly.

Romy sighed. Of all the Sasse sisters, she was the odd one out, dark-haired, dark eyed, and small in stature, if not in figure. Where her sisters were all long limbs and athletic, Romy was curvy, full-breasted, and petite. She still worked out as much as her siblings, but her figure was always going to be soft instead of athletic like them. Juno and Artemis took after their mother; Romy didn't know where she'd gotten her curves from. She barely remembered what her father looked like. Oh, she knew people considered her beautiful, but she never played it up. Slightly myopic from a young age, she wore glasses instead of contacts, and stuffed her long, thick chestnut hair up into a messy bun more often than not.

Juno poked her with a foot now. "Will you be coming to our traditional Thanksgiving run this year?"

Giving her sister a cheesy smile, Romy said, "Sadly, I'll be working."

"Roms!"

"Sorry," Romy sang in a not-so-at-all voice. She loathed running, unless it was towards something. Like pizza.

Juno sulked while Artemis grinned at Romy. "Nice work, Romy. And what with my broken ankle ..."

"What broken ankle?" Juno shot her eldest sister a confused look.

"The one I'll mysteriously acquire on Thanksgiving." Artemis laughed and high-fived Romy.

"Don't blame me when the pair of you get old and fat." Juno sighed dramatically, then, lowering her voice, she nodded towards the kitchen where Stuart and their mother talking. "What do you think?"

"Too early to say."

"He looks like Blue a little. Same eyes."

Juno grinned. "You got a little crush, Romulus?"

Romy threw a pillow at her. "None of your business, quisling."

Dinner was a fun affair, and Romy decided she liked Stuart very much. He was charming, intelligent, and seemed to adore her mother. Romy noticed, however, that Artemis was a little quieter than normal and when she questioned her sister afterward, Artemis shrugged.

"I'm just reserving judgement is all, Romy. We don't know him that well yet."

Romy went to work the next day, wondering if she should mention Stuart to Blue, but when she walked into the locker room, the place was in a chaotic state with people running every which way.

"What's going on?" she asked, preparing herself mentally and physically for what would likely be a long haul.

"There's been an attack at a sorority house," Mac told her, his face pale. "Really nasty stuff. Eight girls, three dead. The rest are being brought in here. Allende is already operating."

Every time she thought she was used to the darker side of

her profession, Romy got a reality check. Because truthfully, there was no way to ever get used to innocents slaughtered.

Reaching for her scrubs automatically, she asked, "Does he want us in the observation room?"

"No." They heard Blue's voice behind them and turned. Clad in bloodstained scrubs, the handsome surgeon looked weary and grim-faced. "Romy, you're with me in OR3; Mac, with Dr. Fredericks in OR7; Jim, Molly, and Flynn, emergency room until we can find theaters for the less injured girls. Come on, Romy."

She changed and was back in under a minute. Blue briefed her on the way to theater. "Patient is Yasmin Levant, nineteen, multiple stab wounds to the abdomen, shattered left femur, looks like the killer stamped on it, possibly to incapacitate her. We've got Ortho coming in but her abdominal wounds are catastrophic, at least twenty-nine separate wounds."

"God, poor girl."

Blue nodded as they went to scrub. "Look, Romy, we're going to do everything and anything to save her, but I have to warn you. The odds are against us."

She'd expected as much, sadly, but appreciated the warning anyway.

After scrubbing, Romy followed him into the operating room where the victim lay on the table. She was covered in blood and barely breathing, blood bags and saline trying to keep her alive. Automatically, Romy avoided looking at anything but the injuries. Looking at the faces right off the bat when the situation was so dire ... it didn't help things.

For hours they operated, trying to repair the damage the knife had caused, pumping her full of blood, but at midnight, Blue called it. There was nothing else to do ...

Yasmin Levant was dead.

CHAPTER THREE

The adrenaline leaving her system, Romy felt weirdly emotional, horrified, and drained by the experience. She waited until almost everyone had left the room before walking up to Yasmin's head. Finally looking at the young girl's still, pale face, her dark hair blood-soaked to an auburn color, Romy saw herself reflected in the victim's silent, still features. She whispered a silent apology for her failure and started removing the tubes from her throat.

"The nurses will do that," Blue said gently, putting his hand on her back. Romy, unable to speak, just shook her head and eventually Blue began to help her, both working in silence until all the medical equipment had been cleared away and Yasmin lay on the table silent and still, but at least with slightly more dignity.

"Can I wash her face?" Romy found her voice breaking as she asked, but Blue, his eyes sad, shook his head.

"No, we have to keep her secure for the forensic team now. Even all of our equipment will need to be saved. The police will probably want a statement from all of us."

Romy looked back down at Yasmin and a sob choked its way out of her. "Who would do this? Why?"

She felt Blue draw her away from the victim then and wrap his arms around her. It wasn't what colleagues usually did, but Romy allowed it because she needed it. She leaned into him, tears filling her eyes.

"I wish I could tell you it gets easier in these cases, Romy, but it doesn't," he said softly, his voice achingly sad and kind. "The vile things people do to other humans—sometimes there is no reason why. Sometimes people are monsters."

Romy nodded and looked up at him, wiping her eyes. "I know the type."

Blue stopped, and his green eyes were intense on hers. For a long moment they gazed at each other before, blushing, Romy gave an awkward smile and stepped away. "I'm okay now. We'd better go talk to the family."

"Of course." There was pain in that beautiful voice of his and Romy wanted to hold him and comfort him as he had done with her, but Blue walked away. She followed him, running slightly to keep up with his long stride. He dwarfed her five-foot two by at least a foot, and suddenly he slowed down. "Sorry, *piccolo*, I'll try not to walk so fast."

"*Piccolo*?"

"*Little one*," he explained, the tenderness in his voice tugging at her heart as much as the hint of a smile. Then as they neared the relative's room, his smile faded. "Is this your first one?"

"First murder." Romy's heart began to beat out of her chest.

Blue nodded, squeezing her hand. "Just follow my lead."

They knocked and walked in. A middle-aged woman, terrified, was sitting down, her arms wrapped around herself, and when she saw their faces, she moaned. "*No, no, no, no...*"

A man, her husband, his face etched with pain, stood. "Doc? Please don't tell me ..."

"I'm so sorry, Mr. and Mrs. Levant. Despite our best efforts, Yasmin's injuries were too severe and she died a short time ago."

The woman collapsed in a sobbing, weeping huddle, and Blue kept talking to her husband as Romy moved to try and comfort Yasmin's mother.

"There are no words for the regret I feel, *we* feel, at your loss."

Trying futilely to soothe the mother's unsoothable grief, Romy listened to Blue talk first to Yasmin's father, then watched him take a turn gently addressing her bereft mother, comforting both as best as he could, answering all of their questions patiently and as fully as possible. But the truth was the one question would never be adequately answered.

Why?

Romy's chest was tight with sorrow but she maintained her composure. Afterward, they talked to the police, those questions prolonging the endless night even further. Finally, as dawn began to break over Seattle, Romy went back to the locker room to change out of her bloody scrubs. The room was empty and echoed with each footstep and slam of the locker door.

Somehow managing to drag on her jeans and shirt, Romy slumped onto a bench afterward and put her head in her hands. The adrenaline from the surgery was long gone and now she felt wrecked. Her hip and leg ached from standing too long but she ignored the pain, trying not to break down. She failed, and silent, hot tears poured down her face. She buried her face in her hands to cry, her entire body trembling.

She heard him come in; it was impossible not to in the silence, but she didn't expect to feel his arms go around her for the second time that evening. Gently, he drew her head to his chest. His clean soap-and-spice smell was familiar now and Romy pressed her face into his sweater, breathing him in. He stroked her hair and whispered soft Italian words, resting his chin on her head and just letting her weep.

When she finally stopped crying, she looked up at him. His eyes were sad, but he held her gaze for a moment before brushing his lips against hers just briefly. It was clear from the look on his face that he'd intended it as no more than a reassurance, but the heat that instantly flared between them changed those intentions. They both felt it, so there was not even the slightest chance of denying the chemistry.

Blue framed her face with his big hands. "Are you sure, Romy?" His voice was low and sent shivers of desire through her body.

"It is wrong?" she whispered, looking up into his intensely compassionate eyes. "She just died. How can we ..."

"Life has to go on, *piccolo*," he said softly. "We honor those who go before us by continuing to live fully. But if you prefer not to, I understand absolutely—"

"No. Yes." Romy slid her hand into his dark curls and kissed him hard, needing this. Needing him. Their mouths moved together hungrily, and when Blue stood and picked her up, it was like she belonged in his careful embrace. He carried her as if she weighed nothing, kicking open the door to the on-call room and locking it behind him.

He set her down on her feet and gently pulled at the drawstring of her pants, drawing them down her legs then pulling her top over her head. "God, you're beautiful," he said softly, and she could see the lust and admiration in his eyes. Her own hands went down to his groin, cupping his hard-on through his jeans. Damn, he was huge ...

Blue pulled down the lacy cup of her bra and fixed his mouth on her nipple as he slid her panties down her legs, then expertly flicked her bra clasp open, letting her full, ripe breasts fall into his hands. The feel of his skin on hers was sending tingles racing through her body and she pushed his sweater over his head and ran her hands over the hard planes of his chest. Naked, Blue Allende was even more godlike, tall, broad-shouldered, and slim-hipped. He swept her onto the small bunk, kissing her as he kicked off his pants and underwear. Romy reached down to stroke his cock, the skin so silky, the hard, hot length of him filling her hands.

Blue was kissing her breasts, her belly, as he made his way down the bed and hooked her legs over his shoulders. He smiled up at her. "I'm going to lick you until you scream, beautiful girl ..."

Romy moaned, drawing in a sharp breath as his tongue lashed around her clit, his fingers massaging the soft flesh of her inner thigh as he expertly pleasured her. "God, Blue ... Blue ..."

A rush of emotion flooded her system as she came and she began to cry, much to her embarrassment. His mouth was on hers then, tender, loving. "Don't cry, *piccolo*," he murmured, his eyes soft. Romy stroked his face but said nothing, drinking him in.

"Do you want me inside?"

She nodded and as she watched him slip a condom onto his straining cock, Romy knew she had wanted this man from the first moment she had seen him.

Blue hitched her legs around his waist. "Okay?"

She nodded and he smiled, pausing to stroke her belly, before she helped guide him into her. With one long thrust, he entered her, and Romy gasped with the thrill of him filling her, the rhythm that he found so quickly. She moved with him, meeting and holding his gaze until they were both trembling and panting for air. She tightened her vaginal muscles around his pulsating cock, making him groan her name. And as she came, her back arched up and she cried out as he kissed her throat, her breasts.

Afterward, he held her as she tried to stop her body trembling, kissing her forehead and the tears that still lingered at the corners of her eyes from the emotion of everything. "Are you okay, *piccolo*?"

She nodded, stroking his face. "I am very, very okay. Surprisingly so. Should we have done that?"

Blue smiled wryly. "Probably not ... but I admit, I've wanted to do that since I first met you."

Romy was amazed. "*Me*?"

He laughed. "Yes, why is that hard to believe? You're beautiful, smart, funny, the whole package. Who *wouldn't* want you?"

"But you could have anyone you want, Blue. Anyone."

"And I want you, Romy." He sighed. "Although I'm not naïve that this will be complicated, not just at work, but with our families."

Romy groaned. "I didn't even think about that ... God. Maybe we should keep this," she gestured to their naked bodies, "to ourselves."

Blue nodded, then grinned at her. "I'd like to keep your body all to myself."

Romy laughed as he covered her body with his, feeling his cock hardening again. "I'm serious."

"Secret liaisons? That's pretty hot." He kissed her neck, then moved again to her lips. "I can't get enough of these lips."

She smiled, her mouth curving up as he kissed her, but when he broke away, her eyes were serious. "This is so complicated, Blue. You're my boss to begin with, then there's our families. I mean it. We should keep this between us ... assuming, um, assuming this isn't a one-night thing." She blushed again, but he laughed.

"It isn't, not for me, but I do agree with you. Maybe next time we'll keep it out of the hospital, but tonight, heightened emotions, I needed this. I needed you."

Touched, she cupped his cheek in her hand. "You have me. Just ... on the down-low. I can't risk my career, Blue, as much as I want you."

"I agree, Romy." He sighed and leaned his forehead against hers. "And I hate to do this, but I have to be back on rounds in three hours and so do you."

"Yeah, we'd better go home. I mean to our *own* homes," she added, smiling as he chuckled.

Somehow they managed to keep their hands off one another long enough to get dressed and walk outside.

Down in the parking lot, he stole one more kiss. "You're heavenly," he said quietly, but with intensity in his eyes. "I'll see you in a few hours. Take some time. I'll cover for you."

Romy saw him watching her car as she drove away, her emotions in turmoil. The man knew how to make her body respond like no one ever had. More than that, he seemed to see something in her that she'd thought Dacre's assault had stamped out permanently. There was a goodness to Blue, a tenderness to where it wasn't just red-hot searing sex but also something more, even this very first time.

She wasn't sure she'd be able to keep the secret, but it was sure worth giving it a damn good try.

A t home, Romy set an alarm for two hours and fell onto her bed still fully clothed. She groaned when the alarm went off and hauled herself out of bed, finally discarding her work clothes and stepping into the shower. As she ate a quick breakfast, she flicked on the television and watched the reports of the murders. It was an awful idea but she needed to see it somehow, as though it helped atone slightly for being unable to save Yasmin. As thought it might help her understand even slightly.

THE FOUR DECEASED YOUNG WOMEN, savagely attacked in their sorority house, have now been named as Rebecca Fulsome, 20; Oona White, 19; Madelaine Culpepper, 21; and the youngest victim, Yasmin Levant, who at just 18, died last night of her wounds at The Rainier Hope Hospital. Hospital officials say that their best surgeons worked tirelessly to save Miss Levant, but she succumbed to her injuries in the early hours of this morning. Police say the attacker broke in through an open window and attacked each girl in her bedroom, before leaving the premises. So far, no suspects have been identified, but the murders mirror a similar case in New York two years ago.

ROMY SWALLOWED the last of her cereal, feeling sick. She'd forgotten all about the murders in New York. God, there were monsters everywhere. She remembered her own personal monster, the midnight beatings, the forced sex.

Rape. Call it what it was, Sasse. He raped you. Bastard.

She drove into work and was assailed by her friends, wanting to know about working with Blue in an emergency situation. Romy, exhausted, was grateful when Mac rescued her, shooing everyone away and bearing her off to the cafeteria. "Allende sent me. He saw you come in and knew you'd get caught by the pack. Damn hyenas."

Romy smiled at him and at Blue's thoughtfulness. "Mac, if it had been someone else but me, we would have been hyenas too."

Mac shrugged. "Fair point. Are you okay? You look done in."

"It was a long night." In more ways than one. "Is Dr. Allende all right? He had it worse than me."

"He looks good, but then he always does."

"True story."

Mac grinned at her. "So you're not immune to the good doctor's charisma then? I thought you were the one hold-out."

Romy cursed silently but faked a smile. "I'm here to work, not get laid."

"I'm just saying ... out of all us, I reckon you'd be his type."

Romy shrugged off the conversation. "Did you hear the news this morning? The murders in New York? The same as here?"

"Yeah. Jesus, humans, huh?"

"Humans." She agreed. Her pager went off a second before Mac's. "We're summoned."

.   .   .

I⊤ WAS evening before she even saw Blue again. There was so much paperwork from the murders and the subsequent medical procedures that Romy was sequestered with a police team most of the day. They went over everything again and again. Romy told them again how Yasmin Levant had been stabbed so viciously that her abdominal artery had been shredded, that she had simply bled out before they could attempt any kind of repair.

"What about her left femur?" Det. Halsey asked her eventually. "Did your orthopedic department attend the surgery?"

Romy nodded. "But, to be honest, it was secondary to the abdominal wounds. I'm not an expert, but I assume he—or she —broke her femur to subdue her enough that she couldn't fight him—or her—off."

"We're pretty sure it's a him," Halsey said quietly.

Romy, overtired bristled. "Because women aren't strong enough to do that to a person?"

Halsey held his hands up. "I meant no offense, Dr. Sasse. We found DNA on the victim. Male DNA."

Romy backed down. "I'm sorry. Bad day."

"Of course. Look, we need to talk about the survivors' injuries. We got the report that they weren't as serious as the deceased victims."

"No, that was strange," Romy said. "They were badly beaten, and they'll probably need serious psychiatric counseling, but yeah, it is odd that he didn't finish the job, so to speak. God."

"And Ms. Levant was the only one with a broken femur?"

Romy's own leg ached and she rubbed it unconsciously. "Detective, the femur is the longest, strongest bone in the human body. The force it takes to break it ... it would take anger.

Rage. It's sadistic too ... but then, that's what we're talking about here, isn't it? He's a sadist."

"He is," the detective agreed, then smiled kindly at her. "You'll tell your friends to be careful when they leave at night?"

Romy gave a hollow laugh. "Detective, you're talking about everyday life for a woman in this world."

NOT EVEN HALFWAY THROUGH her shift, Romy was hollowed out through and through. She didn't know if she even had the strength to walk out of the hospital for a breath of fresh air, when Blue appeared in the breakroom. He didn't say a word, helping himself to coffee nonchalantly before stepping into the supply closet.

She knew he was giving her a chance to choose, and choose she did. Dragging herself out of her seat, she joined him in the small room and locked the door.

"This isn't 'keeping it out of work' Dr. Allende."

Blue reached for her. "Shut up and kiss me, woman."

He crushed his lips against hers, his arms snaking around her waist, pulling her hard against his body. Romy moaned as she felt his erection, hard against her belly. For just a moment she let herself sag, let him carry her weary weight ... "God, I want you, but ..."

Reality reasserted itself and gently she extricated herself from his arms. "Bad boy." She wagged her finger at him and he laughed.

"Come home with me tonight and I'll show you just how much of a bad boy I can be."

Romy hesitated, but then the lure of his green eyes, his dark curls and that body ...

"*Piccolo*, unless you want to sleep," he said softly, studying her face and holding her more gently. "No pressure, you under-stand. It's been a long two days. Another day, if you prefer ..."

"No." Romy made up her mind. *The best way to honor those who have gone before us is to continue living our lives fully.* "I'm off tomorrow, so I can risk it."

Blue flashed a huge grin. "Oh, you're off tomorrow ... funny thing ... so am I."

Romy started laughing. "I wonder how that happened?"

"Come here."

They kissed again, and Romy reached down to squeeze his diamond-hard cock. He groaned and buried his face in her neck. "It's a good thing we're off, because I'm going to make sure you can't walk straight for the entire day."

"Is that right?"

"God, yes."

Romy giggled as he pretended to ravish her. "Easy, soldier. You're the one who's not going to be able to walk properly, and we still have rounds."

"Spoilsport."

"Get over it, Doc."

ROMY'S BODY felt electrified all day at the thought of what Blue had promised. That electricity gave her a much-needed boost that, paired with caffeine, got her through the remainder of the long hours. But as the day wound down and she walked down to the concessions stand to grab a new toothbrush, she groaned inwardly as she saw a tall, blonde, and very familiar figure looping towards her.

"Yo, sis." Juno grinned, flinging her long arms around her diminutive sister.

"Hey, Boo ... what are you doing here?"

"Just finished a class and wanted to say hi. Also, to check out the famous doc ... is he here?"

Romy opened her mouth to answer just as Blue came toward her, grinning. She gave a quick, almost imperceptible shake of the head, and cut her eyes to Juno. Blue slowed his pace, his smile faltering in confusion.

"Dr. Allende, do you have a moment?" Romy said formally. "My sister Juno would like to meet you."

Understanding now, Blue smiled at Juno, shaking her hand. "Hey, nice to meet you at last."

"You too." Juno's amazed expression was written all over her face as she took in the gorgeous man. "Can I call you Blue?"

"Of course. Listen, would you ladies like to grab a coffee?"

Romy was gesturing wildly behind Juno's back, but Blue didn't understand her signal, and when Juno agreed—a little too enthusiastically—Romy sighed. She knew Juno—any excuse to stay at Romy's place overnight in the city, especially if there was a chance to gossip. *Damn it.*

They went for a coffee at a little independent place on 6th Avenue. Blue smiled at Juno. "So, we're about to be siblings?"

"Looks like." Juno was stuffing a Danish pastry into her mouth. "We haven't met your brother yet, either. Mom's looking forward to Thanksgiving dinner—just a warning, she cooks brussels sprouts, and given it's ..." she checked her watch, "two weeks until Thanksgiving, she'll be putting them on to boil about now."

Blue laughed. "Duly noted. Dad and I are looking forward to spending that day with you."

"And your brother?"

There was a pause, a beat too long. "And Gaius. Of course."

"You don't mention your brother much," Romy said and saw a flicker of something in his eyes before he gave them a half-smile.

"We're not as close as you three appear to be. I always wanted a sister. Juno, Romy tells me you're quite the musical prodigy."

"Ha." Juno grinned at him. "She flatters me. But it is my passion, and I'm about to start working for the Gabriella Renaud Foundation down in New Orleans."

"Just when I move back to Seattle, she moves out," Romy grinned. "I might take it personally."

"Then you'll have to make the most of me while I'm here. Like tonight ... I could stay over at your place?" Juno looked hopeful, and Romy had to work to keep the disappointment out of her face.

"Of course, Boo." She shot an apologetic look at Blue who winked at her and mouthed 'don't worry' at her. "But," Romy added, thinking quickly, "I have to be out early tomorrow for a training seminar. All day, I'm afraid."

"Yes, she does," Blue caught on, trying not to smile. "I'm leading that seminar, and I'm very strict about time. One of my things, I'm afraid, punctuality."

"He is."

Juno shrugged, surprisingly clueless. Usually she picked up on these things with a terrifying radar. "What's the training about?"

"Orthopedics," Blue said smoothly, "mostly about the recovery time of someone's gait after strenuous exercise."

Romy snorted her coffee from her nose and was embarrassed, wiping her nose. "Sorry, went down the wrong way."

"That's not like you," Blue said innocently, and Romy had to hide her laughter in her tissue. Juno still didn't notice anything, already making inroads on Romy's carrot cake, which she'd left alone. Romy, trying to stop her giggles, cleared her throat.

"So, yeah, if you don't mind being left alone in the apartment."

"Of course not." Juno shrugged.

Blue's eyes were twinkling. "Don't forget we also have that patient we might need to check in on overnight too. I'll page you if I need you."

"Please do," Romy was enjoying their little game, "I'd like to make sure the patient is, um, responding to stimulus."

It was Blue's turn to hide his laughter now. "Do excuse me, I have to use the bathroom."

When they were alone, Juno turned to Romy. "Well, he's gorgeous and sweet and cute. How do you concentrate on work with a man like that around?"

"A man who will soon be our brother," Romy reminded her, cringing inwardly. She hated lying to Juno, who was so trusting that she would believe anything Romy told her. "Also, he's my boss."

"Ha, flirty boss." But Juno didn't push it. She gave up on the carrot cake, licking cream cheese frosting from her fingers. "Look, maybe I will go home tonight. Seems like you're preoccupied with work anyway. But we must, must, must have a sisters' night before I leave for New Orleans."

"Are you going before Christmas?" For some reason, Romy was confused about the timeline. Had Juno told her and she'd just forgotten?

"Only for a couple of weeks, just so Livia can get me trained before she gives birth. Can you believe she's having a baby?"

"I'm just glad she's well enough to." Their friend Livia had been stabbed and shot by a psychopath the year before and had barely survived. "Give her and Nox my love, won't you?"

"Speaking of gorgeous men." Juno muttered, then grinned as Blue returned. "It was so good to meet you, bro, but I think I'm going to head back home, leave you your second-in-command." She threw her arms around his neck and hugged him. Faintly surprised, Blue smiled and returned the embrace. "You're coming to Thanksgiving, right?"

Blue nodded. "Just try and stop me. I'm a sucker for over-boiled sprouts."

Laughing, Juno kissed Romy's cheek and then loped out, garnering the appreciative looks of a table of young men as she walked out of the coffee house.

Blue grinned at Romy. "So ... you're free, after all?" He sat down next to her and slid his hand along her thigh. Romy wiggled with pleasure.

"Dr. Allende?"

"Yes, Dr. Sasse?"

"I believe you prescribed me some bone-shattering sex earlier ... how about you fill my prescription?"

Blue laughed. "That was the worst doctor dirty talk I've ever heard ... but yes, I need to do that immediately ..."

GAIUS EAMES TAPPED on his father's office door, not waiting for a reply before he opened it. "Hey, Pa."

Stuart looked up over from his computer, annoyed. "Gaius, why bother to knock if you're just going to come in anyway?"

Gaius was unrepentant, shrugging as he flopped into the chair opposite his father. "I just get into town and that's the greeting I get? What would I have caught you doing? One of your secretaries?"

"That's enough, Gaius." Stuart glared at his eldest son.

Gaius grinned widely, knowing his barb had hit home. "*Jeez*, Pa, take a chill pill. I was *kidding*. How is the lovely Magda?"

Stuart's face softened. "She's wonderful, and looking forward to seeing you at Thanksgiving —you are coming, I take it?"

Gaius nodded. "Although Mom's not happy, yes, I'll be there."

Stuart sighed. "At this point, I really don't care what Hilary thinks anymore, Gaius. She burned her bridges long ago."

"I don't want to fight, Pa." Gaius held his hands up. "So, Thanksgiving. Will I meet the daughters? I've done my research, two blondes, one brunette —have they got the same father? I'm just asking," he added as his father looked annoyed, "no judgement."

"As far as I know, yes. Artemis and Juno take after Magda, and Romy after her father, I understand. Anyway, you'll meet all of them then. Have you spoken ..."

"To the Italian?" Gaius finished his father's sentence. "No, but then that's nothing new."

Stuart sighed. "Blue is your brother, Gaius, and it's about time you both grew up."

Gaius stayed silent. He would never, ever bond with Blue Allende, and not just because he was his bastard half-brother. The jealous that squirmed in his gut when he thought about Blue's success, his devastating good looks, his decency ... goddamn.

"I hear he's working with one of the Sasse girls."

Stuart nodded. "Romy. She's in her last year of residency. Blue says she's the best he's ever seen."

Gaius chuckled darkly. "Is he fucking her?"

Stuart's blue eyes went gray, and Gaius knew he'd gone too far this time. "Don't ever talk about one of Magda's daughters like that again. Ever."

"Forgive me." Gaius tried to keep the sarcasm out of his voice. "Look, I just got into town —can I use the condo? I'm assuming you've moved in with Magda already?"

"Close enough. I spend every night there. Here," Stuart reached into his desk drawer and threw Gaius a set of keys. "You know the rules."

"Pa, you realize I'm forty-two, right?"

"And Charlie Sheen is fifty-something. No whores, no drugs. Not in my condo."

Gaius sighed and got up. "Fine. Well, I guess I'll see you at Thanksgiving."

Stuart relented a little. The man had a soft spot that made Gaius respect him even less. "Look, have dinner with me, just me, on Tuesday."

Gaius masked a smirk. "It's a date."

At his father's condo, Gaius unpacked, then grabbed a beer from the refrigerator and stretched out on the couch, flicking through the television channels disinterestedly. It was gnawing at his gut the way his father talked about Blue, the pride, the love in his voice. Gaius had been seventeen when his father had revealed his affair with Blue's mother. He hadn't blame his father for straying—he knew his own mother Hilary hadn't been faithful at any point during his parents' marriage, but he'd resented the fact that there was a child.

Blue, twelve at the time that his father brought him into their family, was quiet, kind, intense, and everything Gaius wanted to be. Even as a child, Blue's big green eyes, full of intelligence and compassion, garnered him quick acceptance into their family circle, something Gaius had struggled with. However much Blue had tried to befriend his new brother, Gaius, ridden by jealousy, had been uninterested.

Gaius gave a humorless laugh. Now Blue already had an 'in' with his father's new wife and her daughters too. *Fuck him.* Gaius grabbed his iPad and typed in a name in the search engine.

Doctor Romy Sasse. Her photograph came up immediately on the alumni page at Stamford's website, and Gaius studied it. Long, dark hair falling in waves past her shoulders, Romy was a doe-eyed beauty with her olive skin, that faint blush of pink in her cheeks, and the curve of her breasts in her white coat was promising.

Yeah, Gaius thought, if Blue isn't fucking her, *he's a fool.* Gaius read everything he could on the young woman, but there was a surprising dearth of information. Weren't doctors always publishing research? Why were her name and profile not on the website of the Rainier Hope Hospital, but only on the alumni page of Stamford? Did she not want people to know where she was?

Intrigued, Gaius took out his phone and dialed. "Yeah, Greg? It's Gaius Eames. Yes, good, thanks. Listen, I have a job for you, if you're interested. Yeah, I want you to find out everything you can on a Dr. Romy Sasse. She's a resident at Rainier Hope Hospital. Find out what she's hiding ... or who she's hiding from."

CHAPTER FIVE

At the same moment that Gaius set out to find out more about Romy, his half-brother was doing the same thing—albeit in a more physical way. He trailed his lips up the length of her spine, feeling her shiver. Her skin was so soft that it drove him crazy. "Turn over, baby."

Romy rolled onto her back, hitching a leg over his body. Her lips crushed against his as he buried his rock-hard cock deep into her, and he heard her moan of pleasure. He couldn't get enough of this woman; she was so soft, her skin silky, the color of milky coffee. The way she looked up at him with those dark chocolate eyes ...

He found his rhythm, moving in and out of her, feeling her sweet cunt contract around his cock, loving the way her breasts and belly undulated with the movement. He'd never been one for skinny girls and Romy had the kind of curvaceous body men salivated over. He'd wanted her the moment he saw her, and he hadn't felt that way in a long time.

Blue was aware that his physical attributes meant people thought he was a man whore, and he himself had done nothing to dissuade that image but the truth was ... he was careful with his heart. So many women wanted him to look good on their arm, or wanted his cachet as a superstar surgeon to show off. Very few wanted Blue for who he really was underneath the movie-star looks, a funny, unabashed geek, who just wanted to find someone to laugh with.

And very quickly after she'd arrived in Seattle, Romy had shown herself to be just that woman. That they would soon be related by marriage and be siblings, well, they'd have to deal with that later.

For now, all he wanted to do was make love to her. He stroked the hair back from her face as they moved together, marveling at the beautiful flush in her face as she came, trembling and sighing his name. They smiled at each other as they caught their breath.

"I've never had sex this good," Roy said, stretching her limbs and then curling into him.

For a long moment, Blue stared at her. "I wish we could go public," he said regretfully. "I want to tell the world about this brilliant, beautiful woman who somehow wants me."

Romy laughed. "First, thank you for complimenting my intellect first; you get extra points for that. Second, you know you could have any woman you wanted, Blue Allende. Don't be modest. You know it's the truth."

"It's the accent," he said playfully before letting loose with a string of Italian. "*Ho incontrato la ragazza più gloriosa e voglio portarla in tutte le mie parti preferite d'Italia e farle vedere da dove vengo.*"

"Holy crap, that's unfairly hot!" Romy exclaimed, kissing him hungrily.

"Ah, a weakness," he teased, tickling her ribs and enjoying her writhing against him.

"Mmm, *yeah*. Now ... what did you say? There was something about a ho and glorious ravioli?"

Blue grinned. "I just said I met the most glorious girl, and I want to take her to all my favorite parts of Italy and show her where I came from."

"Wow. Where *did* you come from?" she wondered. "I mean, I know Stuart had an affair with your mom ..." she trailed off, apparently realizing that wasn't the hottest of pillow talk conversations.

"He did," Blue nodded, long ago having come to terms with that aspect of his DNA.

"Technically he was—and regretfully still is—married to Hilary." Just mentioning her name made his gut tense for reasons no one knew but him. "But the marriage has been over for years. Mom was a widow; her husband was killed in a car wreck three years after they married, and she was in mourning for years. Stuart went to Rome for a conference, met my mother, and it was, according to her, like a thunderbolt."

Blue rolled over onto his back and gathered Romy back into him, enjoyed her pressed tight against his chest. "I was conceived on that first meeting, accidentally, of course, and my mom even gave Stuart an out, said she would raise me alone. Stuart was a stand-up guy. He and my mother ... their chemistry was plain to see even when I was a kid, so when my mom died, Stuart didn't hesitate to bring me to the States."

"That makes me very happy to hear," Romy nodded. "Not the affair, obviously, but it doesn't seem like he'll break my mom's heart."

"No," Blue assured her. "He will not, Romy. He made mistakes, yes, but he is a genuinely good man."

Romy's face clouded. "What is your stepmother like?"

"Hilary?" Blue gave a humorless laugh, feeling that wrench again. "Hilary Eames is an unremittingly vile piece of crap. Sorry if that sounds harsh, but it's the truth. She treated—and continues to treat—my dad as an ATM machine, but gives the world the impression she's a God-fearing charitable Christian woman. Ugh. That woman has never believed in anything in her life."

"She's that bad?"

Blue nodded. "Thankfully, Dad saw the light and filed for divorce, but it hasn't stopped her from trying to control him. And Dad's so desperate for the divorce to be final, he gives in on everything. She's bleeding him dry. I haven't met your mom yet, Romy, but I would warn her ..." he looked at her intensely, willing her to feel the depth of his warning, "don't let Hilary in, even an inch. She's like a cancer, and I haven't even told you the half of it."

Romy propped herself up on her elbow and studied him. "She won't get a chance, I promise. No one messes with my mom —they have to get past me and my sisters and we can throw down, I tell you."

Blue smiled fondly at her. "I bet you can. I really look forward to meeting Magda. She's made my dad happy, and I owe her everything for that."

"Thanksgiving."

There was a tiny pause before he nodded at the invitation. "Thanksgiving. Yes." He bent his head to kiss her. "Now, Romy, be a good girl and lie back for me ... I'm going to kiss every inch of your spectacular body."

Soon, he was hooking her legs over his shoulder and burying his face in her sex. She tasted so good to him, the crimson blush of her swollen cunt so beautiful as his tongue teased and tormented her hardening clit until she was bucking, and coming. He gave her no time to recover before he plunged his cock deep into her and fucked her mercilessly until she was crying with ecstasy, arching her back and pleading with him to never, never stop.

· · ·

ARTEMIS SASSE DROVE into the city to do some early Christmas shopping. Her partner, Glen, had called her to say he would be late home and Artemis was enjoying the time alone. She and Glen had not been getting along too well lately, and she knew in her heart that it was over. Still, the thought depressed her. She and Glen had been together since high school, nearly twenty years, and the thought that they would not be in each other's lives much longer was a deep sadness within her. It turned out that it was true, the whole thing about people outgrowing one another. He'd grown one way and she'd grown the other. There was no longer any chance of them meeting in the middle, though they'd tried for a long time.

At thirty-six, Arti had worked her way up in the otherwise male-dominated faculty and was now a tenured professor at the university. There was something missing though, something that wasn't satisfying her in her life, but she couldn't figure out what. She loved her family—she was close to both her sisters and her mother—she had great friends, and ye t...

Something had been bugging at her for a few weeks now, and she couldn't quite reconcile it with her stoic and practical nature. It was Romy, she realized. She felt her middle sister was heading towards trouble and she couldn't figure out why she felt like that. Certainly, Romy was fitting in well at the hospital, or so she said, and she was happy in her small apartment, but Artemis couldn't help feeling scared for her sister.

Why, though? she asked herself again as she browsed around the department store. *Why do I feel like that?*

Maybe it was Dacre, Romy's ex. He was still out there, still angry with Romy for leaving him. The way he had beaten her the last time still haunted Artemis. The hospital in New York had called her and she had flown with her mother and Juno to see Romy. Walking into that room, seeing her sister almost unrecognizable, her face bloodied and bruised, eyes swollen, her leg smashed ... Romy, thankfully, had pressed charges, but Dacre, thanks to his wealthy parents, had hired the best lawyers money could buy and the Sasse women couldn't compete. Dacre had been fined and gave an outward expression of regret, but Romy and her family knew he was enraged by the court case and by the subsequent divorce.

Artemis shook herself. *Romy is an adult and doesn't need you worrying about her. Get a grip.* Artemis asked herself whether she was distracting herself from her failing relationship by focusing so much attention on her sister. She pushed everything to the back of her mind and went to her favorite coffee shop.

A gingerbread latte and a pastry later and she felt the tension leave her body. She was flicking through a book she'd purchased for Juno for Christmas when she felt a hand on her shoulder. Looking up to see a very tall, handsome man, she smiled delightedly. "*Dan?* Dan Helmond?"

Her old friend grinned back at her. "The very one. Hey, kiddo."

Artemis stood and hugged him. Dan had been a couple of years old than she and Glen at school. Now he was a big bear of a man, his dark hair shot through with silver, his beard full. Plaid shirt and camo pants and ear piercings, and Dan looked more like a Hell's Angel than the architect he was. He'd always been a kind, gentle man though, and all the Sasse sisters had had a crush on him at one point or another.

"Can I get you a coffee?" Artemis asked hopefully.

"Nah, I just ordered. Can I get you a top up ... *ugh*, woman, what is that monstrosity?" He peered into her half-empty mug and Artemis grinned.

"It's a gingerbread latte, you philistine, and no, thanks. One sugary hit is enough for me."

Dan excused himself to pay for his own coffee—Americano, no sugar, no cream—and sat down with her. His brown eyes twinkled merrily at her. "Well, now, girl. You're looking good. How's life?"

"It's good, thanks. I'm tenured at my college, family's good. My mom's getting married soon."

Dan looked surprised. "Wow, really? Someone's tamed Magda Sasse?" He always deliberately pronounced their surname 'Sassy' rather than 'Sass,' Artemis remembered.

"I wouldn't say tamed, exactly; you know Mom. She's still a head-in-the-clouds nutso, but wonderful with it." Artemis sipped her coffee. "She's marrying Stuart Eames."

With satisfaction, she saw the amazement on Dan's face. "No freakin' *way.*"

"Yes, way."

Dan let out a long breath. "Wow. *Wow.*"

"One of his sons is in property ... Gaius Eames. You know him?"

Dan shook his head. "Heard of him, and that star doctor brother of his, but I don't know either. How about you? Still with Glen?"

Barely. "Yes, we're still, um, still ... together."

"You don't seem so sure."

Artemis shrugged, not wanting to talk about Glen with Dan and ruin the atmosphere. "How about you?"

"Wife passed a few years back, cancer." Dan stirred his coffee, clearly lost in those memories for a long moment, such that Arti reached over and touched his hand.

"I'm sorry, Dan."

He nodded and looked up, briefly covering her hand with his and then going on as if he hadn't missed a beat. "I have a seventeen-year-old daughter, Octavia. She's heading off to Harvard next year."

"That's exciting."

Dan beamed and Artemis felt her stomach flutter. *That smile*

... "She's my angel." Dan went on, digging out his wallet and showing her a photograph of a pretty teenager with long dark hair and big soulful brown eyes like her father.

"She's gorgeous. She could be Romy's twin."

"She could. How is your sister doing? Last I heard, she was in New York."

Artemis felt her chest tighten. "She's back now, working as a resident at Rainier Hope. Surgical superstar in the making, so they say."

"I'm not surprised. And Juno?"

"About to work for a charitable foundation in New Orleans."

"Man, the Sasse sisters done good."

Artemis smiled. "We're doing okay."

Dan glanced at his watch. "Listen, Missy, I hate to cut and run but I have a meeting in town —don't suppose you'd like to make this a regular thing? Meeting up for coffee? Tavia's always telling me to slow down, take some time to chill, and I'd like to see you again."

"I'd love to ... here." She pulled a business card out of her pocket, a little worse for wear. "It has my cell phone number on it. Call anytime. It was really great to see you."

Dan bent down and kissed her cheek. "Soon, yeah?"

"Soon."

ARTEMIS FELT ABSURDLY CHEERED as she walked back to her car. *A new friend,* she thought to herself, *a new friend that's an old friend.* She pushed away any thoughts of anything beyond friendship, although she kept rerunning Dan calling her 'Missy'—she'd forgotten that was his name for her back in high school.

When she got home, Glen was in a cheerful mood, and they enjoyed a pleasant meal together for the first time in a long time.

When Glen had gone to bed in his own room, where he'd moved a long time back, Artemis checked her phone to see Dan had already sent her a text message, a photograph of him and his daughter giving her the thumbs up. Sweet and funny.

She went to bed with a huge smile on her face.

FROM ANOTHER COFFEE house across the street, Dacre Mortimer had watched his ex-wife's sister chatting with the tall man. He knew Artemis wouldn't hesitate to call the cops on him if she saw him, and he couldn't risk being caught, not while Romy was still out there in the world, alive. He didn't much care what happened to him after she was dead, but for now, he had a job to do.

Find Romy. Find his beautiful, sexy, love-of-his-life, ex-wife Romy.

And kill her.

CHAPTER SIX

"Dr. Allende, can I see you about a consult, please?"

Romy hid her grin as Blue looked up from his paperwork and his eyes twinkled at her. "Of course, Dr. Sasse. Where to?"

In less than a minute, they had locked themselves into a supply closet on the quietest floor in the hospital. Blue's lips were against hers, his hands hitching up her skirt as she freed his cock from his pants. He lifted her easily, his strong arms supporting her as she guided his cock inside her. They fucked hard but silently, their eyes locked on the others, their mouths hungrily seeking the other's.

"God, you're amazing." Romy moaned, burying her face in his shoulder to muffle her cry of release.

Blue groaned as he came, panting for air, kissing her so furiously he tasted blood. "You think everyone knows about us?"

"I've been careful ... but we really *should* stop doing this ... God, Blue, that is *not* what I meant by stop, you lunatic."

He was stroking her clit now, relentless until she shivered through another orgasm. "I'm addicted to watching you come," he murmured, his lips against hers, "Your skin flushes such a beautiful color when I'm fucking you. My cock in your cunt is all I think about all day, all night, and the way you squeeze my dick when I'm inside you."

"God, *Blue!*" Romy's head rolled back as she came again, his dirty talk making her wet and shivery and weak. Blue, grinning, triumphant, thrust his rampant cock back into her and Romy almost screamed with pleasure.

Finally, as they caught their breath, Romy, laughed and shook her head at him. "You are a machine, Allende."

"Love machine." He gave her the finger pistols and she chuckled.

"And you are so cheesy, so, so cheesy."

He kissed her, then helped her straighten her clothes. "Listen, I was thinking ... we should talk about birth control."

"*How to Kill a Mood in Ten Seconds* by Dr. Blue Allende." But she grinned at him. "What are you thinking?"

"We're both doctors, and we both have access to, um, tests. You're right, this isn't sexy, but what I'm leading to is, hopefully."

"And what's that?"

"I want to feel you. Really feel you when I'm inside you. I want to know that when we're doing rounds, you're carrying my seed around with you. Does that sound selfish? I don't mean it to, I just ... I want to be close to you. Oh, damn, I sound like a creep. I'm not explaining this well."

Romy shook her head. "No, but I understand what you're trying to get at. And I want that too." She leaned into him and nuzzled his nose with hers. "Skin on skin," she said in a low, chocolatey voice, "you and me, together." She slid her hand onto his groin, feeling him hardening again.

"Damn, woman, how come I couldn't put it like that?"

Romy chuckled. "Dr. Allende?"

"Yes?"

"When we get back to your apartment tonight, I'm going to suck you dry."

With that, Romy grinned, picked up her files, and headed for the door. "By the way," she said to Blue, who was waiting until his hard-on dissipated, "I had a full work-up last year in New York. I'm clean as a whistle, so to speak. Your move, Doc."

She blew him a kiss and left him in the closet.

ROMY WAS STILL GRINNING when she was called to the emergency room forty-five minutes later. A nervous young intern came to find her. "Hi, Dr. Sasse, I'm sorry to call you personally but there's a patient asking for you. He's in curtain six."

"Name?"

"He won't give me it."

Romy's heart began to thump unpleasantly. *Surely, not.* Surely Dacre hadn't found her already? She smoothed her face out and nodded at the intern. "No problem, I'll see him."

For one awful moment before she pulled back the curtain, she imagined it was her violent ex-husband, that he would lunge for, get his hands around her throat, choke the life out of her.

The relief when she saw the patient was immense, and she smiled at the man, who was cradling a bloody hand. He smiled at her. "Dr. Sasse?"

"That's me, Mr. ...?"

The man grinned, his handsome face lighting up, his blue eyes intense. "Eames. Hey, Romy, I'm Gaius, your soon-to-be stepbrother."

Her eyebrows shot up as she searched for a resemblance to Blue and definitely saw it, now that she was looking for it. The high cheeks and sculpted jaw were apparently genetic. "Hey, well, hey," she stammered and then laughed. "Wow, you caught me off guard. Nice to meet you at last, even if unexpectedly."

Gaius held his hand up. "I was careless while fixing my car."

"Let's take a look."

Romy pulled up a chair and took his hand. "You didn't want to see Dr. Allende?"

"I wanted to meet you. Something good to come out of this. Ouch."

"Sorry." Romy examined the nasty gash. "Well, it's deep, but you won't need surgery. I'll clean it and give you some local anesthetic. Then we can stitch the wound, or even glue it."

Gaius nodded, his eyes never leaving her face. "Thank you, Romy."

As she worked, he asked her questions about her work. "Do you work closely with Blue?"

Was there an edge to his voice? She kept her tone neutral. "Well, he is our General Surgery attending, and that's my chosen specialty. It's strange to think he'll be my brother soon."

"I bet. I didn't think to ask Dad ... have they settled on a wedding date?"

"I don't think so, but Mom's being really secretive about it. Lord knows why; she's not usually shy about anything. Of course, your father's divorce isn't quite final yet, so there's that to consider."

Gaius laughed. "Secrets are overrated. Do you have any secrets, Dr. Sasse?" His voice dropped lower, quieter, and Romy flushed, not out of pleasure, but awkwardness.

He was *flirting* with her, and it was freaking her out. For a second, she imagined saying *Well, your half-brother just reamed me real good in a supply closet, but apart from that ...* "Nope. Boring, I know, but that's me. We're all done here." She gave him a smile and pushed away from him. "The nurse will come to stitch you up."

He reached out and took her arm. "Romy ... thank you. To say thank you, I'd love to take you to dinner. What do you say?"

Romy stepped gracefully away from his grip. "Well, we'll see you at Thanksgiving in a couple of days, and I'm afraid I'm pretty much working until then."

Gaius reached for her hand and kissed the back of it. Instead of the heat that flared through her when Blue touched her, Romy felt her skin go weirdly cold. "Then I shall have to be satisfied with that."

AFTER HE LEFT, Romy felt unsettled. Gaius was all charm and politeness, but there was something underneath the façade, something that made her feel uneasy. She wondered if she should tell Blue that his brother had been in, but eventually decided not to. It was nothing, after all.

She didn't regret her decision that night when Blue dropped a sheet of paper in her lap as he was pulling off his tie. Blood tests. She scanned them and grinned up at him. "Dude, some of these tests take weeks. How did you manage this?"

"Well, honey, let me just say there's a very happy guy in testing right now."

Romy giggled at the mischievous look on Blue's face. "Blue Allende, did you pimp yourself out for tests?"

"Kinda, but not in the way you mean. He might have needed half a week off for a family destination wedding and I might've pulled some big strings."

"Allende, bribery?" she teased. "That's all kinds of wrong."

"I know. I'm disgusted with myself," Blue was grinning widely as he pulled her jeans off of her and knelt between her legs. Romy watched him lazily as he slid her panties down her legs.

Romy hooked her legs over his shoulders. "Lick my pussy, doctor, or I'll forget my promise to milk you dry."

Blue, grinning, buried his face in her sex and Romy closed

her eyes, moaning softly as his tongue lashed around her clit, then delved deep into her cunt. He made her come, then she made good on her promise, taking his cock into her mouth and sucking and drawing on him until he came, swallowing down his seed.

Blue scooped her into his arms and carried her to bed, tugging off her sweater and his own, feeling her full breasts soft against his hard chest. He lay on top of her, gazing down at her, stroking the hair back from her face. "So ... do we need to use a condom today?"

Romy shook her head. "I'm on birth control ... let's go for it. I want to feel you inside me."

Blue crushed his lips to hers before slowly burying his cock deep inside her. Romy shivered and Blue groaned. "God, you feel good. Your cunt is so velvety, baby."

They began to move together, Romy savoring every sensation that he sent through her body. A deeper connection was being forged and they gazed at each other, murmuring sweet words to each other as they made love. Romy tilted her hips up so he could go deeper, harder, digging her nails into his buttocks, urging him on. God, this man ... his cock, so big, so thick, reaming her into submission, his intense green eyes soft with love, with desire, with fire, for her ... Romy couldn't quite believe it.

She cried out his name as she came, shuddering and trembling, then felt his seed explode out of him, filling her belly. This man, this incredible man ... she wanted to scream at the top of her voice that she was falling in love with him, that he was her destiny, her dearest desire.

But Romy settled for his sweet kisses, not wanting to spoil the moment with too-soon declarations. But she knew it was true; she was falling for him. Not just his handsome face, his glorious body, or the way he fucked her, both animal-like and yet so tender. It was his sense of humor, his utter lack of ego when he could rightfully claim to be one of the best, his playfulness.

More than anything, Romy felt she could trust him, and after what Dacre had done to her ... it was a big thing for her.

She did tell him that she felt she could trust him (leaving out the parts about Dacre) and to her surprise, Blue looked utterly moved. "I'm glad, *piccolo*. I'm honored by that, and you should know ... I feel the same. Whatever this is between us, whatever it becomes ... you are my person. My lover, my muse, my best friend ... and my family."

Romy's eyes filled with tears. "And you, mine."

Blue kissed her tenderly. "Thank God you came home to Seattle, Romy. Thank God."

And they began to make love again, loving each other long into the night.

GAIUS SMILED GRIMLY to himself as he sat in his car outside his half-brother's apartment. He had followed Romy from the hospital and could hardly believe it when she drove here. He saw Blue come down to greet her, saw them kissing. So his bastard half-brother was fucking his almost- stepsister. Gaius' gut churned with jealousy. Romy Sasse was beautiful, sweet, and of *course*, Blue had gotten there first.

Damn you.

Still, it would make for extra sport, Gaius grinned to himself. Romy Sasse had a whole lot of secrets that he would bet his life Blue didn't know about. The abusive ex-husband, for one.

Dacre Mortimer. Son of New York socialites, a billionaire in his own right. So, Romy liked the money ... that would be useful, although Gaius could see from the divorce papers that she had not asked for a penny from Mortimer, not even the prenup money she had been entitled to. That was interesting.

Gaius also knew Romy had been hospitalized a year previously as she was about to enter her last year of her residency program at Johns Hopkins. Smashed left femur, multiple wounds from a beating, bruised liver, and a burst ovary from being kicked in the stomach. Mortimer's parents had done a good job hushing it up in the papers, but their son had gone to town on Romy when she'd asked for a divorce.

Why the hell had she married him? Gaius couldn't figure it out but if he could find Mortimer, he would ask him. Romy had fled New York as soon as she was well enough and applied to Rainier Hope to finish her residency. A new life.

Hmm. Gaius began to see a whole campaign of terror he could unleash on the couple—especially if he could find Dacre Mortimer and lead him to his ex-wife. He smiled when he thought of watching Dacre confronting his ex-wife, of Blue finding out what had happened. Blue would defend Romy, of course, and maybe Dacre would get rid of Blue, once and for all.

Gaius got excited now. *Yes, yes, this was perfect.* If he could manipulate Mortimer into killing Blue, then he, Gaius, could sweep in and 'save' the day. Poor Romy would be devastated — unless of course, she too was dead. Gaius shrugged. Either way, he would win.

He picked up the phone and called his detective, thanking him for finding out all the information he had already collected, then paused. "I'd like you to do something else for me, and I'm willing to pay you double if you can do it."

"I'm intrigued. Go ahead."

Gaius smiled. "Find out where Dacre Mortimer is, and ask him to meet with you. I have a very interesting proposition for him."

CHAPTER SEVEN

On Thanksgiving morning, Magda took one look at her fiancé's somber face and sighed. "Uh-oh. What did she do now?"

It had almost become a joke between them; Hilary Eames' attempts to draw out her divorce from Stuart were creative, Magda had to give her that. But Stuart was being worn down by it, his usually merry green eyes losing their sparkle. Magda stood on her tiptoes to kiss him; she was a tall woman herself, but Stuart was a big man, broad-shouldered and long-limbed.

He wrapped his arms around her now. "I can't make head or tail of it, Mags. She's dropping her objections to the divorce."

For a moment, Magda was so shocked, she couldn't speak. After months and months of vicious back-and-forth between Hilary and Stuart, Hilary was dropping her claim for seventy-five percent of Stuart's wealth? How? And more importantly, why? Magda had only met Hilary on two occasions, but it was enough to get a measure of the woman. She liked power, and she loved money. Hilary Eames would not drop her claim to Stuart's billions.

"What the hell?" Magda studied Stuart, who looked lost.

"I just don't know... but I don't trust it."

Magda shook her head. "No. Did you call Gaius, ask him if he knew anything?"

"I did, and he doesn't. He's as bemused as I am. He said he would call her and report back later at dinner."

Magda blew out her cheeks. "So ... she's signing the divorce papers?"

Stuart smiled now. "She is ... which means, my beautiful Magda, we can get married. And soon. I was thinking ... Christmas?"

"It'll be finalized that soon?"

Stuart gave a wry grin. "Sometimes, being rich helps."

"Moneybags." But she kissed him, laughing softly. "I love you, Stuart. If you didn't have a penny, I would still love you to the moon and back."

"Mushy." But he kissed her tenderly, tangling his fingers in her short, steel gray hair. "God, woman, you are beautiful."

She smiled up at him. "Well, you're old. Your eyesight is fading and ... ouch, ouch, no, stop that," she shrieked as he tickled her.

Juno wandered in, hopping up onto the counter and watched them. "Is this some kind of Cocoon foreplay?"

Magda shot her youngest daughter a withering look. "We're not that old. Maybe I don't mind so much that you're moving out after all ..."

Juno smirked and blew her mom a kiss. "You looooove me ..."

Stuart laughed at their antics. "Hey, kiddo," he said to Juno, "I'm trying to persuade your mother to marry me at Christmas. Help me out, would you?"

Juno's eyes went wide. "Vampira's signed the divorce papers?"

"Yup."

Juno did a seated dance of victory, hands raised high in the air. "Yeah, baby! Then, hell yes, Ma, snag this dude before I steal him away from you. Can I officiate?"

Magda and Stuart looked at each other. "Can you get ordained before Christmas?"

Juno looked smug. "Already am. I was waiting for you to announce your wedding day then I was going to surprise you. What do you say?"

"I say I forgive you for the Cocoon crap," Magda beamed, hugging her youngest tightly. "Stuart ... yes? No?"

Stuart grinned. "I think that would make the day even more perfect, yes. Now all we have to discuss is where."

Magda laughed. "Okay, you two, slow your roll. Let's get today over and done with. Juno, are your sisters on their way?"

"Arti is, but Romy said she might be a little late. Emergency at the hospital, and she said that she and Blue might come together for convenience's sake."

"That's cool ... but I hope they don't get tied up."

ROMY WAS INDEED TIED up but not in the way her mother meant. Blue's tie was wrapped around her wrists, her hands behind her back as she lay on his dining table, her legs wrapped around his waist as he plunged his cock in and out of her, thrusting harder each time as he fucked her, his strokes brutal but his hands on her body, caressing her breasts, her belly, were soft and tender. Romy came explosively as Blue pulled out and came on her skin, shooting thick reams of creamy white come onto her belly.

Romy begged him not to stop, and so he turned her onto her stomach, pulling her hands, and she cried out with pain and pleasure. He pushed into her perfectly rounded ass and fucked her slowly this time. "God, Romy, you're so beautiful, so exquisite ... I'll never get enough of you, not ever..."

He made her come over and over before, exhausted, they showered together then fell onto his bed. They had been working an all-nighter and had gotten home just after dawn. After sleeping for an hour, they both woke, horny for each other and for the next three hours, fucked each other's brains out, clawing at each other, desperate for that connection.

Now they lay side by side, sleepy and exhausted. Blue grabbed the alarm clock and set an alarm for two p.m. "Don't want to be late for your mom." He grinned, but then saw Romy had fallen asleep, her head resting in the crook of his shoulder. Blue studied her face, so lovely, so expressive even in repose. He knew he was in love with her, had been for weeks now, almost since the first, but Blue struggled with whether to tell her or not. They needed to get this dinner with their parents over with, then decide whether or not to go public.

The only person Blue had told was his chief of surgery, Beau Quinto, not wanting any improper behavior on his record, nor to let his mentor and friend down.

"It isn't a fling, Beau," he'd told him seriously, "I'm crazy about her, but it won't affect either my work or Romy's. We're professionals. Yes, Romy and I work closely together, but I assure you I don't favor her above the other residents." He grinned slightly. "Even if she is the best general surgery resident I've ever seen."

Quinto had rolled his eyes. "Blue ... I've been where you are. When I met Dinah, she was a patient, so I know all about improper relationships. I trust you and Romy not to let your relationship interfere with your work. Don't let me down."

"I won't, I give you my word. Thanks, boss."

Blue laid his head on top of Romy's and closed his eyes. Feeling her in his arms was like a drug to him; he loved her brain, her commitment to her work, to the hospital ... God, he'd dreamed of finding a woman like Romy all his adult life. The only person who had ever gotten close was Julia, his college sweetheart, but she had had an affair with Gaius during their final year at Harvard. When a vindictive Gaius had dumped her soon after, Blue had had no interest in resuming the relationship though he hadn't wished his brother's cruelty on her. He wouldn't wish it on anybody.

Gaius had always been resentful of Blue, of anything he had that Gaius didn't. Success, focus, commitment —Gaius thought these things were something one either had or didn't have, rather than things one would work for. Blue had no time for his feckless older half-sibling, and even less time for his stepmother. Hilary had made Blue's mother's life a misery while she was alive, and continued to besmirch her memory after death.

He shook himself now. Later, he would have to see Gaius and not give away that he was in love with Romy. He had nightmares about Gaius setting his malevolent sights on the beautiful young woman in his arms. Of course, they were nothing to the other nightmares that had plagued him ever since the eight young women were brutalized in the city, since Yasmin Levant had died on his operating table. She *had* looked like Romy, too much for Blue not to imagine it was his love bled out and dead in the O.R.

His arms tightened reflexively around her now and he pressed his lips to her forehead. Romy murmured in her sleep and opened her eyes, smiling up at him. He kissed her soft lips, treasuring every moment, before she sighed and went back to sleep.

God, I love you, piccolo. He hadn't exaggerated when he'd told her he wanted to whisk her away to Italy, to show her every place he'd loved as a child, everywhere he had been at his happiest until he'd met her.

He closed his eyes and slept then, with that happy dream in mind, until the alarm went off at two p.m., and he and Romy made love again before finally dragging themselves from their beds to go celebrate Thanksgiving with their blended family.

. . .

He had been following Artemis for weeks now, and finally, she had led him to the Sasse family home. When he and Romy had been married, she had been cagey about where her mother lived, scared of him even on their wedding night. Dacre smiled to himself, remembering. She hadn't wanted to sleep with him, and as she'd held out until they were married, Dacre had been certain of one thing. He would fuck Romy on their wedding night if it killed him ... or her. It had taken his forearm across her throat before she gave in, tears pouring down her face as he forced her legs apart.

"You are *mine*," he growled at her continually. He'd worn her down over the months to be able to get her to agree to marry him, destroying her confidence, isolating her from her friends.

By the time of the wedding—fifteen minutes at City Hall—Romy had been a shadow of her former self. Dacre still wasn't certain how he'd scared her so much that she'd actually agreed to be legally bound to him, but such was his power, he now remembered proudly. That, and keeping her away from her damn nosy family so they couldn't run interference.

She'd spoken her vows in such a quiet voice the judge had had to ask her to speak up twice, but when she had seen the barely concealed rage on Dacre's face, she had quailed and recited them louder, but in a monotone. Dacre had seen the two witnesses, strangers he had wrangled from a bar, exchange concerned looks. The woman with them had slipped Romy her number. *If you need anything.* He knew Romy hadn't called her. It would have made no difference if she had.

Dacre killed the woman, Regan, a few weeks later, catching her unawares as she stepped out into a dark alley in the back of the bar where she worked to have a smoke. Hand across her throat, knife in her belly, one, two, three.

Dead. God, the feeling, the rush it gave him, and every single time he imagined his victim was Romy. His cock would harden and he would smell the blood, imagining it to be hers. That sweet gasp of shock and pain as the knife sliced through flesh was Romy's ... she never made any noise when they had sex, would never kiss him on the mouth. She didn't fake orgasm and it made him crazy. When he'd found out she was back in touch with her family that had been the last straw and when the beatings had started.

That last one, the final one, had begun when she was late home from the hospital and he'd been drinking. Such a normal thing, but he'd heard her coming up the stairs and for a moment, he had just been joking around, hiding behind the door to spook her.

He had hooked his arm around her neck and she had screamed in fright. Pulling away from him, she'd rounded on him with wide, frightened eyes, so beautiful in her terror, and told him she was leaving him for good. Dacre had lost it. He'd beat her mercilessly until she could no longer stand, blood pouring from cuts above her eyes, her nose broken, her mouth bleeding. He'd pulled her hair until she sobbed, then, as she slumped to the floor, he had stamped on her left thigh and they'd both heard the decisive crack as her femur shattered. Romy, choking on her own blood, could no longer scream for help.

Dacre had studied her dispassionately, then, grabbing a knife from the block, had raped his broken wife. He had intended to kill her, he knew that now, but when he'd heard his neighbors shouting, banging on the door, he'd chickened out. Instead, he'd called an ambulance for Romy, turning on the waterworks, apologizing over and over, begging her to live.

At the hospital, the police had arrested him and he'd made a great show of not protesting. Secretly he had been waiting for his lawyer to tell him Romy was dead, that her injuries were too bad. The police had discovered who he was and their whole attitude had changed. His father had friends high up in the NYPD. He had been cautioned and told that if Romy pressed charges, they would have to revisit.

His mother and father had been beside themselves with grief. They had adored Romy and had thought she would be able to tame some of Dacre's excesses. When it became clear Romy would live and that she would be throwing the book at him, Dacre's father, Hubert, had paid off the people he needed to drop the charges in return for a plea deal. No jail time for Dacre. Romy and her family had fought back, but they were no match.

In return, Romy had been given her divorce but would not take a penny from the Mortimers. Hubert Mortimer had given his son a check for three million dollars and then cut him off. His parents had disowned him entirely.

And you are to blame, Romy Sasse. You shouldn't have made me angry.

Dacre parked his car behind the tree line of the forest which bordered Magda Sasse's property and stepped out to slink closer to the house. He saw a car pull up and saw a dark haired-man and Romy get out. They were laughing and joking. God, Romy looked so beautiful. Dacre's cock twitched at the sight of her long dark hair tumbling around her lovely face. Who was this guy with her?

The next moment, he watched as the man pulled Romy into a small corner of the house, shaded from the windows, and kissed her. Romy gazed up at the man with love in her eyes and it made Dacre's insides twist in rage.

Damn fucking bitch. How dare she cheat? Because she was still his in spite of the divorce. She'd vowed forever and she would always be, no matter her whoring ways.

"She's exquisite, isn't she?"

Dacre started and turned to find a tall, amused-looking man with piercing blue eyes staring at him. Dacre was lost for words. The man held his hand out.

"You must be Dacre Mortimer," he said in a friendly tone. He nodded towards the couple who were now disappearing into the house. "And that's my bastard half-brother Blue Allende kissing your ex-wife. And yes, they're fucking each other. Sickening, isn't it?"

"And who the fuck are you?"

"Gaius Eames. Hello, Mortimer. I think we're going to have a lot of fun together."

CHAPTER EIGHT

Romy was beginning to feel really uncomfortable. The meal had started off well. Everyone had been formally introduced, and the food was out of this world. If there was one thing Magda excelled at apart from parenting and sculpting, it was cooking. The turkey was juicy and plentiful, the side dishes of creamy mashed potatoes and yams sweet and heavenly, the gravy well-seasoned. Even the cranberry sauce was made from scratch and Blue grinned at her as she went in for another helping.

She shrugged unrepentantly. "It's my favorite."

The worst part of the meal was not giving away that she and Blue were together, not sharing those intimate glances or private jokes between them. They'd slipped a couple of times but had written it off as 'work jokes.'

Everything had been going really well until Gaius turned his attention to her.

"Nice to see you again so soon, Romy."

Oh, fuck. "How's the hand?" She could feel Blue staring at her curiously.

"Much, much better, thanks to you." Gaius appeared

friendly, even if there was an undercurrent. He looked at Blue. "She's quite remarkable, Blue. Have you noticed?"

"Of course," Blue smiled smoothly, but the edge in the smile was one Romy hadn't seen before and it made her cold. "Romy is by far the best resident at Rainier Hope this year. And for many years, come to that."

"You sound impressed, brother."

Blue fixed Gaius with a searching stare. "I am, Gaius. When did you and Romy meet?"

Romy opened her mouth to speak but Gaius got there first. "A couple of days ago ... you didn't mention it, Romy?" His face was a picture of innocent confusion.

"Patient privacy," Romy said quietly. She risked a glance at Blue, who met her gaze steadily. *There will be questions later*, his eyes said, and she gave a quick, almost imperceptible nod, believing with every fiber of her being that he might be upset but would not hurt her as Dacre had done anytime he was enraged.

"The consummate professional," Gaius said.

Artemis cleared her throat, picking up on the sudden tension. "I actually have some news."

Romy shot her a grateful smile. "Is everything okay?"

"Oh, yes ... well, no, but yes, and I know that doesn't make sense. Glen and I have decided to break up. Now I know you'll think this is a bad thing, Mom, but for both Glen and I ... we've grown apart. Neither of us thinks badly of the other, it's just we no longer fit as a couple. Glen's moving out ... today, actually, which is why he couldn't be here. It's entirely amicable, I assure you, so there's no need to pick sides, etc."

"I'm glad," Juno said immediately, "but you know we've always got your back, Arti."

Artemis grinned at her.

"I know you do, Bubba. But, yeah, so ... I guess I'm just saying, I'm single, and happily so for now."

"As long as you're happy, darling," Magda looked a little upset, but smiled at her eldest daughter, always supportive. Artemis leaned over and squeezed her hand.

"I am, Mom, and so is Greg. So, can anybody cheer proceedings up? Mom, Stuart?" She grinned at them. "I hear someone very special is going to marry the two of you?"

Juno beamed as Romy and Blue looked surprised. "Really, Juno? That's awesome. Hey," Romy said in a stage-whisper to her sister, "When they get to the kissing bit, can you leave that out? I don't want to see that."

Magda threw a brussels sprout at her daughter. "Cheeky girl."

THE REST of the meal passed in easy conversation and laughter, but Romy could feel the tension rolling off Blue's body. It didn't help that Gaius, pretending there was a friendship between he and Romy, made jokes with her, flattering her as if they had known each other for more than a few moments. Romy saw her sisters looked confused at the strange behavior and when they got her on her own, clearing the dishes, they questioned her about it. Romy shrugged.

"I don't get it either. I treated him for his hand wound, that was it. I don't know the man. Perhaps he's just trying to, I don't know, ingratiate himself."

"Then why isn't he all pally-pally with me and Arti?" Juno shook her head. "Guy's a creep."

"For God's sake, Juno, lower your voice." Artemis hissed at her and Juno rolled her eyes. Romy felt a lump of misery settle in her chest. She should have told Blue; that he was pissed was obvious—to her, at least. *Damn it.* She looked at Artemis and for a moment debated telling her about how she felt about Blue. No, it wasn't fair to him; they had vowed to keep it quiet, at least until after Stuart and Magda's wedding. She turned back to the dishes, only half-listening, as her sisters chatted.

Eventually she was alone in the kitchen, making work for herself. She felt a hand on the back of her neck and turned hopefully, expecting to see Blue. She jerked backwards when she saw it was Gaius instead. He held up his hands.

"Sorry, I didn't mean to startle to you, Romy; it just seemed like you were tensed up there."

Romy was trembling. "Gaius, please don't touch me unless I ask you to."

"Sorry." His smile was innocent, but his eyes sparkled with malice. "Guess you're always a little jumpy these days. After what your husband did to you in New York."

Romy was so shocked that she didn't see Blue enter the kitchen behind her as Gaius started to grin. It was only when she heard him put down the casserole dish he was carrying that she turned—and saw the hurt in his eyes. He gazed back at her for a beat then turned and walked out. Romy stared after him in dismay.

"Was it something I said?" Gaius asked, and laughed coldly.

CHAPTER NINE

Blue was silent as he drove Romy back to her apartment. Romy sat in miserable contemplation as he followed her into her small apartment and shut the door. In spite of her total trust in him, her nerves were tightly wound, fear unavoidable. She waited for the storm as they walked into the living room, but he just grabbed a bottle of scotch from her kitchen with two glasses and sat her down next to him.

"Now," he said quietly, calm and patient, the utter antithesis of Dacre, "tell me everything."

Romy took a deep breath in, pressing her hands tightly together. "It's true, I was married, although I don't know how the hell Gaius knew. Incidentally, he's an asshole for behaving as if he and I were better acquainted than a five-minute consult the other night."

Blue nodded slowly. "But you didn't tell me about it."

"No, and right now, I don't know why. Blue, he's a creep, and he came onto me then as well as tonight. He makes my skin crawl."

Blue looked slightly mollified. "That's Gaius, all right. But why didn't you tell me you were married?"

"We weren't—aren't—there yet. You've never told me about your past lovers either."

"Don't do that, Romy. No games. Husband is a lot different from girlfriend. Who was he?"

Romy looked at him steadily. "He was a violent, ignorant spoiled rich boy who tried to kill me. There. Now you know."

"What?" Blue said in obvious horror.

Romy was glad he was shocked. "That's why I didn't tell you. I don't like to talk about it, frankly. It's a lot more complicated than just 'I was married.' He regularly beat me and raped me, then when I told him I wanted a divorce, he assaulted me so violently that I nearly died. He comes from a rich family. He's arrogant, entitled ... Dacre Mortimer is a monster and if he finds me, I'm dead. So, the fewer people that know about him, the fewer people there are both in his firing line, and who can help him find me. Why do you think my photo and name aren't on the Rainier Hope website or in promotional material? He knows I live in Seattle, he just doesn't know where." She sighed and rubbed her face. "Obviously, Gaius has done his homework."

"*Jesus*, Romy." Blue got up and paced around. "Why did you marry him in the first place?"

"That's a question I still can't answer fully for myself," she said softly. "He ... cowed me. Separated me from my mother and sisters. I guess after months of nonstop abuse, you get broken down to where a person can make you do just about anything. Even marrying the devil himself."

To Romy's great relief, Blue came back to her and put his arms around her, holding her tightly. He buried his face in her hair and Romy was shocked to feel him shaking.

"Blue?"

"The thought of anything happening to you." His voice was muffled and his arms tightened around her.

"It's okay, baby; nothing's going to happen to me." Romy

made him look at her and she stroked his face, wondering how she could ever have wondered even slightly if this man would hurt her. He was such a good man, God. How had she gotten so lucky this time? "I'm sorry I didn't tell you about Gaius. I just didn't want to upset you. That's clearly want he wants, to drive a wedge between us."

Blue pressed his lips to hers. "Romy ... that won't ever happen. I won't let it. I'm in love with you. The thought of anyone hurting you kills me."

It was Romy's turn to cry now. "I love you too, Doc," she smiled through her tears and he kissed her passionately. Romy pressed her body to his. "Take me to bed, Dr. Allende."

He undressed her slowly, kissing each piece of exposed skin until her whole body vibrated with longing. Naked, she wrapped her legs around him and took him in, his cock thrusting deep into her cunt in long, measured strokes. His lips moved with hers, tender and loving as they made love. Blue's eyes were intense on hers.

"Let's tell our family, tell them we're in love. I'm shocked they didn't guess." He began to smile as Romy moaned with pleasure as he buried himself deeper inside. "I want to tell the world about the woman I love, the brilliant, beautiful Romy ... I promise you. I'll keep you safe and loved. So, so loved ..."

Romy cried out his name as she came, her back arching up, her thighs tightening as he came inside her, his lips at her throat. "Yes," she said, as they caught their breath, "Yes, Blue ... yes ..."

IN THE MORNING, Romy was changing into her scrubs when Mac came to find her. "You look different," he remarked. "Glowing. You're not knocked up, are you?"

"No, definitely not," she rolled her eyes in amusement.

"What's going on today? It's like a ghost town." Virtually none of the regular staff had been present when she'd walked into the hospital.

Mac's smile faded. "You haven't heard? Another massacre. Four women found in the grounds of the Gasworks. All stabbed. They were brought to the ER, but they were all D.O.A. Everyone is cleaning up that mess and/or doing paperwork and/or talking to police. Again. I'm so sick of police."

"Oh God, not again." Romy felt sick. She followed Mac out of the locker room as he headed for rounds.

"And get this," he went on. "None of them knew each other. Police think they were all picked for some reason and then left together. One of them had her femur smashed like Yasmin Levant."

Romy stopped. "What did you say?"

"Left femur smashed. Why?"

A curl of horror was beginning to form inside of her, a doubt, a horrific idea. Murders in New York and now Seattle ... smashed femur ... *no, you're being paranoid and ridiculous, Sasse.* "Can I see the records?"

Mac shrugged. "Sure." They walked down to the ER, Romy assuring Mac she'd smooth things over with Blue if they were late for rounds. Romy picked up the files from the desk and read through them. There were multiple stab wounds, and all of the women were dark haired and dark eyed, with olive skin.

"Huh."

She looked up at Mac, who was studying the files with an odd expression his face. "What?"

"I just noticed. Their names. *Roberta, Ornella, Margaret, Ynez.* Their initials spell your name."

Romy felt like she'd been hit in the chest by a sledgehammer. No, it had to be a coincidence. She turned to the computer and brought up the case files for Yasmin Levant and the other women who had died with her. Reading through the names, she looked at Mac, whose eyes were now troubled. Drawing in a deep breath, Romy logged on the Internet and Googled the murders in New York. "Oh God ..."

All of the victims had names whose initials spelled her first name. Mac put his hand on her shoulder. "You know, Roms, this really could be coincidence—"

"It isn't." Romy began to tremble. "I need to talk to the police."

Mac looked alarmed. "You don't know who it is, do you?"

Romy nodded grimly. "I do. I have to find Blue."

Upstairs, Blue looked up, but his smile faded when he saw her face. He stood up and walked over to her immediately, reaching for her. "What is it, sweetheart?"

Romy drew in a deep breath. "It's Dacre. He's in Seattle. He's coming for me."

CHAPTER TEN

Artemis tried not to feel too excited as she made her way through the icy streets of Seattle to the coffee house. She and Dan had met up a few times but this day was the first time when she was a free agent. Glen had moved out over the weekend, and although they had both been sad, even cried a little, Artemis had never felt so convinced they were doing the right thing.

And now she was going to see Dan, the man who had been haunting her dreams for weeks now. She'd repeatedly told herself it was just a friendship, but she couldn't mistake the look in Dan's eyes when he was with her, and she was sure it was reflected in hers. Desire. A bond. She had never felt so comfortable with a man in her life, so at ease and relaxed—at the same time, every time she was with him, all she wanted to do was rip his clothes off and kiss him until she couldn't breathe.

She felt some guilt—after all, she and Glen had only just split—but then again, they'd lived separate lives for so many years. It was time to move on, and today was a big step forward doing just that. Today Dan was bringing his teenage daughter to meet her. He had asked Artemis if she wouldn't mind, his face going red, and Artemis knew she was being assessed for ... something. God, she hoped she would pass the test, and it wasn't helping her nerves but as soon as she pushed open the door to the coffee house, Dan and his female mini-me both grinned at her and Artemis relaxed.

Octavia was a delightful mix of typical teenager and nerdy geek. She reminded Artemis both of Juno with her confidence and Romy in her dark looks. She told Octavia that and the young woman smiled. "Dad said the same thing. He's always talked about the Sassy Sasse Sisters—you're almost legendary in our house."

"Really?" Artemis was absurdly flattered and Dan rolled his eyes.

"Way to ruin my game, kiddo."

Octavia chuckled. "Sorry, Pa, but it's the truth. I'd love to meet your sisters."

"We can arrange that, though Juno is leaving for New Orleans soon. Romy is still here, though, at the hospital."

They chatted easily for an hour then Octavia got up. She kissed Artemis's cheek. "Sorry I have to cut and run, but I have study group."

Her father coughed something which sounded suspiciously like 'geek.' Octavia grinned. "I am what you made me. Bye, Missy, I hope we see each other again soon. Pa, I'll probably stay over at Gail's tonight, so don't wait up."

"Just text me if you are."

"Will do. Bye." And she was gone.

Artemis grinned at Dan. "She's great."

Dan grinned, delighted. "I know, she's a good kid. I think you have her approval."

"Ha, I hope so." Artemis met his gaze and held it, blushing furiously, but Dan, his dark eyes twinkling, smiled in a way that made her stomach flutter.

"Missy?"

"Yes?" Her heart was beating out of her chest and she felt breathless.

"I'm gonna kiss you now." Dan leaned over and brushed her lips with his, lightly, before the kiss deepened and went on for a long moment. Artemis sank into his embrace, feeling his hands cup her face. "God, Missy, if you knew how long I've wanted to do that."

Artemis smiled. "Me too. What happens now?"

"Well, option A ... we stay here kissing all day. Option B ... I take you back to my place, undress you slowly, and kiss every inch of your perfect skin, before we make love tenderly. Option C ... we throw caution to the wind and fuck each other's brains out. Feel free to mix the last two options." He was grinning, and Artemis started to laugh.

"Dan Helmond, I say ... Option C first, then option B. Option A can go hang."

Before she could finish her sentence, Dan had grabbed her hand and they were running towards his car. In thirty minutes they were naked in his bed, and Dan was thrusting his enormous, thick cock deep inside her as they fucked hard. Artemis threw every caution to the wind; she had an animal desire in her for this man, his huge, muscled body making her feel so small and precious, his kisses both tender and feral.

Afterwards they ordered pizza and ate it in bed, feeling like lovesick teens again. Artemis grinned at Dan's self-satisfied expression. "Don't think for a minute, Helmond, that I left Glen for you."

"Yeah, you did." But she could tell he was joking around, and laughed. "Admit it, woman, you had to have the Dan-Dan-Man."

"Oh, jeez, I'm leaving," she groaned and giggled as he pulled her back into his arms and kissed her. "Marinara kisses."

"Think I got some mozzarella action going on in my beard if

you're interested." His smile was so wide, Artemis couldn't help giggling until she cried.

"That's so gross. Your seduction game is poor, Helmond."

"You love it, Missy Sassy."

She kissed him then. "I do. You may be crazy, but I'm crazy about you. If I'm honest, I'm kind of relieving a high-school fantasy right now."

Dan grinned, smoothing her blonde hair back from her face. "Except this is no fantasy. This is real, Missy." His face was serious now, but Artemis could see the love in his eyes. "I'm all in, Missy. You and me, this is all I want."

Artemis sighed happily, leaning into his embrace. "Me too, big guy, me too."

"Stay with me tonight."

She nodded, her lips suddenly too busy to speak, and they made love again, slowly this time, exploring each other's body, forgetting the time, long into the night.

ROMY SIPPED HER NOW-COLD COFFEE. She had been with the police most of the day and now she and Blue sat together in the interview room as the detective in charge of the homicides questioned her again.

"I'm sorry if I'm repeating questions, Dr. Sasse, but it's important. Now, it could be a coincidence, but we always look for patterns and we had noticed the women who died shared the same first name initial. But until you came forward we didn't know who the message was intended for."

Blue groaned in dismay and the detective looked at him. "Don't worry, Dr. Allende. We have a state-wide BOLO out for Dacre Mortimer. If he's here, we'll find him. In the meantime, we'll assign you protection, Dr. Sasse."

"I can handle that." Blue said, his voice gruff. "The best protection money can buy. He won't get near you, Romy."

God, was this really happening? Romy closed her eyes and asked herself if she was really that shocked. Dacre would never have accepted her leaving him ... but to kill all these innocent victims to send her a message? "Why didn't he just kill me?" Her voice was quiet and surprisingly calm.

"Don't." Blue was barely holding onto his composure. The detective smiled at them.

"You've been unbelievably brave and helpful in coming forward. Go home and get some rest. I'll be in touch."

ROMY ASKED Blue to drive her to her mother's house. "I want them all to know what's going on—it's not fair to them not to know that they might in danger too. Dacre is a monster."

Her heart sank, however, when they got to her mother's house. Gaius was there too, meeting with his father.

Magda knew something was wrong, clearly, as she gazed at her middle daughter. "Romy?"

Blue took Romy's hand. "Magda, Dad ... we have something to tell you. Two things. One, we hope you'll be happy about, because we are. Romy and I have been seeing each other for a while now, and Magda, I'm so in love with your daughter ..."

Magda exclaimed in delight and threw her arms around them. "I thought I sensed something!"

Stuart grinned widely, clapping his son on the back. "Son, I'm delighted for you both."

"Oh, Romy ... sweetheart, finally. I'm so happy you found a good man at long last." Magda was in tears, and Romy teared up a little too before adding to the overall level of emotion.

"Mom ...There's something else."

Gaius, smirking in the background, leaned forward, his eyes glittering with spite. "Don't be shy, sis, tell us."

Romy flushed at the jibe, but she felt Blue squeeze her hand. "Shut the fuck up, Gaius; this isn't the time for your malice. Magda, Dad, I'm afraid that it isn't all good news. We think Dacre Mortimer is in Seattle."

"God, no." Magda went pale and clutched at her daughter's hand. "Sit down with us, sweethearts, and tell us what's going on."

As Romy told them about the murders, about the signature that had led her to suspect Dacre was behind them. "I knew, or I should have known, he would come after me. He has nothing to lose by murdering me. His family has already cut him off; revenge is all he has left."

Blue cleared his throat and Romy looked at him. His beautiful eyes were deeply troubled and she could feel the tension in his body. "Dad ... I've already set the ball rolling for added protection. I know it's inconvenient, especially with the wedding coming up, but I won't risk any of us getting hurt." He paused, then glanced at his half-brother. "Gaius, you too. And I think perhaps you'd better clue your mother in, too."

"That's very thoughtful of you." Gaius's voice was a monotone and Romy couldn't tell whether he was being sincere or not. She studied him ... the malice had gone from his eyes and he didn't smile. He looked at her. "As long as you're okay, Romy, that's all *I* care about."

Fucker. That tone was back in his voice, the intimate one, the one that said *I know you better than you know.* His smirk was back too. Romy looked away from him. Blue pressed his lips against her temple.

"*Piccolo*, I know this is fast, but I'd feel a hell of a lot better if you moved in with me."

"I would too, Romy," her mother added quickly, and Romy nodded.

"Fine. Yes, of course. God, I'm sorry about this, everyone."

Magda looked angry now. "Listen here, my girl, you have nothing to be sorry about. It's that ... asshole. He should have gone to jail when he hurt you last year. Bastard. I could kill him with my bare hands. I will if he ever comes in spitting distance of me."

LATER, when Blue and Romy got back to his apartment, Blue made her drink some hot tea, Romy shivering uncontrollably. "I thought it was all over," she said in a low voice, "I was so stupid."

"No." Blue wrapped his arms around her, kissing her gently. "There are crazy people all around. It has nothing to do with any choices you've made in life. I won't let anything happen to you."

Romy leaned into him. "It's weird. I'm scared, but at the same time, I can't recall ever being as happy as I am with you right now. I love you, Blue."

"And I love you, baby. Maybe we should go away for a while."

Romy shook her head. "He'll just kill more people. If he knows I'm here, he can try and get to me and then we'll have him."

"Christ, Romy, you're not bait, here." Blue's voice rose and then fell just as quickly. "Sorry, I didn't mean to snap, but we have to take this seriously. You saw what he did to Yasmin Levant."

"I did see," Romy said quietly. "I watched her die, remember? Right alongside you."

Blue blanched and yanked her hard into his chest. "I'm sorry, baby. Forgive me, *piccolo*. I didn't mean—I just—the thought of you in harm's way makes me insane."

She curled into his warm, hard strength. "I won't deliberately put myself in his sights, but once we confirm it is him ... maybe, just maybe I can help catch him. I need to do *something*, Blue. Those poor girls."

Blue drew in a deep breath. "For tonight, let's just ... try and forget him. This place is secure. Tomorrow I'll call in a security team. Baby, do you feel safe?"

"With you, always." She kissed him and he stroked her face, half-smiling.

"Regardless of the circumstances, I'm glad you're here. I was thinking about asking you to move in this morning, but then the sensible part of me said it might scare you off."

Romy smiled at him. "It might have done this morning, although I loved waking up with you." She sighed. "I hate that the reason I'm here is that bastard."

"No," Blue said, his lips brushing her, "the reason you're here is that we love each other."

"You got that right, Doc." Romy pressed her body against his, and Blue held her tightly.

"Are you tired, *piccolo*?"

Romy smiled. "No ... but I am starving."

Blue laughed. "Of course, forgive me. Well, how about some old fashioned Italian comfort food?"

"Pasta? Sold. Shall we order in?"

Blue pretended to look affronted. "How dare you?"

Romy giggled. "You can cook?"

Blue got up and pulled her to her feet, throwing her over his shoulder and carrying her to his state-of-the-art kitchen. "Can I cook? I'm Italian, *piccolo*. Sit here," he dumped her onto a stool, "and watch the maestro at work."

Romy watched him cook pasta, rolling out the dough and making the ravioli with deft efficiency. He kept up a stream of instructions, just as he did in the operating theater, and when the pasta was cooked, Romy almost swooned at the garlicky, oozy, buttery taste.

"God, Allende," she mumbled over a huge mouthful, "is there anything you're not good at?"

He pretended to consider, then shrugged. "Nope." He laughed as she threw her napkin at him.

"There's one thing you didn't think of, Dr. Wonderpants. I now have garlic breath."

"Ha," he said, "so do I." He pressed his lips against hers and they both decided that it wasn't an issue as the kiss deepened and soon the remnants of the pasta were forgotten as Blue tumbled her to the floor.

FOR THE NEXT FEW HOURS, Blue did his best to make her forget everything else but the blissful release of making love, but as the night wore on and he fell asleep, Romy lay awake.

Just as I find happiness, Dacre comes for me. Bastard.

Now that the fear had dissipated a little, she felt anger at the injustice of it. All those innocent girls. Romy eased out of Blue's arms and got out of bed, walking to the huge picture window that looked out over Seattle. Romy leaned her forehead against the cold glass and stared down at the streets below.

Wherever you are, Dacre, come for me. I'm ready for you, you piece of shit. Come for me.

I'm ready.

CHAPTER ELEVEN

N*ew Orleans*

JUNO SASSE SPRAWLED on her friend's couch and watched as Livia balanced a plate of cookies on her huge, pregnant belly. Juno grinned at her. "I can't believe you're having a baby, Livvy. When you think where you were a year ago."

Livia Chatelaine smiled at her friend. "You're not the only one who can't believe it, darling. When Sandor stabbed me, then put that bullet in me, I thought that was it. I was a goner. Still, that's in the past." She smoothed her dress over her bump. "And this little girl is almost here. I cannot wait."

Juno grinned. "My first niece."

"You betcha. Speaking of which, you haven't filled me in on what your sisters are up to. Has Arti married Glen yet? What about Romy? Does she like the hospital in Seattle?"

"So many questions," Juno laughed. "Okay, in order, *no, they broke up; she's fine*; and *yes*."

Livia almost spat out her cookie. "Glen and Arti what?"

"They split," Juno repeated. "It wasn't a nasty breakup or anything, they'd just grown apart."

"Wow. So much for fairy tales," Livia muttered in dismay. "Except mine. I won't deny I'm living the dream. Poor Arti though."

"I think she's much happier, actually," Juno said. "Now, the real gossip is Romy. Talk about fairy tales. She's in love ... with our soon-to-be step-brother Blue. Here ..." She grabbed Livia's iPad and typed something in, then showed Livia the photo of Blue Allende. Livia's eyes opened wide.

"Wow, he's gorgeous ... and he and Romy?"

"Are fucking each other's brains out. They've only just told Mom and Stuart, but I knew a while back."

Livia grinned at Juno's smug expression. "They told you?"

"No, I went for coffee with them unexpectedly, and it was so obvious." Her smile faded. "After what Romy's ex did to her ..."

Livia nodded, her eyes sad. "And they think he's the one behind the murders?"

"Yup. God, the thought of something happening to her again ... she's so tiny, Liv, and she can kick ass, believe me, but Dacre is a sick fuck."

Livia pushed herself from her chair, somewhat awkwardly, and came to hug her friend. "Juno, you can't let it rule your life. I bet Romy is back at work today, saving lives. I remember when Sandor was waging his campaign ... the thought of him hurting Nox or Odelle ... if Romy feels half the anger I did, she won't let Dacre near her or anyone she loves."

Juno felt comforted by her friend's words and when she was in bed later, in the sumptuous guestroom of Nox and Livia's mansion, she called Romy, surprised when her sister picked up straight away.

"Well timed, Juno Boo." Romy sounded cheerful, "I just got

out of a four-hour surgery and am on a break. How's NOLA? How are Livvy and gorgeous Nox?"

"New Orleans is warm," Juno teased, hearing Romy's jealous groan. "Livvy is blooming, about to pop any second, and Nox is, well, delicious as always. You okay, Romulus?"

"I am good," Romy said determinedly. "No fucker is messing with me."

"You got seriously laid last night, didn't you?" Juno laughed as her sister giggled.

"Last night, this morning, and as soon as Blue finishes up, in about five minutes. The on-call room is free."

"Babe, you've turned into a nympho. Seriously, though, are you okay?"

"I really, really am, Boo. Please don't worry."

Juno heard voices in the background and then the familiar voice of Blue. She heard her sister laugh. "I guess you need to, um, get off ... the phone, I mean."

Romy laughed. "You guessed, right. You're okay, though, right?"

"I am. I really am. I'll talk to you tomorrow."

"Okay. I love you."

"Love you too."

Juno clicked off her phone and snuggled down in her bed. Romy sounded happy, and not cowed by what was happening, and Juno had to be happy with that. She fell asleep and was woken three hours later by Livia shouting to Nox that the baby was coming.

SEATTLE

Romy moaned as Blue's cock thrust deeper and deeper inside her, his lips hungry on hers, on her throat, sucking at her nipples as he fucked her. She gripped his dark curls tightly, their lovemaking animal and feral.

"Christ, woman, you drive me crazy," Blue groaned, slamming his hips against hers, sinking balls deep into her ready and swollen cunt. Romy was almost delirious with pleasure and her orgasm hit hard, leaving her breathless and with her head swimming. Blue came, shooting thick, creamy cum deep inside her belly and she clamped her legs around him, keeping him locked inside of her. His dark brown hair was damp with sweat, his skin salty, his eyes sleepy with love and pure desire. He was so beautiful, Romy wanted to cry.

She stroked his face, tracing a small scar on his cheek. "How did you get that?"

Blue smiled. "I wish I could tell you something cool, but I fell off my bike when I was a kid."

"That's not *un*cool."

"The bike still had training wheels. And I *still* fell off of it." Blue looked aggrieved as Romy started to laugh.

"Klutz. Sexy klutz, but still."

Blue shrugged, grinning. "I wasn't as suave as I am now."

Romy snorted. "Suave. You didn't realize at dinner two nights ago that you had marinara sauce all over your pretty face, Allende."

"I did. I was just hoping to entice you to lick it off."

"Ah," Romy nodded wisely. "You know me well, doctor."

"I know you well enough to know that food, any food, can charm you like a snake."

Romy kissed him as he looked smug. "Speaking of snake, put that incredible cock of yours back in me, boss."

Blue laughed. "Hmm, boss, I like that." He hitched her legs around his waist again, his cock already hard again. He slid into her and Romy sighed happily, winding her arms around his neck.

"You know, boss, if you like that ... I'd be willing to be dominated ... in bed. For you? God, yeah, that would be such a turn on."

He pinched her nipple hard and she yelped in surprise but it made her cunt flood with arousal. "Oh, you're wet, baby girl," Blue said, and slammed his cock deeper into her. They made love, clawing, biting, hungry for the other until they both came again, then, making sure their pagers were on, they wrapped their arms around one other and fell asleep.

Just after midnight, the door to the on-call room opened and Mac peered in, spotting them in the small puddle of light from the hallway. Romy heard the door open and she and Mac smiled at each other. Mac touched his hand over his heart and blew her a kiss, backing out of the room, and Romy felt safe and loved. *No one is going to take this away from me,* she thought, and closed her eyes, locked in the embrace of the man she loved.

DACRE HAD SEEN Romy go into the on-call room with Blue Allende and his gut had twisted with rage. He knew the police were looking for him but they had old photos of him, photos before he'd shaved his head and grown a thick beard, adding piercings, a neck tattoo, and thick spectacles. He'd bulked up too; it made the killings easier if they couldn't match his physical strength.

Gaius Eames had arranged the new identity so he could apply for the orderly job at Rainier Hope. Dacre still didn't trust the man; he wondered why he hated his half-brother so much when Gaius seemed to have unlimited resources. Maybe Gaius wanted Romy too, and if so, Dacre wouldn't stand for that. Romy was his. She hadn't even recognized him the time she'd asked him direct questions; she was friendly and polite, joking around with the patients and with him. He'd changed his voice too, whiskey and cigarettes lowering his register. No one, not even his damn parents, would recognize Dacre Mortimer, preppy Harvard grad, now.

Gaius Eames had asked of him one favor. "Don't kill your ex-wife yet," he'd said. "I want Blue to really fall for her so when she dies, he'll be destroyed."

Dacre gritted his teeth. "The thought of his hands on her …"

Gaius had smiled. "Think of the ways you could punish her, Mortimer. Those girls you killed had it easy compared to what you're going to do to the lovely Romy."

Dacre had liked the sound of that, so he'd agreed. Working at the hospital was another one of Gaius's ideas as was the small studio apartment close to the hospital.

Now, as he heard the door of the on-call room click closed, he knew that Allende had his hands all over his Romy and it made him rage. Dacre checked his watch—his shift was over in five minutes. He paused, entertaining the fantasy of storming into the on-call room and butchering his ex-wife and her lover. Instead, he finished up his shift and left the hospital. His body tingled with rage and the need to kill. Gaius had told him his little game of killing women with Romy's initials had been found out—good, it meant she was scared.

Dacre went home, ate a sparse meal of microwave hot dogs, and sucked down a couple of beers. He watched TV mindlessly for a few hours, then, just after midnight, headed out into the city. He was careful always to wear black so that the blood of his victims would not show up on his clothes and when he returned home, he would seal those clothes into a sack and burn them in the furnace at work.

Tonight, he looked for anyone who resembled Romy. He found her working at a bar downtown, followed her when she closed up for the night, took her at the end of an alleyway, and dragged her into the darkness. She was beautiful, with long, dark, wavy hair, doe-eyed, petite. He overpowered her easily and as the knife sank deep into her flesh, Dacre felt the usual release. Staring at the girl unseeing, all he thought of was how it would feel to kill Romy like this, his blade slicing through her tender flesh, severing arteries, destroying her vital organs. This girl died too quickly, his knife cutting through her abdominal aorta clumsily, though he usually liked to draw it out.

He lowered her to the ground as she struggled for life, ripping her shirt open, and finishing her with a few brutal stabs. The girl, her eyes wide with terror and agony, made a gurgling sound as blood filled her throat, then went still. Dacre stood, breathing heavily, staring down at her, only seeing Romy's face on this girl's brutalized body.

Dacre sucked in lungfuls of air, smelling the rust-and-salt smell of his victim's blood, then, leaving her for others to find, walked slowly back home and feel into a deep, peaceful sleep.

CHAPTER TWELVE

Stuart Eames looked up as his soon-to-be-ex-wife approached the table. He stood, dutifully kissing her on the cheek, and pulled out her chair for her. Hilary Eames smiled and sat down.

"Always the gentleman."

Stuart tried not to roll his eyes. Hilary was obviously in one of her seductive moods. "You look well, Hilary."

She smiled. "You too. Magda Sasse is obviously looking after you ... and I hear her daughter is looking after the Italian, too."

Stuart sighed. "His name is Blue as you well know, Hilary, and yes, he and Romy are seeing each other."

"Keeping it in the family."

He grimaced in disgust. "I didn't come here to talk about Blue's love life, Hilary. We agreed to meet to finalize the divorce, so shall we stick to that topic?"

Hilary smirked. Stuart studied her. Hilary had once been considered a beautiful woman, but now she was stick-thin, gaunt, brittle. Her dark hair, once her crowning glory, was now coiffed to hide the hairpieces she used to create the illusion of lustrousness, her blue eyes ringed with kohl, hard lines. Her full lips—enhanced by fillers—made her look slightly ridiculous. Her cheekbones were jutting out and even the amount of make-up she wore couldn't conceal the greyness of her skin, the pinched look from denying herself food.

Being rich and thin was the overriding reason Hilary lived— that and to cause misery to those she felt envious of. Stuart wondered how he could ever have loved this woman; she was Magda's antithesis.

"So, you dropping your claim to the financial settlement has me wondering—what are you up to, Hilary?"

Hilary hid a smile behind her water glass. "I thought you'd be happy."

"Who is he? I know there must be a 'he' because otherwise there isn't a chance in hell you'd relinquish my money unless you had someone else lined up."

"You think so little of me?"

Stuart stayed silent rather than lie. Hilary shrugged. "Not that it's any of your business, Stuart, but Giles is ..."

"Giles?" Suddenly Stuart started to laugh. "You mean Giles St. Clement? *Lord* Giles St. Clement? Oh, Hilly, you really are so transparent."

Hilary's face contorted in anger. "If you must know, Giles and I are in love, and as soon as the divorce comes through, we are to be married."

"And you're moving to London? I can see it now. High tea with the prime minister as you peddle your faux-manitarian causes. Blow jobs abound and suddenly, Lady St. Clement, you're receiving titles of your own. Honorary damehoods, perhaps?"

Stuart hadn't meant to be so cutting—it wasn't his style, and this meeting was, after all, to make sure Hilary did sign the divorce papers—and now he realized he had gone too far. Hilary's eyes glittered with spite.

"What's it to you who I marry, or who I 'blow,' as you so crudely put it? This is what I want, Stuart, just like your pathetic little hippie is who you want. Aren't you glad I'll be out of your life for good?"

Stuart shrugged. "Sure ... I just hope Giles knows what he's let himself in for."

"Fuck you, Stuart. I never loved you; I was stupid to think I did."

Stuart's smile faded. "You think I don't know that? And you made Bianca's life a misery too."

"She spawned your precious lovechild, the saint-like Blue. If you only knew, Stuart, about your bastard son."

"What the hell is that supposed to mean?" Stuart was irked now but Hilary just smiled.

"You have two sons, Stuart. Isn't it about time you concentrated on your firstborn? Gaius tells me he feels shut out of your new family."

"That's not even close to true, Hilary. Gaius just tells you what you want to hear, because it suits him to feel like the redheaded stepchild. Magda has made great efforts to include him. Far more efforts than you made with Blue."

"You're just surrounded by saint-like people, aren't you?"

Stuart gritted his teeth. This was more like the Hilary he knew—spiteful, resentful, vindictive. "I really think we should stick to signing these papers. Do you want lunch, Hilary?"

She shook her head, dismissive. "I don't have time." She took the papers from him and scrawled her signature where he indicated. Stuart put the signed papers back in his jacket pocket.

"Thank you. I wish you well, Hilary."

Hilary smiled at him and for a brief second, Stuart could see the beautiful woman she had once been. Then the malice crept back in her face. "Tell your girlfriend's daughter to watch out for Blue ... he isn't what he says he is."

.   .   .

HILARY'S last words were still bugging Stuart as he drove back to Magda's home. They had decided that he would move in with her after the wedding, selling his massive condo. "I don't need it," he'd told her, "this is home to me now."

Magda saw the preoccupation on his face and Stuart told her what Hilary had said. Magda shrugged it off. "She's just trying to upset you. Blue is a good man; we all know that."

Stuart sighed. "I know. I just don't trust Hilary not to go screw things up for him. She loathed Bianca, and barely even spoke to Blue —until, get this, until he was a young teenager and started to blossom into his looks. Then she would show him off like a trophy. Blue isn't like Gaius. He hated being paraded around like a prize. As soon as he was eighteen, he left home, just to get away from her. I confess, I helped him move out." He sat and rubbed his face, but then smiled at Magda. "But all that aside, she signed the papers."

Magda grinned and sat down on his knees. "You're a free man?"

"I'm a free man ... so, officially, Magdalena Helen Sasse ... would you do me the great honor of marrying me?"

Magda laughed, and nodded. "I will, Stuart Gregory Eames. I really will ... and if you'll have me, on Christmas Day."

Stuart grinned, knowing the arrangements were almost in place for their wedding. He kissed her tenderly, gazing up into her navy-blue eyes. "I can't wait, my darling. I can't wait."

Romy was concentrating so hard on the practice dummy she was performing a surgery on that she didn't see Mac sidle into the room until he poked her side and made her jump. "Dude! You just killed my patient."

Mac laughed. "Nah, she was a goner anyway. So ..."

Romy hid a grin. "Yes?"

"You and Doc Allende?"

Romy flushed, but smiled. "Pretty much."

"How long?"

"A couple of months."

"Rom?" She looked up to see his smile. "Is it love?"

She nodded, flushing again. "It is. I'm crazy about him."

"Good. You get your man, girl. It's not like it's a huge surprise to anyone."

Romy looked at him sharply. "What?"

Mac held his hands up. "Slow your roll. I didn't tell anyone. But the chemistry between the two of you speaks for itself."

He watched her for a few minutes as she worked. "Rom? Did you hear? More murders."

Romy's hand slipped and she cussed, ripping off her gloves to see the small gash in the top of her finger. Mac helped her to clean it up. "Girl, why were you wearing gloves to operate on a dummy?"

"Habit," she said, "ouch."

"Sorry. Look, it just needs cleaning and a stitch is all. No biggie. Want me to do it?"

"Please."

Mac studied her face as he helped her. "I know you think these killings are your fault. They're not, babe. They are the work of a very sick, very bad man. Do you know how many times I thank God that he didn't kill you that day? And I didn't even know you back then. You're a survivor, Romy."

"But what does that mean when innocent women are being killed because of me?"

"It's not because of you!" Mac said angrily. "God, I could kill Dacre Mortimer with my bare hands. Have the police told you anything about their search?"

Romy shook her head. "He could be anywhere, Mac."

"Except here. We have his picture up at every entrance, all

the security team has been advised to look out, all the reception staff."

"I know, and I'm grateful. Thanks, Mac."

He finished treating her finger. "You deserve happy, Romy. We can all see that you and Blue make each other happy. Live that, not the past."

Romy hugged her friend. "Thanks, Mac."

ROMY WENT to find Blue afterward, eager to see him and kiss him but as she approached his office door, she could hear him arguing. "No ... no way. I do not want to see you or talk to you. Why can't you get that into your head?"

Romy stopped, listening but she couldn't hear anyone replying. It must be a phone call. Feeling guilty, she hovered just outside the door. She heard him sigh. "Look, I don't know why you're bringing this up now. Perhaps you heard I'm in love with someone else? I thought so. Keep your less-than-subtle threats and go fuck yourself." She heard him slam the phone down and mutter to himself. Romy waited a beat then knocked at his door.

Blue looked up and for a second, his face was stormy, dark, beautiful—and terrifying. When he realized who it was, the storm cleared and he grinned at her. "Why are you knocking, baby? Come here."

Romy went into his arms and he kissed her tenderly, his eyes never leaving hers. "God, I love you, woman."

Romy chuckled. "Right back at you. I just came to see the schedule of surgeries—and to kiss your face off, of course.

"Of course." He pulled her onto his lap and reached for the schedule. "Light, today, unless we get any emergencies." He stroked her hair back from her face. "After the lap, you could duck out and go Christmas shopping if you want. I'll cover."

"Nah. That's what Amazon.com is for." Romy leaned her

cheek against his and closed her eyes. She was so curious as to who he had been talking to, but couldn't bring herself to ask. "I did some serious shopping at lunch. Speaking of which ... I have no idea what to get you."

"All I need is you, baby." Blue kissed her. "If I have you, I have everything."

Romy grinned. "Mushy. Okay, so I'll ask your dad."

"Like he'll know. Honestly, Romy, I don't need anything." He twirled a lock of her hair around his finger. "How about this? Instead of exchanging gifts, we go away together after Christmas."

Romy smiled. "Is this you trying to get me out of Seattle again?"

"A little," Blue admitted with a wry smile. "But also, I keep dreaming of us in a rustic Italian villa, making love in the olive groves. My fantasy is you in a summer dress, no underwear, and me fucking you against a cypress tree, my cock buried deep in your silky cunt, my fingers stroking your clit, my tongue in your mouth ..."

Romy, turned on, groaned. "God, Blue ..."

Grinning wickedly, he snaked his hand into her top, pulling it down over one breast, sliding the lacy cup of her bra down and taking her nipple into his mouth. His other hand slid slowly up her thigh, under her skirt, caressing her through her increasingly damp panties, then slipping underneath to stroke her clit. "I'll fuck you so hard that the whole of Tuscany will hear you come, beautiful girl."

Romy buried her head in his neck. "Blue ... God, I'm so wet for you."

In a flash he had swept her onto the couch, locked the door, and flicked the light off. The whole back wall of his office was glass and Romy glanced quickly to see if anyone could see in. Blue grinned down at her as he unzipped his pants and tugged her underwear off. "Maybe we'll get caught, baby."

His smile, his words, sent a thrill through her and he plunged his ramrod-hard cock into her and they fucked deliriously, not caring if they were caught. Romy sighed as she came, feeling him pumping his seed deep inside her. "God, we're such a pair of sex fiends."

Blue chuckled. "Yes, we are."

Laughing and talking, they tidied themselves up and went back to work. The routine laparotomy went easily and afterwards, Blue took Romy out to dinner.

ROMY DIDN'T KNOW when she started to feel uneasy, but in the car on the way home, she kept looking behind them, as if she had seen something. Blue frowned at her. "You okay, baby?"

Romy nodded, but her chest was tight. "I don't know why but I feel like ... someone was watching us."

"In my office?"

She shook her head. "No, at the restaurant. I went to the bathroom, and I could have sworn ... no, never mind. I'm just being paranoid." She glanced behind them again.

Blue looked in the rearview mirror. "Sweetheart, if your instincts are telling you something, we should listen to them. Do you think we're being followed?"

Romy didn't want to sound insane but Blue's expression was serious. "It's crazy, but yes. There's a dark sedan that's been following us all the way from the restaurant."

"Gotcha." With deftness and skill, Blue pulled the car off the freeway and onto a side street. He made a circuit of the almost deserted business district, and then circled back towards his apartment. "How about now?"

Romy was watching carefully. "I can't see it anymore. I'm sorry, honey, maybe I was imagining it."

"Better safe than not."

She smiled gratefully at him. "I promise I'm not a hysterical female."

Blue laughed. "Would never have crossed my mind that you were."

As they parked the car in the garage beneath his building, Romy couldn't resist checking out the other cars there. Blue grinned at her. "Still being super spy?"

"You got me."

He took her hand. "Come on, Black Widow, let's go home and cuddle some."

In the elevator, alone, he kissed her tenderly. "You know, if you want, we could look for somewhere together. We don't have to stay here."

"I love your apartment," she said, leaning into him, feeling his arms tightening around her. She reached down and squeeze his cock through his jeans and he grinned.

"Insatiable."

"You know it."

He was still laughing when he unlocked the door to his apartment and held it for her. "After you, ma'am."

Romy's laughter echoed through the hallway but when she got into the living room, her smile faded. She heard Blue cuss behind her.

"What the fuck?"

The naked dark-haired woman slowly spread her legs with a wide smile on her face. "Hello, darling Blue. Is this your new toy? Would she like to play with us?"

Romy's whole body was icy cold. She slowly turned to Blue. "I take it back. I hate your apartment."

She pushed past him, wrenching her arm free when he grabbed it. "No, baby, wait, this isn't what it—"

But Romy ran, slamming the door behind her, her sobs wracking and desiccating.

HILARY EAMES STOOD up and sashayed over to her stepson. "Flighty, isn't she?"

Blue, his anger threatening to overwhelm him, glowered at her. "What the fuck do you think you're doing, Hilary?"

She touched his cheek and he flinched away. She smiled. "Just reclaiming what is mine, Blue."

"Get *out*." Blue clenched his fists to stop himself from physically hauling her out of his apartment. "Now, Hilary, and don't ever come back."

Hilary pretended to pout. "Come on. Don't you remember the fun we used to have? God, you were like a Roman god back then." She studied him. "Now ... you look tired, Blue. She's exhausting you, making you pretend that you're good enough for her when you and I know differently, don't we?"

"Get out now, Hilary, or I won't be responsible for what I'll do."

Hilary smirked. "Fine. I'll go. You know where to call me."

"Don't hold your breath. You know what you did to me. Don't pretend it was anything more than ..." Blue squeezed his eyes shut, trying to erase the memories, the feelings from back when he was just a kid.

"Call it what you will, Blue." Hilary reached down and squeezed his groin. "You may tell one story, but your magnificent cock told another."

Blue did lose his temper then, and taking her by the upper arm, hauled Hilary to the door and threw her out. A bright flash blinded him, and he realized that a paparazzo had been waiting outside his door to take a photo of him throwing a naked and grinning Hilary from his home.

But Romy was all he could think about, out there, unprotected. Blue called the security firm. "Find her. Protect her. She won't want to see me at the moment and that's fine. But, please, keep her safe."

"Will do, boss."

CHAPTER THIRTEEN

Running out into the midnight streets, Romy kept going until she could not breathe any longer. Stopping, dragging much needed oxygen into her lungs, she allowed herself to feel the pain of what had just happened in and it bent her double. "God ... *God.*"

Slowly, as her breathing returned to normal, she began to walk, dazed. She knew it wasn't safe to do this but at this moment, the pain of Blue's betrayal seemed to overwhelm any fear that Dacre might catch up with her.

Come for me now, Dacre, and end this pain for me. I don't care anymore.

She sat down on a low wall and put her head in her hands, willing the tears to stop.

God, how stupid was I? To think a man like Blue wouldn't have a fleet of women in his past. How long ago had he slept with this one? Who the fuck was she? She was beautiful, if skinny as hell, but way too old for him. Jesus, that's what you're focusing on, Sasse?

Fuck. Romy wiped her eyes. She'd call a cab and get them to pick her up at the end of the street. She was dialing when a silver Audi pulled up beside her. She began to walk quicker, nervous now.

"Romy?"

She stopped, turning towards the speaker. Gaius smiled at her. "What on earth are you doing out here so late?"

"I ..." Romy didn't know what to say. "Blue was called in for an emergency and I decided to try and find a cab." Lame as hell.

"Girl, get in. With your rabid ex on the loose, you really do not need to be out on the streets alone."

"I'm fine." Her voice shook, betraying her. Gaius got out and came to her.

"Come on, sweetheart. I'll take you home."

Romy let him put her in his passenger seat and drive away from Blue's neighborhood. Gaius looked over at her, concerned.

"Are you okay?"

Romy nodded. "Would you mind taking me to my sister's place? To Artemis's place?" She gave him the address and then smiled tentatively at him. "Thanks, Gaius."

"It's no problem ... but are you sure you're okay? You look upset."

"I'm fine."

"You said that already."

Romy gave a half-hearted laugh. "Just tired."

She stared out of the car window. The shock was dissipating now, and Romy was beginning to regret running away. She should have stood her ground and gone toe to toe with the whore in Blue's flat. Romy gritted her teeth. Then again, why the hell hadn't Blue come after her?

Was it the guilt of being caught? God. Romy closed her eyes. The pain in her chest was killing her. Had she gotten him so wrong?

No. She was sure of Blue's love for her, utterly sure. There had to be some kind of rational explanation for it.

Gaius left her alone on the journey, only turning to her as they turned into Artemis's street. "Are you sure I can't do anything else for you, Romy?"

"No, thank you again, Gaius." A thought occurred to her. "What were you doing in Blue's neighborhood tonight?"

"Just hoping to see my brother for a few minutes. Nothing important."

That didn't ring true, but Romy didn't have the energy to press the point. She got out, then bent down to thank him again.

Gaius smiled at her. "It's no problem. If you need anything, I'm always here for you, Romy. Always."

She watched him drive away, then dug in her purse for the key. All of the sisters had keys to each other's houses and Romy was glad she wouldn't have to wake Arti up. She snuck into the house, but halfway up the stairs her phone beeped. She knew it had to be Blue.

Baby, where are you? I swear it wasn't how it looked—but of course I would say that. Please believe me, her being here was nothing to do with us. Please just let me know you're safe. I love you.

Romy sighed, all her anger dissipated.

We'll talk tomorrow, Blue. That's all I can promise right now. I'm at Arti's for the night. I'm safe.

Of course. Just know I love you.

I love you too. Tomorrow.

Tomorrow.

Romy climbed up the stairs wearily, and slipped into Arti's guest bedroom. She stripped down to her underwear and into bed—only to encounter bare flesh. She shrieked, as did the other person in the bed, and Romy skittered across the room to switch the light on.

A young woman with dark hair and huge brown eyes was staring at her, her hand clamped over her mouth.

"Who are you?" Romy asked, breathless, but the girl didn't

have time to answer before Artemis burst into the room, followed by a giant of a man who looked familiar. Romy gaped at him. "Dan? Dan Helmond?"

The man grinned widely, a strange counterpoint to the three women all in shock. "Romy Sasse, as I live and breathe. I take it you've met my daughter and your mini-me, Octavia. Tavia, meet Romy Sasse, Artemis's sister."

Romy and her younger double stared at each other for a long moment before Romy, not knowing what else to do, burst out laughing.

CHAPTER FOURTEEN

Romy shrugged, recounting the story to her sister. "So I just walked out. Wouldn't you?"

Artemis, sitting opposite her sister at the breakfast bar, chewed on her toast thoughtfully. "Maybe. No, probably not. You know me, I would have demanded a full and detailed explanation."

"With color-coding."

Artemis grinned as Dan and Octavia laughed. "And, you, sis, are the firebrand, so I guess I can't blame you for walking away."

Romy sighed. "I told Blue I'd meet him this morning in the city. Don't suppose you could give me a ride?"

"I can." Octavia said, spooning the last of her cereal into her mouth, "I have to go to the library, it's no problem."

Romy grinned at her. "Thanks, dude. I still can't get over how alike we look. Daniel, are you sure you didn't fool around with my mom when we were back in high school?"

The women laughed as Dan held up his hands. "All I'm saying is Magda is a beautiful woman."

"Dad! God, you're so embarrassing." Octavia hid her face in her hands as her father smirked.

Romy snorted with laughter and poked Octavia. "Come on then, twinsie, let's get going."

ON THE DRIVE into the city, Romy and Octavia chatted easily, then Octavia smiled at her.

"Artemis told me you are actually a twin. I'm sorry about your brother."

Romy felt a lump in her throat. "Thanks ... I miss him still, even though it's been over twenty years."

"What happened? If you don't mind telling me."

Romy cleared her throat. "Not at all." Her voice quivered a little but she ignored it. "It was so quick, such a normal moment in a normal day. He fell over in the school yard. He was playing with some friends and tripped and hit his head. For a few hours he was okay, and then the next morning, Mom found him dead in bed from a hemorrhage."

Even now, Romy remembered the agony of seeing her twin, the person closest to her, blue- lipped and lifeless.

Octavia had tears in her eyes. "I'm so sorry, Romy."

"You know what it's like to lose someone, Tavia. It never gets easier; you just get used to the pain."

Octavia nodded. "I know. Mom fought cancer twice, once before she had me. That time she won, and was determined that it wouldn't stop her and Dad from having kids. They went through seven rounds of IVF before one took. Sometimes I wonder if having me, putting her body through all of that, made her weaker and allowed the cancer back in."

Romy squeezed her hand. "No, honey, it doesn't work like that. And, believe me, she would have taken the cancer over and over again if it meant having you in her life."

Octavia looked tearful. "Thank you, Romy." She laughed a little through her tears. "I wish you *were* my sister."

"How about we pretend we are? After all, it looks like Arti and your dad are pretty much solid—so that makes you family. Of course, I would technically be your step-aunt—but sister sounds better, right?"

Octavia grinned at Romy. "Deal."

OCTAVIA DROPPED Romy off at the breakfast place and waved goodbye. Romy drew in a deep lungful of oxygen and went inside, seeing Blue was already waiting for her. His green eyes were troubled, wary, but Romy allowed him to pull her into a hug. "Thank you for coming, baby."

Romy leaned into him, breathing in his woodsy, clean scent. "Let's talk."

They ordered eggs and toast with strong black coffee and Romy waited. Blue looked at her. "I have no idea how she got into my apartment, but I swear to you, Romy, I'm not sleeping with her."

"Who is she?"

Blue hesitated. "An ex-patient who got a little too close."

"Did you sleep with her before you knew me?" Romy was watching his expression carefully. *Don't lie, please don't lie.*

Again, Blue paused. "It's more complicated than that."

His answer irked Romy. "Either you had sex with her or not, Blue."

His expression was unreadable then in a low voice. "Technically, I did have intercourse with her."

"What does that mean?"

"Romy ... I have a past, and some things are too painful, too scarring to discuss. You should know that."

Ouch. "Don't try and weasel out of this by bringing up Dacre, Blue."

"I'm not trying to weasel out of anything. It is what it is."

Romy sighed. She wanted to believe Blue, but there was something in her gut instinct making it difficult. "But you're no longer involved with her?"

"No, nor any other woman. Believe me, Romy, you are my love, my life." He leaned forward and brushed her lips with his. She didn't pull away. "Nothing will ever change that. As far as I'm concerned, you and me? We're endgame."

Romy felt a rush of warmth inside her at his words. "We are?"

"*Yes.*" This time his words were defiant, determined. Blue held her gaze steadily. "I love you."

Romy half smiled. "I love you too, Doc."

"Can we move past this?"

She considered for a long moment then nodded. "I guess we can. But no more beautiful naked women in the apartment."

Blue grinned. "Unless it's you."

Romy laughed then, her tension falling away. "Unless it's me. And get your locks changed, would you? If she could get in that easily, anyone could."

"Already done," he said grimly, "And the building's security team got a tongue-lashing as well."

"Maybe we should look for somewhere together."

Blue nodded. "I'd like that. I want to be somewhere of both our choosing."

Romy was dreaming now. "Maybe out on one of the islands? I ..." Her attention was suddenly caught by the flat screen TV in the corner of the diner. Blue's face flashed up, followed by a photograph of the naked woman being thrown out of his apartment, and Blue's shocked, angry face behind her. With a sledgehammer-like shock to her heart, Romy read the headline.

. . .

Prominent Seattle surgeon in late-night tryst with naked step-mother, socialite Hilary Eames. Photographer captures moment lover's tiff escalates into public humiliation.

Romy felt her throat fill with vomit. "Oh my God ..." She breathed and turned on a shocked Blue. "An ex-patient, huh? You sick, perverted *fuck ... Jesus,* Blue, your own stepmother?"

"It wasn't like that, I swear." Blue's voice was gravelly, broken, his shoulders slumped, but Romy had no sympathy.

"How could you?" She didn't wait for an answer but darted to the bathrooms and threw up and up until she was sobbing and dry-heaving. She sat on the bathroom floor and cried, her heart shattering. *What the fuck is wrong with the world?*

A young waitress came to find her. "Are you okay?"

Romy shook her head. "No."

"Your friend asked me to come see if you were okay." The waitress crouched down beside her, her kind face concerned. Romy tried to smile.

"He's no friend of mind." She wiped her face. "Is there a back way out of this place?"

The waitress led Romy through the kitchens and Romy thanked her, pressing a large tip into her hands. "Give me a few moments before you tell him I'm gone, would you?"

"Of course. I hope you're okay."

"Thanks, honey."

Romy went out into the cold December streets and walked to work. How the hell were they going to resolve this? Everything was so fucked up. *You should never have slept with him to begin with.* Would she have to transfer to a different hospital? *God.*

She was in the locker room when Mac came and hugged her. "You okay? I saw the crap on the news."

"No, I'm not okay, but I have to work, so ... here I am." She lowered her voice. "Is he here? Have you seen him?"

Mac nodded, glancing around at the other residents. "He looks broken, Romy. Utterly devastated. I saw him talking to Quinto."

"You defending him?"

"No way. Team Romy all the way. I'm just saying, he's not out there preening."

Romy felt a little better and a little worse at that. She almost wanted Blue to be unrepentant so she could keep being mad at him. *He was sleeping with his stepmother*, she told herself, you *have plenty to be mad about*. A few minutes later, just as they were leaving for rounds, the Chief of Surgery, Beau Quinto, came to find them.

"Okay, people, so a bit of news. Doctor Allende has requested and been granted some personal time. Therefore, I'll be your lead for the time being. Sasse and Jones, if you could still keep to the general surgical schedule you had planned, I'll be stepping in to replace Doctor Allende."

Quinto's eyes flicked to Romy's face briefly and she couldn't read the expression. Was he mad at her? She bristled then told herself to calm down. The man was a professional—and she hadn't done anything wrong.

Quinto gave out his orders to the rest of the residents and they all scattered throughout the hospital. Romy was relieved that she had some breathing space. Mac nudged her as they walked down the OR's. "Wonder how long Allende will be away."

She shrugged. "Until he gets his life sorted out."

"Does that include you?"

Romy didn't know how to answer him.

CHAPTER FIFTEEN

Christmas Eve, and Romy finished late in the evening, wanting to catch up with her files before she took some time away for her mother's wedding. If she was honest, she was delaying going home. Going home meant facing Blue for the first time since the Hilary incident, but there was no way out of it. In the morning, her mother would marry Stuart, and there was no way either she or Blue would let their parents down.

Maybe we should just shake hands and live as step-siblings, she thought now. The thought depressed her, though, and she suddenly felt tearful. *Distraction is what I need.*

She walked through the floor, checking on all her post-surgical patients, chatting to the few who were still awake, wishing them a Merry Christmas even if it was spent away from their families. The hospital always made sure that, if at all possible, they could have an enjoyable time. There was one patient who wouldn't even know it was Christmas. Kelly Yang, a young woman who had been in a car accident a few weeks previously, lay in a coma. No family, no visitors, and so Romy had taken to sitting with her, holding her hand, and talking to her, trying to reach into the young woman's locked-in mind.

"Hey, Kels," Romy said now, pulling a chair up to the side of her bed. "How you doing, kiddo?" She checked Kelly's vital signs, flicked her light in the girl's eyes, then sat down. "Merry Christmas, sweetheart. Wish you were awake to share it, but I promise, when you do wake up, I'll make sure you have your Christmas."

She sat with Kelly nearly an hour, almost falling asleep, when she heard someone at the doorway. "How is she?"

Romy turned to see one of the orderlies, a huge, hulking man, nodding at Kelly. He was bald-headed with a thick dark beard, multiple piercings and thick spectacles, but his smile was friendly. Romy wracked her brain for his name. Wally? Warren?

"The same," she replied, looking back at Kelly, "although I live in hope she'll wake up."

"Fingers crossed. Sorry to bother you, doc, but we just needed to check in, see if you needed us anymore tonight."

Romy smiled at him. "No, thanks ... Warren. Have a good Christmas."

"You too, Doc. Thanks."

Left alone again, Romy squeezed Kelly's hand. "Do me a favor, kiddo. Give me the best Christmas gift by waking up, huh? Sweet dreams, sweetheart."

THE HOSPITAL WAS SO QUIET, so still, that as Romy walked through the reception area out to the parking lot, her heels echoed on the polished floor. Outside, the temperature was dropping fast and thick, fluffy snow falling from the sky. *A picture-perfect Christmas for us,* Romy thought, pulling out of the lot and turning the car towards her mother's house. The roads were almost empty as the snow began to thicken, and Romy drove with extra care, her heart thumping painfully all the way home.

When she got home, she only saw one light on—Artemis' old room. Breathing a sigh of relief that everyone else seemed to be in bed, she snuck through the house to her old room. Juno, back from New Orleans, was curled up in one side of the bed, fast asleep.

Romy pulled her wet boots and jeans off, changing into her fluffy brushed cotton jammies and pulling her robe around her. Despite the time, she wasn't tired, and so, instead of waking Juno up with her restlessness, Romy tugged a comforter from the closet and went back downstairs. The living room had been transformed into a winter wonderland by her mother, thousands of tiny white lights, white ribbons, and tasteful Christmas decorations everywhere.

It really is going to be a fairytale wedding, Romy thought, with a pang of both sadness and joy. Her mother deserved every happiness and now Romy nodded to herself. She would not let this thing with Blue ruin her mom's day. She would tell him they could talk—after the wedding. In the meantime, they would plaster smiles on their faces and be a family.

She felt, rather than heard, the person behind her. Romy turned to see Blue, shirtless, barefoot, and in jeans, staring at her. In the blue light of the early hours, he looked like an apparition. His eyes were wide and sad. Romy gazed back at him for a long moment, then slowly pulled her top over her head, releasing the drawstring on her pants and stepping out of them.

Wordlessly, he came to her, hesitant at first, then as his cold hands touched her skin, she shivered with desire and he crushed his lips against hers. Romy could not help but sink into the embrace, her longing for him almost debilitating. Her hands went to the fly of his jeans and soon he too was naked, his cock standing proud against his belly, quivering as she stroked it. There was a question in Blue's eyes and Romy answered it with just a nod. She lay down on the couch and opened her arms to him.

Blue went into them, hitching her legs around his waist and thrusting into her in one long, quick movement. Romy gasped as he filled her, her cunt contracting around his cock, moving with him as they made love. Romy did not think of anything else at that moment but of her own needs, her desire for the man in her arms.

Blue held her gaze as he braced himself and moved quicker, harder, deeper, Romy tilting her hips up to take him in as deep as she could. Blue's thrusts were almost violent now, making Romy's hips burn as he slammed his cock into her. He was angry, Romy could tell, but right now, she wanted that anger, needed it to fuel her own. Blue came inside her, burying his face in her neck as he groaned, his cum pumping out of him, filling her belly. Romy dug her fingernails into his buttocks as she too reached her climax, gasping and moaning softly.

Afterward they gazed at each other. "I hate how much I love you," she said, and he nodded.

"I promise, Romy, I will make this right between us. We need to talk."

"I know," Romy closed her eyes as he kissed her throat. "But after the wedding."

"Agreed. I love you, Romy," he said, his voice trembling with emotion. "I've never loved anyone or anything as much as I love you, beautiful girl. Please don't ever leave me."

Romy was moved beyond words and hot tears dripped from her eyes, splashing on her naked body. Blue stroked her face, wiped away her tears. "I promise, I'll tell you everything. *Everything.* There will be no more secrets between us."

Blue lifted her into his arms and carried her upstairs to the guestroom. They entangled their limbs, in a bid to get as close as possible, lips on lips, belly to belly, her soft breasts pressed up against his hard chest, and fell asleep together.

Romy's last thought before she gave into sleep was that maybe, just maybe, everything would be all right.

GAIUS HAD WATCHED his step-brother and Romy make love, his hand down his own shorts, jerking off, as he gazed at Romy's spectacular naked body. She was so beautiful that Gaius thought it would almost be a shame when Dacre Mortimer killed her. What a waste ... then again, the thought of seeing her confused and in agony as Mortimer murdered her was also a turn-on. If Dacre could see them now, Gaius thought with a smile. Romy riding Blue, her large, pillowy breasts moving in rhythm, her flat belly soft and sensual. Gaius imagined putting a bullet into it as she rode Blue, watching the horror in his hated stepbrother's face as she bled out on top of him.

He muffled his grunt of release, wiping his hand on a bunch of tissues. *God* ... he would love to fuck Romy before she died, but what would the insanely jealous Mortimer do if he did? End him? Probably. No, he would have to settle for voyeurism when it came to the middle Sasse sister. The more important thing was that Blue was destroyed ... Gaius gritted is teeth. When he had seen that photograph of Blue throwing Gaius' naked mother out of his apartment, the rage had been like nothing he'd ever known.

Gaius had been so mad that he had ignored his mother's phone calls, staying silent as she'd begged outside his door.

How could you, Mom? With the man I have hated all my life ... fucking whore.

Gaius watched now as Blue swept Romy into his arms and

gritted his teeth. *You took the woman I loved, brother, and now I'm going to do the same to you. Romy is a dead woman, Blue, and you know what?*

It's entirely your fault.

CHAPTER SIXTEEN

Romy woke feeling more at peace that she'd expected to. Blue's arms were around her and she stayed locked in them as she gazed up at him. Yes, she loved this man. Whatever he had done in the past was the past. He'd said he would tell her everything, and she believed him.

Romy was amazed at herself. After Dacre, she had struggled with trust, and yet here she was risking her heart once again for this man.

As they dressed for the wedding later, Romy smiled at him. "Damn, man, you wear a suit well."

He was wearing a dark gray, exquisitely tailored suit which brought out the green of his eyes. He was grinning at her. "Woman, you should see what I'm seeing."

The dark gold shift dress clung to her curves, simple in its design but perfectly matched to her olive skin tone. The lightest makeup and her dark hair falling in waves down her back completed her bridesmaid look. Blue couldn't keep his hands off of her, kissing her tenderly.

She stroked his face. "Blue, today is all about Mom and

Stuart. That's all I care about today, so let's put everything else aside for after they've left for their honeymoon."

"I agree ... but can I just say one thing?"

"Go for it."

"I love you, Romy Sasse, and there are things in my past I'm ashamed of, but nothing, nothing means more to me than earning and deserving your love and your trust."

DOWNSTAIRS, Artemis was arranging everything and everyone and Romy saw that some of the guests had started to arrive. She welcomed them in and made sure they had drinks before heading up to see how Magda was doing.

Her mother was uncharacteristically calm. "Hello, darling. Could you help me with this hair comb?"

Magda was dressed in a simple pale cream dress too, with only some ornate beading around the neck and sleeves. The hair comb was encrusted with rubies—a present from Romy's grandmother when Magda had graduated from college.

"You look breathtaking, Mom." Romy hugged her gingerly and Magda beamed. She studied her daughter.

"You look happier, darling. Did you and Blue talk?"

Romy half-smiled. "A little. But today isn't about us, it's about you and Stuart. As the reckless middle daughter, I think it's probably up to me to ask the awkward question. Are you sure, Mom?"

Her mother met her gaze steadily. "I am, Romy. I truly am."

Romy smiled. "Then I wish you nothing but utter happiness and joy forever. I love Stuart; he really is a good man. Oh, here. Dad sent a message too."

"He did?" Magda read the card James Sasse had sent. "That's sweet. Your daddy is a good man, Romy. In spite of everything"

"I know, Mom. And now I have a stepdad too."

Magda laughed. "Not quite yet." She glanced at her clock. "Wow, that came around quickly. Forty-five minutes and then the nerve-wracking stuff will be over with and we can party."

A HALF-HOUR LATER, Romy walked her mother down the wooden staircase and to the front of the aisle, Artemis serving as matron of honor, and a grinning Juno, resplendent in a man's tuxedo, welcoming the guests to the wedding.

Blue and Gaius stood at Stuart's side as he married Magda, Blue's eyes twinkling with happiness as he winked at Romy.

God, I love you, she thought as she smiled back, and felt the weight of the last few weeks fall away from her. This was all that mattered, love, family, celebration. As Magda and Stuart said their vows, she wondered idly if she and Blue would ever get here. She didn't even know if he regarded marriage as a goal. Romy never had—until she'd met Blue.

Her mother looked so overwhelmingly happy that as Juno declared them husband and wife, Romy burst into tears, making everyone laugh.

THE RECEPTION WAS a laidback affair of chatting, casual speeches which made everyone laugh, soft music, and a buffet of such delicious food that it was soon gone and the caterers were thanked and sent on their way.

Blue sat with Romy on his lap in one of the armchairs. Juno sprawled on the sofa, one of their guests' toddler asleep in her arms. Artemis, Dan, and Octavia sat on the carpet, teasing each other.

Romy watched her mother circulate the room, taking time to chat with every guest, introducing them to her new husband.

Blue grinned at Romy. "Some of Dad's friends are maybe a little too ..."

"Snooty?"

Blue laughed. "I was going to say reserved, but snooty works. They can't figure out what they're supposed to do in such a relaxed gathering."

Romy shrugged and snuggled into his arms. Blue pressed his lips to her forehead. "Romy?"

"Yes, baby?"

"Will you come to Italy with me for New Year's?"

Romy looked up at him. "Blue, we need to resolve things between us first."

"I know, I'm just saying ... we'll talk today, tomorrow, maybe the next day. It's going to be hard for me to talk about some of this stuff. So, I just thought, if, and I mean, if, no pressure, if we can reach a resolution—let's have a few days of us, away from all of this."

Romy kissed his neck. "How soon do I have to confirm?"

"A couple of days."

She nodded. "Then, once Stuart and Mom leave for honeymoon, let's go back to your apartment and lock ourselves in and get through this. I want to go with you, baby, I really do, but not until everything is out in the open."

"That's fair." He pressed his lips to hers. "I love you."

MAGDA HUGGED HER DAUGHTERS, tears flooding down her face. "I love you, Arti, Romulus, and JunoBoo. So much. Thank you for making my day so perfect, so beautiful."

Stuart, himself moved deeply, also embraced them. "I will never replace your dad but just know—to me, you are already my daughters, and I think myself the luckiest man on Earth."

Even the stoic Artemis was crying as they waved them off.

"God, Barbados for a month ..." groaned a jealous Juno. Octavia giggled with her; the two of them already fast friends. "Come on, people, let's ignore the tidying up and go drink the contents of Mom's liquor cabinet."

ROMY AND BLUE excused themselves and drove through the cold night back to the city, making it to Blue's apartment just after midnight. Blue opened the door for her, and Romy couldn't help but brace herself for another unwanted intrusion. This time though, they were totally alone.

They sat down at his kitchen table, Blue finding a bottle of scotch and some glasses and pouring a finger of the dark tan liquid into each.

"So," he began and Romy took his hand.

"So."

Blue breathed in a deep lungful of oxygen. "Hilary Eames. Hilary Eames is a vindictive, manipulative piece of human excrement. We all know that. That's not all she is. She ..." His voice broke and he looked away from Romy's gaze. "She likes young men, Romy. *Very* young men."

It took Romy a second to catch on, and her heart sank. "Oh, God."

"Yep. After Mom died, after I came to live with Stuart, at first, she wouldn't even look at me. Then, one night, when I was fifteen, she came to my room late at night, just in her robe."

Romy didn't say anything, swallowing over the lump in her throat. Blue gave her a humorless smile. "That night, she didn't do anything but stroke my face, tell me what a handsome boy I was. How I looked like a carved statue in one of Italy's great palaces. The next day, she went back to ignoring me. Then a couple of weeks later, she came to my room when I was asleep and got in beside me. I woke to find her ... sucking my penis. I was fifteen."

"Oh, no ..." Romy was horrified.

Blue looked desolate. "Of course, she told me if I told anyone, she would deny it and I would be cast out with nothing and nobody. The next night, she put my hand on her genitals and told me to stroke her. I did, because I was so terrified of her."

Romy's tears were flooding down her face. "Oh my God, Blue, I'm so sorry ..."

"She raped me for the first time three weeks shy of my sixteenth birthday. By then, she had threatened me so many times that I was a shadow of my former self. I was completely under her control. I still can't smell her perfume without being taken back there. The last time was when I was eighteen, just before I went to Harvard. She knew she was losing control over me, and so was even more threatening. She would have me killed if I told anybody. I didn't doubt she had both the means and the viciousness to do so."

He sighed, rubbing his eyes. "So, I kept the secret, both out of fear of what she would do, shame over feeling that fear, shame over what had happened. I always felt like I would never have been able to say anything, because how would I prove it?"

"So she showed up at your apartment because she was trying to exert influence? Still?"

Blue nodded. "She's wildly jealous of you, of Magda. We still haven't gotten to the reason why she suddenly dropped her bid for more of Dad's fortune."

Romy stood up and paced, her sorrow now turning to anger. "That fucking bitch." She stopped and turned to Blue. "And I'll bet all the money in the world Gaius knew she was going to do it."

Blue looked surprised. "How?"

"He picked me up that night, outside your apartment. He said he was coming to talk with you. I was so intent in getting away that I didn't question it, but ..."

"Fucker. Conniving motherfucker." Blue was angry now too but Romy put her arms around him.

"Tonight is not the time for retribution. Tonight we're talking, remember. Just you and me."

Blue stared down at her. "I've never told anyone about what Hilary did to me. Not one person. I was stupid to think I could keep it from you, especially after you trusted me enough to tell me about Mortimer."

"There are bad, bad people in the world," Romy said quietly. "And they all have their reasons, however fucked up, to want to hurt us. It's up to us to make sure they can't."

Blue stroked the backs of his fingers down her cheek. "You're right."

Romy leaned into his touch. "Blue ... we're going to get through this, I swear we will." She took his hand and led him to their bedroom. "Let's go to bed, baby. In the morning, we'll talk more, and we'll make a plan where to go from here."

Blue kissed her tenderly. "You got it, beautiful."

IT SEEMED ONLY a few moments after they closed their eyes that the call came, and they knew it was about to be one of the worst days of their lives.

CHAPTER SEVENTEEN

So much blood. The floors of the emergency room were covered with it, making the rushing staff slip and slide in it as they tried to cope with the influx of seriously injured and dying patients.

A high-speed train had missed a stop signal, plowing into another passenger train at the station. Hundreds were injured, dozens dead, and worst of all, as Mac told Romy as they hurriedly changed into scrubs, there were a lot of families.

"There are kids," he said, dead-eyed, and Romy felt sick.

It was worse than she'd expected. Blue, some of his fellow attendings, and Beau Quinto, were all down in the ER or in the operating rooms desperately trying to save people with horrific injuries. The first few hours saw so many people brought in dead that Romy lost count.

The ER was overrun, a warzone, and she yelled out to Mac, "Why aren't the other hospitals taking in emergencies?"

Mac gave a steady look. "They are ..."

"Jesus." Romy could not fathom the scope of the accident. On Christmas night too.

Warren, the orderly she vaguely knew, helped out, arranging

places for the treated to go, and she threw him a grateful glance. "You're the best, Warren."

He nodded shyly. Romy caught sight of Blue, his face pale and stressed. He nodded to her and mouthed, "You okay?"

She nodded. If she let her feelings take over, she would scream.

Beau came over. "Romy, we're sending a team into the field. You, Mac, Blue, and myself will go to begin with. Get some supplies together, as many as we can spare, and let's go."

As they rode in the ambulance down to the King Street Station, Beau briefed them. "The station building itself is undamaged so there's a triage area that has been set up inside. Look, there are a lot of dead and a lot of injured, as you know, but we still have people trapped who might need surgery in situ. It's going to be upsetting and dangerous, but I trust all of you. Stay safe."

Even Beau's words could not have prepared them for the horror of what they found in the mangled wreckage. Romy felt her composure slip when she saw the dead bodies of two children, rendered unrecognizable by their injuries, being lifted from the train, and she turned away, taking in deep breaths. *People need you. Get a grip.*

The doctors went to work with the same efficiency they had employed in their own emergency room. Romy worked closely with the first responders both on the track and in the train's vast waiting area.

Hours passed, night turned into day turned into night again. Drooping from exhaustion, the medical staff nevertheless kept up their treatment, dispatching as many patients as they could to hospitals in the area. The less injured were ferried down as far as Portland to get beds.

Blue came to find Romy as the second night drew on and they grabbed a couple of private moments together.

"You okay, bub?"

She nodded, but she could tell he wasn't convinced. "First major incident?"

She half laughed. "Yep, having a lot of 'firsts' this year."

He hugged her tightly. "Beau says another hour and he'll call it."

"Okay. I'm just going to do another sweep of the place."

"Okay, I'll take the other end of the station. See you in a few."

ROMY CLAMBERED BACK down onto the tracks, careful to avoid the third rail even though they had been assured the power had been switched off. She scooted behind the pile of wreckage and searched around in the dark. Her foot slipped on some blood and she wobbled, falling backwards—but thankfully, was caught by two strong arms.

"Thanks," she said breathlessly, turning to face her savior but before she could see who it was, he grabbed her head and slammed it hard against the steel of the wreckage. Romy didn't even have time to cry out as he attacked her, hitting her head repeatedly against the steel until she was almost unconscious. Blood was pouring from her forehead into her eyes and she could feel herself weakening.

"Hello, my darling," a familiar, horrifying voice growled in her ear as she blacked out. "How ironic that your life should end here, Rome, as you do your Florence Nightingale thing."

No ... no ... it couldn't be, this wasn't how it ended. Romy found she couldn't move her arms to fight him off and as he slipped his hands around her throat, all she could think of was Blue.

God, Blue, I'm sorry, I love you ...

"Romy!"

The pressure on her throat stopped and she heard Dacre's muffled. "Fuck!" Suddenly she knew she was alone and that her would-be killer had gone, but now the darkness was beginning to cloud her vision and the last thing she remembered was Blue's anguished cry.

Beau's handsome face was set and grim as he faced the television cameras. "As you know by now, we have confirmed seventy-eight deaths, one hundred and fifty-three seriously injured, and forty-seven minor injuries in the King Street Station Rail crash. I and my team were on hand to help the first responders, and I would like to thank them for their exceptional service. My team, both with me at the station and here at Rainier Hope, has worked tirelessly for over forty-eight hours since the accident, and I applaud every one of them."

He looked down for a moment, trying to rein in his anger. "Unfortunately, shockingly, during the operation to save the lives of as many victims as possible, one of our doctors, Dr. Romy Sasse, was attacked and seriously injured by an unknown assailant. Dr. Sasse is currently being treated at Rainer Hope for head injuries. We ask anyone who was in the vicinity of the King Street Station on the twenty-sixth of December to come forward with any information they may have." Quinto looked directly into the camera. "Whoever you are, you should know. No one attacks my staff and gets away with it. Whoever you are, you will be brought to justice."

Blue clicked off the television, grateful for his boss's support. In the bed next to him, Romy opened her eyes as she'd been doing intermittently for a while, but this time her eyes focused on him. "Blue?"

He let out a shaky breath. "Thank God ... baby, I was so scared. How do you feel?"

"A little woozy."

"Do you remember what happened?" Blue asked, leaning down to stroke her hair gently.

Romy nodded, then winced.

"Dacre was choking me until he heard you call my name. You saved me, baby."

"I shouldn't have taken my eyes off of you," he said, his eyes sorrowful.

"You can't watch me twenty-four seven, and we had a job to do. Who knew Dacre was psycho enough to do that? Come to think of it ... how the hell did he know I was down there? And why would he risk trying to kill me there with the police all around? He's insane."

"Well, we knew that. Anyway, don't think of that, just get well. That's all I care about right now."

Romy leaned back further into the pillows. "I honestly feel okay, which surprises me. He really did a number on my head."

"They gave you a CT scan before anything. No brain bleeds, thank God, but you'll be concussed for a few days."

Romy pushed the covers on the bed back and swung her legs over the side. Blue was up in an instant.

"Whoa, whoa, whoa. Where are you going?"

"A concussion, I can deal with at home, Blue," Romy said, frowning as he caught her and made her sit again. "I'm taking up a bed when I don't need it."

Blue sighed. "You're not going anywhere, Romy. Beau wanted to keep you in for observation and he's the boss."

"You need the beds for the train victims."

He shook his head. "Honey ... the less seriously injured were taken to hospitals out of the city in anticipation that we would need more beds." His voice was gravelly. "We didn't need as many beds as we hoped we would."

"Oh God," Romy groaned. "How many?"

"Seventy-eight dead, over one-fifty serious, and more than a third of those critical. It was a bad smash, baby."

"Merry fucking Christmas."

"Indeed." He stroked her face and she leaned into his hand. "You might not feel it now because you still have morphine in your system, but honey, you're going to have one hell of a headache when it wears off. So, bed rest. I'm going to be here the whole time."

Romy sighed and got back into bed, reaching up to feel the pattern of butterfly stitches on her head. "Will I at least have some awesome scars?"

Blue chuckled softly. "No, you bled a lot, but the wounds in themselves weren't too serious. The bruising is the main thing."

"Can I see?"

Blue looked at her askance then nodded. He went into the en-suite bathroom to fetch a mirror. "You were one of those kids who bragged when you skinned your knees, right?"

"Hell, yes." She took the mirror from him. "Whoa." Her entire forehead was an angry thundercloud of purple, black, and red, crisscrossed by the white of the stitches. "Yup, this is the look."

"You kind of look like that chick from that film with the road race."

"Penelope Pitstop?"

Blue laughed. "No, the Charlize Theron character from *Mad Max*."

Romy looked impressed. "Furiosa. Yeah, baby." She pulled Blue over to kiss him. "Now that's some roleplay I could get into."

"Ahem."

They both looked up to see a tired-looking but smiling Beau at the door. "Am I interrupting?"

"Not at all." Romy smiled at him. He came into the room, winking at Blue before checking Romy's vitals.

"Good. That's all good."

"So, I can go home?" Romy looked hopeful as Blue rolled his eyes.

Beau grinned. "Not on your life. At least overnight, Dr. Sasse, your chief's orders. Listen," his smile faded and he pulled up a chair, "the police will want to talk to you. I've spoken to the hospital board; we're going to be intensifying the security around here. There will more scrutiny on visitors, on staff. I can't tell you how sorry I am about the attack."

"Thanks, boss."

Beau left them alone a little while later and Blue kissed Romy's hand. "When they let you out, we're going away for a few days. I've cleared it with Beau."

Romy sank back onto the pillows. Her head was beginning to pound painfully now. "Okay." She closed her eyes for a moment, then let out a distressed gasp. "God, Mom. You didn't call her, did you?"

"It was on the news; I had to call Stuart. He told me he would break it to her gently."

"I don't want them coming back and ruining their honeymoon."

Blue stroked her sore head. "I think I persuaded them not to."

"Thank God." Romy leaned into Blue's touch. "I think I need to sleep now."

"You go right ahead. Do you want some painkillers?"

Romy nodded, wincing, and when Blue came back with the tablets, she swallowed them gratefully, draining her water glass. She felt exhausted, drained, and now that the adrenaline had left her system, the shock of the attack was getting to her. She closed her eyes before they could fill with tears and fell into an uneasy sleep.

GAIUS WAS beside himself with rage. "You damn fool! Do you know how many cops were at the accident? You tried and kill her *there*?"

Dacre waited until Gaius had ranted himself out, then narrowed his eyes at the other man. "I didn't intend to *kill* Romy, just scare the crap out of her. I promise you, it worked."

"But you could have been seen; all the work we've done to get you close to her could have been undone."

"You mean like if someone had tried to split them up before we got to finish what we set out to do? Like your slut mother?" Dacre enjoyed the dark rage in Gaius' face.

"Believe me, my mother and I are going to have a serious talk. *God.*" Gaius' express was pure disgust. "How could she have slept with that Italian son of a bitch?"

Dacre said nothing, just smirked. Gaius stared at him in dislike. "Yeah. You laugh, but it's Romy's mouth wrapped around his cock now."

Dacre growled and Gaius smirked. "Yeah, that sticks in your craw, doesn't it?"

"Not for much longer."

"Well, this time, stick to what we planned and we'll get everything we ever wanted."

Dacre nodded, but said nothing. Gaius had been useful up to now, but there was no way Dacre would tell him what his real plan was. Something that would make Romy's last moments on Earth a living hell.

CHAPTER NINETEEN

After three days, Beau discharged Romy, and Blue immediately whisked her onto his private jet and flew them both to Italy. As she stepped out into the mild Italian winter and felt the sun on her skin, Romy sighed happily. "Yeah, this is what I needed." She smiled at Blue, who was loading their cases into the big hire car. She loved that rich as he was, Blue preferred to do things himself rather than hire a staff.

He drove them through the Tuscan countryside, past olive groves, vineyards and avenues of cypress trees until he pointed out a large villa on top of a hill. "There it is."

Romy saw a terracotta-colored stone villa nestled into the hill and as they approached she sighed. "God, it's beautiful."

"And ours," Blue grinned at her surprise. "Merry Christmas, baby."

Romy gaped at him. "You *bought* this place?"

Blue laughed. "Almost ... I wanted you to have a say, so I'm holding off until you give the final say as to whether I sign the papers. But yeah. I wanted to surprise you."

"You certainly did that."

At the villa, Blue dumped their cases in the lobby. Then,

taking Romy's hand, he walked her through the villa. Exposed brick, billowing white drapes, bookcases, hand-turned wooden furniture—the whole place was a romantic dream. Romy went from room to room, open-mouthed. "God, Blue, I thought these types of places only existed in the movies."

"You like?"

"I *love*."

Blue laughed, delighted. "Good. I'm glad you think so. Come see the kitchen."

The kitchen was a vast open-plan room with an open fire as well as a state-of-the-art stove and range, and a huge wooden table, marked from years of use. Dried herbs hung from the walls, and there were three comfy couches at one end. "This is the heart of the house," Romy said, "you can just tell this is where the people congregate, eat, drink, love. God, can you imagine our family here? Everyone bustling around, Mom taking over the cooking, Juno flopped on the one of the couches."

"Our kids running around." Blue smiled as she looked up at him.

"Someday, hopefully."

He kissed her softly, then as she responded, the kiss became fiercer before he broke away, breathless, studying her. "Do you feel okay?"

Romy nodded. In truth, the injury was still giving her headaches, but she wanted Blue so badly, she pushed aside any doubts. She pressed her body against him. "Take me to bed, Allende."

Blue swept her into his arms and strode through the villa, grinning down at her. "I'm going to kiss every inch of you, pretty girl."

. . .

BLUE MADE love to her tenderly, a little hesitantly, conscious that she wasn't fully recovered. The bruises on her lovely face were a daily reminder of how close he had been to losing her and it gnawed away at his gut. Who attacked a doctor at the scene of an accident? Why the hell would Dacre Mortimer risk so much?

Fucker.

When Romy fell asleep, Blue lay awake, his mind whirling with anger and love and confusion. He'd hired the security team —even, here, in Italy, they weren't far away. He hadn't wanted Romy to feel trapped so he'd kept that information to himself, but it reassured him that no one could get to them here. He could relax and Romy could heal.

He eventually fell asleep and was awoken by soft kisses from Romy. He smiled without opening his eyes. "You taste so sweet, baby."

He heard her throaty chuckle, then felt her move down the bed and take his cock into her mouth, running her tongue along the hard shaft and up to the sensitive tip. He gave a soft groan as his cock stiffened and quivered under her touch. He stroked her soft hair as she worked on him, then as he came, she gripped his hips tightly, and he came onto her tongue.

"God, Romy ..."

She climbed up his body and straddled him. Blue opened his eyes and smiled at her. "Good morning, beautiful."

"Morning, handsome. Touch me, Allende."

He grinned at her order and cupped her full breasts in his hands, feeling the pillowy softness of her skin, the small nipples hardening under his touch. "Have I told you how much I love your breasts?"

Romy grinned, her dark hair falling over her shoulders, her makeup-free face ethereal in the early morning light. She guided his cock inside her and Blue sucked in a sharp breath.

"And your cunt ... your glorious, silky, tight little cunt ... *Jesus*, Romy ..."

She moved on top of him, taking him in deeper and deeper, clenching her muscles around his cock until he was bucking and shuddering beneath her. As she cried out with her climax, he flipped her onto his back and began to thrust harder and harder, pinning her hands to the bad, holding her gaze as he fucked her.

Romy came again and again and Blue, not able to get enough of her, shivered and shot thick, creamy cum deep into her belly. They collapsed against each other, not caring about morning breath, and kissed passionately. "God, I love you," Blue said, his voice gravelly with emotion.

"I love you, Blue. Let's just keep doing this for the rest of our lives." She was breathless, and Blue admired the way her breasts and bely moved with her breathing. He stroked his hand over the soft curve of her belly.

"You've got a deal," he grinned and kissed her again. She pressed her breasts against his hard chest.

"I've never felt like this, ever," she said in a whisper, touching his face tenderly.

"Probably just the concussion," Blue chuckled, and she laughed.

"No way. This is it for me, Blue. This is real. This is what life is meant to be about."

"I couldn't agree more, Romy Sasse." He wrapped himself around her, looking deep into her eyes. "Marry me. Marry me today, or tomorrow, or however soon we can arrange it."

Romy stared back at him and for a long moment, he thought she might say no. *If she is sensible,* he thought, *she will say no. But God, please, please, Romy, say ...*

"Yes."

For a moment, Blue didn't comprehend her answer then as it sank it, he whooped loudly, overwhelmed, as Romy giggled. He rolled her around on the bed, cheering and laughing until they were both breathless.

After they'd calmed down, he stroked the hair away from her face. "Really?"

"Really."

"God, thank you, thank you, thank you. *Mio Dio, mio Dio.*"

"One condition."

"Yes?"

"We have the ceremony in Italian. It's only fitting."

Blue grinned at her. "I'll coach you on the language."

Romy giggled. "I'll have people check that you haven't made me agree to some kind of sexual deviancy."

"Damn, you caught me." Blue propped himself up on his elbow, grinning down at her. "And I thought you'd like that."

"Oh, I would," Romy laughed. "But you don't have to make me agree to it, it's implicit." She reached down and stroked his cock, which twitched into life again. "Let's do this, Allende. Make me your wife."

And two days later, that was exactly what he did.

CHAPTER TWENTY

O ctavia Helmond grinned at the message on her phone, and her friend, Mandy, nudged her. "What is it?"

"My sister just got married on a whim in Italy."

"That's romantic. Wait, what sister?" Mandy, who had known Octavia since the beginning of high school, looked confused. "I thought you were an only child."

Octavia grinned and explained her relationship to Romy and the Sasses. "Huh," Mandy said, when Octavia saw a photo of Romy. "She does look like you. Sure she didn't donate eggs seventeen years ago?"

"I think not; she would have been twelve." Octavia rolled her eyes at her friend.

"Her mom could have, though. I'm just saying." They were sitting in the cafeteria of the library, waiting for two of their friends to join them. The new year had brought even more snow and the girls were heading out to do some sledding before retreating to Octavia's house for hot chocolate and pizza.

Rebecca, a fiery redhead, yelled over to them as she entered the café, always one to show off, but good natured, and then quiet but sweet Yelena followed her in. The dark-haired girl had been an emigre from Russian five years ago and before meeting the others, had felt left out and lonely. Octavia had brought her into their fold of tomboys and book nerds and now Yelena was thriving.

They set out in Octavia's four-by-four to go to her father's cabin up in the mountains. Dan hadn't been wild about the idea of four teenage girls alone out there, but Octavia had gently reminded him, they were all adults now.

"Almost," he said, with narrowed eyes but Octavia had stared him down. "Dad."

Dan sighed. "Fine ... but you call me when you get there and text every morning and night."

"Deal."

They reached the cabin after dark and hurriedly brought their luggage inside. Octavia lit the fire and Yelena made some hot chocolate. They sat around chatting and laughing until late, then Octavia stretched her long limbs. "Gonna turn in, I think. Want to be ready for a full-on day tomorrow."

"Hell, yes!" Rebecca raised her mug, cursing as she slopped it all over her. Mandy rolled her eyes and helped her clean it up.

Octavia was the last to fall asleep. She was sharing the room with Mandy, her friend curled up beside her, fast asleep. Octavia snuggled under the covers and closed her eyes.

IT WAS ALMOST dawn when she heard it. A soft cry from the other bedroom woke her. She sat up, listening intently. She heard a strange noise, like a thumping into something soft. What the hell? She swung her legs over the side of the bed and crept out into the hall, moving silently along. As she approached the other room, she began to tremble—something didn't feel right. The door was slightly ajar and to her horror, she saw the hooded figure of a tall man bending over her friends' bed. He was moving his arm up and down and in the moonlight, Octavia saw the glint of steel. Oh god, no ...

For a second she was frozen, not believing what she was seeing then, with nothing else to do, she gave a banshee scream and run to tackle the assailant. She hit him full force but he threw her off easily, sending her crashing back to the wall, banging her head viciously. As she recovered, she heard Mandy running to help.

"No, Mandy, run, get help."

But it was too late. Mandy came crashing through the door, flicking the light on, and then Octavia saw the horror of what had happened. Rebecca and Yelena, both gasping for oxygen, covered in blood, were clutching at the vicious stab wounds in their bellies.

"Oct, Mandy, *run*," Rebecca croaked before the killer shoved the blade into her throat, and she fell back, choking and dying. Octavia scrambled to her feet pushing Mandy back out into the hall, but then there was another masked man, easily picking Mandy up and driving a knife deep into her abdomen so many times, so quickly that Mandy had no chance. The killer dumped her body on the ground and then both of them came after Octavia.

She almost reached the cabin door but then one of them tackled her to the ground, the other grabbing her legs and straddling her. He ripped the top of her pajamas open, then to Octavia's disbelief, he pulled his mask off.

Gaius. He grinned down at her. "Well, now, I guess I'm quite the surprise."

"Please don't kill me, Gaius, please."

He laughed, looking at the other assailant. "Well, it's always worth asking, isn't it?" He slowly pushed the knife into her navel and Octavia gasped at the horrific pain. Gaius buried the knife into her to the hilt.

"I did some research, little Octavia, some digging around in the files of the surrogacy place. Seems like we're related. Magda Sasse *is* your biological mother, which makes you Romy's sister —which means we're going to kill you the same way we're going to kill her. Slowly. Painfully. Without mercy." He wrenched the knife from her and Octavia could feel her blood pumping from the wound. Gaius smiled.

"Ah, damn ... I think I've gone and severed your abdominal artery. You'll bleed out in a few minutes, so we'd better make the most of this ..."

Octavia screamed as the other killer drew his own knife out of his pocket and both men stabbed her again and again until there was nothing left but darkness.

CHAPTER TWENTY-ONE

Romy Sasse-Allende rolled over in bed and smiled at her husband. "Hey, hubby."

Blue opened his eyes and grinned. "Hey, wifey." He leaned over to kiss her and she wriggled into his arms, hooking a leg over his body. She could feel his cock stiffening as she pressed her body against him.

"Fuck me, husband."

With a chuckle, Blue rolled her onto her back, and hitched her legs around his waist. "Damn, you're so wet."

Romy grinned up at him sleepily. "I've been dreaming about you." She moved her body so her breasts and belly undulated and with a growl, Blue plunged his cock deep inside her ready and swollen cunt, pining her hands to the bed, and thrusting with measured but brutal strokes into her. Romy moaned and encouraged him as he fucked her, loving it when he got rough, coming over and over as he shot his load inside of her. He flipped her onto her stomach and eased into her ass, pulling her hair as she screamed his name.

They tore and clawed at each other, the bed moving with the violence of their lovemaking. Blue fucked her against the wall of the shower, lifting her easily in his strong arms, Romy bracing herself against the cool tile as his cock reamed her cunt until she thought she might not be able to take it anymore.

As they made breakfast, he bent her over the counter and took her from behind, telling her over and over how much he loved her, then later, as they walked in the olive groves, he had her again, staking his claim of her body as well as her heart, fucking intensely until they were both breathless and sated.

Evening was falling as they made their way back towards the villa. Blue was picking grass and twigs from her long dark curls, and his eyes were so soft with love, that Romy couldn't help but stop to kiss him. He ran his hands down her body.

"How did I ever exist before you, Romy Sasse?"

Romy grinned up at him. "Romy Sasse Allende. And I don't know, Blue, because there was nothing before you."

He grinned. "I think we just exceeded our cheese quote for the year."

Romy laughed. "I don't care. This is our honeymoon, gorgeous man; cheesy is a requirement. You know what's also a requirement?"

"What?"

"Food. I'm *starving*."

Blue drove them into Florence to a favorite restaurant of his, and they dined on lobster and pasta and garlic bread, moaning over the delicious food. Blue ordered some wine and they lingered over desserts of Zabaglione with fresh berries.

The coffee was strong and dark, and they sat talking long into the evening. Romy leaned her head on Blue's shoulder. "I'm so chilled right now. This place is heavenly."

"I'm glad you think so. So, what's the verdict? Should I close on the villa?"

Romy nodded, smiling. "Blue, we haven't discussed kids, but I think the villa would be the perfect place to bring them up."

He smiled warmly. "I do too, baby."

Across the street was a row of stores, each different, none of them brand names, all family owned, some of them still open this late in the evening. There was something so pure and natural about this place, Romy thought. Her eye was caught by the flickering of a television in the bar across the street. For a moment, she couldn't believe what she was seeing.

"Tavia?" No, it couldn't be. Her young friend's face flashed up again, and Romy saw now that the news channel was focusing on a snowbound crime scene, police tape fluttering around a small log cabin. Romy stood up to move closer to the television and Blue, hurriedly throwing a wad of Euros down to pay for their meal, followed her.

They had been cut off from cell phone and Internet access for a few days and both had enjoyed it, but now, Romy stared in horror at the television. "Can you turn that up, please?" she asked anyone who would listen.

Blue repeated the question in Italian and the bartender grabbed the remote and increased the volume.

The four young women, all aged seventeen, were found stabbed to death this morning by the owner of this isolated log cabin. It is believed he is also one of the girl's father, local businessman Daniel Helmond.

"No!" Romy's legs gave way as Blue dived to catch her. "No, no, no, not Tavia, please, *please, not Tavia.*" She was screaming, not caring that the entire street was staring at her.

THE VICTIMS HAVE NOW BEEN OFFICIALLY IDENTIFIED as Rebecca Moore, Octavia Helmond, Mandy Fitkins, and Yelena Shostakovich. All the women were from Kings County, Seattle; all were brutal stabbed to death. Police say the killer or killers left very little physical

evidence of themselves and have asked that anyone with any informa-
tion come forward. Back to the studio.

TWO HOURS LATER, when Romy had finally gotten through to a devastated Artemis, she spoke with her sister for a few minutes then came back to the table. She was calm now, too calm, Blue thought as he stood to take her in his arms. The restaurant was officially closed but the owner was a kindly man who told them to take all the time they needed to make calls. He kept them supplied with hot, strong coffee, and pastries although neither Blue or Romy could eat.

Romy leaned against her new husband's body. "We have to go back. It's Dacre. He'll keep killing innocent women. We have to draw him out."

"Romy …"

"No, Blue. No objections. It's the only thing left to do." She looked up into his eyes and he could see the endless sorrow in them. "I won't go down without a fight. And I'll play dirty, Blue, believe me."

"You're not in this alone."

"I know." She sighed, squeezing her eyes shut to stop them from tearing up again. She felt raw from screaming. "For tonight, let's go home."

"I'll book the plane for tomorrow."

"Thank you, baby."

DACRE AND GAIUS watched the news with satisfaction, then Gaius grabbed a couple of beers from his fridge. Dacre clinked his bottle against Gaius' and then sat back, studying the other man.

"How did it feel? Your first kill?"

Gaius smiled. "Godlike."

Dacre laughed. "I'll drink to that." He took a long swig. "Romy will be on her way back to the states now."

"So her sister says."

Dacre sighed. "It's time, man. When we were killing those girls, all I could think of was doing the same thing to Romy. Sticking that knife into her gut over and over. I got hard just thinking about it."

Gaius nodded. "I agree, it's time."

Dacre was deep in thought. "The best place to do it will be at the hospital. No one suspects me there; hell, she doesn't even recognize me."

"Well, you did do a transformation from preppy asshole to redneck psycho." Gaius smiled as Dacre laughed. "Yeah, she won't see you coming."

"God," Dacre grabbed his cock and squeezed it. "The anticipation of that pop, the moment when my knife cuts into her skin."

"Dude, don't jerk off in front of me." Gaius' nose was turned up in disgust, but Dacre just laughed.

"Don't flatter yourself, asshole." He took another long drink of beer. "So, what about you? You gonna fuck your brother up? Or are you going to leave him alone to mourn Romy?"

"Both." Gaius' eyes glittered with malice. "I'm going to beat him to within an inch of his life, then drag him to watch you kill Romy. How does that sound?"

Dacre's smile spread slowly across his face. "Dude ... that sounds just about perfect."

CHAPTER TWENTY-TWO

The funeral was well-attended and as painful as they all expected. Octavia's coffin was lowered into the cold January ground; Dan, her father, had such a look of desolation on his face that Romy could barely look at him. The guilt she felt was overwhelming, and since she and Blue had flown back to Seattle, a week ago, she had been working with the police to try and smoke Dacre out.

At the hospital, she and Blue had had a conference with Beau and the head of security and decided the measures would stay for now. "I'm not risking your life or anyone else's, Romy." Beau said. "I've had experience at the vengeful ex thing—my Dinah nearly died."

"I know, Beau, and thank you." Romy looked between the two men. "I'm so sorry for bringing this all down on your heads."

"It's not your fault," Blue repeated for what seemed the hundredth time, but Romy couldn't help but feel it pressing down on her. Octavia's horrific murder had affected the whole family —Dan, to his credit, hadn't blamed her, or Artemis but Romy almost wanted him to yell and scream at her.

At night, after she and Blue were in bed, after her adored husband was asleep, his arms tight around her, Romy would lie awake, thinking up ways to bait Dacre into revealing himself, and then coming up with increasing violent ways to kill him herself. Her rage was all-consuming. She would sleep for a couple of hours then get up, grab her laptop, and go through all the information she could find on Dacre, his family, the murders. On more than one morning, Blue had found her asleep on the couch, her laptop still open.

She knew Blue was worried about her and couldn't blame him for being so. Never, even after the attack of the previous year, had she felt so on edge, like she was on a tightrope and nothing could stop her from falling.

Only at work could she focus on what she was doing. She and Blue were even more in tune in the operating theater, and even their recent marriage hadn't affected her relationship with her colleagues—much to her relief.

Mac was the only other resident who knew everything. Romy found she was leaning on him more and more, someone outside their family, a friend, a sounding post. She had told him —then told him to forget it.

"Everything I talk about now seems to be about Dacre," she said, with a sad smile. "Promise me that when we talk, we'll bust each other's chops or just talk about work, or our love lives— rather, your love life."

Mac smiled, his smile splitting his handsome face and lighting it up. "You got it, gorgeous."

And he kept his word, joking with her, relieving some of that stress. Romy had never been so grateful to someone as she was to Mac.

. . .

MAGDA, back from her honeymoon, was stressed out and hyper when Romy went over to her house to visit. After Magda had hugged her for way too long, Romy escaped her mother's arms and rolled her eyes. "Mom, I'm fine. It's Arti and Dan you should be worried about."

"Oh, I am," Magda said, grim-faced, "but Dacre's not trying to kill them, is he?" She sighed and covered her face and, to her distress, Romy saw her mother was crying. She went to her.

"Mom, I have protection coming out of my ears. Look at the two hulking guys I had to bring with me to come visit. Dacre's not going to get to me unless I let him."

Magda dropped her hands and glared at her daughter. "What does that mean? Unless you let him?"

Romy silently cursed herself for the slip. "Just a figure of speech, Mom, chill out."

Magda sighed, her usually youthful face seeming older.

"When you were in the hospital last year," Magda said, "I sat with you, and in my head, I was making up ways I could kill Dacre Mortimer. Some pretty hardcore things."

Romy half-smiled. "You and me both, Mom."

Magda nodded, hesitated, then fixed Romy with a steady look. "Could you? Could you do it? Kill him?"

Romy, grim-faced nodded. "I wouldn't even hesitate."

Magda nodded. "Good. God, Romy, I hate that I couldn't protect you then and can't protect you now."

"What are you talking about? You gave me and Arti and Junebug the best childhood ever. Ever, Mom. The love in this house, that was all down to you. That we've all followed out dreams, that's all because of you. You are my superhero, Mom."

Magda was openly crying now and Romy wrapped her arms around her mother. "Mom, we will get through this."

Magda nodded. She looked at Romy. "Darling, there's something I have to tell you."

Romy, trying to lighten the mood, smiled at her. "Did Stuart knock you up?" She regretted the joke immediately when she saw her mother wince. "God, Mom, what is it?"

"Darling, come sit down. This isn't going to be easy."

LATER THAT NIGHT, Blue came home to find Romy sitting in the dark. He knew at once that something had happened and he sat down beside her. "What is it?"

Romy looked at him and the sorrow in her eyes was bottomless and searing. "Octavia was my sister. The police told Artemis and Dad that she matched Mom's DNA. Mom told me that twenty years ago she donated her eggs after she'd had Juno. She knew she was done, so she and Dad had eggs fertilized and donated. That's why Tavia looked just like me. We *were* sisters."

"God, no." Blue felt the shock reverberating through his body. Romy looked at him, eerily calm.

"This ends now, Blue. No more. If it kills me, Dacre Mortimer is going down."

Blue looked at his wife unhappily. "This won't end well, Romy."

"I know, baby, but we will prevail. We will be ready."

Romy had no idea how soon she would have to put her theory into practice.

CHAPTER TWENTY-THREE

Beau wasn't happy, but eventually he agreed to Romy's request that her protection at the hospital be removed. "At least the visible protection," Blue amended, with a glance at his wife. "Romy's determined to draw him out."

"He knows I'm in Seattle; he knows I work here." Romy looked at Blue. "Blue's arranged for a journalist to interview me about the murders. I'm going to goad him in the press so that he has no option but to come after me."

Beau exchanged a look with Blue and Romy sighed. "Fellas, it's up to me. I'm the one he wants, and I won't let anyone dictate my life."

Later, she was working in the resident's lounge when Warren, the friendly orderly, knocked on the door. "Hey, Dr. Sasse, can I run something past you?"

Romy smiled at him. "Go for it."

Warren came in and sat down. "Staff's been talking. About what's going on with you and this jerk ex of yours."

Romy felt a little awkward. "People are talking."

"Yeah ... sorry if that's inappropriate, but we look after our own around here."

Romy smiled at him. "That's sweet, but I think we got it handled."

"I'm just saying ... I'm around. You ever feel threatened, I got your back."

Romy was moved. "Warren, you're the best, but I think I got this. I can be pretty badass."

Warren laughed. "I have no doubt. Well, I said what I wanted to, so ..."

"Thanks, Warren. I do appreciate it."

After the orderly had gone, Romy felt strange, like somehow her friends and colleagues were looking at her as if she were a victim. God, that was the last thing she needed. Her stomach roiled and she pushed away from the table and got up, determined to stop feeling sorry for herself.

The hospital was quiet now as the day ended and Romy checked the surgical schedule, seeing that Blue was still operating on an elderly woman with appendicitis. She checked on all of their post-surgical patients and set out about updating the medical records.

She'd just glanced at the clock and seen it was nearly two a.m., when she heard the first shot. Freezing, for a moment she wondered if it was a car backfiring in the lot, then when she heard the screams starting Romy began to run towards the sound of the shooting, joined quickly by other staff and the hospital's security team.

More gunfire and security stopped the medical staff. "Shooting's coming from the OR floor."

Romy's heart nearly failed and she darted forward only to be stopped by one of the security guards. "Sorry, Doc, we can't let you go down there."

"But Blue is there," Rom said, her voice rising as the panic set in.

Mac grabbed her upper arm. "Romy, come on. We need to take care of our patients. Let the security team do their job."

"Hospital is on lockdown," the security chief was telling them all, "go back to where you were and secure your patients as best you can."

Mac dragged Romy back to the post-surgical patients. Some of them were awake now, wondering what was going on. Romy tried to reassure them but when the gunfire came closer, there was a palpable sense of panic.

"Let's get the patients who can't walk and can't hide into secure rooms," Mac said and Romy nodded, her stomach roiling with panic. She grabbed her cell phone and texted Blue.

Are you safe?

There was no answer. When she saw the head of security again, she grabbed him. "What's going on?"

"Shooter." He looked at her as if she was stupid and Romy rolled her eyes.

"I know that ... where is he or she? Is anyone hurt?"

"I don't know, Doc. It's a developing situation."

He moved away before she had a chance to ask any more questions and she hissed in frustration. She tried to call Blue, but knowing he switched off his cell phone when he was in surgery, prayed that was the reason he wasn't answering.

Please, please, be okay.

God, how much more horror would they have to put up with? Romy did her job, helped patients, made sure the floor was secure, but she couldn't help wondering how the hell a man with a gun got into the hospital. Was it because Beau had reduced the security at her request?

Don't be stupid—this has nothing to do with you.

But her instincts were telling her otherwise. Romy felt her composure slip, and she darted into an empty room and dragged some deep breaths into her lungs. *He's fine, he's okay.*

There was a soft knock on the door. "Yes?"

Warren opened the door and gave her a hesitant smile. "You okay, Doc?"

She shook her head. "No. There's a shooter down on the OR floor and Blue is there. No, I'm not okay, Warren. They won't let me go to him."

He stared at her for a long moment, then said, "I can get you down there."

Romy's eyes widened. "You can?"

Warren nodded, his eyes watchful as he gazed at her. "I can. Come with me."

Romy didn't even think twice, such was her need to get to Blue. She followed Warren into the far end of the floor, raising her eyebrows as he opened the fire escape.

"No alarm."

"No, they shut the power down on the doors to contain the shooter, which knocked out the alarms. But this door has always been tricky."

She followed him down two flights of stairs then as he passed the OR floor, she faltered. "Warren?"

He turned and grabbed her hand, pulling her after him. "We have to go down to go up, Rome."

It took a second to process what he'd called her and a wave of utter horror swept over her. "What did you call me?"

Warren's hand tightened on her wrist as he turned back towards her. "Miss me, Rome?"

It couldn't be ... Romy stared at the big man in horror, and began to see it. Dacre had completely changed his body type; his hair was gone; the thick beard; the piercings ... but yes, it was her ex-husband.

"How did I not see it?" she said out loud and as Dacre pulled her into his grip, he laughed.

"Because you didn't want to. You've only had eyes for the Italian, haven't you, whore? His hands all over you?"

He was dragging her down the stairs, her petite body no match for his strength. "They'll find your body in the basement, Rome, gutted, bled out. Of course, by that time I'll be long gone. They'll still be looking for whoever is shooting up the hospital."

"Motherfucker, that was you? Killing more innocent people?"

"Dumb bitch, there is no shooter. The dumb security team is going through the hospital trying to find someone who isn't there. I set it up so someone would fire blanks nearby and panic everybody."

Confused by his certainty, Romy was trying desperately to put her hand in her pocket. She had a hypodermic needle in there—if she could just reach it, she could use it as a weapon ... her fingers closed around it and with all her might, she gripped it in her fist and plunged it backwards, aiming for Dacre's face. She felt resistance then, as Dacre howled and released her, she knew she'd hit her mark. Dacre jerked back, the needle piercing his left eye. "Fucking bitch!"

Romy didn't wait around. He was blocking the way upwards, so she went down, practically flying down the staircase. In her pocket, her cell phone began to buzz. *Blue.*

"Baby, where are you? The freakiest thing, there's some kind of ..."

"Blue! It's Dacre ... he's here, he's after me... I'm in staircase C and I don't know where I can get away from him."

"God, baby, go down as far as you can, to the basement, you can get to the foyer. From there I ..."

There was a scuffling noise and she heard Blue cry out in anger and pain and Romy screamed. "Blue!"

"Romy ..." And then the phone went dead. What the hell was

going on? Behind her, she heard Dacre crashing down the stairs after her. What the hell had happened to Blue?

She pushed her way into the basement of the hospital, a vast labyrinth of pipes and dank corridors. Romy ran as fast as she could, towards what she thought was the front of the hospital. Dacre was almost on her as she flung the door open and ran out into the foyer of the hospital.

Dacre grabbed her and they both tumbled to the floor, Romy struggling with his vast weight on top of her. Even a glimpse at the blade of the knife he pulled out made her mad rather than scared and she kicked and bit and clawed at him as he tried to subdue her.

"No," she screamed at him, "You don't get to win this time, Dacre. Never again."

He laughed at her, cuffing her viciously around the face. "Give it up, bitch; it was always going to end this way."

He was winning, his sheer physical size overpowering her. He bounced Romy's head off the cold hard floor and as she reeled, he pinned her. His mouth ground down on hers, his tongue penetrating her mouth. Romy bit down on it as hard as she could, tasting blood, and Dacre roared in pain and anger.

He drew back his arm, ready to stab her, but then everything stopped. Dacre's eyes widened suddenly as blood began to pour from his chest. Romy whimpered as he fell forward onto her, then kicked him off of her, her eyes whirling wildly around the room.

Behind them, Gaius Eames lowered the gun he was holding. Romy hadn't even heard the shot.

"Gaius!"

He came to her immediately, helping her to her feet, his expression incredulous. "Are you all right? Are you hurt? Who the fuck was that?"

Romy leaned against him, relieved to find a friendly face even if it was Gaius. "My ex-husband. And no, I'm not hurt."

"Good." He pressed his lips to her temple, wrapping his arm around her, and Romy felt comforted.

"Blue. I have to get to Blue."

Gaius nodded and tucked his gun in his pants. Romy blinked. "Gaius, why do you have a gun?"

"I have a permit to carry a concealed weapon," he said, shrugging. He nodded at Dacre's body. "Thankfully."

"Amen to that, but you might want to be careful. He set it up so it sounded like someone was shooting up the place, and if security sees you with a weapon ..."

Gaius nodded. "Yeah, let's get out of here. Find Blue and get out."

They made their way carefully to the OR floor. It was dark, silent, and Romy felt a coldness settle over her. She could smell cordite in the air. OR3. That was where Blue had been operating. She led Gaius towards it, the smell of gunsmoke stronger.

Romy pushed her way into the scrub room and looked through the window. The OR was a mess, blood, instruments, drapes everywhere. She pushed into the room—and saw him.

He was covered in blood and Romy screamed, dropping to her knees by his side. "Blue?"

He opened his eyes, the bright green stark against the blood on his face. He smiled. "You're here."

"Are you shot?" Romy was running her hands over his body, trying to find wounds. Blue shook his head.

"No, he only hit me. God, Romy, I never knew. I never knew he hated me that much."

Ice flooded through her veins. "Dacre didn't even know you, Blue; he just wanted you out of the way."

Blue looked confused. "No, not Dacre, Romy ..." He trailed off as he looked behind her and his face went pale. "Romy ..."

Romy whirled around to find Gaius, smiling at them both, and aiming the gun at Blue. "No, Romy, Dacre didn't know much about Blue. He wanted to kill you, beautiful, and I offered to help—as long as Blue was made to witness your murder. Then, well, Dacre became a loose end. After we killed your ... what was she ... sister? Octavia, anyhow, and her friends, I knew I wanted to do you myself, but Dacre wouldn't hear of it. So he had to go."

Romy was staring at him aghast, then with a scream, she threw herself at Gaius. He had anticipated it and easily threw her off, but not before Blue had a chance to scramble to his feet and go after his half-brother.

"You bastard! *Figlia di puttana!*"

Gaius was a big man but nothing to Blue's strength. The two men crashed to the floor and Romy cast around desperately for something to help Blue. She grabbed a scalpel and leapt at Gaius, slashing at him. She caught his arm and he yelled as Blue landed a punch so hard that Gaius fell backward. As he scrambled away from them, he pulled out his gun.

Blue stopped as Gaius aimed it at him. "Gaius, don't be stupid. Killing me won't help you. This place is crawling with cops. They'll cut you down in an instant."

Gaius stared at him as Blue and Romy, holding their breaths, stood still. Then Gaius's mouth hitched up in a smile. "You're right." And he swung his arm and shot Romy.

The bullet smashed into her belly and she dropped as Blue, half-crazed with grief, went for Gaius. Gaius was too quick for him, putting the gun to his own temple. "You fucked my mom," he said, sounding like a child.

Blue shook his head. "She raped me, Gaius."

"No."

Blue, seeing the half-crazed expression in Gaius' eyes, but desperate to get to Romy, crouched next to his half-brother.

"Don't do it, Gaius. Your mom is a bad person, but she loves you."

Gaius half-smiled. "She's nothing anymore. I strangled her to death the day after I found out she fucked you. They've probably found her body by now."

Blue was horrified. "Jesus, Gaius."

Gaius was staring at Romy now, who was clutching at her bleeding stomach, but calmly, deeply breathing, watching the scene play. "She's lovely, Blue. So lovely. I'm glad I got to kill her before I died." And he put the gun in his own mouth and pulled the trigger.

Blue didn't hesitate. He went to Romy and gathered her into his arms. Romy stared up at him, still unnaturally calm. "Blue," she said in a steady voice, "Blue ... save our baby. Please, save our little one. I love you so much." Her eyes closed and she passed out.

Shell-shocked, Blue swept her out of the room and into an unused OR. Keeping his hand pressed to the bullet wound, he grabbed his phone. "Beau, the shooter is dead. But Romy's been shot. I need a team in OR2 right now. Please, help me save my girl ... and our child. Please ..." His voice shook, but he knew that to lose control now was to sentence Romy to death. "Please, Beau ... I need you right now ..."

CHAPTER TWENTY-FOUR

Romy opened her eyes and wondered why she felt no pain. *It's the morphine, doofus.* She breathed in a lungful of sweet pure air and smiled. Looking around the room, she saw Blue checking her chart. He glanced up and grinned. "Hey, beautiful."

"Get over here and kiss me, Allende."

"Such a nag." But he pressed his lips to hers and they kissed until they had to break away to breathe. He stroked her cheek. "How do you feel?"

"Good, really good. Blue ... how's ...?"

"Our baby? He or she is doing just fine. How come you didn't tell me?"

"I was going to, but I hadn't even taken a test yet." Romy sighed, putting her hand on her belly. "I can't be more than a couple of weeks; I just had a feeling."

"Three weeks to be precise," Blue grinned, covering her hand with his. "I can't wait to meet him or her."

"We're really going to do this, right?" Romy felt nervous and excited and Blue laughed.

"You bet your sweet ass we are. We got married on a rollercoaster ride; we're gonna start our family the same way. You in this adventure with me?"

Romy gazed up at her husband and grinned. "Just try and stop me."

THREE MONTHS LATER...

BLUE SMILED at his excited wife. "I honestly thought you'd fight me on this."

"Are you kidding? This is our honeymoon, Blue. We earned this."

They were flying in Blue's private jet down to the Caribbean, and to one of the lesser-known islands, owned by a friend of Blue's.

Romy had recovered quickly from the shooting and now, their child growing in her belly, she was ready to return to work. Blue, however, had insisted on them taking some time together first, and so for the next two blissful weeks, they would make love, laze in the sun, eat whatever they wanted.

"I cannot wait," Romy stretched out her body and rubbed Blue's groin with her foot, "to get naked and rude with you, Blue boy."

Blue laughed and went to her. "Why wait?" He pulled her gently to the cabin floor and kissed her until they were both breathless. Romy tangled her fingers in his dark curls as he unbuttoned her dress, parting the fabric and pressing his mouth to her soft skin. Blue freed her breasts from her bra, taking each nipple into his mouth in turn and teasing them into hard peaks. Romy sighed happily as he moved down her body, kissing the soft swell of her belly as he gently slid the panties down her legs.

"I want you inside me," she whispered and grinning, Blue moved to kiss her mouth as he freed his cock from his pants.

"You want me inside, pretty girl?"

Romy giggled, seeing the mischievous lust in his eyes. "Always ... *Oh!*"

Blue thrust his cock deep inside her, pinning her hands above her head and kissing her with animal passion. Romy hitched her legs around his waist, tilting her hips up to take him in deeper. Nothing else in the world existed for them as they made love, their gazes locked, their bodies perfectly in rhythm.

As she came, Romy's back arched up and Blue buried his face in her neck as he shot his seed into her. They collapsed together, panting for air and laughing. Blue kissed her and Romy stroked his face. "I love you so much, Blue Allende."

"You and me forever, baby."

Romy grinned and squeezed his butt playfully as she nodded. "You bet your sweet ass, gorgeous man."

And they made love again as the plane came in to land in their Caribbean paradise ...

The End.

THE NAUGHTY ONE EXTENDED EPILOGUE

*Five years after they met and fell in love, Romy Sasse and Blue
Allende are both loving parents to Grace, and at the top of their game
in the surgical world. As Blue is named as Chief of Surgery at Rainier
Hope Hospital, Romy is courted by another hospital, eager to have her
come on board with them as their own Head of General Surgery.
Romy has to make the decision whether she wants to stay working
under her husband and suffer career setbacks because of internal
politics, or take the job, work away from her family and possibly risk
her marriage.*

*With only a week to decide over Christmas, Romy, Blue and Grace
head for their mountain hideaway to enjoy the holidays together, and
Romy comes to a decision which will change all of their lives forever...*

B lue lifted his four-year old daughter onto his shoulders,
grinning as Grace giggled, clutching onto her father's
dark curls. "You okay up there, slugger?"

"Yes, Papa."

Romy smiled at them both. Grace looked so much like her

father, all bright green eyes and dark brown curls, though Grace's were long and wild, and Blue's were shot through with silver now. Romy marveled at her beautiful family, at the two people who meant the most to her in the world. "You ready, kids?"

Both Blue and Grace laughed. "Let's do it."

The SUV was loaded with their bags, and boxes full of gifts, mostly for Grace. Blue strapped his daughter securely into her car seat as Romy climbed into the driver's seat and set up the Sat-Nav. They'd bought the lodge in the Olympic Mountains only this year and Romy still wasn't sure of the way. In fact, she'd only seen photographs on the realtor's website – Blue had been the one to visit it and give the final verdict.

She still remembered when he'd come home the night he'd viewed it, shining eyes and enthusiasm making him seem manic. "It's perfect, Romy, just perfect."

"Is it cozy?"

He'd hesitated and Romy had grinned. She knew the lodge was beyond what most people would dream of, all carved wood furniture and fittings, huge picture windows, a state of the art kitchen as well as huge bedrooms. "*We'll* make it cozy." Blue promised and Romy hadn't doubted it.

Now as they began the long drive from Seattle, Romy was both excited and nervous. Excited for Christmas with her loves, but also nervous about the decision she had to make.

Since their Chief of Surgery Beau Quinto had resigned from his position to move away from Seattle, Blue had been Beau's first and only choice to replace him. Romy was thrilled for her husband – Blue had worked tirelessly and with utmost loyalty for Beau and Rainier Hope, and he deserved every bit of his success.

It was only after they'd really thought about the implications of his new job that reality had hit. Romy was the best Attending the hospital had, but she was also his wife. To others, it might look as if Blue was favoring her if he promoted her, and Romy was worried her own reputation could suffer. On the other hand, she was one of the best, and so if Blue didn't promote her out of fear of impropriety, Romy's career would suffer.

"I'll tell Beau no," Blue had declared, determined. "There's no way I would ever put my career above yours, baby. No way."

Romy smiled at him, moved. "You will *not* tell Beau no. We'll find another way, but I'm not letting you hold yourself back for me. You earned this, Blue, you paid for it with your blood. You *are* the Chief of Surgery."

It took her a few weeks to persuade him but finally, Blue had acquiesced. Then, two weeks later, Romy got a phone call from Portland General.

We want you to be our new Head of General. We won't be the first or last to headhunt you, Dr. Sasse, your reputation precedes you.

Portland. Yes, it was only three hours away by car, but that meant six hours traveling time a day – or she could fly, which meant two of three hours traveling. And that was on the days when she wasn't delayed by surgeries or emergencies or just by the workload of a Chief Attending. The excitement she'd felt after their phone call and offer dissipated quickly. It would mean barely seeing Blue and Grace, never being there for bedtimes or bath-times or after school plays. *God.*

Portland had been right. More offers came in thick and fast but she dismissed them all – except Portland. Now they had given her until New Year's Eve to decide.

Blue had been her champion, and they talked about it one night, after Grace was asleep. Romy lay in his arms, her naked body pressed against his. Blue kissed her tenderly. "You deserve this, baby. Look, I'll do the commute. We'll move home, go to Portland. We both love it there, anyway, so it won't be a wrench."

"But then the exact problems I face will be yours. And you're the Chief, dude. Beau was a workaholic and so are you." Romy had sighed. "And I *love* our home. And I don't want Gracie in the hands of childminders all the time. I want to be able to pick her up from school, play with her, help her with her homework."

Blue grinned. "Yep, she needs all the help she can get with trig at age five."

Romy laughed. "The younger she starts...but seriously, no. Look, there are other things I can explore...maybe even going out on my own."

"Private practice?"

Romy nodded. "But not elitist. Something where anyone could come and be treated, regardless of financial restrictions."

"So, a free clinic?"

"Yeah...but I haven't thought it all through yet so, in the meantime..."

Blue stroked her face. "Whatever you decide, we'll make it work." He suddenly grinned. "Have you ever used trig at work?"

"Never. Not once in my whole adult life."

Blue kissed her, running his hands down her body. "The only 'triangle' I'm interested in right now is *this* one." And he slipped his hand between her legs as Romy wriggled with pleasure. "Well, doc, I may need to find out the angle here, but, oh no, it seems to be widening..."

Romy was giggling, tears in her eyes. "No, Allende, you can't make trig sexy, no way...*oh!*"

Blue thrust his diamond-hard cock into her and they made love slowly, leisurely until they were both exhausted. Blue fell asleep in her arms, but Romy lay awake thinking. *What do I want from my life? Do I really have to choose this, my family, or my career? Why can't I have it both ways?*

She'd fallen asleep without making a decision and now, as they drove through a snowy Washington State, she wanted nothing more than to just relax and enjoy this time away with her family.

BLUE HAD ARRANGED for the lodge's fires to be lit and the huge kitchen supplied with everything they needed for their vacation. The windows glowed with warm welcome as they finally reached the lodge after dark. Grace, asleep for most of the journey, was eager to be let out to play in the thick blanket of snow that surrounded the home. Romy freed her daughter from her restraints and held her hand as Grace yelped with joy and threw herself into the snow.

"Little lunatic." Romy said fondly, then shrieked as Blue dumped a snowball down her back. The three of them then spent twenty minutes play-fighting, before Romy ordered them indoors to get dry and warm.

After a supper of hot steak sandwiches and fully loaded baked potatoes, they sat in front of the fire in the living room, cuddled together on the huge, comfortable couch.

"Tomorrow, we'll decorate the tree," Blue told Grace, nodding to the bare spruce tree in the corner of the room. Grace smiled.

"Lots of twinkle lights?"

"Of course, Boo."

Blue wrapped his arms around his girls, meeting Romy's gaze. He pressed his lips to hers and nuzzled her neck. "Later," he murmured in her ear and Romy knew exactly what he meant. Her heart beat faster – still, after all these years, he could do that to her – and she smiled, her eyes lazy with lust.

"Later."

Grace was overexcited and stayed up way after her usual bedtime, but Romy shrugged. "It's Christmas."

Finally, just after midnight, Romy crept out of Grace's room and closed the door. She padded quietly downstairs to see that Blue had switched off the overhead lights and draped strings of tiny white lights around the room. He'd dragged the sofa back and laid a comforter on the floor in front of the fire. Romy smiled at him as he offered her his hand and pulled her gently into his arms.

The moment his lips met hers, Romy closed her eyes, feeling any tension leave her body. They kissed for a long time, Blue's fingers stroking her face as she pressed her own hands on the hard planes of his chest.

"God, I love you, Romy Sasse."

"I love you too, Blue Allende."

His fingers were at the buttons on her dress now, and as he gently undressed her, he kissed her exposed skin, making her shiver with desire. She pulled his sweater over his head, making his hair even messier, then freed his cock, so thick, hard and long, from his pants. She stroked the length of it, feeling it twitch and harden in her hands.

Blue stroked her clit until it was hard, then slid two fingers inside her. "You're so wet, baby."

"For you, always."

He swept her onto the floor, kissing her mouth. Romy lay under him, enjoying the weight of his body on hers, feeling the tip of his cock nudging at her sex, then as it notched into her cunt, Blue thrust his hips hard and sank deep inside her.

"God, that feels so good," Romy moaned as he moved slowly in and out of her, never taking his eyes off hers. Romy tightened her thighs around his hips. "Fuck me *hard,* Allende."

Blue grinned, increasing his pace, as Romy dug her fingernails into his buttocks. "*Mio Dio,* you're so goddamn sexy, baby... I'm going to fuck you all night long, ream your silky cunt until you beg me to stop..."

"I'll *never* beg you to *stop,*" Romy said, breathlessly, her breasts moving, her nipples brushing his chest as they fucked. "Take me, Blue, take me like you want to hurt me..."

Blue gave a growl and pinned her hands to the floor, slamming his hips against hers, his cock plunging ever deeper and harder into her. Romy tilted her hips up to take him in as far as she could, her eyes on his, tasting blood as he kissed her ferociously.

In these moment, Romy saw nothing else but her love, her Blue. Their connection, forged so quickly all those years ago, had only grown stronger, through the horrific circumstances that nearly killed them both, to the ecstatic joy of Grace's birth. She had never known what it meant to be truly a partnership until Blue, and she thanked the heavens for him every day.

Blue's cock, buried inside her, seemed to grow even larger as she neared her orgasm and they came together, Blue groaning as he shot thick reams of creamy white cum deep into her belly. Romy muffled her cries by biting his shoulder – which only served to make Blue even more aroused and after a few minutes, he was inside her again, almost feral in his desire for her.

It was almost dawn before they finally feel asleep, having made it to their bedroom at last. Blue wrapped his arms around Romy as they slept, and when they were woken a few hours later by Gracie climbing into their bed, they greeted their daughter happily, listening to her talk excitedly about decorating the tree.

After breakfasting on way too many carbs, they took Grace out into the woods to explore a little. They were surrounded by spruce, and deep fluffy snow, but the sun was out and the air was cold but refreshing.

Later, as Blue gave Grace her lunch, Romy drove down to the little farmer's market in the town at the bottom of the mountain. As well-stocked as their lodge home was, there were still a few pieces that Romy wanted to get by herself – small gifts for Grace's stocking, and some fresh produce.

She browsed the aisles slowly, knowing Grace would have a nap before they decorated the tree anyway, and that Blue had some emails he wanted to catch up on. The farmer's market was full of home-grown produce and freshly butchered meat. Romy bought a large chicken for their Christmas day supper, and grabbed as much fruit as she could handle. She saw some adorable little wooden bears, and was selecting one for Grace when she heard her name.

"Romy? Romy Sasse?"

She turned to see a tall, handsome man with short brown hair and merry hazel eyes twinkling at her. She gaped at him. "Atlas? Atlas Tigri?"

"The very one. How are you, small fry?"

Romy threw her arms around him, hugging him tightly. Atlas Tigri had been one of her best friends from school but she hadn't seen him for years. He had been a quiet, studious type, shy until one got to know him, then he showed his whip-smart intelligence and quick-wit. He had been best friends with her sister Artemis's husband, Dan. Romy studied him now.

"So, Tigri, what gives? I heard you were living in London."

He grinned. "Mostly. But I came home for Christmas this year. Mom is, well, let's say less spry than she used to be, and so I thought I'd lend a hand. My sister's kids are a handful. Luckily Mateo's kid keeps them in line." Atlas, like Romy, was a twin, but unlike Romy, Atlas's twin Mateo was his exact copy – tall, broad and drop dead gorgeous.

"Any kids of your own?"

"Not yet. I hear you're married?"

Romy told him about Blue and Grace. "God, it's good to see you. Why don't you come up to the lodge and have drinks with us? We're here all week."

They swapped cell-phone numbers and Atlas promised to call, kissing her cheek. "So good to see you, small fry."

She was still smiling as she took her groceries to the checkout. The man behind the counter, his lank black hair unshaped and too long, smiled at her. "And how are you this morning?"

Romy gave him a polite smile. "Good, thanks. Just these please."

She was digging around for her wallet when she realized he was staring at her. Uncomfortable, she glanced at the register. "What do I owe you?"

"Seventeen-fifty-three...and maybe your cell-phone number?"

Oh, lord. She tried not to pull a face. "Ah. Sorry." She waved her wedding ring finger. "Very, *very* married."

"Shame."

Annoying creep. "Not for me. Thanks." She went to pick up the brown paper bag, then recoiled, as he placed a very cold, sweaty hand on hers.

"Don't be so hasty. You gave your cell number to that man – why can't I have it?"

Was he for real? Pulling her hand away sharply, Romy glanced around the store and realized they were alone. "Look, you're being completely inappropriate. I don't want to ask for your manager, but I will."

His smile was nasty. "He's out sick today. You're really pretty."

Romy took her bag and headed for the door. In a flash he was in front of her, slamming the door shut and leaning against it. "C'mon now...it's Christmas. Give me some sugar."

Give him some sugar? Romy, despite her unease, had to laugh aloud at that one. "Listen, *boy*," she said, steel in her voice. "Get out of my way right now, and I'll *think* about not reporting you to the police."

He grabbed her shoulders. "I just want to have a little fun. You don't need to be a bitch about it."

What the hell was happening here? Romy calmly put her bag down on the floor then stood to face him. Without warning, she brought her knee up sharply, and smashed it into his groin. The man buckled, cussing her out. Romy calmly picked up her bag of groceries, and walked out of the door, leaving him with a "Go fuck yourself, creep."

It wasn't until she was in the car and driving back up the mountain that she realized she was trembling so violently that she was making the car slide on the icy road. She pulled over and calmed herself down. Closing her eyes, she dragged great lungfuls of air in, feeling her breathing steady, her heart slow. *What the fuck was wrong with the world?*

She heard the whoop of a police car siren as it pulled up behind her and a tall deputy get out. She rolled down the window.

"You okay, ma'am?"

She nodded, then shook her head, the words spilling out, telling him exactly what had happened. His mouth set in a grim line. "Yeah, we've heard rumors. Are you sure you're okay? He didn't hurt you?"

"No, I'm okay, just a little shaken. Why on earth do they employ him?"

The deputy rolled his eyes. "He's the owner's daughter's boyfriend. Look, I'm going to escort you home, Ma'am. If you'd like to make a statement..."

Romy considered. "Actually, I would. There's no reason other women should suffer that creep."

AT HOME, Blue looked alarmed as she introduced the deputy, Jim, to him and told him what had happened. "That son-of-a-bitch! I'll deal with him." Blue was enraged but both Romy and Jim blocked his way.

"We'll deal with him, sir, don't you worry. Mrs. Allende wants to make a statement and we'll press charges of assault and harassment."

Romy looked slightly guilty. "I'm probably guilty of assault too. I might have kneed him in the balls."

Blue and Jim both grinned. "Did he put his hands on you first, Mrs. Allende?"

Romy nodded and Jim shrugged. "Then it's self-defense. Now, let's take that statement."

AFTER JIM HAD TAKEN her statement and bid them farewell, Blue hugged Romy tightly. "Trouble follows you, *Piccolo*," he said, but laughed, and Romy could see it was mostly from relief.

His use of her nickname reminded her of meeting Atlas. "It went completely out of my mind. I've invited him for drinks one night – I hope you don't mind."

"Not at all, I would like to meet him. It's a pity you didn't walk out of the store with him."

"Ha," Romy said, mildly, "I took care of it."

"Yeah you did, sexy ninja wife." He eyed her appreciatively. "Gracie will be up soon...but I think we could still get one in under the wire."

Romy burst out laughing. "Now, *that's* sexy," she dead-panned, but giggled as Blue swept her into his arms and placed her on the kitchen counter. He pushed her skirt up to her hips, shimmying her panties down her legs, over her boots, which he insisted she kept on. Romy had to admit that they did add to the sensuality of the moment. As Blue thrust his cock into her, she gave a small moan of release, forgetting all her upset, knowing that this man loving her now was all she would ever need.

. . .

THEY HAD JUST FINISHED DECORATING the tree when the deputy called. "We've arrested him – apparently there are other female customers who have made complaints too. He'll be out on bail soon, I expect, but it's handled."

"Thank you so much," Romy said. "I'm sorry you had to deal with it."

"No problem at all. Been aching to book that creep for years. Merry Christmas, Ma'am."

"And to you, Deputy."

ROMY HUNG UP THE PHONE, gave a thumbs up to a relieved Blue and watched as her daughter was surreptitiously poking at the wrapped gifts under the tree. "I can see you, Gracie Allende."

Gracie gave a chuckle. "Momma, why has Santa brought these ones early?"

"Ah, because you've been a good girl."

"Then I can open them now?" She looked at her parents hopefully.

Romy laughed as Blue picked his daughter up. "Not a chance, monkey. Come on now, Christmas day is only tomorrow, kiddo. Enjoy the anticipation."

"Yes, we're going to watch Christmas movies and eat enough sugar to give us all diabetic comas." Blue said with a grin at his wife, who rolled her eyes.

"Look, Gracie, we're going to make a gingerbread house – want to help?"

ROMY PUT the upsetting incident at the Farmer's market to the back of her mind as she enjoyed the evening with her family.

After making a tall but rather crooked gingerbread house, they sat down to watch *Home Alone* and *Home Alone 2* with Gracie – their favorite Christmas movies, before gorging on mac and cheese for their supper.

Despite her assurances that she wouldn't be able to sleep a wink, Gracie fell asleep in Romy's arms just as the second movie finished and Romy carried her daughter up to bed, tucking her in. She sat on the bed, stroking her daughter's soft face, marveling at the sweet beauty of her. She felt Blue follow her in and they both watched their daughter sleep for a while.

"Isn't she perfect?"

"Just like her mother," Blue said softly and took her hand. He led her quietly out of Gracie's room and to their own bedroom. Inside, he kissed her tenderly, stroking his thumbs over her cheeks, gazing at her with such love-filled eyes, Romy felt weak. "*Ti amo.*" His voice was soft, and sent tingles down her spine.

"*Ti amo*, Blue."

Their love-making this night was slow and leisurely, soaking every moment of sensuality up, enjoying each other's bodies as they moved in perfect rhythm with the other. Romy sighed and shivered through multiple orgasms as Blue made love to her in the indigo moonlight streaming through their window.

Before they fell asleep, Romy and Blue lay talking softly, mostly about their daughter and how excited she would be in the morning.

Blue tucked a lock of hair behind her ear. "I still can't believe we're parents, Romulus."

She grinned at the nickname her family had always given her. "I know, it's just so grown up."

They were quiet for a while, then Romy said "Do you think it's the right time to try for another? Do you even want another?"

Blue grinned. "Baby, I want a *bunch* of kids with you. I was ready for another about three seconds after Gracie was born."

Romy laughed. "Even after I threatened to 'Bobbitt' you if you ever got me knocked up again?"

"Even then. What do you think? I mean, let's be practical, I'd love to carry the kid for you but that ain't gonna happen. So, we're talking about a year of your life, a year out of your career. And with this other thing..."

"Yeah, it'll be complicated. But, I'm thirty-four now. There's a time limit here – okay, so it's not pressing but it's still there. And I want another child, Blue, so badly. I want to give you your son."

Blue kissed her. "I'll be happy as long as they are healthy. I quite like being outnumbered by women."

Romy laughed. "I bet you do. Listen, this isn't the time to make huge decisions like this...let's save that for after tomorrow. But by the end of the week, one way or another, I'm going to have to make some difficult decisions."

"I got your back, beautiful, whatever you decide."

Romy smiled gratefully at him. "As long as I have you and Gracie, I'm good. That's all that matters."

THE NEXT MORNING was a riot of laughter, torn wrapping paper, way too much sugar and one very excited and happy little girl. Romy and Blue played with Gracie, helping her put together her toys, taking her directions (Blue was put on diaper duty for her new doll, Romy sneaked some chocolate spread into the diaper and giggled when she saw his horrified face).

Romy and Blue took turns in playing with Gracie and cooking their celebration meal. Outside, the sun was hidden behind gray clouds heavy with snow, and as evening fell, it began to snow thick flakes and they turned off the lights in the lodge and watched it fall.

A picture-perfect Christmas, Romy thought, and felt a tug in her chest. She didn't want to be away from Blue and Gracie most of her time. And yet her career was so important to her that she couldn't see a way out. She hadn't realized her sadness showed on her face until she and Blue were alone again that night and he asked her what she had been thinking.

"Just about work," she said with a half-smile. "And the thought of leaving you and Gracie in Seattle while I work in Portland...god. No. I can't do it. Especially if we decide to have another baby. I love my job, I *love* it, it's my calling...but I love you and Gracie more. I think I'm going to stay at Rainier Hope. I know it's not the best thing for my career but it is the best thing for me, and our family."

Blue was thoughtful, but he looked unhappy. "I hate that you're having to choose."

"Don't. I got to choose, I wasn't dictated to by you or anyone else. *I* made this decision."

Blue wrapped his arms around her. "I promise, everything I can do that doesn't fall within nepotism or favoring, I will do. I won't let you slip behind your peers."

"You bet your ass I won't," Romy said with a grin. She tangled her fingers in his hair. "I know you'll be the best Chief ever, and I also know you're fair, balanced – with only a hint of bias."

"More than a hint, but thanks." Blue was chuckling.

"Baby...all I really care about is us. I won at life when I met you, when we had Gracie. My Mom is happy, my sisters are doing so great and I get to wake up with you. *God*, I'm a lucky woman."

"Well, shucks." Always unassuming, Blue's face was red, but he grinned anyway. "Then how about we go practice making another baby?"

"I say *yes*," Romy laughed and laughed as he bore her upstairs. "Merry Christmas, baby."

"Merry Christmas, beautiful."

TWO DAYS LATER, her decision made, Romy felt a weight fall from her shoulders. She called the hospital in Portland and expressed her regrets but turned the job down. They were disappointed but offered her any position she wanted should she change her mind. Romy watched Blue and Gracie playing and knew she had made the absolute right decision for her.

ROMY OPENED the door and greeted Atlas as he trudged through the snow. "Hey, small fry," he said with a grin as she hugged him.

"Come and meet Blue and Gracie."

A half hour later, and Atlas, with his natural charm, had won over both Romy's husband and daughter. Gracie climbed onto Atlas's knee and told him all about her Christmas presents and Atlas chatted easily with her. He and Blue found common ground easily, both men's sense of humor jelling almost straight away.

Later, the adults shared a late supper. Blue opened some champagne. "To old – and new – friends," he grinned and they tapped their flutes.

"Well, I do have some news. I didn't mention it the other day because it was still being worked out but...I'm relocating back to Seattle permanently." Atlas grinned at Romy's surprise.

"That's wonderful...but what about your business in London?"

"My partner has just bought me out. He knew my heart didn't lie in it anymore, selling pharmaceuticals. More and more I felt like I was taking from the world rather than giving back."

Romy nodded. "Fair enough, but what will you do now?"

"I'm glad you asked because I might need some advice." Atlas pulled out a crumpled piece of paper. "A couple of years ago, one of my nieces was assaulted. She was at college, alone in a study room, and her boyfriend, who she'd just broken up with, found her and... You can guess. Since then, it's been bugging me that there isn't a safe house in the city that also helps those battered women – and to a lesser extent, men, who can't afford medical expenses. So, me, and a couple of other local entrepreneurs are doing just that. Seattle's first secure hostel with a full medical staff. I also want to make sure that we have a fully operational surgical facility – and an emergency room. Basically, somewhere to go when things are desperate. Eventually, I'd like to extend it to the homeless too."

Romy and Blue looked at each other in amazement. "But that's fantastic," Romy said, shaking her head in amazement. "God, Atlas...if I had had that when I left Dacre..." There was a lump in her throat. "Atlas..."

Blue rubbed her back, seeing she was close to tears. "And you need us to headhunt medical and surgical staff?"

Atlas nodded. "Please...obviously, this is a voluntary role, so asking docs to give up their time and pay-packet to do so might be difficult and there'll be no recriminations if candidates decide they can't make it work. I do need a chief of surgery though."

"I'll do it."

Both Blue and Atlas looked at Romy. She returned their gazes steadily. "It's perfect. Look, Atlas, these past few days we've been going around and around trying to find a role for me which doesn't smack of nepotism but also won't tamp down my career. This is it. Don't you think, Blue?"

Blue nodded slowly, and Romy could see him working things out in his head. "Yeah...yes, I think it is perfect. What do you think, Atlas?"

Atlas looked a little shell-shocked. "Well, I mean...god, really? You would do this? Train my staff? Be our head of surgery? For free?"

Romy started to laugh. "Are you kidding me? *Of course.* There is just one thing. There's a good chance I might be pregnant again soon, so we'd have to work around that."

Atlas held his hands up. "Girl, even an hour of your time would mean the world to us – I think we can accommodate a pregnancy." He laughed. "But we should slow down, discuss this more fully when we're not hopped up on your good champagne."

But Romy could see how excited he was and later, after Atlas had gone home, she smiled at Blue. "This is it, isn't it? This is what I *should* be doing. Everything has been pointing towards this."

Blue studied her. "You know what, Romulus Sasse? You are my freaking heroine; do you know that? My absolute superstar Wonder Woman. Yes, baby, I agree. Everything's has been leading to this. It's not only a way to give back, but to finally get the stain of Dacre from your memories."

"Exactly. Honestly, baby," Romy wrapped her arms around her husband's neck, "I can't wait to get started."

"Let's go celebrate."

"Take me to bed, Allende."

THREE MONTHS LATER, Atlas's clinic opened its doors.

. . .

SIX MONTHS AFTER THAT, Zachery Stuart Allende was born, with his twin sister Rosa following six minutes later. Their mother and father looked down at their newborn twins and knew their family was now complete.

THE END.

HER DARK MELODY

A CHRISTMAS ROMANCE (SEASON OF DESIRE 3)

On the worst day of my life, she was there...
Ebony...her voice enchanted me, her beauty made me
breathless. When she sang for me and my twin brother Mateo at
our Halloween party, I knew I had to make her mine.
I wanted her in my life, my arms, my bed...
Nothing could stop how we felt about each other, nothing...
But then a terrible tragedy struck and suddenly life came to a
halt.
Ebony is the only reason I carry on now, the only reason I
breathe in and out.
When we make love, it's the only time I can feel happiness...
But someone wants to take her away from me.
I can't let it happen, can't let my beautiful girl be ripped away
from me.
She's all I have left...

CHAPTER ONE

New Orleans

EBONY VERLAINE STARED at the plastic stick in her hand in dismay. *God, no.* She leaned her head against the cool tile of the bathroom and let a few tears escape, feeling utterly hopeless. Her whole world shifted at that moment as she saw everything she'd worked so hard for disappear.

Pregnant. Pregnant and alone at twenty-six. God dammit.

Outside the bathroom, she heard a voice and pulled herself together. She was at the Gabriella Renaud Foundation, the charitable organization which had been mentoring and supporting her over the last two years. Her best friend Juno Sasse, now her sister-in-law, had at first been her tutor, guiding her through singing lessons and songwriting, preparing her for a career in the music industry.

Since she was young, Ebony had loved singing and performing. It was a no-brainer that she would follow that love into a career, but while the executive she had met had praised her smoky, rich voice, and been even more enthusiastic to exploit her dark beauty, all of them had balked at releasing jazz and blues. She'd lost count of how many of them tried to steer her into a pop career – something she had no interest at all in.

As word spread and she was painted unfairly as a diva, the offers dried up. Despondent, she continued to sing in New Orleans's jazz clubs until Livia Chatelaine approached her.

Herself a musician, Livia was the head of a charitable foundation which focused on giving opportunities to musicians outside the mainstream, along with those who couldn't afford a place at a traditional college. To Ebony's amazement and delight, Livia was crazy about jazz and a real kinship developed between the two women.

"We're moving toward releasing our own recordings in partnership with Quartet," Livia told her at that first meeting. "We're keeping it small, keeping our roster tight and exclusive, and we won't release anything until we're sure you're ready."

Ebony laughed. "You realize you're handing me my dream... for free? It's incredible."

"Don't get too complacent," Livia teased. We ask for full commitment. We'll work your ass off if we think you're worth it – and I do. Your voice is once-in-a-lifetime, Ebony. It would be a crime not to champion you."

Ebony sipped her iced tea, her mind whirling. "Livia...you must have heard the rumors about me. That I'm a diva? That I'm never satisfied?"

Livia's smile faded. "Let me put those rumors into perspective. They were put around by old white men who run recording companies that only deal in profit. They also like to tell women what to do, how to dress, what to eat...I don't believe the rumors. You're clearly a strong woman who follows your passion, and who is unwilling to compromise to make a quick buck. That, Ebony Verlaine, is why I reached out to you."

Ebony remembered her mentor and friend's words now as she dumped the pregnancy stick in the trash – carefully hidden. This wasn't going to derail her life, she decided firmly. She could only be two weeks pregnant – she'd only been with one man in *months* – so she had plenty of time to think about her next steps. She washed her hands and splashed water on her face before making her way back to her small recording studio.

Juno was waiting for her, and to Ebony's delight, Livia was there too. She hadn't seen her friend for a few weeks – Livia had just given birth to her fourth child, a girl called Amita. It was an odd feeling, holding the gorgeous little girl, knowing she could one day have one of her own. "She's so beautiful...and so tiny!"

Livia and Juno laughed. "They come like that," Livia said, "although they don't feel so tiny when they're coming out."

Both Ebony and Juno winced, and Livia grinned. "You wait and see."

Ebony turned away, pretending to grab some work from her bag. "Hey, I finally finished that song we were working on." She handed over the score to Juno, who rolled it out.

"This looks good...maybe a couple of tweaks, but we'll run it through. Anyway, before we start work, there's a reason Liv is here. We have a proposal for you."

"What's that?" Ebony asked, putting aside her worries about the future in favor of curiosity.

Juno grinned. "Romy called me last night. The organization she works for is having a huge fundraising event and they need someone to perform at it."

"Juno called me, and we both agreed – it *has* to be you, Ebony. You are so ready for this. You've been working your ass off, now it's time to get some more actual experience. It's going to be a pretty big deal." Livia looked as excited as Ebony felt.

"Really? God, that's incredible." Ebony had missed performing, but the next moment she was filled with anxiety as Livia told her the scope of the event.

"Although the facility is for people with few means, this event is high society – it's a few thousand dollars a plate, all the money going to the facility, of course."

Ebony felt her legs shaking and had to sit down. "So, I'll need to perform a song?"

"A set, maybe seven to ten tracks. It'll be in Seattle," Juno added as an afterthought, "and it might mean spending Christmas in Seattle. Romy says she'd be happy to have you stay with her if you don't want to be stuck in a hotel."

Ebony smiled. "Back home to Seattle."

Juno grinned. "Word. Obe and I will come up for the holidays so you won't be alone, but we can't actually be there for the performance, sadly."

"Atlas Tigris is the chairman of the event. He told me that if the performance goes well, he might need you for more charity events and has offered to pay you twice the going rate. You can do this, Ebony, you could do it in your sleep, and working for the Tigri family comes with immense benefits. Their step-dad, Stanley Duggan, is a heavy hitter in the music industry, and he's a sweetheart too."

"You don't have to sell me on this, I'm in. When is the gig?"

"December 20th, for the fundraiser, but Atlas may need you for the New Year's Eve party too. Think you can handle that?"

Ebony felt a wave of relief flood over her. Worrying about the pregnancy could wait until after this. "I can handle it." she grinned at her friends. "I won't let you down."

. . .

ATLAS TIGRI GLANCED at the clock. Almost ten p.m. Even when he had been in pharmaceuticals, he'd never worked this late, this often.

"It's because you're doing something you love," his brother Mateo had once said to him mildly. "You're going to go that extra mile."

Mateo was right. Ever since Atlas had decided to set up this facility to take care of battered men and women who needed surgical and medical help, he'd been putting in twenty-hour days but never once felt exhausted.

The only time he felt lonely was when he spent time with his friends, Romy and Blue. Both surgeons, they were madly in love with the other. They welcomed him as part of their family, but as much as he adored them, their happiness made him realize how much he missed having someone in his life. Someone for just him.

His family was his life. His twin brother Mateo was the person he was closest to; he shared not just the same glorious handsome face, black curls and green eyes with Atlas, but a similar personality – although Mateo tended to be louder than Atlas. Mateo had a seven-year-old son, Fino, whose mother had dumped the newborn on Mateo and taken off, never to be heard from again. Mateo adored Fino, and his son worshipped his father.

Seeing them together made Atlas yearn for kids of his own, but the truth was, he didn't have time to seek a partner out. At various fundraisers for the facility, he'd attracted the attention of some of Seattle's socialites, but he just couldn't create a spark that wasn't there. He found them shallow and vapid.

"Hey, you. Still awake?"

Romy Sasse was at the door to his office now, her long hair pulled up into a messy ponytail, spots of fresh blood on her white coat. She flopped into a chair opposite him. Atlas studied her pale, drawn face.

"You okay?"

"Just had an emergency brought in. Women got cut up pretty badly by her ex. Asshole." Romy's jaw tightened. "She didn't make it."

"God, I'm sorry, Romy." Atlas saw how exhausted his friend looked. Romy had given birth to twins only three months previously but had eschewed most of her maternity leave. Now Atlas wondered if she regretted leaving her job at Rainier Hope Hospital to come here. It wasn't like she got paid to do this – not that Romy or her husband needed the money.

For the last nine months, she had worked tirelessly with Atlas to set up this center for abused partners, and for the most part, they knew they had done a great thing for Seattle. Days like today, though, and Romy looked downhearted. "You can't save them all, Romy." Atlas got up and poured her a cup of hot coffee. Romy took it gratefully.

"I know, boss." She sighed, sipping her drink. "Look, let's focus on something else. Harriet told me that everything is planned for the fundraiser?"

Atlas smiled. "It is indeed. Juno called me, told me her singer friend was all set."

"Ebony? That's great...honestly, Atlas, when you hear her sing...she's incredible. Such a lovely person too."

"Stanley told me she had impressed some recording people in L.A. but they didn't pick up her option because she wouldn't change her genre to pop?"

"That's right."

"Good for her, sticking to her guns. Shows integrity."

Romy nodded. "You got that right." She ran a hand over her

face. "Good, so it's all settled." She glanced at the clock. "Do you mind if I take off? Clark's in to cover, and my babies will already be asleep."

"Of course, small fry."

Romy grinned at him. "And you go home too, Atlas. Don't think I haven't noticed how late you've been working."

"I haven't got the impetus to go home as much as you," he brushed away her concern but got to his feet anyway. "Come on. I'll walk you to your car."

MATEO WAS STILL awake and eating a ridiculously overstuffed sandwich in their huge kitchen when Atlas walked in. He offered the other half to Atlas, who, suddenly starving, thanked him.

"How's business?" Mateo asked, his mouth full. Atlas's brother's curls were even shaggier and in need of a cut than Atlas's own. He wore a simple white cotton shirt, even in the middle of a Seattle winter. Mateo's business, wine importing, took him all over the world, and he still retained a tan from a family holiday in Italy. The twin's mother was Italian, and their elder sister, Clelia, lived in Sorrento with her husband and five children.

"How's Fino?"

Mateo grinned. "He aced his test today. Molly says she's never had a harder-working kid. Sometimes I wonder if I do the right thing, homeschooling him, but it's the only way I can do my job and still see him every day. Do you think I'm selfish?"

Atlas got up to grab a beer from the refrigerator. "Not at all. Fino's the most well balanced child I've ever met." He grinned at his brother. "Just please, don't go and screw Molly, like you did the last one."

"Oops." Mateo drained his beer and Atlas groaned.

"*Really?*"

Mateo sat forward, his smile fading. "Okay, I'll come clean. I'm crazy about her, Atlas. I swear, nothing happened for a couple of months, but when we were in Italy...I don't know. Something happened to us, a moment. We talked about it, what the implications were and decided we couldn't do anything about it, for Fino's sake."

"So, what changed?"

Mateo sat back, regarding his brother with a steady gaze. "I fell in love with her."

Atlas' eyebrows shot up. Now there was a word Mateo didn't use often, particularly not in conjunction with women. He wooed them swiftly and just as swiftly moved on.

"Yes, love," Mateo repeated, undoubtedly noticing Atlas' expression. "Not just because she's gorgeous, Atlas – although let's face it, she is – but when we talk, we really *talk*. No barriers. She doesn't treat me like the rich boy playing at being a dad. She encourages me, she adores Fino, and she pushes him too, to the best of his abilities."

His voice gravelly with emotion, Mateo smiled a little shyly. "We decided that we would take things slowly – Fino is the priority, after all. But, god, Atlas...I think about her all the time."

"Calm down, bro," Atlas laughed and punched his brother lightly on the shoulder. "It's about time. Go for it. We all love Molly – even *Clelia*, which is a modern miracle."

Both brothers laughed – their older sister was fiercely protective of them, to the point of being blunt and rude to people she thought were taking advantage of the twins' good natures.

Mateo nodded, his eyes shining. "I think I would like to make it formal, Atlas. Bring it out into the open. We have to tell Fino first, of course, and it's really his opinion that counts here. And yours, of course," he added hurriedly.

Atlas grinned. "You have my blessing, bro, but what the hell do I know about love?"

ATLAS LAY awake until just after midnight. Mateo had been the one who had always slept around – his drop-dead gorgeous looks making sure that he could have any women he wanted – but when Fino had come along, Atlas had seen his brother grow up overnight, becoming a man. Now, he was clearly crazy about the lovely Molly. *Yeah, you go for it, bro. If she's the one, go for it.* He was proud of his twin.

Atlas turned over, trying to find sleep. He wasn't someone who dwelled on his single status, but lately, he'd been feeling it.

You're a billionaire, you have the looks, the charm...why is love so hard to find? Atlas shook his head. *Because I want a best friend as well as a lover, someone who* gets *me.*

He sighed, turned over and tried to get some sleep.

CHAPTER TWO

Ebony stepped off the plane and walked quickly through the airport. In the Arrivals hall, she saw Romy waiting for her and waved excitedly. Romy threw her arms around her. "Hey, girl. Thank you so much for doing this."

"So good to see you, Romy." Ebony hugged her back. She'd only met Romy a few times since Juno had married her brother, but she liked the petite brunette very much. "And I'm so flattered to be asked to perform for you."

"You're going to blow them away. Now, I do have to warn you, Zach and Rosa are screaming the place down at the moment. We've put you at the far end of the house, but we can always arrange a hotel suite for you."

"I don't want to be any trouble."

Romy rolled her eyes and smiled. "Girl, I've been *dying* for some girl talk. Grace tries, but you know, she's five."

Ebony laughed. "I'll do my best."

Sitting around the Allende's dinner table over homemade lasagna, surrounded by three gorgeous kids and her two friends,

Ebony felt a pang of longing. This family was so happy, so loving, that Ebony wondered if she would ever find anything as good.

"Child, calm yourself. Jeez." Romy wrestled with a very wriggly Zach.

Blue took his son from his wife and immediately Zach chilled out, smiling up at his father. Romy rolled her eyes. "I swear you're the child whisperer, Blue." She grinned at Ebony. "Are you excited about tomorrow?"

Ebony nodded. "Excited and nervous. I hope Mr. Tigri approves of the set list."

"I'm sure he will, especially when he hears your voice. And he'll insist on you calling him Atlas, by the way."

"That's different," Ebony remarked. "What's he like?"

"Atlas? The sweetest. When we were at school together, he and Arti's husband Dan were everybody's school crush – along with Mateo. That's Atlas's identical twin, and when you see Atlas, you'll know why that's only a good thing."

"Ahem," coughed Blue.

"You're still my number one," snickered Romy, then groaned as Rosa spit up on her. "Oh, great timing, kiddo."

"I'll get the cloth, Mama." Grace Allende, a shy, intelligent girl with a concerted crush on Ebony, darted off and came right back.

"I don't know how you do it all, Romy," Ebony said, watching her friend tidy herself up and wipe her younger daughter's mouth.

"We are a well coiled machine," Gracie said proudly, making the adults laugh.

"*Oiled*, not coiled, sweetie." Romy said, kissing the top of Gracie's head. "But she's right. It just works. Sure, it's exhausting with newborns, but worth every moment. And I have the two best helpers in the world."

Blue grinned at Ebony. "What about you? Anyone on the horizon?"

Ebony shook her head. "Happily single. Concentrating on my career."

"Good for you," Blue said, but then stroked a hand down Romy's hair, twisting a lock of it around his fingers. Ebony could have cried at the love in his eyes as he gazed at his wife. *Oh, to have that,* she thought.

SHE WOKE up early the next day and found the whole family in the kitchen. Romy grinned at her. "Atlas just called. He's sending a car for you at ten a.m. and wondered if that was too early. I heard the shower running, so I told him that was okay – was I right to?"

"Definitely." Ebony felt nervous all of a sudden.

"I must give you a key," Romy said, grabbing her purse. "We're heading out about nine to drop Gracie off at kindergarten."

"I can count *this* much!" Gracie informed her, holding both hands out. "One, two, three ..."

"Don't get her started or we'll never leave the house," Romy warned, handing Ebony a key. "Help yourself to anything you need. You have my number – I'm sorry I can't be there for your meeting with Atlas."

"It's no problem. Honestly, you've done enough."

As the various members of the family were rounded up, Ebony sat quietly in the kitchen, sipping a cup of decaf in deference to the pregnancy she was trying not to think about. The sudden lack of chatter was peaceful, but at the same time, oddly lonely.

· · ·

AT TEN A.M. SHARP, a navy-blue Mercedes pulled up to the gates of the Allende home and Ebony buzzed him through. She went slowly down the front steps of the mansion, feeling oddly out of place. The driver got out of the car and Ebony drew in a sharp breath. If even the chauffeurs were this gorgeous...he was tall, had wild dark curls and merry green eyes and a smile that lit up his handsome face.

"Miss Verlaine?"

Ebony smiled at him. "That's me. Nice to meet you."

The driver opened the passenger door for her and Ebony was relieved. She would hate to sit in the back seat like some rich mukety-muck. The driver helped her in, and she thanked him.

As he sat in the driver's seat, she breathed in the scent of his cologne: clean linen and fresh air. He grinned around at her. "I hear you're from these parts."

Ebony nodded, hearing an accent in his voice, but unable to place it. "Born and bred, although sadly, all my family is either gone or scattered. My brother lives in New Orleans."

"I know – he's married to Juno, Romy told me."

Ebony was a little confused. He was very forward to be a driver. Maybe that's how it worked in Atlas Tigri's world—Romy had said he was a sweetheart—unless...

"I'm really sorry, I should have asked your name. Forgive my rudeness."

The driver laughed, and something flipped in Ebony's stomach. God, he was *gorgeous*...

"No problem. Atlas Tigri, at your service."

Ebony felt her face burn. "God, I'm sorry, Mr. Tigri, I thought...Romy said you were sending a car, not picking me up yourself."

Atlas grinned. "Atlas, please. I changed my mind, thought it would break the ice faster to come get you myself. I hope that's okay."

Oh, god, yes. Ebony smiled at him. "That explains the accent. Italian."

"Yes, indeed. So, now that we've met officially, would you spend the day with me, Miss Verlaine? I thought I would show you the facility then take you to lunch. After that, we can go to the party venue and talk more about your performance."

"Ebony, please, and that sounds perfect."

ON THE WAY to the Haven facility, Ebony was impressed even more with Atlas Tigri – it became apparent very quickly that he wasn't just a rich, pretty boy, but someone really passionate about helping victims of domestic abuse. "I wanted somewhere, a safe space for abuse victims to go and get the medical help they needed, but also the psychiatric help, the comfort, compassion," he told her as they pulled up to the building. It was sleek and modern, but also had a warm atmosphere to it, which Atlas commented on as they walked up the steps, greeted by various employees with friendly nods.

"I want this placed to be somewhere they feel secure, well fed, warm. It needs to be somewhere they can regroup and plan the next steps in their lives. A kind of home, if you will." He smiled at her ruefully. "It's grown far beyond what I envisioned, and quickly, too. We now have lawyers on hand, as well as top surgeons, such as Romy. I'm also hoping, eventually, to be able to rehouse people, but at the moment, my accountants won't let me fund that."

There was a flash of real frustration in his green eyes and if Ebony had missed it, his next words made it clear it wasn't imaginary. "It's my money. I should be able to use it for any purpose," he muttered, sounding distinctly less rich financier than frustrated philanthropist. "But that's why I have financial counsel, to make sure there's money available for many years."

She nodded, walking inside the building as he held the door for her. "Long-term planning instead of a flash in the pan."

"Precisely." He stepped in and smiled at one of the residents as she walked by, a look of tension on her face that relaxed under Atlas' warm smile. "We're not struggling by any means, but this fundraiser will bring in vital money for supplies, food, medicine. If it goes well, we may make it a regular thing."

Moved beyond words, Ebony looked around as they walked through the clean, freshly painted hallways, to some of the residential halls. The rooms, though dormitory style, were painted in warm colors, decorated with carefully curated artwork that made them feel simultaneously homey and stylish.

Ebony's eyes glistened at the obvious care that had gone into the smallest detail. "It's incredible, Atlas...wow."

"We never have enough beds," he told her soberly, "and it breaks my heart."

Impulsively, she rested her hand on his forearm and looked up into his handsome face. "What you've done here—beside the physical appearance of things, all the programs you offer, the highly trained staff, the overall dedication to helping them help themselves—" she shook her head. "It's incredible, Atlas. Far and beyond the expected or even the usually possible. But you can't save everybody."

Atlas laughed softly, lightly covering her hand with his own and sending a tendril of warmth straight into Ebony's heart. "Romy tells me that all the time." His smile faded. "We had an emergency brought in the other night, and Romy had to operate. The victim didn't make it. That's the hardest part of all of this."

"But you're making a difference," she said intently, keeping her gaze locked with his. He was mesmerizing, this man; a mirror of sorts to this facility where the exterior was as handsome as everything inside. Ebony felt a surge of adrenaline, inspired by this man's heart, by his vision. "It's incredible, Atlas, it really is. Any way I can help, even if it is just by singing for you, I'd love to be a part of it. I know, from working with GRF, how a foundation can change a life. It changed mine when I met Livia Chatelaine. It changed *forever*, and I'm just a singer."

"You're not *just* a singer, Ebony. You bring pleasure to people with your natural gift."

"You haven't even heard me sing yet," she flushed but felt the shift in atmosphere between them. Suddenly there was a tension, and she could feel his body heat. For a long moment, they gazed at each other, then Atlas smiled, his eyes soft.

"I can't wait to hear you," he said softly and touched a finger to her cheek. Her skin burned where he made contact, and her stomach was filled with butterflies. "I can't wait."

HE TOOK her for lunch to an independent burger joint, and she loved that he had no airs, enjoying the fast food as much as she did, chatting easily. She took her time to study him; the way he dressed, a dark blue sweater which brought out the color of his green eyes, blue jeans which highlighted his long, slim legs and – much to Ebony' approval – a firm, tight bubble-butt. It was his eyes which really drew her, though. The color of them, so bright against the thick, long, black eyelashes which she wanted to brush her fingers across. They were so dark that they made him look as if he were wearing eyeliner. His face, boyish, with rounded cheeks, and his smile which made her weak.

Do not get a crush on him, she warned herself, then realized it was too late. To be fair, Atlas Tigri was flirty, funny, and held her gaze for a beat too long when they talked. She was used to being noticed by men, but this was somehow totally different.

Built like a pocket Venus, Ebony was all curves, her dark

skin glowing with vitality, her face a callback to 1940's glamour; something she played up by styling her hair in the style of Josephine Baker. When she performed, she would slip into skin-tight flapper dresses which highlighted her curves. But off-duty, she was pretty much a jeans and t-shirt kind of girl.

Now, as she looked at this man in front of her, she felt her entire body ache for him. She wondered what he would be like in bed; if he unleashed all that wild Italian sexuality or was more reserved. She wondered how he would look naked, how his cock would feel inside of her...

Jesus, stop. She could feel herself getting wet and tried to distract herself by talking about her set list for the party. It was difficult when Atlas was looking at her like he wanted to fuck her right there, though.

Somehow she forced herself back into the conversation. "I have a mix of jazz standards and original pieces planned, but we can arrange them any way you want. If you'd prefer a set of songs that your guests would recognize, we can do that. Or, as another idea, I could do jazz versions of modern classics."

"I love that idea," Atlas nodded. "I can see you doing some jazz Pearl Jam."

They both laughed, and Ebony nodded. "I never thought of them as classic, but if that's your *jam*, so to speak, I can make it work."

"I bet you could."

There was a pause, a beat where they just smiled at each other. Ebony laughed softly. "How is it I feel I've known you for more than a few hours, Atlas?"

He smiled. "That crazy thing called chemistry."

"That must be it."

They gazed at each other for a long moment before Atlas leaned over and kissed the side of her mouth. "Mustard."

Ebony snickered, her body tingling with anticipation. "Of course, thank you."

Atlas cupped her face in his palm. "Can I tell you you're beautiful without sounding like a creep?"

"You just did," she whispered and moaned softly as he pressed his lips to hers again. This time, the kiss went on and on until they were both breathless and trembling. Atlas drew away, taking her hands in his.

"I don't want to take advantage," he said in a low voice. "Nor do I want to behave unprofessionally or put you in a position where you feel uncomfortable. The party is in two days..."

He didn't have to finish his sentence. As much as Ebony wanted him right here, right now, she agreed with him. They needed to press pause on whatever this was until after the fundraiser. She kissed him again. "I understand, and I agree, Atlas." She grinned. "After all, isn't anticipation sexy?"

He nuzzled his nose to hers. "It is. As sexy as you are, and that's so goddamn sexy I could cry."

They both laughed then. "Come on, Tigri, let's go see this party venue."

As they were walking out of the restaurant, Atlas stopped her. "We might be being grown-up and sensible about this, but I have to warn you. I'll be stealing kisses whenever I can."

Ebony laughed, feeling so at ease with this gorgeous man. She slipped her hand into his. "You can't *steal* something that would be given willingly."

He immediately pressed his lips to hers. God, he tasted so good, and the way his lips moved against hers sent vibrations through her entire body. She wanted to tell him to fuck her *now* and fuck her *hard*, but she kept her countenance – just. The thought of after the party, of being naked with him, of his cock plunging into her. She shivered. Atlas smiled at her. "Cold?"

"No. Just...anticipation." Summoning her courage, she slid her hand down to his groin. God, he was *huge* and ramrod-hard.

His green eyes were now dark and hungry as he lifted her hand away and turned it palm-side up, kissing it heatedly. "Soon, baby."

Her skin went up in flames at the touch of his lips and she immediately imagined them so many other places. "Soon."

They made it across town somehow, their hands increasingly wandering over one another, their lips meeting frequently. Walking into one of Seattle's most exclusive and expensive hotels, they were forced to stop until the elevator, at least, which they took full advantage of.

By the time they reached the penthouse, Ebony's legs were like jello from his passionate, tender kisses. He held her hand with warm possession as they walked into the beautiful space and she immediately spotted the small but well-situated stage. Not much could have derailed her thoughts from Atlas at that point, but music had always held the upper hand in Ebony's world and it reasserted itself just enough now that she managed to step away, assessing her performance space.

Walking back and forth, she mentally mapped where she would stand, where instruments might be, the distance between herself and the audience..."Will I meet the band beforehand?"

"Oh, yes, I've arranged for you to spend the day with them tomorrow if that's okay. The hotel will bring you all food and refreshments all day, but Juno said you might need the day to arrange things with them."

"That would be great, thank you. Just perfect—" Her eyes found the magnificent piano at last and she gasped. "Is that a Bösendorfer Imperial Grand?"

As she spoke, she was already walking over to run her fingers over the keys and knew as soon as she heard the depth of tone color that she hadn't been mistaken. Swooning for an entirely different reason now, Ebony slid onto the seat and played a few bars.

"My accountants had fits," he whispered into her ear. "But after Romy told me about your magnificent voice—and when I heard it for myself—there was no way I could stand for anything less."

She sank into a slow melody, losing herself in the magic, as always, until he trailed his lips across her shoulder.

"Romy and Blue have asked me to come to dinner tomorrow night."

Ebony moaned slightly, the collision of music and man—this man—making her dizzy with need.

"If you do that, I'm not going to be able to control myself."

Atlas tipped her chin up and kissed her softly. "Come to dinner?"

"Oh God." She closed her eyes for a brief moment before opening them again and reaching up to cover his hand with her own. "I want you, Atlas Tigri, but we made a deal. Unless you want me to leave you with blue balls," she added with a mischievous grin.

Atlas groaned and rested his forehead against hers. "Woman, you just wait until the party is over. I'm going to rent a room in this place, and take you there. And believe me, you won't be able to walk straight the next day."

The marble floor suddenly looked like the most inviting mattress ever, but Ebony managed to get up and avoid the thought of being tumbled onto it. "I think we'd better go mingle with other people before we break our rule."

Atlas stood but pulled her to him. "One last thing."

Ebony smiled up at him, feeling his erect cock pressing against her belly. "And what's that?"

He bent his head and kissed her thoroughly. "When I get

you into bed, I'm going to fuck you so hard, woman, that you'll see stars."

She shivered. "You'd better keep that promise, Atlas Tigri."

HER BODY FELT as if it had been electrified, but later, back at Romy's house, she had a stark reminder that her body was no longer just her own. Lying in bed, reading, and trying not to think about Atlas Tigri, a wave of nausea hit her just as she switched off her lamp, and she staggered to the little en-suite bathroom and threw up. She groaned, leaning her head against the cold tile. The nausea kept coming for the next two hours and eventually, Ebony heard the door to her bedroom creak open and Romy's soft voice calling her.

"In here," Ebony croaked, her throat sore from vomiting. Romy, her sweet face creased with worry, came in and crouched next to her.

"Sweetie, are you sick?"

Ebony tried to smile as Romy swept a hand onto her forehead. The coolness of Romy's fingers felt nice against her hot skin. "Must have eaten something at lunchtime that didn't agree with me."

"Hmm. I don't think you're feverish, but you feel hot. Can I get you some Pepto?"

Ebony didn't know if Pepto was good for pregnant women, so she shook her head. "Honestly, I think it's just a bad oyster."

"You had oysters?"

"No." Ebony suddenly laughed. "But I'm okay, really. My stomach's settling down now."

Romy helped Ebony back to bed, but Ebony could see she was worried. "Honestly, Romy, I'm fine."

Romy hesitated. "I'll be just down the hallway if you need me."

"Thanks, honey. I'm sorry to wake you."

"No problem, I was awake for the twins anyway. I won't miss the midnight feeds, I can tell you. Night, sweetheart."

"Night, Romy."

As her friend slipped away, leaving Ebony alone once more, she wondered if she should confide in Romy about her pregnancy. She hadn't told anyone yet, and it was eating away at her. Today. Atlas had been a wonderful distraction, and she couldn't wait to see him again – and certainly, the thought of a night with him was making her excited. But she couldn't ignore what was happening to her for much longer.

No, I don't want to think about this, she thought resolutely. *Not tonight. Give me these next few days and then I promise, we'll figure it out.* Ebony realized she already thought of her child as a person, as them both as a team, and sighed. It would make it so much harder for her to decide what to do about the baby.

She turned onto her side and closed her eyes, and dreamed of Atlas Tigri, smiling at her as if he loved her, and holding *their* child.

CHAPTER THREE

Fino Tigri looked between his father and his uncle. Mateo shrugged at his son. "I think he heard you, *Cucciolo*, but I'm not sure. Atlas?"

Atlas blinked and broke his reverie. "I'm sorry, I was thinking of...nevermind."

"What could you have been thinking about, I wonder..." Mateo smirked knowingly. "Fino was asking you a question."

Atlas turned to his nephew who was spooning cereal into his mouth at a rapid speed. "Sorry, Fino. I missed what you said."

Fino grinned at his uncle. "I just asked if you were looking forward to seeing Papi and Vita. Bella texted me to tell me to tell me she's going to take me horse-riding."

"Sure, I am." Atlas exchanged a loaded glance with Mateo, whose expression was no longer mischievous.

'Papi' was the twin's step-father, Stanley, and Fino adored both him and Stanley's step-daughter, Bella. Stanley's wife, Vita, was an entirely different prospect, unfortunately. She was the very definition of a gold digger, having married Stanley mere weeks after the death of her first husband. Stan, mild-mannered and kind, had himself been reeling from the death of the twin's mother from cancer, and both Atlas and Mateo had been shocked at his quick wedding.

He'd apologized to them on the day of his wedding. "I need a distraction," he said, shrugging hopelessly, "because it just hurts too damn much."

The twins had accepted his new wife, mostly because of her daughter, Bella; a shy, awkward teenager, who suffered at the hands of her mother's ambitions for her. Vita was constantly bugging Stanley to sign Bella to his record label despite her tone-deaf voice and utter lack of desire to be in the music industry. Atlas and Mateo had taken her under their wing, shielding her from the constant belittling of her mother and she, in turn, adored them and Fino.

Stanley's own biological son was another tricky situation. Cormac Duggan was a billionaire in his own right, working on Wall Street, and he had little time for the two beautiful Italian twins, thinking of them as pretty playboys and nothing more. Atlas had tried to reach out to him for Stan's sake, but Mateo had told his twin not to bother.

"He's a jerk, At. Don't waste your time."

Atlas knew there had almost been a fight once between Mateo and Cormac, but Mateo would never tell him the details. "It was nothing, brother."

So, when Cormac announced he would be spending Christmas with them, Mateo had rolled his eyes but said nothing. To his credit, the one person Cormac was devoted to was Fino, who adored the older man. Mateo didn't understand it, but shrugged it off.

Atlas heard a female voice and then Molly, Fino's tutor, and Mateo's love, her sweet face breaking out into a smile, came into the kitchen. A tall, willowy blonde, Molly had been a godsend for Fino, who had struggled to connect with any of the other tutors Mateo had tried. Molly had changed all of that, and now, as Atlas watched his brother stand to greet her with a hug (no kissing in front of Fino yet, clearly), he could see the love in his brother's eyes and immediately thought of Ebony Verlaine.

Christ, she was so sexy, it killed him. Not only that, but she was bright, and funny and kind, and everything he had been looking for. He told himself to calm down, step back, but if he was honest with himself, it was taking all his strength not to call her right now and say 'Hang the fundraiser, let's spend the day in bed.'

Atlas smiled at Molly, dragging his thoughts away from Ebony's magnificent body. "You'll be spending Christmas with us, I hope."

Molly smiled shyly, and Mateo nodded. "I already asked her." Mateo turned back to Molly, who was gazing at him with utter adoration. "You're part of this family now, Mols." He drew his finger down her cheek gently.

They were so sweet Atlas felt like he was intruding. With a smile, he stood up. "Well, I'd better get to work. Molly, we'd love to have you for the holidays – and I hope Mateo is bringing you to the fundraiser tomorrow?"

Molly nodded shyly, and Mateo grinned. "You bet your a... butt I am." Atlas laughed as Fino giggled at his dad's near cussing.

"See you later, kids."

ON THE DRIVE into the city, he noticed snow was beginning to fall and smiled. Fino would love a white Christmas. When he and Mateo were younger, they would always have winters in Italy, where the weather was much warmer, so even at thirty-five, Atlas loved the prospect of a picture-perfect Christmas. Last winter, he had spent some time in the Olympic Mountains, where he had run into his old friend Romy.

. . .

WHAT A LIFE-CHANGING MEETING THAT WAS, he thought now. And how far they had come. He loved working with his old friend and was eternally grateful that she had given up a surgeon's salary to come help him build the Haven. She was so much more than just his Chief of Surgery. She was family, and part of Haven's very heart. He was looking forward to dinner tonight, with Romy, Blue, and Ebony.

HIS MIND DRIFTED BACK to the beautiful young singer. She could only be twenty-four, a decade younger than himself. Was the age-gap going to be a barrier? He didn't think so. Their shared sense of humor, at least on yesterday's evidence, defied any generational misgivings.

He couldn't wait to see her again.

AT HAVEN, however, his attention was taken up entirely as a young woman, beaten and stabbed by her abusive husband, was rushed into the operating theater where Romy desperately tried to save her life.

"Mr. Tigri?"

Atlas wasn't an angry man by any stretch, but the interruption in the middle of life or death surgery—not that he was helping, standing helplessly by watching, praying – disturbed him. Checking his temper, he turned to the security guard questioningly.

"I'm very sorry," Noah Valdez said hastily. "But we have a... situation. It's unnerving some of the residents and the police have been delayed."

"Go," Romy said tersely, not looking up from the table, and Atlas didn't dare distract her by arguing.

Still in the scrubs he'd donned to observe, he strode outside and found a man in his late twenties, railing at the security guards, his face distorted with fury as he screamed to be let inside.

"My wife is in there, and I want to see her!" he shouted as he spotted Atlas. "*Now*, motherfucker."

"I don't think so." The anger he so rarely felt now moved through Atlas like ice as he contemplated the piece of shit who had put Romy's patient on the operating table. "In fact, since I've called the police, I think it very likely you're about to be arrested for her attempted murder. You stabbed your wife *seventeen* times. And you expect us to let you in? You're lucky I don't put you in the ground, *motherfucker.*"

He knew he shouldn't be saying this stuff to the man, that he should let the police deal with him, but it was rare the abuser turned up at Haven. Was the man an idiot?

The assailant narrowed his eyes at her. "I did no such thing... I found her like that."

Atlas's eyes swept over the man's hands. "And those cuts and bruises on your own hands?" He grabbed the man's arm as the man reached into his pocket.

The man screamed in pain as Atlas squeezed hard. He would have been more than happy to crack the bastard's ulna clean in two, to leave him writhing on the floor wailing, but fortunately the Haven security guards intervened and hauled the husband away. As they pulled backwards and he let go with extreme reluctance, a bloody knife skittered to the floor from beneath the guy's hoodie. In the distance, sirens began approaching.

"You're about to be arrested for attempted murder," Atlas growled at the man, his fists balled up tightly. "Don't make it worse for yourself."

Romy appeared by Atlas's side, wearing bloodied scrubs. "Make that murder," she said in a dead voice. "Kiersten didn't make it."

Kiersten's killer smirked and before he could help himself, Atlas landed a powerful punch to the side of the man's head, knocking him backwards and onto the concrete. He lunged forward, intent on breaking the guy's arm, face, whatever he could reach, even as Romy shouted for him to stop.

"Atlas! This isn't helping!" She dragged him away with all the strength in her small body as the man cussed them out.

"Fuck! Fuck you, and fuck that bitch. I'll kill all of you, all of you. You, pretty doc, want me to gut you like I did her? My fucking pleasure..."

So much for being the usual soul of calm. Atlas erupted in a white fury and it took three huge police officers to eventually manhandle him away. Romy bore him off while the police arrested the killer and a few minutes later, while Atlas was still spitting nails, a detective came to interview them both.

"He could press charges of assault, Mr. Tigri, but as he had just threatened your life, I can't see them sticking."

"He didn't just threaten me, he threatened Doctor Sasse. He threatened to do to her what he did to his now deceased wife." Atlas's protective instincts had always been hardwired, but the notion that anyone would lay a finger on Romy in anything other than kindness made him livid. "He's a sick *fuck*."

"No doubt, but we have to follow due process. We'll need access to the body, and to your premises while we investigate."

"Of course, whatever you need," Romy told him. Her hand was on Atlas's back, rubbing him, comforting him. Atlas drew a deep breath in as the detective left them alone. He marshalled his temper at last, embarrassed.

"I'm sorry, Romy. Such behavior is acceptable from no one. I just saw red. Are you okay?"

"I'm fine." She nodded, letting his arm go at last. "Just upset at losing another one. But, that's what I signed up for. We knew this kind of thing was a possibility."

Atlas shook his head, grief for the dead young woman leaving him as numb as he'd been furious. Always even keeled, unaccustomed to such mood swings, he found himself suddenly exhausted. "Blue's going to kill me for putting you in danger."

"You didn't do anything," Romy replied. "I chose this job. I knew the dangers. Besides, our fortress home is just that. You know how Blue is about our family's security."

"I think we should go ahead and escalate our protection at Haven."

"Well, let's see what the police think. In the meantime, let me fix your hand up."

ROMY DIDN'T KNOW whether to tell Blue about the incident later, and when he came home in a good mood because of a successful surgery, she decided against it. Also, she didn't want to scare Ebony. When she got home, she knocked at Ebony's door. "Eb? Honey, how are you feeling today?"

Ebony opened the door, smiling. "I'm good. Must have just been a bad burger or something. Look, can I help you with dinner? I feel bad just sitting around."

"Actually, that would be wonderful if you don't mind. I want to get the kids fed and in bed by the time Atlas gets here."

She said nothing when Ebony's face flamed scarlet, too tired to ask questions just yet. As they both worked in the kitchen, Ebony smiled at Romy. "I thought all billionaires had staff."

Romy laughed wearily. "Oh, Blue has staff, but we don't like to have people around us permanently, especially during family time. Obviously, we have our nanny, who is wonderful, and essential if I want to work, but both Blue and I love to cook. So, no fancy schmancy chefs for us. Speaking of fancy, I hope Atlas treated you well yesterday."

"He's a great guy," Ebony said. "So much fun and I'm really looking forward to the fundraiser."

"Not your typical billionaire, is he?" Romy noted, still shocked at Atlas' anger earlier. It was a side of him she'd never known existed.

"Not at all. He brought me to Haven, and I have to say, the work you both do there...so inspiring."

"Thank you. So, you got along great?"

Ebony nodded, and this time Romy hid a smile at the two pink spots high on her friend's cheeks. While it hadn't been her intention to play matchmaker, if Atlas and Ebony got along, she would love to see her two friends happy. Ebony could only benefit from having such a devoted partner, and Atlas had long needed a good woman by his side. She knew what Blue would say. He would roll his eyes and tell her that she couldn't make *everyone* in the world love each other.

If only I could, she thought now, and her mind flew back to the horrific incident earlier. Another woman lost to her partner's violent jealousy. Romy's own experience with her murderous ex was never far from the surface, still after almost six years. Dacre Mortimer had vowed to kill her, *had* killed several women in order to get to her. She had to remind herself every day that Dacre was dead and couldn't hurt her anymore. Ironically, it hadn't even been Dacre who had almost killed her in the end. It had been Blue's stepbrother Gaius, insanely jealous of his brother, who had shot Romy in an attempt to make his half-brother suffer.

"I'm still here." That's what she told herself every morning, and she murmured it to herself now as the door opened and Grace came in, yelling happily, to greet her and Ebony.

. . .

BLUE CAME HOME from the hospital early, as he had promised, and as the nanny fed Grace, he and Romy sneaked off to their room to 'get changed for dinner.' Of course, the second the door was closed – and locked – they were the parents of a five-year-old, after all – Blue's fingers were at the zipper of Romy's dress. Romy enjoyed his lips against her skin as he kissed her then, and as she freed his cock from his pants, she smiled up at him before falling to her knees and taking him in her mouth. She sucked and teased him until his cock was quivering and rock-hard, then Blue lifted her and lay her on the bed, hitching her legs around his waist and stroking his cock into her ready and swollen cunt.

Romy moaned with pleasure as they made love, Blue kissing her passionately, leaving her breathless. She would never get tired of this, never get tired of his glorious body, the way he loved her. The way he looked at her when he was inside her...

"I love you so much," she whispered to him, and Blue nuzzled her nose with his.

"You are the reason I breathe in and out every day," he said simply. "You are my world, Romulus."

She started to giggle, and Blue grinned, watching her breasts jiggling with obvious appreciation. Then she was coming and gasping his name, arching her back up, pressing her breasts and belly against his body. Blue groaned, his cum shooting deep into her belly. Collapsing together, they kissed as they caught their breath. Blue stroked the hair back from his wife's face.

"You know, when the kids are a little older, we should try and get away, just the two of us. Even for a weekend."

Romy nodded. "I would love that. Mom and Stuart would kill to have the kids."

"For two whole days?" Blue grinned as Romy laughed.

"Let's be honest; Gracie would actually be the one in charge."

"Our little adult," Blue said fondly. He studied his wife. "Are you okay?"

Romy nodded. "Yes, of course. Why'd you ask?"

Blue traced a little line between her eyes. "Haven't seen this for a while. Not for a few years."

"I was frowning?"

"Well, not right now, but when I came home, there was a moment. I might have imagined it."

Tell him. Romy swallowed hard and shook her head. Blue still hadn't forgiven himself for her near-death years ago, though he had been in no way to blame and had actually saved her life. Why resurrected old nightmares? "I do have a small headache, so it was probably that."

"Can I get you some aspirin?"

"I'm fine, honey, it'll go when we have dinner. Speaking of which, we'd better get ready."

They showered together, taking way too long, kissing and caressing each other then got dressed slowly. Romy shimmied into a lilac tea-dress that she knew Blue loved her in and left her long dark hair down, pulled over one shoulder. Light make-up and she was ready. She turned to see Blue watching her.

"Come here."

She went to him, and he kissed her. "I love you, Dr. Sasse."

Romy gazed up at her husband and wondered how she had been so lucky as to have found him. "I love you, Doc. Let's go and have fun with our friends."

CHAPTER FOUR

Ebony, wearing a dark red dress, her short, dark hair combed into a bob, and a long gold chain around her neck, was both nervous and excited about seeing Atlas again. She wondered if she'd somehow managed to imagine the sizzling chemistry between them, but then he walked in the door and the heat crackled immediately once again.

His green eyes met hers, warm with desire that he reined in as he simply leaned in and kissed her cheek. That small gesture alone left Ebony trembling with need.

She breathed in the scent of his expensive cologne, woody and spicy, and felt her pulse quicken. "Tomorrow night," she whispered.

Atlas brushed his fingers over her jaw, leaving no doubt that if there hadn't been an audience a few feet away he would have been kissing her thoroughly. "Tomorrow."

AT DINNER, which was a fun, laid-back affair, Ebony sat with her friends and felt happier than she had in a long time. Atlas was sitting next to her and not hiding the chemistry between them as if they had known each other for years, and she was grateful to him for that.

"Listen," he was saying to Romy and Blue now. "Christmas. Are you going to the cabin?"

Blue shook his head. "No, Arti and Dan are taking Grey up this year, and we didn't want to intrude. So, it'll probably be a quiet one at home."

"In that case, I'd like to invite you all to come celebrate with us at the house. We have a houseful already – Stan's there, and I believe the Angel of Death is showing his face as well."

Ebony raised an eyebrow curiously and mouthed *Death?* to Romy, who shook her head.

"Well, you make it sound *unmissable*," said Blue dryly. "I assume you're speaking about the always delightful Cormac?"

"The very one." Atlas grinned. "Mateo's delighted as you might guess. But Vida is less annoying at Christmas, I'll admit, and I know Fino, Mateo, and Stan would love for you to be there."

"Done and done," Romy said as Blue nodded.

Atlas looked at Ebony. "Yes?"

"Me what?"

"You, Christmas, us ..." he gestured at everyone at the table. "Together."

As elated as she was surprised, Ebony nodded slowly. "Of course. If I'm not imposing—"

"You're part of our extended family now," Atlas cut in, and the way he was looking at her, there was no way Romy and Blue didn't notice, but Ebony didn't care. "I'd love to, but I think Juno and Obe are coming from New Orleans."

"Then they are invited too." Beneath the table, his fingers grazed her knee. "Please come."

Ebony couldn't look away from Atlas's gaze. "Then I'd love too."

. . .

AFTER DINNER, Ebony noticed Romy and Blue excused themselves, a little pointedly, to take care of the dishes and left Ebony and Atlas alone in the living room. Atlas sat next to her, his arm along the back of the couch. Ebony had to resist the urge to snuggle with him.

Atlas glanced out of the room and risked leaning in to kiss her. "I thought about you all day," he said softly, "and all night too."

She traced her fingertip around his mouth. "Me too...when I wasn't busy working with your band. What a great bunch of guys."

"They are. Mike called me just before I left for here, telling me he's never heard such a wonderful voice. Tomorrow night is going to be so special, Ebony...in more than one way."

Ebony shivered in anticipation. Risking another kiss, she shimmied closer to him, and Atlas slid a hand up her thigh, his fingers coming perilously close to her hot sex. Ebony couldn't help but grab his hand and pressed it between her legs.

"I want you so badly," she whispered into his ear and heard his low rumble of laughter.

"If we don't stop, I'm going to fuck you right here, right now, and that's just not good dinner party etiquette." But he kissed her back passionately, moaning when she squeezed his ramrod cock through his pants.

"Don't make any plans for the day after tomorrow," he said, "because we're spending all day in bed and I'm going to kiss every inch of your heavenly skin, Ebony Verlaine. You have crept into my brain and the things I want to do to you...most of them are *barely* legal." He said all this with a wicked grin on his face and Ebony felt herself getting wetter and wetter.

She leaned in. "The anticipation is killing me."

"Me too."

Romy and Blue made a lot of noise out in the hall to make it obvious they were about to join them, and when they came in, Ebony saw they were both grinning from ear to ear. Atlas didn't move his arm, or make any effort to hide his desire for her, and Ebony smiled at him.

IN THE MIDDLE of the night the sickness returned, but this time, she tried to be as quiet as possible. Ebony threw up then rinsed her mouth out and sat on the cool tile, placing a hand on her belly. Was morning sickness supposed to hit this soon? Ebony drew in some deep lungfuls of air. How had she been so stupid that night, which was still only two weeks ago? A hot night out on the town with her friend Kate had turned into something else entirely.

Ebony could barely believe she'd done the things she had that night. Kate, always the more adventurous one, had dared her to go to that sex club. At first, Ebony had resisted, but then later on, after way too many drinks, she'd agreed. "Just to see what it's all about."

Kate nodded, grinning. But of course, what it was about was *sex,* and she'd found herself in a room, bound and being fucked by a man whose face was obscured by a rubber mask. He had a great, hard body, a little too ripped for her taste, but she liked his back tattoo, a red phoenix. He didn't speak at all. He'd used a condom, so it was just unlucky that she'd gotten pregnant, but her shame at what she had done had overwhelmed her the next day.

Kate came to see her the next day, deeply apologetic. "I'm sorry, Ebony. I was just trying to get you to loosen up. I didn't know that would happen."

"It's okay," Ebony said, "I was fully consenting, it's just..."

"I know. But I also know you're not into that scene and I should've stopped you."

"Who's to say I would have listened?" Ebony reassured her friend. "It's okay, you know, it's life, it's an experience, it's not like I'm some virgin. I just generally like to be in control of when I'm going to sleep with someone."

"I know, and I feel wretched."

Ebony had hugged Kate, who genuinely seemed ashamed. "Dude, look, sex is great, and I'm sure there are people who dig that whole scene. It's just not for me."

She'd told herself that it was fine over and over, that sex clubs definitely had their place in the world, but she couldn't help feeling a little dirty, a little sordid. She hadn't even seen the guy's face, and now she was carrying his child. God.

But the thing was...it was something she tried not to admit to herself, but a small part of her was excited to be a mother. *Lots of women have children young,* she thought to herself, *but it's just the timing sucks. If I hadn't met Atlas...*

But she *had* met Atlas, and she was so excited about where this could go. So excited that she refused to think about the complications pregnancy would add to an as-yet nonexistent relationship. Why worry before anything had actually happened?

Dragging herself up from the floor, she glanced at her phone. Just after 4 a.m. in Seattle, and she wondered if her brother, in New Orleans, would be awake. She went back to bed and texted Obe.

You up?

Hey, sis.

She called him immediately. "Hey Bubba, sorry to bother you so early."

"No sweat. What are you doing up so early?"

"Just ... stuff on my mind," she deflected. "How's our old hunting ground?"

"Stuff like your performance, I'm guessing. The hunting grounds are beautiful, but cold. You with Juno?"

"Yeah, she's still asleep. I was about to go to the gym but I'd rather talk to you. Miss you, kiddo."

Ebony smiled down the phone. "Miss you too. Listen, the guy who's working with Romy is a sweetheart, and he's invited us to spend Christmas with him and his extended family. So, it's something to think about, thought I'd mention it. Juno knows him...Atlas Tigri."

"Yeah, she's mentioned him. That's cool. I'll talk to Juno about it, but I'm sure we can make it work if that's what you want to do."

"It is." Ebony wondered if she should share the growing attraction between her and Atlas with her brother, but decided against it.

"So. Nervous about your performance at the fundraiser?" Obe asked again.

"A little," she admitted, letting him keep thinking that was what was keeping her awake even though she didn't know the meaning of stage fright. Never had. "I don't want to let Atlas and Romy down."

"Not possible," her brother gave a short laugh, "you'll kill it, sis."

Ebony thanked him and ended the call. She lay in bed, her mind whirling with how much, in such short of time, her life was changing. She had no idea what was coming next, but she knew one thing for certain: This time tomorrow she would be in bed with the most gorgeous man she had ever laid eyes on...and she couldn't wait.

CHAPTER FIVE

I t was a habit of hers to always check out a venue early on the day of the performance, just to get the vibe. A place felt so different the day of something than on any other day.

Ebony walked into the party venue and stopped. Talk about a different vibe. "Wow." Though elegant as ever, the large room had been transformed into a white and silver Christmas wonderland, with thousands of tiny, twinkling white lights. Ebony looked around the room as the staff set dinner tables and prepared the room.

The money Atlas had put into this – his own money, Romy had told her – was a little unsettling. The man was rich – *very* rich, and it freaked her out a little.

On the stage, there was a curtain of crystals hanging like rain behind where she would sing. Ebony suddenly felt overwhelmed, an unfamiliar feeling she didn't enjoy in the slightest.

"Miss Verlaine?"

She turned to see a young woman smiling at her. "That's me, hello."

"Hi there, I'm Felicity. Mr. Tigri suggested you might drop by early."

Ebony looked at her in surprise. "He did, did he?" The way he seemed to know her so well when they'd barely just met could have been unnerving, but she found it somehow only amplified how hot the man was.

"He asked whether you'd like any changes made. Any at all, and I'll make them happen."

Ebony didn't even need to look around. The place was easily the nicest venue she'd ever been in. "No. It all looks fantastic. Just make sure the jazz drummer has a screen, please." She elaborated at Felicity's confused look. "The plastic cage you see around them sometimes. Helps avoid drowning out quieter instruments, and my voice. It's not standard use in jazz, but at rehearsal this morning the drummer requested one."

Felicity made a note on her phone. "I'll take care of it," she promised. "Mr. Tigri also said you might want a new outfit for tonight. Because it's special, he asked me to tell you specifically."

For one second Ebony found herself offended at the suggestion that she didn't have the right outfit for this upscale joint, and then Atlas' 'because it's special' hit home and she realized he was flirting with her. Through his unwitting assistant, no less.

"I love dress shopping," Felicity confided with a shy smile. "Especially with no budget. I'd be happy to help you pick out something. Mr. Tigri told me to take the day to help and to warn you to spare no expense."

Ebony smiled. "He said that, did he? Well, all right, then. Take me to your favorite place, Felicity."

Standing in the exclusive boutique a short while later, Ebony's eyes widened at the designer clothes. "This is too much."

Felicity laughed. "Not at all. Now, what's your aesthetic?"

Ebony hesitated then said. "I'm a retro girl. I love anything from the Twenties, Thirties or Forties."

Felicity nodded. "Then we're in the right place. Carmen is one of Seattle's up and coming designers, and she loves anything retro. This is going to be amazing..."

Over the next hour, they talked with the designer herself, who brought out several pieces that Ebony almost swooned over. Eventually, she chose a form-fitting gold dress which skimmed her curves and looked sensational against her dark skin. Felicity then took her to a beauty salon where they worked on her hair, shaping it into pin curls around her face. Ebony had to admit – she didn't recognize the stunning woman in the mirror.

"Now," Felicity said, "Underwear?"

Ebony flushed. "Um..."

Felicity grinned impishly. "Top to toe was what Mr. Tigri suggested, but only if you wanted it. He's not trying to Eliza Doolittle you – his words."

New, sexy underwear was definitely appealing, but Ebony felt awkward. "On one condition...I'm allowed to pay for my own underwear."

"Entirely up to you."

They went to a small boutique, and Ebony picked up some sultry, dark red underwear that cost way too much for something that just might end up shredded in three seconds. But God, she hoped it did end up in pieces on the floor. It'd be worth the expense. Every cent of it.

"Good choice." Felicity approved, then smiled. "Okay, lunch?"

Ebony enjoyed Felicity's company at lunch, getting to know the young woman. "How long have you worked for Atlas?"

"Five years," Felicity said, her mouth full of sandwich, "he recruited me as an intern – a paid intern at that – and after his long-time secretary left, I became his assistant. I think he likes me because I'm not star struck by him. I tell him the truth."

Ebony smiled. "I get that about him. He's a good guy."

"He really is." Felicity studied Ebony. "He told me you come from Seattle originally?"

Ebony nodded. "Born and bred. I moved away from Seattle when my brother moved to New Orleans. Serendipitously, it turned out, because the Foundation who mentored me and my career is based there."

Felicity nodded. "My girlfriend's brother is involved with them too. Ben Faldo."

"I know Ben, he's a wonderful musician and a sweet guy."

Felicity beamed. "He is, thank you."

Ebony decided she liked Felicity very much and after Felicity dropped her back at the venue, she gave her cell phone number to her. "In case you want to go for drinks sometime."

Felicity grinned. "Would love to. Knock them dead tonight."

"You're not coming?"

"Sadly, not this time, I have a family thing, but I have no doubt you'll rock it."

EBONY HUNG her performance dress up behind the door of her dressing room and, covering her hair with a cap carefully, stepped into the shower. She wasn't sure if all dressing rooms had showers, but it sure was convenient. She scrubbed off, shaved, massaged moisturizer oil into every part of her body, then slipped her new underwear on. The oil had a gold shimmer to it which made her dark skin glow, and the dark red underwear was the perfect color for her. She slipped her day dress back on, not wanting to get her performance dress rumpled – it was a couple of hours until she was on.

Happily, she began to warm up her voice, even though the

performance was way too far away for it to make a difference yet. In the middle of a scale, there was a knock on the door.

Opening it, her heart began to beat faster. Atlas grinned at her. "Hey, gorgeous."

She couldn't help herself; she grabbed his tie and pulled him into the room, pressing her body against his as he bent his head to kiss her. She tangled her fingers in his dark curls, savoring every moment of the kiss, his lips firm and gentle, but with a fierce passion.

Breaking away finally, gasping for air, Ebony laughed. "God, Atlas Tigri...what you do to me."

"What I'm going to do to you later tonight," he said, sliding his arms around her waist, "will put even a kiss like that in the shade."

Ebony moaned in anticipation. "Am I in a dream? I think I must be."

Atlas laughed, his green eyes shining. "Then I'm in it with you, beautiful. Now, tell me, did Felicity spoil you like I asked her to?"

It was Ebony's turn to laugh. "Yes, she did. I felt like Julia Roberts in Pretty Woman, except for the whole hooker thing."

"Just as long as you weren't offended. I tried to have her explain, without giving it away."

"I got the message," she promised as he kissed her again, then swept a lock of her hair over her ear. "Are you nervous?"

Ebony shook her head. "No. Not about *anything,* Atlas."

He groaned. "I've never wanted a party to be over so badly. I'm just going to be the worst host."

Ebony smiled. "I don't believe that for a second."

Atlas grinned. "Hey, you hungry? I have pizza coming."

"You read my mind."

Somehow they kept their hands to themselves as they ate, and Ebony figured they both qualified for some kind of sainthood by the end of the hour when Atlas kissed her cheek and left her alone to get ready. "Get dressed." He leaned in and whispered into her ear, "So I can undress you later."

Leaving her utterly on fire, he departed.

Pulling herself together after he'd all but melted her bones, Ebony slipped into her couture dress and went through a full vocal warmup as she prepared to be called by the floor manager. As she approached the stage, she heard the chatter of the guests and peeked out at the crowd. Scores of beautifully and expensively dressed people, none of whom she recognized, were milling around, glasses of champagne in hand, talking and laughing with each other.

She saw Atlas, breathtaking in his Armani suit and bow-tie, step up to the microphone. Ebony felt another curl of desire in her stomach as she listened to his low, sensual voice thanking the guests for coming. He talked with such passion about Haven and what his ambitions for it were that Ebony was almost moved to tears.

She realized Atlas was coming to the end of his speech and was about to announce her. Her skin tingled as she registered the fondness in his voice as he talked about her, and when he announced her, she walked onto the stage to warm applause. Atlas kissed her cheek, winking at her. "Go get 'em, kiddo."

Adrenaline pumped through Ebony's system as she greeted the crowd and introduced her band, and then, as the music swelled, she began to sing.

ATLAS STOOD to the side of the stage, unable to take his eyes off of Ebony. Her voice, low, tremulous and sensual, sent shivers down his spine. The way the gold dress clung to her body was driving him crazy, and when she glanced over at him and smiled as she sang, his heart thudded against his chest.

Atlas had questioned himself over the last two days whether he was doing the right thing, getting involved with Ebony. Not because of who she was, but because of who he was. Was he taking advantage? He would hate to think so, but Ebony was very young. His gut was telling him that she was special though and for now, he would go along with that. He had dreamed of her creamy dark skin and deep brown eyes since the moment he met her, and when he kissed her, he'd never been so sure about anything.

Last night, he'd told Mateo how he felt about her, and Mateo, ever the romantic, had been delighted. "Brother, as long as neither of you gets hurt, what's the harm? Live, Atlas. You've been surrounded by sycophants and gold-diggers all your life. If your instinct is telling you this girl is different, go with it. *Leap.*"

Now, Atlas closed his eyes for a moment, immersing himself in the sound of her voice. It wrapped him as smoothly and softly as he imagined her body would later. Ebony made even much-performed standards sound fresh and original, her smooth voice with that touch of gravel entrancing the gathered party-goers. After every song, they applauded her loudly, some even whooping their approval, and Atlas could see the confidence in Ebony's eyes growing. Her sweet smile, the friendly, easy way she chatted with the audience between songs...she was a star, that much was obvious. Atlas made a mental note to talk to Stanley – his step-father, with all his contacts, could help Ebony immeasurably, and she deserved every opportunity.

He felt someone touch his arm and found Romy, beautiful in a midnight blue column gown, smiling beside him. "Girl did good, huh?"

"Unbelievably good," Atlas agreed, still half wrapped in Ebony and her song. "How're you doing?"

"Very good. Blue's grabbing us some drinks. Listen, I wanted to thank you for not spilling about the guy at Haven yesterday. I don't want Blue worried about me every second – he does that enough, anyway."

Atlas's smile faded. "The detective called. Dude was bailed. Keep your security team close."

Romy didn't look worried. "We will, don't worry. I can't believe they bailed that motherfucker. He *killed* her."

"Apparently his family is well connected."

Romy looked angry. "God. Preppy entitled assholes. Dacre was the same."

Atlas squeezed her head. "Dacre's dead."

"I know." Romy sighed. "But there's always another one and another..."

"Which is why we do what we do." He put an arm around her shoulders and hugged her. Ebony was about to start another song, and Romy smiled again.

"God, I love this song."

It was a cover of Etta James' *At Last,* always a crowd pleaser, and the audience began to sing along with Ebony, who grinned and encouraged them. She had them in the palm of her hand, that was obvious, and Atlas felt a surge of affection. In a life and career where he saw so much pain, so much of the worst of people, it was a salve to the soul to see someone connecting with others so much. He felt Romy grinning at him and looked down at her.

"You're smitten," she said, nudging him with her shoulder and he laughed.

"I admit, I am," he said honestly.

Romy smiled and gave him an affectionate sideways hug. "I'm happy for you, Atlas. I adore Ebony, and you both deserve happiness. She feels the same way, believe me."

"I hope so. It's the very beginnings of *something,* Romy. I hope it becomes more but at the moment..."

"I know, I know. Just enjoy it. God, her voice is like velvet, isn't it?"

ATLAS WAS SPELLBOUND – as was the audience – as Ebony finished up her set and he, like them, applauded her long and hard. He got up onto the stage as she shyly took her bow. "Ladies and gentleman, it's a cliché, but tonight, I think, a star was born. Miss Ebony Verlaine, everybody."

Ebony chuckled, her face red as Atlas kissed her cheek. "You were sensational, baby. Utterly sensational."

CHAPTER SIX

A t the dinner after the show, Atlas had seated her next to him, with Romy and Blue at their table too. "I thought you might want some friends around."

Ebony smiled at him gratefully. "I can't thank you enough for this opportunity," she said to him and Romy. "If there's any more I can do to help, please, just ask. I'd be happy to."

"I think you'll be fighting the offers off now," Blue said, with a wink. "In fact, if I'm not mistaken, Roman Ford is here somewhere."

"Of Quartet?" Ebony almost squeaked. Quartet was one of the biggest record companies in the world – but they were very, very picky about who they had on their roster. To be a Quartet Artist was to have a cache in the business like no other.

"That's him...I can introduce you if you'd like." Atlas nodded to a table where Ebony saw Roman laughing with a beautiful blonde woman who looked familiar. Ebony recognized her as Kym Clayton, the guitarist in The 9th and Pine, a Seattle rock band she and Obe loved and had been to see play live many times.

Ebony swallowed nervously. She'd just spent hours working

out her voice, but her throat was suddenly dry as sand. "Maybe another time, I don't want to use this night to shill for myself."

Atlas and Blue laughed, and Romy squeezed Ebony's hand. "Darling, the second you opened your mouth up there, that was your introduction, believe me."

Romy wasn't wrong. After a luscious dessert of champagne sorbet with strawberries, Roman Ford came over to their table and shook her hand. It was all Ebony could not to stutter when he complimented her. "That voice is astonishing, Ebony." And when he casually added, "Call me. I'd like you to meet my partners," if Atlas hadn't been discreetly propping her up with a hand on her back, she might have sagged at the knees.

He handed Ebony a business card, then stayed to chat with them for a time. Ebony sat, listening to her friends talking and laughing, feeling Atlas's fingers stroking up and down her bare back, Quartet's business card in her purse and surrounded by friends. A small twinge of something fluttered in her belly – a new life in more ways than one. *Is this all really happening?*

As the guests started to drift away toward the end of the night, Atlas and Ebony said goodbye to their friends and hand-in-hand rode the elevator to the penthouse suite. They gazed at each, no words needed, and when they walked into the suite, Atlas took her in his arms and kissed her.

"You were amazing, the party was a success...but, god, I'm glad it's over..."

Ebony gave a moan as he buried his face in her neck, his lips against her throat, his fingers gently pulling the straps of her dress down her shoulders. The gold fabric slithered down her body to the floor and it was Atlas' turn to moan at the sight of her curves. "Even more beautiful than I dreamed."

Ebony's trembling fingers pulled at his tie, then unbuttoned his shirt. She pressed her lips to his chest, his hard pecs with a smattering of black hair, trailing her fingertips down his flat stomach, feeling it contracted with desire under her touch. As she unzipped his pants, Atlas stroked her stomach. She gazed up at him as she freed his huge, diamond-hard cock from his underwear, and stroked it against her bare belly.

Atlas muttered something in Italian and cupped her face as he kissed her passionately. His hand slipped between her legs, caressing her through her panties, then gently sliding them down her legs. With an expert twist, he unclasped her bra, letting her full, ripe breasts fall into his hands. Stroking a rhythm over them with his thumbs, Atlas kissed her again, then swept her into his arms and into the bedroom.

On the bed, he covered her body with his, kissing her, then moving down to take her nipples into his mouth one by one. Ebony tangled her fingers in his dark hair as he moved down her body, rimming her deep navel with his tongue, then, making her gasp, his mouth found her sex.

Teasing, biting, tasting her, he expertly brought her to a mellow orgasm, flooding her sex with desire. "I want to taste you too."

Smiling, she pushed him onto his back, as she took his cock into her mouth. He really was so big that she couldn't take him all, and so with her hand, she fisted the root of him as her mouth worked, her tongue running up and down the silky skin, feeling the hardness underneath.

"God, Ebony..."

She knew he was close, but she didn't pull away until he shot his cum onto her tongue, shuddering and groaning her name. She swallowed him down, salty sweetness on her tongue, then moved up to straddle him as he recovered.

Atlas stroked her belly, cupped her breasts. "Your body is heaven," he said breathlessly and laughed as she bent to kiss him, pressing her breasts and belly to his.

He flipped her onto her back. "I'm going to fuck you so hard, Ebony, all night long."

Ebony smiled. "Tell me more," she purred as he sat back and grabbed a condom, rolling it onto his stiffening cock. "You're so big, baby."

"And you're going to take it all, my darling." He slipped his hands between her legs. "You're so wet, sweetheart."

"I've been wet all day, thinking about this moment," Ebony whispered. "Thinking about you, how you'll feel inside me... *oh...god...*"

Atlas slid into her slowly, filling her silky cunt with his rock-hard cock. For a moment he paused as they gazed at each other, savoring the moment, then a frenzied need took over them both, and they were fucking hard and fast, tearing at each other, Ebony's nails digging into the skin of his back and his buttocks as she urged him on, gasping and panting.

Atlas slammed his hips against hers, forcing her legs wider until her hips burned, but Ebony loved the pain of it. She wanted him, wanting all of him, the feeling of his cock driving deeper and harder inside her was ecstasy. Her head swam with delirious desire as Atlas pinned her hands to the bed, reaming her harder until she cried out, her orgasm hitting, making stars explode in her vision. She felt Atlas' cock throb hard inside her, and he groaned her name as he too reached his peak. They collapsed together, breathing hard.

"Stay inside me for a while," she said, and Atlas grinned.

"I'd stay inside you forever if I could, beautiful." His mouth was gentle on her lips now, tender, loving. Ebony swept damp black curls away from his forehead.

"God, you're one gorgeous man," she said, chuckling. She still couldn't believe he wanted her, but she adored the soft look of love in his eyes. "I hope I didn't disappoint you."

Atlas laughed aloud, rolling his eyes. "Baby, disappointed is not even in my vocabulary tonight. Call it overwhelmed, call it blown away...even better than what I've been thinking about solidly for the last forty-eight hours. Man...I love the way your body fits perfectly next to mine...do you get that?"

Ebony wiggled, reveling in the fact his cock, still semi-hard, was still buried deep in her cunt. "Fuck me again," she said, nipping his bottom lip with her teeth. "Make me scream."

Atlas grinned. "Your wish is my command..."

He excused himself for a moment to get rid of the used condom, then returned quickly to her arms. He hooked her knees over his shoulders then sat up. "Is this uncomfortable?"

Ebony shook her head. Atlas retrieved a new condom, and as he buried his face in her sex, Ebony rolled the condom down his long, thick shaft, feeling the steely muscle inside quiver at her touch. She cupped his balls in her hands, tickling them, teasing them until Atlas groaned, his voice resonating against her clit, then he was inside her again.

This time was even more intense. Their gazes at each other never faltered as they fucked, Ebony bucking up against him, Atlas's hands rough on her skin. They came again and again, fucking on the floor, against the walls, and even up against the wall-to-ceiling glass window, Atlas taking Ebony from behind as her breasts and belly pressed against the cool glass.

Even in the shower, as dawn approached, they couldn't get enough of each other, Atlas parting her pert, rounded buttocks and easing into her ass as Ebony urged him on. They explored every inch of each other with their eyes, their hands, their mouths. For the few times they were recovering, they talk and laughed and joked, and Ebony felt something shift in her soul. She had never had this kind of connection, this chemistry with anyone before.

Atlas stroked her face as dawn broke outside the window. "I cleared my schedule for today. Are you free?"

"I am." She wiggled closer to him, and he wrapped his arms around her.

"Would you like to come to my home, meet my brother and nephew?"

Ebony smiled. "I would love to." She loved the hopeful look in Atlas's eyes – he really wanted her to be part of his family, didn't he? The feeling touched her on a totally different level than he had for hours just now, but no less deeply.

"First, though, being an old man..."

"At thirty-four..."

Atlas laughed. "But, as jazzed as I am, how about we try and get some sleep? I want to hold you in my arms and rest."

Ebony tucked her head into his shoulder. "I'm always up for a nap."

Atlas chuckled, pressing his lips to her forehead. "I knew we had a lot in common."

"Sweet dreams, Atlas."

"Sweet dreams, baby."

CHAPTER SEVEN

Felicity knocked on Romy's office door. "Romy? Detective Halsey is here to see you."

"Thanks, Felicity." Romy got up as the detective entered and shook his hand. "I'd say it was good to see you, but I can the see the expression on your face."

She motioned for him to sit and the detective thanked her. "Yes, unfortunately, I come bearing bad news. Carson Franks was released from jail this morning, on a three-million-dollar bail. Apparently, that's short change for his family."

"Ugh." Romy sighed. *Another rich fuck getting away with murder.*

"Quite. Franks had to relinquish his passport, but..."

"But with his kind of money, getting counterfeits will be no problem."

Det. John Halsey looked at her. "Dr. Sasse...I read about your ex-husband, so I know you have experience with these kinds of things."

"Sadly, I do. The reason I became involved in Haven was because of that situation. The victim, Kiersten Merchant, was sadly typical of our residents here. At the moment it seems particularly bad, the deaths, the ones we can't save." Romy sighed, rubbing her face. "I'm sorry, Detective, did you have something else?"

He nodded. "Dr. Sasse, we have reason to believe that Franks meant what he said. I came to make sure you and Mr. Tigri are taking the security issue seriously."

Romy nodded. "We are. We've more than doubled our security presence here, and at our homes. He won't get near our facility, I assure you."

"I'll be checking in with you, keeping you updated about the situation." He glanced at the big picture window in Romy's ground floor office, and Romy read his mind.

"It's bulletproof," she said, "but if you think we ought to take extra precautions."

John Halsey nodded. "It's just...I've dealt with obsessives before. Carson Franks blames this facility, Mr. Tigri, and you, for Kiersten's death. It's just the way a psychopath's mind works. Never mind that he stabbed her seventeen times. It's always someone else's fault."

Old memories worked their way through Romy and she pushed them aside firmly. Dacre had long been out of her life and she wouldn't give him one more second of fear.

At home, later, after the kids were in bed, Romy and Blue shared a soak in the tub. Romy lay back against Blue's hard chest as he trailed his fingers up and down her stomach, and cupped her breasts. She giggled as he pretended to bite her shoulder.

"How was your day, beautiful?"

Romy hesitated before she answered, unaccustomed to hiding anything from her husband. Her desire to protect him won out though. "Oh, same old, same old. No new intake, which is always a blessing, so I had time to catch up with paperwork."

"Boring."

She laughed. "Ever the surgeon. Any big cases?"

"Actually yes. We have a domino surgery soon."

"Woah." A domino surgery was a rare and risky procedure, involving multiple donor-recipients receiving organs in a simultaneous procedure. "Is this your first one?"

Blue kissed her temple. "It is...you want in?"

"Hell, yes I do...if we can make it work."

"Getting you privileges at the hospital is no problem, obviously."

Romy looked around at him. "Perks of getting busy with the boss."

Blue laughed. "Obviously."

Romy turned around, straddling him. Blue immediately reached for her breasts, and she grinned, then sighed happily as he took a nipple into his mouth. She reached down to stroke his cock, feeling it swell and harden under her touch. Blue lifted her up and impaled her on his shaft. "God, your cunt is so silky," he said, kissing her mouth, crushing his lips against hers as she began to ride him, rolling her hips towards his. His fingers bit into the skin of her hips as she took him in deeper and deeper. "Romy, Romy, Romy..."

The whisper of her name made her whole body tingle, and she increased her pace, looking down to watch his cock slide in and out of her. "A beautiful sight, eh?" Blue whispered, "I love watching us fuck."

"God, yes..." Romy was close, and when Blue started to stroke her clit, she shivered and gave a little cry as she came, then smiled as she felt him pump thick, creamy cum deep into her belly. "I love you so much, Blue Allende."

"And I love you," he said, kissing her passionately. As she caught her breath, Blue was gazing up at her with such love in his gorgeous green eyes that her eyes filled with tears.

"Hey, hey, hey..." he said in concern, pulling her in for a kiss. "*Perché piangi, bella?* Why are you crying?"

She smiled as the tears dropped down her cheeks. "They're happy tears...I swear...I've never been so happy as I am right now. Our beautiful family...and you. Blue, I don't know what I'd do without you."

"You'll never have to find out, baby. I couldn't live without you."

Romy pressed her lips to his again. "Let's get out of this tub and go to bed, baby. I want to fuck you all night long."

As they dried themselves, Romy massaged moisturizer into her body. As she stroked the cream into the skin on her belly, she traced the faint scar of the bullet wound she had sustained all those years ago. She'd been lucky; the bullet hadn't hit any major organs and arteries, and their daughter, at the time only a tiny, tiny embryo, had also survived.

Blue came up behind her and swept her into his arms making her giggle, and carried her off to their bed. As he covered her body with his, she gazed up at him and knew she had everything she had ever wanted right here, right now. No one could touch them.

VERY SOON, she would discover, in the worst way, that she was wrong.

CHAPTER EIGHT

A boy, not older than seven or eight, skidded to a halt in front of Ebony and gaped at her. He had the same shaggy black hair and bright green eyes as Atlas and Ebony smiled at him. "You must be Fino."

A moment's hesitation and then the boy smiled, the same wide, friendly, devastating smile as his uncle, and presumably his father. A moment later, Ebony saw his father, Mateo, as he came down the steps of the Tigri mansion to greet them.

"Hey, At, hey, Ebony, great to meet you."

Ebony thought he was going to kiss her cheek; instead, Mateo picked her up and twirled her around, making her shriek with laughter. Atlas chuckled, shaking his head. "He likes to surprise people."

"Ebony isn't people, she's family," his brother corrected, setting Ebony back on her feet and grinning down at her. "You said it yourself."

"Did you?" Ebony looked at Atlas and smiled, touched all over again even though he'd said as much at the dinner table.

"That's the last time I tell you a secret," Atlas teased his brother, while wrestling with his nephew.

"I've never seen him so enchanted," Mateo went on, smirking.

Ebony flushed as Atlas sighed. "Dude."

Mateo grinned, unrepentant. "Sorry, bro. Fino, come give Ebony a hug."

Ebony was about to say he didn't need to when Fino threw himself at her. She hugged the young boy, feeling slightly over-whelmed by the warmth of the Tigri's greeting, but she soon realized it was par for the course for the Tigri twins. Their house, while as palatial as she would have expected, was also a place of love and laughter. Mateo introduced her to the sweet Molly, who clearly adored both Mateo and his son, and enjoyed a jokey relationship with Atlas. Their chef, Annalise, prepared a delicious buffet for their lunch, and afterward, Atlas took Ebony on a tour of the grounds.

It was bitingly cold, but Ebony hunkered down in her thick wool coat, and Atlas offered her his arm. The grounds looked like a Winter Wonderland – a hoar frost was clinging to the vegetation, the trees, and the fences around the property.

"You grew up here?"

Atlas nodded. "Most of the year. We spent a lot of time in Italy, too, Padua, where we were born." He smiled down at her. "Maybe I can take you there sometime."

Ebony grinned. "One thing at a time, Atlas, I'm still processing that someone like you could want someone like *me*."

Atlas frowned. "I don't understand what you mean."

"I mean, look at this." She gestured around the grounds, and to the house. "I'm just a kid from St. Anne's. Obe and I went to regular high school, we brown-bagged our lunches, we worked three jobs through college to pay for it. I'm...ordinary, and you are...a god."

Atlas chuckled, but his eyes were serious. "Ebony, you are anything but ordinary. And what does all this mean except we got lucky to be born wealthy? Yes, both Mateo and I have made our own fortunes, but we had doors opened for us to help us achieve that. Believe me, I am the last person you should consider a god, whatever that means. I have plenty of demons."

Ebony wiggled her eyebrows at him. "Sexy."

Atlas laughed, but his eyes were serious. "We don't know each other yet, Ebony, but I won't hide anything from you. I want to know everything about you, and there's nothing about me, or my life, or my past I want to hide from you. Ask me anything."

Ebony chuckled, pushing aside the fact that she was very definitely hiding something from him. "Um, okay. When did your parents pass?"

"Our dad when we were kids, Mom a few years ago."

She nodded. "And your step-dad remarried?"

"On a whim, we think, but Stan practically brought us up, so we support him no matter what."

"And he has a son who looks like death."

Atlas half-smiled, but there was a serious edge to the curl of his lips. "It's not that I don't like Cormac, rather that we have nothing in common with him. The man has no sense of humor, and he's a shark. He's engaged to the heiress of a very, very wealthy New York family, because," and he continued in a dead-panned voice, "inheriting Stanley's billions won't be enough."

Ebony snickered. "Must be hard for him."

"Right? Corman will always take the easy way to quick money – as long as it's legal. I give him that, he's a straight shooter. He doesn't hide his ambition." Atlas pulled her abruptly into a warm hug. "Ebs, he's coming for Christmas, and I wanted to warn you about him. He has very little tact, and he'll grill you endlessly. I'll protect you, but he has a habit of being tenacious when he wants to know something."

She read easily between the lines. "You're saying he'll imme-diately assume I'm a gold-digger?"

"I'm afraid so."

Ebony shrugged. "Atlas, I wouldn't care if you were poor and lived under a bridge. Your money is of no interest to me."

Atlas stopped and tilted her chin up so he could kiss her. "I know that, Ebony." He pressed his lips to hers, his tongue massaged hers gently. "God, you're beautiful."

Ebony's mouth curved up in a smile. "I'm glad you think so."

Atlas chuckled, then grabbing her hand, moved away from the house. "Come with me."

He led her further into the grounds to an area shaded from the house, and Ebony gasped as she realized they were in a maze. "Wow. It's like Harry Potter."

Atlas laughed. "Fino thinks so too. But what I have in mind right now is way more R-rated than even JK Rowling's adult books."

"Adult what? She wrote books post-Harry? I think I'm brokenhearted," Ebony joked breathlessly as he took her in his arms and kissed her, as his hands slid down the length of her body.

"Good idea to wear a skirt, baby."

"In this cold?" she teased. "I *knew* you had skills."

His hands slid her panties down her legs and over her boots as she unzipped his fly. Atlas produced a condom from his back pocket, and Ebony laughed. "So, this was a plan?"

"Oh, god, yes...Ebony in the snow...man, I've dreamed about this."

She freed his cock from his underwear, and he cussed little at the cold, making her giggle furiously. Nevertheless, he was inside her in a flash, supporting her, as they fucked against the maze's thick hedge. It wasn't an entirely successful pairing; Atlas wobbled as their pace quickened and they tumbled to the snow, both laughing furiously. "Damn," Atlas said, shaking his head, "In my head, that was so erotic."

Ebony had tears of laughter in her eyes as he helped her to her feet. "Worth a shot," she said as she helped him tidy up. "I'll make it up to you tonight."

"Yeah, you will," he leered at her comically, and she giggled.

"You are so silly for a billionaire businessman. Aren't you all supposed to be arrogant and aloof?"

Atlas shrugged. "That sounds like way too much effort. Mateo can do that to a certain extent, but he's a better actor than I am."

"You're the softy of the two of you?"

Atlas considered as he took her hand. "In different ways. Mateo is quicker to anger, whereas I'm the one who will take a lot until I blow, then it's like Armageddon."

Ebony studied. "I can't imagine that."

"I lost my temper at work the other day," he admitted. "A man showed up, one responsible for his wife's death on Romy's operating table. If she hadn't been there to restrain me ..."

She kissed him softly. "There are places and times when exploding is understandable."

"I'm so glad you agree." He grinned at her and rolled his hips, playful once more as he tumbled her back into the snow and kissed her over and over, their laughter ringing through the vast property.

THE REST of the day passed quickly, playing with Fino, who Ebony was madly in love with, and joking around with the Tigri twins. As she and Atlas left for the city, Mateo hugged her.

"So, we'll see you in two days for Christmas?"

Ebony nodded, kissing his cheek. "You will, thank you, Mateo. Thanks for making me feel so welcome."

"My pleasure, honey." He winked at his brother. "I always

said my brother had good taste. You'll meet my Molly then, too. I know you will get along."

Fino also clung to her and Ebony felt something shift inside her. Was this what having a child would feel like? This joy, this wonder of the new? "Come back soon," Fino ordered, and Ebony grinned at him.

"How can I resist such a request? Bye, Fino, next time I see you, you'll have to teach me how to play chess."

Mateo coughed something that sounded suspiciously like 'geeks' and Fino grinned at his dad.

In the car, Atlas looked over at Ebony. She was smiling to herself. "Did you like my family, baby?"

She nodded. "Very much, Atlas. Mateo and Fino have such a wonderful relationship."

"They do. No one was more surprised than me when Mateo stepped up to be a father. He astonished me. He was always the playboy of the two of us, reckless, and sometimes irresponsible, but when Fino came along, it was almost instantaneous, the change in my brother. He's incredible."

Atlas smiled at Ebony but was surprised to see tears in her eyes. "Hey, hey, hey..."

Ebony half-chuckled. "It's okay, it's just so moving. And Fino is such a wonderful little kid."

"He is." Atlas touched her cheek. "How about you? Do you want kids?"

Her faint hesitation surprised him, given how well she'd gotten along with Fino. "In time. And I want a guarantee he or she will be *exactly* like Fino." Ebony colored. "I mean...I'm not presuming...oh god, I really stuck my foot in my mouth."

Atlas grinned at her. "No, you didn't. I already know I would love to have kids with you. Does that scare you?"

Ebony gave a strange half-laugh, which almost sounded like a sob. "A little."

"No expectations," Atlas said lightly, trying to ease the sudden awkwardness, "Just a fact."

Ebony was quiet for the rest of the journey and Atlas wondered if he'd scared her off. "Look," he said, as they rode the elevator to his apartment. "All I meant was..."

"It's okay," Ebony interrupted him, her hand on his face. "I know what you meant, and I feel the same. But we're in the very early days of whatever this is."

Atlas smiled ruefully. "You're discovering one of my many faults – I get overexcited, and overreach. I'm just happy we met."

Ebony smiled at him. "Me too, Atlas."

They sat up talking until late, cuddled together on the couch until Atlas swept her into his arms and carried her to bed.

Their lovemaking was tender and slow-burning this time, Atlas's thick, long cock thrusting in measured strokes as they kissed and caressed each other. Atlas admired Ebony's luscious body as she writhed beneath him, the dampness on her skin making it glow, the way her full breasts, her softly curved belly undulated with their movements. Atlas loved the feeling of being buried deep inside her velvety cunt. Her vaginal muscles contracted around his shaft, milking him, caressing him until he was shooting cum deep into her belly.

"God, you're amazing," he gasped, shuddering and groaning as he came, admiring the way her back arched up as she came, her thighs clamped around his waist. They fit together so perfectly.

They fell asleep wrapped in each other's arms, but in the early hours Atlas woke suddenly. Finding the bed empty beside him, he sat up, listening. From the bathroom, he could hear violent wretching and immediately swung his legs out of bed in concern. "Ebs?"

Receiving no response, he got up and went to the bathroom door, knocking gently. "Ebony? Are you okay?"

The wretching began. "I'm coming in."

"No, it's..." But her words were cut off by more vomiting. Atlas pushed open the door, glad it hadn't been locked, and crouched next to her as she hovered over the toilet. Reaching for a washcloth and wetting it with cold water, he gently wiped her face the next time she came up for air.

"Are you okay?" he asked with deep concern at her pallid, gray, sweating countenance.

"Yeah, I'm so sorry, Atlas. I just woke up and felt nauseous."

"Why are you apologizing?" He smoothed her damp hair back, lingering on her flushed skin.

"This," Ebony indicated herself, "is the opposite of sexy."

Atlas rolled his eyes. "God forbid you should be human. Do you want me to call a doctor?"

Ebony shook her head. "No, thank you. I'll wait it out – hopefully it's nothing more than a twenty-four-hour thing."

Atlas frowned. "I hope so, baby. Look, let's get you back to bed, I think I have some Pepto somewhere."

LATER, back in bed, Ebony pretended to fall asleep, and then when she heard Atlas's breathing settle into a steady rhythm, she opened her eyes. *You can't put this off any longer,* she thought, *not if you want a future with this man. You're pregnant, and it isn't going to magically go away. See a doctor. See someone. Make a decision.*

The thought of abortion made her feel wretched, even though she supported the right to choose; at the same time, how could she tell this wonderful man she was pregnant with another man's child? What would he think of her if he knew the circumstances of the conception? Would he think she was a whore?

God, you stupid, stupid woman, she berated herself and felt her eyes fill with tears. *No. I will not wallow in self-pity. In the morning, I'll call Romy and ask for her help, her advice.*

Decision made, she snuggled back into Atlas's warm embrace and finally fell asleep.

CHAPTER NINE

R omy pulled off her latex gloves and patted Ebony's shoulder. "Yup, about two to three weeks, I would say. You can get dressed now, honey."

While Ebony tidied herself up, Romy sat down. Ebony had called her this morning and asked to come see her somewhere private. Romy had invited her to her home, and now, Ebony smiled at her gratefully.

"Thank you for doing this, Romy. I wouldn't ask, but I'm conflicted."

"I should say." Romy gave her a warm smile. "Look, it must be a confusing time, what with this thing with Atlas, and I can totally see why you're hesitant to tell him. That being said, Atlas is far from the oblivious billionaire. He knows stuff happens which isn't convenient, or perhaps the way society states things should happen. It's life."

"So, you think I should tell him?"

"It's not my decision, but I always think honesty is the best way to go. Do you want the baby, Ebony? That's the big question."

Ebony sighed and sipped the decaffeinated tea Romy placed

in front of her. "That's just it. I don't know. My head is saying no, but the thought of getting rid of it...I just don't know. And I have no way of contacting the father, I didn't even see his face."

She felt her face burn red and looked away from Romy, who leaned over to pat her hand. "You know what? Blue and I have been to one of those clubs before, just for the adventure of it. Nothing to be ashamed of."

"Unless you accidentally get knocked up."

"Which reminds me, there are other considerations. We'll need to do some blood tests."

Ebony closed her eyes. "I didn't even think about STDs or worse."

"I'm sure you're fine, but we need to make sure."

"God."

Romy got up and came to hug her. "Sweetheart, listen. It's under control. You and Atlas are using protection, right?"

Ebony nodded. "Definitely."

"So, stop worrying. Take each step as you go, but I would talk to Atlas at least. Get things out in the open."

Ebony smiled gratefully at the other woman. "You're so great, Romy. All of you Sasse women, I adore you all."

"You're our family, Ebs," Romy said with a shrug, "it's what we do. We look out for each other."

EBONY WAS STILL THINKING about what Romy said two days later as she and Atlas drove to the mansion to celebrate Christmas with everybody. Ebony was a little nervous – Juno and Obe had called to stay they wouldn't be able to make it to Seattle after all, and so Ebony felt one of her anchors was missing. *Romy will be there, it's okay,* she told herself. They were the first to arrive, and Fino immediately bore Ebony off to see his presents. She was sitting on the floor with him, playing a game when she heard a girl's voice called him. "Fino?"

"Bella!" Fino got up and scooted out of the room, re-emerging a few moments later with a young woman, a little younger than Ebony, long red hair and a shy smile. "Ebony, this is Bella."

Ebony clambered to her feet and shook the girl's hand. Bella smiled at her. "Atlas has sung your praises," she said, her voice soft, "especially about your singing."

Ebony laughed. "He's biased. It's lovely to meet you."

"You too." They both heard a more strident voice outside, followed by a mellower male chuckling, a low melodic sound, and two other people entered the room. The man, in his sixties, had a warm smile and big soulful brown eyes behind spectacles. His brown beard and hair were speckled with white. He introduced himself to Ebony. "Stanley Duggan, my dear, and this is my wife, Vida."

Vida Duggan was exactly how Atlas had described her – a faded beauty queen type, with dark ruby hair and sharp silver eyes which darted around the room and up and down Ebony, appraising her.

"Hello, dear," she said, "We've heard a lot about you. Perhaps you'll be able to help Bella with her singing."

Bella rolled her eyes. "*Mom.*"

Ebony smiled at Bella. "I'd be happy to help in any way I can."

"See, Bella? Don't look a gift horse in the mouth. Hello, Fino, dear."

Fino gave Vida a cheesy, insincere smile which nearly made Ebony burst into giggles. Instead, she suppressed a smile, catching Stanley's eye. He too looked amused, and Ebony felt they had shared a private joke. Stanley clearly had the measure of his wife and knew what she was like. It made Ebony warm to him, though she didn't understand why such a kind man would have married such an obvious harpy.

Atlas returned with a tray of drinks for them all, followed by a slightly-irritated-looking Mateo, and a tall, dark-haired man with a stony face, clearly The Angel of Death.

Swallowing a burst of laughter at the nickname, Ebony heard him saying something about Harvard to Mateo, and Mateo, his green eyes flashing, sighed in annoyance. "He's seven, Cormac. I think we have plenty of time to think about college."

"I'm just saying, it's never too young to start preparing him for the rigors of the university experience."

"I don't even know if he'll want to go to college, Cormac. Fino will find his own path."

Cormac opened his mouth to say more, but Atlas interrupted, probably hoping to head off a full-blown argument. "Cormac, this is my Ebony. Ebony, Cormac Duggan."

Hearing herself referred to as his sent a bolt of delighted heat through her. It had never occurred to her to want to be claimed, but it turned out she loved it.

"Pleased to meet you." Ebony stepped forward with her hand outstretched. Cormac Duggan looked at her but made no attempt to take her hand, and after a beat, Ebony dropped her own, flushing red and glancing at Atlas, confused.

Cormac shook himself. "I'm sorry, yes, hello. You're the singer?" He offered his hand now and took hers, holding it for a beat too long. Ebony drew her hand away, gently, not wanting to slight him.

"I'm a singer, yes."

"More than just a singer, Cormac." It was Atlas' turn to sound irritated now. "A once-in-a-lifetime singer. Stanley...I have your next superstar here...if you can fight off Quartet, that is. Ebony, Roman Ford called me yesterday, wondering why you haven't called him." Atlas grinned. "I took the blame, said I'd been hogging your attention and time, rather selfishly."

"Dear one," Stanley put his hand on Ebony's arm, "if Quartet offers you a contract, take it without hesitation. If not, then I'd be happy to help. Otherwise, the truth is, I'm retiring. I've done my time, and now I just want to enjoy my life."

Vida looked at her husband sharply. "What about *Bella's* career?"

Mateo mumbled, "God, not this again," under his breath and hooked his arm around Bella's shoulders. "Bells, what do you say we go check on the food? And by the way, everyone...Merry Christmas."

The atmosphere in the room changed in an instant as they all remembered why they were all there. As more guests arrived, Romy, Blue, and their kids included, the house filled with laughter and chatter, and when they all sat down to a magnificent dinner, Ebony felt more relaxed. Atlas was sitting next to her, Blue on her other side.

Atlas leaned in to kiss her cheek. "I think Cormac has a little crush on you. It's quite funny."

Ebony glanced over at the man and flushed when she saw him staring at her. She honestly didn't find it amusing. There was something about him that was weirdly unnerving. Next to him, his fiancé, Lydia Van Pelt, was chatting to Vida, and Ebony heard them trying to one-up each other talking about designer clothes that had been gifted to them. Mateo, on Vida's left, caught Ebony's glance and rolled his eyes. She grinned at him.

"So, where do you hail from, Ebony?" Cormac's booming voice cut across all of the conversation at the table, making everyone else fall silent. Ebony blushed a deep scarlet.

"From here, actually," she said, "I'm a Seattle girl, but I've been living in New Orleans for a few years. My brother is a dance teacher down there."

"So, you came back for Atlas?"

Ebony shot a look at her lover who had gone very still. "I came back to perform at the fundraiser for Haven," she said slowly, then firmly, "I stayed for Atlas."

Atlas touched her cheek. "I'm very glad you did, baby."

"Fortuitous." Cormac said with a smirk, his meaning clear. Ebony, instead of feeling hurt, fixed him with a glare.

Oh, I do not *like you*, Ebony thought, and gave him the same insincere smile as he gave her. Mateo winked at her and mouthed 'Ignore him.' Atlas squeezed her hand, and she saw Romy shoot daggers at Cormac. *I am amongst friends,* she thought, her body relaxing. She looked at Atlas. "Darling...later, I need to talk to you about something. Something important that I should have told you before."

"Of course, sweetheart." Atlas looked curious but not worried. "Are you okay?"

Ebony smiled, suddenly at peace. "Totally and completely."

AFTER LUNCH, Molly arrived, having had lunch with her own family, and Ebony could immediately see the love between her and Mateo. She and Ebony got along immediately, chatting easily as the twins took them all on a walk through the snowy grounds as evening began to fall, and thousands of white twinkle lights suddenly turned on, making the walk even more magical.

Mateo and Molly strolled ahead, arm-in-arm, but Atlas stopped Ebony and kissed her, tender and loving. "Thank you for spending Christmas with me, my darling."

"Thank you for inviting me." She stroked his dark curls, gazing up at him. Had it really only been a few days?

"What was it you wanted to talk to me about?"

Ebony drew in a deep breath. "Atlas...a week or so before I

came to Seattle, I had a one-night stand. It was...a mistake, but it happened. A few days ago, I discovered..." God, could she really say the words? Her stomach clenched painfully. "I'm pregnant."

There it was, out in the open. Atlas stopped. "Oh."

"Yeah. Look, I haven't decided what I'm going to do. But I didn't want us to go any further without you knowing. It wouldn't be fair."

Atlas's expression was unreadable, and Ebony studied him, her heart pounding. "I've just ruined this, haven't I?"

Atlas shook his head. "No, no, no, I'm just a little...taken aback." He gave a short laugh. "Okay, well..." He trailed off, obviously deep in thought and Ebony waited. He was still holding her hand; a good sign, she thought, hopefully.

Atlas took a deep breath in. "Well, let's be logical about this. Have you told the father?"

"No." Ebony shook her head. "Atlas, I honestly...I'm ashamed to say, I have no idea who he is. When I met him...it was in a specialist club, shall we say?"

For a moment Atlas looked confused, then "Ah."

Fear touched her then, and an edge of desperation. "Atlas, I swear, I'm not a whore."

Atlas looked astonished. "Ebs, I never in a million years would think that, and you should never think of yourself like that. You think I've never been to a sex club before?"

Relief washed over her powerfully. "There's no chance you were in one in New Orleans two weeks ago, is there?" Ebony tried to joke, but Atlas grinned.

"No, but right now, I wish I had been, truly." He put his arms around her. "So, first thing is we figure out whether you want to keep the child. Then we go from there. Ebony, I want to see where we go from here, whether we can make it work. If you want the baby, I'll be there for you."

"I can't ask you to do that." Ebony shook her head. "It's too much. We've only known each other a week."

His gaze, locked on hers, never faltered. "I know," his voice was soft, "and already, I'm lost, Ebony. I'm lost."

Her eyes filled with tears at the love in his voice. "I feel the same way," she whispered, and then his lips were crushing against hers, kissing as her hot tears dropped down her cheeks.

Atlas placed a hand on her belly so protectively that she teared up again. "Let's see where this goes," he said. "Let's see if we can do this."

Ebony closed her eyes, her mind whirling. Was he really offering to be the father of her child? Even if it wasn't his own? She felt discombobulated by the conversation as if it had run away from her and nothing had really gotten resolved, at least not responsibly.

For now, though, she would take his kiss, his promise, and enjoy the rest of Christmas.

IN BED that night they made love, quietly as the rest of the house slept. Ebony smiled up at him as Atlas moved in measured thrusts inside her, and knew she was falling in love with him. How could she not? He was everything, he was perfect. Wasn't he?

I don't know, she thought, *but for right now, he is perfect for me. Can we be happy?* She played out different scenarios in her mind and still didn't find an answer. As he slept in her arms, though, she knew she would try, and there was something else.

She didn't know when exactly she'd made the decision, but she knew it was the right one, regardless of anything.

She was keeping the baby.

CHAPTER TEN

In the morning she awoke to raised voices and shouting from downstairs. The bed beside her was empty, and she grabbed her robe and went downstairs.

"You *fucker*," one of the twins was shouting. "You have no sense of family, of loyalty."

"Mateo," Cormac's booming voice echoed around the house, "Who do you think you are to lecture me on my sex life? *You*, of all people. You and Atlas, neither of you are angels when it comes to women. I mean, all of a sudden, you're both coupled up and faithful? Come on."

"Says the man who is engaged for position and money and nothing else. Does Lydia know that's why you proposed?"

"Why don't you ask her? You seemed to have a pretty good idea of what she wants."

"It was six years ago, and we parted on good terms." Mateo was almost growling. "I just don't want to see her hurt."

"Or maybe there's unfinished business between you."

"I'm in love with *Molly*." Mateo sounded dangerous now and Ebony shivered at the ice in his voice.

"Oh yeah, the teacher. You and your brother have really

aimed at the heights with your women. A teacher and a whore singer."

"You fuck!" Ebony heard furniture crashing and realized Mateo had gone for Cormac. "You don't get to call Ebony a whore, and you don't disparage Molly, you asshole!"

Feeling like she needed to do something before someone got hurt, she hurried into the breakfast room to find the two men struggling with each other on the floor. "Stop!"

Both men froze, and Ebony heard footsteps behind her. "What the fuck is going on?"

Atlas stepped around Ebony, touching her cheek, then hauled his brother off Cormac, who got up smirking.

Mateo was still enraged. "Get that bastard out of my sight, Atlas, before I lose it completely. Please."

Cormac held up his hands. "I'll go, don't worry. Another minute in this house playing this family charade would make me sick."

As he left the room, he stopped in front of Ebony, who recoiled, as he ran his eyes up and down her body in such a way as to make her feel naked, and violated. Cormac smirked at her obvious discomfort and left the room.

Mateo ran a hand through his dark curls. "I'm sorry, Ebony, Atlas. I'm sorry I lost it."

"He was trying to goad you all day yesterday," Atlas said, his hand on his brother's shoulder.

"And I let him get to me. *Fuck.*" Mateo looked at Ebony. "Are you okay, sweetheart? Don't let what he said affect you. We all know it's untrue."

Ebony smiled at him. "Thanks for defending me, Mateo."

"Anytime, gorgeous." Mateo looked at his brother. "Cormac is poison. He'll ruin Lydia's life if we let him."

"It's not our battle, Mateo. Lydia is quite aware of what Cormac is like."

. . .

ATLAS AND EBONY drove back to his apartment in the city that night. "Sadly, I will have work tomorrow. What will you do?"

"Juno and Obe are traveling up so I'll probably hook up with them." Ebony told him, stroking a dark curl behind his ear.

"In time for the New Year's parties."

"Indeed."

"Cormac's not invited."

"Good."

Atlas looked over at her. "He's a treat, huh?"

"Oh, yeah," Ebony said dryly, "a real chocolate-covered treat. Gross."

Atlas laughed. "He's considered quite the catch."

Ebony stuck her tongue out. "Ugh. Where? The mental asylum? The Home for Arrogant Douchebags?"

"You have his measure." His smile faded. "Though I do wish Mateo wouldn't engage him. Cormac has a way of getting to my brother, so much so, that Mateo loses his shit. Cormac hates that Mateo slept with Lydia first, even though it was six years ago. I think he's marrying her not just for her money, but to spite Mateo. And now he's annoyed that Mateo doesn't care if Cormac sleeps with Lydia because he's in love with Molly."

"The Love Lives of the Rich and the Famous," Ebony sighed dramatically as Atlas laughed.

"Seriously, though, Cormac hates Mateo, and sometimes, just sometimes, it scares me."

Ebony shook her head. "Cormac is a typical coward if you ask me. All bluster. How he's related to Stanley is beyond me."

"Right? You liked Stanley, huh?"

"Adored him, and Bella too. Vida...yeah could live without her."

Atlas smiled over at her. "I adore you, Miss Verlaine."

"Right back at ya, stud." She squeezed his cock through his pants. "Oh, someone's packing."

They joked and laughed all the way back to his apartment, but once inside, they were stripping each other before they even reached the bedroom.

As they made love, Ebony noticed he was even more careful with her, and realized it was because of the baby. It made her heart warm to him...what kind of man would take so much care over a child that wasn't his?

"I'm so crazy about you," she told him, "so, so crazy."

Atlas grinned. "I meant what I said, Ebony, it's you and me now, right?

She nodded. "Me and you, whatever happens."

And they made love long into the night.

ACROSS TOWN, another couple was making love, kissing and talking. Blue stroked his hands down his wife's body. "Are you looking forward to tomorrow, baby?"

The next day was when their domino surgery was scheduled and Romy and Blue, ever the surgeons, were excited. "I have someone to cover me at Haven for twenty-four hours, so I'm all yours."

She'd read over the patient details again and again until she knew everything by heart. Blue smiled at her now. "I have to say, I cannot wait to be back in an operating theatre with you."

Romy smiled up at him, stroking his face. "Me too...I miss that."

"We make an incredible team. I sometimes consider quitting Rainier Hope and coming to work at Haven, just so I can work with you all the time."

"Ha, don't you dare," Romy laughed, "You are the best Chief of Surgery that Seattle has ever seen."

"Don't tell Beau that, but thanks."

Romy sighed, gasping as she came and Blue buried his face in her neck before shuddering to his own climax. "God, Romy... I'll never get tired of doing this."

"I love you, Blue."

"I love you too, baby."

IN YET ANOTHER part of town, a man, alone, was not feeling loved. Carson Franks sat in his penthouse apartment, gazing at the video of his own wedding to Kiersten, all those years ago, before she had made him punish her for disobeying him, for trying to leave him. He still remembered the moment he'd thrust that knife into her, her shock, her pain, her pleading, and he reveled in it.

He was only sorry that he'd only gotten to kill her once. The feeling of power he'd felt as her life slipped away in front of him...He had thought she was already dead when he dumped her body in the gutter where she belonged, as far as he was concerned, but he should have made sure.

Now, that bastard billionaire philanthropist and his whore surgeon would testify about him in court, and even his father's expensive lawyers wouldn't be able to keep him away from Death Row.

So, he had only two options now. Suicide...or the removal of the witnesses, and that was an easy decision to make. He fingered the knife in his hand and smiled to himself.

By the end of the week, before the end of the year, Atlas Tigri and Dr. Romy Sasse would be dead...and he would be a free man.

CHAPTER ELEVEN

Cormac Duggan swung his legs over the side of the bed and strode to the bathroom. He heard Lydia call his name, but ignored her and stepped under the hot spray. His whole body was still wound tight from his fight with Mateo.

For as long as he could remember, he and Mateo Tigri had hated each other. The more volatile Tigri twin was too much of a playboy for Cormac to ever respect and even his chosen profession of wine importing was, to Cormac, nothing more than a front to a life of idleness and frivolity.

The one thing Mateo had ever done right was to bring Fino up, but even that rankled with Cormac. He hated himself for loving the boy, despite the hatred of his father, but Fino was a special kid, and Cormac was envious of the bond that had formed between father and son.

Because Cormac would never have that. A year ago, on a routine medical check-up, Cormac had asked the doctor to test his sperm count. "Lydia and I want to try and have kids as soon as we're married."

He hadn't expected the doctor to call him and tell him that

he was sorry, but it turned out that Cormac had a troublingly low sperm count. "Do the tests again," he had ordered, and the doctor complied, but the result was the same.

"I'm afraid it's very unlikely you'll have children naturally, Mr. Duggan, but don't give up hope. Low sperm count is not the same as *no* sperm count."

Since then, resentment and anger had grown within him, and seeing Fino at Christmas had only made that resentment, that hatred, toward Mateo fester. Cormac wanted kids more than anything, even money. He clung to that wish, knowing it was the one thing that saved him from being a complete asshole.

Cormac closed his eyes, trying to calm himself down. He heard the door of the shower stall open and felt Lydia's slender arms snaked around him. There was a flash of irritation, but it subsided quickly. None of his rancor towards Mateo was Lydia's fault. He turned and smiled down at her.

"Good morning."

Lydia, her grey eyes shining up at him, was thinner than the women he usually went for, built to walk a catwalk rather than anything else, though she didn't need to work for her living. The Van Pelts were on par with the Rockefellers and Vanderbilts of the world, and Lydia, while maintaining the façade of a fashion editor, was a maven of the socialite scene. She also hated Seattle; found it too accepting and laidback for her refined tastes. Cormac had to agree. The only reason why he'd agreed to come back for Christmas was to rub Mateo's nose in the fact that now he, Cormac, was with Lydia. It had backfired spectacularly, he had to admit, but for one thing. He thought of that one thing now and smiled.

Lydia, mistaking his grin for affection, pressed her lips to his. She'd had lip fillers over the summer which were only now beginning to look settled, but Cormac didn't pay much attention.

"Please tell me we're going back to New York for New Year's Eve?" Lydia groaned now. "Another few days in this place will drive me insane."

"I'm sorry, darling," he said smoothly, shutting off the water and stepping out of the stall, "but I do have some business here. I can't promise I'll be back in New York by then, but you should go if you feel like it."

Lydia, wrapping a towel around her head, narrowed her eyes at him. "So, we'll be apart for the parties? Is that what you're saying?"

"I'm afraid so."

Lydia walked out of the bathroom, and Cormac sighed. It drove him mad that she constantly kept tabs on him – even if it *was* justified. Cormac had no intention of curbing his womanizing ways just because he was engaged – but he was discreet. He never fucked around in New York, always keeping his trysts for his frequent business trips. He almost always used professionals, too, paid for their discretion. He was under no illusions that Lydia wouldn't kick him to the curb if she caught him.

He went to find her now, sitting on the bed in her wet towel, brushing out her long blonde hair. Sulking. He sat beside her. "Darling," he pressed his lips against her shoulder, "I know you hate it here, so that's why I said you should go back. But it's not what I want. I want us to be together on New Year's." He sighed. "I'll even put up with my step-brothers and take you to their party – at least you'll be amongst friends there." Too late, he realized that could sound like a rebuke. Lydia had always adored Mateo, regardless of their break-up. "What I mean is...family. Our family, for better or for worse."

He felt her shoulders relax a little and looked up at her through his dark lashes. She smiled at him. "When you put it like that..."

Cormac smiled, a little triumphantly. He pushed her back on

the bed and hitched her legs around his waist. Lydia was a good if bony fuck, and now she gasped as he launched his cock into her, clinging to him as they fucked, urging him on and on until he came, his cock pumping cum deep inside her as she cried out his name.

ROMY FELT STRANGELY nervous as she scrubbed in beside her husband for their domino surgery. Blue looked over at her. "You're going to rock it, baby."

"You too, my darling. I don't know why I feel so nervous."

"If you weren't, I'd be worried," Blue said, scrubbing his hands with the brush. "Five patients at the same time...it's a big thing. Beau's due any moment and Phillipa and Rex are scrubbing in in OR 5. This is happening, baby."

Romy laughed at the excitement in his voice. "Chief, you know, you're really hot when you're like this."

Blue grinned at her. "If this goes well, I'm so having you in the on-call room later."

Romy chuckled. "Like old times. Remember that first time? We were so unprofessional, but god, it was so good."

"And keeps getting better. I love you, Doctor Sasse."

"Love you too, Chief. Let's do this."

AN HOUR later and the surgery was in full swing. Romy and Blue fell into the same patterns of old, moving around each other like orbiting satellites, reading each other's moves, their wishes. Romy felt a surge of adrenaline coursing through her body. She missed this, the planned procedures, the highly organized routine. At Haven, her work was usually one of emergency surgery, a wide range of skills was required, but the fact the injuries she treated were almost exclusive borne of violence did get to her. Here, trying to combat what disease had done to the patient, she could work methodically, hone her skills.

She didn't regret for one moment working for Haven but they lost a lot of patients, and each one of them haunted Romy. It meant more sleepless nights than she admitted to Blue.

"Okay." Blue lifted a diseased kidney from his patient, "Here we go."

The surgery was a well oiled machine ("A well coiled machine" Romy grinned when she remembered Gracie's mistake), and the donor's kidney was brought in almost as soon as it was required. Blue looked at his wife. "You want to do the honors?"

Romy nodded, her eyes twinkling at him over her mask. With his help, she transplanted the kidney into the young woman on the table and when it began to pink up and respond, they all relaxed. "Great job, baby," Blue said, forgetting the rest of the people in the room, who snickered. "Ah, give me a break," Blue joked, "My wife's a rockstar."

Ten hours later, Blue released his exhausted staff, dumped his bloody scrubs in the bins, and snatched a kiss from Romy. "I'm going to check up on everybody then I'll meet you in the on-call room in an hour."

She kissed him back. "I'll update the charts. Thank you, by the way, that was exhilarating."

Blue winked at her and went to check on the patients. Romy dumped her scrubs then went to find hot coffee and a power bar before settling into the resident's lounge to do her charts. She checked her cell phone and saw a message from her Mom.

KIDS IN BED almost on time, adorable little munchkins. You're raising them well. Love you, good luck with the surgery. Mom xx.

. . .

Romy grinned. Her mother, Magda, had been delighted to look after her grandkids for a couple of days. Still, Romy missed kissing her children goodnight.

She worked solidly for an hour then, checking her watch, gave a grin. She knew Blue would be waiting for her and, as she went into the on-call room, she saw him already shirtless. "Now that is one magnificent sight."

"Get your sweet ass over here," Blue said with a grin, and she went into his arms. She pressed her body up against his, she could feel his hard-on, rock hard, against her belly.

"Hmm, is that all for me?" She said with a grin, then shrieked with laughter as he tackled her to the floor, yanking down her scrub pants and underwear.

"You better believe it's all for you, beautiful."

She helped him kick his own pants off, then pulled her top over her head. He freed her breasts from her bra, taking her nipples into his mouth hungrily. Romy wrapped her legs around his back. "I want you inside me right now, baby."

Impatiently, she helped guide him inside, and as he thrust deep into her, she shivered with pleasure. "God, yes, Blue...yes, yes..."

They fucked hard, not even regulating their cries as his cock drove deeper and harder into her. "Christ, you're so beautiful... your cunt feels so good on my cock...*Jesus...Romy...Romy...*"

Romy cried out as she came, her orgasm blasting through her body, making her vibrate with abandon. Blue groaned her name as his cock pumped thick, creamy cum deep inside her.

"God, Romy...I love you, I love you so fucking much..."

As they collapsed together, Blue kissed her until she was breathless. "I'm the luckiest freaking guy on the planet," he said and grinned at her.

"I love you, Blue Allende, so much. Really mushy, saccharin stuff, you know?"

They both laughed and Blue, withdrawing, scooped her onto the bunk, wrapping himself around her. "I like mushy."

He swept her hair back from her face, gazing down at her. "There is no one else on this planet who makes me feel the way I do when I look at you. Completely lost. Completely loved."

Romy flushed. Even after all these years, he could still make her feel like a giddy teenager. "When I met you, Blue Allende, everything made sense."

They kissed and talked until exhausted, then fell asleep in each other's arms.

CHAPTER TWELVE

Juno and Obe had looked at her in surprise when Ebony told them she was taking them straight from the airport to Atlas's home. "I'm kind of staying there," she said, coloring bright red, and saw Juno and Obe grin at each other, understanding. "It's early days," she told them, admitting her feelings for Atlas, "But I'm so excited. You'll love him, and his family."

Her brother and his wife looked suitably impressed as the limousine drove them to the mansion, but as soon as they arrived, they were greeted by an excited Fino. Mateo grinned at them both. "So good to meet both of you, please, do come in."

After a lunch of steak sandwiches and champagne – luckily, Ebony had never liked champagne, so Obe didn't notice her not drinking – Mateo showed them the grounds. He and Obe strode ahead, talking as Juno held back and looped her arm through Ebony's. "So, you came to sing, and fell for the boss?"

Ebony chuckled. "I know, so cliché, right? But, Juno, when you meet Atlas, you'll know why. He's incredible."

Juno nodded towards Mateo. "If he's anything like that one – *gorgeous,* by the way – then I completely understand."

Ebony nodded. "I hope Livia won't think I'm being unprofessional, it's just...I've never, ever felt this way. It was like instant chemistry, you know?"

Juno grinned. "I do know. It was like that between your brother and me."

The thought of Juno and Obe doing half of what she and Atlas had been doing made Ebony turn bright red. "Didn't hear that," she teased her friend, who smirked.

"There's a whole lot of *that* to hear," Juno said mischievously, and Ebony groaned and buried her face in her friend's shoulder.

"Didn't. Hear. That."

They walked on, noticing that the light was fading. Mateo and Obe were far ahead of them now, almost hidden by a copse of trees that were heavy with snow. Fino ran back toward them, grinning. "I'm going back to the house to switch on the Christmas lights."

"Okay, be careful, Fino."

The boy scrambled past them toward the house, just as Mateo and Obe came back into view, waving at them.

Afterwards, Ebony would try to make sense of what happened next, but still, she could not comprehend. As she turned to see Fino going into the house, a loud noise echoed across the grounds. For a moment everything froze, and then, to her horror, she realized what the sound was.

A gunshot. As she looked around, the next thing she saw was a body falling. Then there were people screaming and a body on the ground, bleeding. So much bleeding.

BLUE WENT to check on his patients for the third time, not quite believing how well the surgery had gone. All of them were responding well – one had a slightly elevated blood pressure, but that was to be expected. He chatted with a couple who were awake, but then handed over to his second-in-command, Bill.

"Go get some sleep with that lovely wife of yours," Bill told him and Blue grinned.

"Sleep wasn't what I had in mind, but I like your thinking. Thanks, Bill."

Blue went to the attendings staff room to find Romy, but seeing it empty, checked the on-call room again, then the cafeteria. Romy was nowhere.

Going back to the surgical floor, he stopped a nurse. "Hey, have you seen Dr. Sasse?"

"Not for a while. She was going down to the lab last time I saw her."

"Thanks."

As he headed toward the stairwell, a very pale man who Blue recognized as one of his patient's husbands, burst through the door. "Please, can you help? I think she's been stabbed."

"Who?" Blue rushed towards him.

"I don't know, I think a nurse, or a doctor, or someone, a young woman...she's on the floor in the corridor, and there's so much blood. I just found her."

His heart thumping, Blue followed the man, trying to quell the panic in his chest. *It's not her, it's not her.* But even before he reached the corridor, he knew it *was* her. Romy. His Romy, laying in a pool of her own blood. Her scrub top was pushed up, multiple stab wounds in her belly, and her eyes were closed. She was so quiet, so pale.

He dropped to his knees beside her with a keening wail and felt for a pulse. Nothing. Blue roared out his pain. "No, no... someone help us...someone help us..."

His scream could be heard throughout the hospital as people began to rush to their aid.

. . .

MATEO'S EXPRESSION was confused for the longest moment, then, as the blood began to bloom across his sweater, across his chest, understanding came into his eyes. Understanding and sorrow, along with a farewell. "Fino..." He gasped his son's name as he touched the blood with his fingertips. "Son ... sorry ..."

"Call 911!" Obe was the first to spring into action, picking him up. While Juno dialed 911, he and Ebony hauled Mateo into the house, locking the door behind them. They had no way of knowing if the shooter was still outside. Laying Mateo on the floor, Obe shoved up his sweater to get a better look at the wound. Blood from his mouth and nose poured out, mixing with the blood from what seemed like every other part of him, so much that it was impossible to tell if he'd been shot more than once

Ebony fell to her knees beside him. "No, no, please...Mateo? Mateo?" She began to blow air into his mouth and pump on his chest. A split second later, they heard Fino returning, and Ebony looked at Juno, panicked. "Stop him..."

But it was too late. *"Dada!"* Fino screamed and ran to his stricken father before any of them could stop him. *"DADA!"*

Juno gathered the boy in her arms, but he struggled, kicking, screaming, clawing and howling in utter despair as she bore the distraught child out of the room.

"What the hell happened?" Obe demanded, watching Ebony perform CPR, waiting to take over when she tired.

More gunshots echoed from outside, followed by loud shouts. "Fuck... Ebony, let's get him away from the windows."

"Can't stop," Ebony gasped out as she kept up the rhythm on Mateo's chest but they could both all see it was too late. His bright green eyes were glazed, his beautiful face pale slack. Ebony checked his pulse again then began to sob, laying her head on her lover's brother's chest as the chaos continued.

Fino was somehow back in the room again then, on his

knees in the blood. He patted Mateo's face, eyes huge and afraid. "Dada?"

"I'm so sorry, Fino," Ebony whispered. "There was nothing we could do."

The boy's wail broke all of their hearts and Ebony reached for him, holding the weeping child in her arms, her own bewildered, brokenhearted tears mingling with his.

CHAPTER THIRTEEN

Two victims, one dead, one clinging to life in a Seattle hospital. Both victims of a suspected revenge attack by a man who allegedly murdered his wife just days before Christmas – then blamed the victims – or in one case, the identical twin brother of a victim – for her death. Tonight, on KOMO, the terrifying story that has shocked America. We'll return after these messages.

BLUE SHUT off the television and rubbed his eyes. He had watched every moment of news coverage he could, trying to make sense of what had happened a week ago. Mateo Tigri shot dead in his own home...and his beloved Romy, stabbed mercilessly and left for dead. How she was still alive was a miracle, but as he watched her, connected up to a myriad of machines, bandages, bruised, torn apart, he wondered if she would ever wake up.

That terrible day, he had been panicked beyond belief, feeling helpless to act as Beau took over, ordering him out of the Operating Room. "No, Blue. We've got this. I saved her once, I'll do it again, I promise you. *Go*."

He'd wanted to swing at his old friend for banishing him, yell at him that yes, he saved her before, but that was one bullet, a bullet which had missed her vital organs, but tonight, this night, her wounds were so much worse.

Butchered.

That was the word which kept coming to his mind, and he winced and tried not to scream as he thought about it.

Romy had been stabbed fifteen times. Her arms, her hands covered with cut and gashes – defense wounds. Her attacker had driven the knife so deep into her belly that it had damaged her spine. Her abdominal artery had been cut, her liver damaged, her gut sliced apart. If she made it, it would have to be a miracle, though she was clinging to life as hard as she could.

And Mateo Tigri was dead. Apparently shot dead by the same man – a man who as of this moment was still free. Carson Franks had been arrested, but he'd had a cast iron alibi for both of the attacks. His smirk at the television cameras told the story. He'd paid someone to murder Atlas – who'd gotten Mateo instead - and had paid him well enough not to roll on him.

Blue knew Carson had stabbed Romy himself. That's what he liked to do, Atlas had grimly told him; he liked to kill women. And with both Atlas and Romy out of action, there would be no one to testify at his trial.

But his hired gun had killed the wrong brother and now Atlas was raging at the press, the police, and his own security team who had failed to protect his family. His anguish at his brother's murder had been further exacerbated by hearing of Romy's stabbing. Blue felt for the man...but...

He was angry. Angry at Atlas, angry at Romy. How the *hell* had they kept this from him? The threats that Carson Franks had been making? If he had known, he would have put the hospital on lockdown. Romy's attacker must have followed her from their safe, secure home to this place, the place that seemed secure. There were things he could have done, had he known... like lock Romy in a bulletproof, knife-proof cube and never let anyone near her ever again.

Jesus. How were they here *again*? Blue got up and went to his wife's side. He stroked her pale, cool cheek, wondering how much she could feel from within her coma. When he had seen her lying in her own blood, torn apart, he had thought she was dead. The attack had been so vicious, so merciless that it had taken seventeen hours to stabilize her.

And then Blue had had the terrible task of telling his kids that Mommy was very sick. The twins weren't old enough to process that Mommy wasn't coming home for a while. It killed him to think of how six-year-old Gracie had looked at him with serious eyes. "Daddy? Is Mommy very sick?"

And Blue couldn't lie to his daughter. "Yes, honey. She's very, very sick, but she's being looked after by the best doctors in Daddy's hospital."

"Can we see her?"

He hesitated. He didn't want Gracie to see Romy attached to all of the machinery, barely breathing, barely alive, but what if Romy didn't make it?

"Gracie...Daddy will take you to see Mommy when she's a little better," said Magda as she touched Blue's shoulder as she passed him, picking up Gracie. Blue smiled gratefully at his mother-in-law. Magda was shattered, utterly devastated by Romy's attack, but she had rallied behind Blue and the kids.

Artemis, Romy's oldest sister, was also on hand and had taken care of the twins, thinking of practicalities Blue hadn't even considered like the fact Romy had been breastfeeding. Artemis had reassured him. "We'll switch to formula, it'll be fine, Blue. Mom, Juno and I will take care of the twins and Gracie. Romy will recover, and all of this will just be another thing we overcame." Her voice had broken at the end of the sentence, and she began to sob, Blue hugging her tightly.

So many people had been torn apart by what Carson Franks had set in motion, he thought now. He kissed Romy's forehead and went to his office. Beau Quinto, the retired Chief, was waiting for him.

"How's Romy?"

"Stable, which is the best we can wish for at this moment. But she lost almost half her blood volume, Beau...if she wakes up, I don't know if she suffered a brain injury due to lack of oxygen and then that spinal injury could mean any number of things—"

"Woah, woah, woah..." Beau held his hands up. "One thing at a time. Romy's stable, Blue. Concentrate on that. No signs of infection?"

Blue sighed. "Thankfully, no. Not yet."

"I think that's a good sign considering where her injuries were."

Blue closed his eyes, the image of Romy's torn belly flashing into his mind again, making vomit rise up in his throat. "Who does that to a woman, Beau?"

Beau, who had suffered his own trauma years before when his wife Dinah had been shot, shook his head. "I'll never understand it, Blue, and I hope I never will." He studied his successor. "Blue...the Board reached out to me. Asked me to step in as interim head while Romy recovers. I told them I wouldn't do anything behind your back."

Blue sat down heavily. "I appreciate your loyalty, but the Board is right. I cannot run this hospital while I wait for my wife to...God, Beau, she might die. She actually might *die,* and if that happens, I don't even know how to exist."

And his friend had no words to comfort him or even hopeful lies to offer about recovery possibilities.

. . .

EBONY WAS SCARED. Atlas, removed from the initial shock of his brother's murder, was a raging automaton, wanting to have sex endlessly, setting up nonstop meetings with record companies, drinking heavily and trying everything in his power to not deal with Mateo's death.

Between them, Ebony, Stanley, Bella and a distraught Molly tried to help Fino through the worst of it, but he was almost catatonic with grief. Atlas could barely look his nephew in the eyes. He applied to the courts for temporary custody and was awarded it, but after that, he stayed away from the boy.

Guilt. He feels guilty, Ebony told herself, but it broke her heart to see this family torn apart. So much hurt. She was glad she could offer Atlas some comfort, but sex felt like revenge rather than lovemaking. The way he touched her now...it was fucking, not making love, and Ebony's body ached from the constant physical demands on it. Atlas would take her in the drawing room, only disengaging seconds before someone else would enter the room, leaving Ebony flushed and embarrassed.

She had no idea what to do. Sex seemed like it was the only thing keeping him from going insane, but at this rate, Atlas was heading for a crash.

And then there was her own child, growing in her belly. A month. Just one month since that night in that New Orleans sex club, and her child was still making her sick at the most inconvenient times, but every day she felt a bond growing with him or her. She'd wondered once, but now there was no longer any question that she wanted this child.

She was still thinking about it when Atlas came to find her. He seemed calmer today, less eager to just fuck her, and when he saw her rubbing her belly, he smiled a genuine smile for the first time in days, albeit one so weary and griefstricken that it made her heart break. He put his hand over hers. "I can see by the expression on your face...you've made a decision."

Ebony nodded. "I have...and I totally understand if you don't want to be involved. I can't ask you for that, however much I want to be with you. I can't get rid of her."

"Her?"

"Just a feeling."

"Baby," Atlas bent his head to kiss her, "as far as I'm concerned, a father is someone who raises a child, not just someone who shares his DNA. If you would let me, I'd like to try and be a father to the little one."

Ebony felt a surge of warmth but cautioned herself. Atlas wasn't in the best frame of mind to make such life-changing decisions. "Atlas, first, we need to try and look after Fino."

Atlas looked away from her, but she turned his head back to face her. "It's not your fault. Mateo wasn't killed because of you. He was killed by a madman."

"Who thought he was killing *me*."

"We don't know that for sure." Ebony sighed. "That being said, the man who actually shot Mateo is in custody. If he rolls on Carson Franks, we've got him. Your security team did what it was supposed to do, baby, they got the shooter."

"But how the fuck did he get in in the first place?"

"Well, that's something your head of security has been looking into." She leaned against him, speaking gently. "Atlas, we need to arrange the funeral."

"Jesus."

His arms went around her, and she could feel his body trembling. She looked up at him, his green eyes troubled and full of bottomless grief. "I love you," she whispered and knew it to be the truth.

Atlas tried to smile. "If you only knew how much I have fallen in love with you, Ebony Verlaine. I could not get through this without you." He kissed her gently. "I want to look after you, care for you, and the little one."

"And Fino."

He nodded. "Of course, Fino. I know I've been disconnected and I cannot thank you and Molly and Juno enough. I'll be better, I swear."

He splayed his fingers out over her non-existent bump. "If it's a father for your child you want, you have it, my love. Always."

They kissed, then heard a small gasp. Breaking apart, they saw Bella, her face pale, but smiling at them. "Are you *pregnant*?"

Too late, Atlas removed his hand from Ebony's stomach, but Ebony sighed. "I am. Very early days." She glanced at Atlas who shook his head.

"We're delighted," Atlas said before Ebony could say anything else. "Obviously, the timing is unfortunate, but we hope that *our* child will help us all heal. Will help Fino heal."

Bella gave a cry of happiness and hugged them both. "I'm so happy for you both."

Ebony smiled; Bella really was a sweetheart. When she went off to find Fino, Ebony looked up at Atlas. "You didn't need to protect my baby and me from the truth."

"As far as I'm concerned, that *is* our child in there," he said softly. He cupped her face in his hands.

Ebony felt wiped out by love for this man, and she was so relieved that he seemed to be calming down, his crazy grief beginning to give way to acceptance. She stroked his handsome face, the lines of sorrow etched deep around his eyes. "Come on, baby. Let's go find Fino."

As they climbed the vast staircase, they heard someone call at the front door, and Atlas's assistant called out to them. "Mr. Tigri?"

Atlas went back down and spoke to the man at the door. Ebony watched as the man handed Atlas an envelope then turned away. Atlas tore the envelope open and cursed loudly, rage consuming him all over him again. Ebony went to him. "What is it, Atlas? What's wrong?"

Atlas waved the letter, his eyes wild. "It's Cormac. He's suing me for custody of Fino."

CHAPTER FOURTEEN

Ebony rubbed Fino's back as he struggled with his math homework, then glanced at Molly. The other woman was staring out of the window, her face etched with such a bottomless grief that Ebony couldn't help but feel terrible for her.

"Molly, honey, why don't you go grab some private time? I'll look after Fino."

Molly turned to her as if she hadn't heard what Ebony had said, but then nodded, wordlessly, and stumbled from the room. Fino, dark circles under his eyes, looked at Ebony. "She misses Dada."

"She does, baby, we all do." She stroked Fino's dark curls away from his face. "You know, if you want to talk about Dada, anytime, you can always talk to me, or to Uncle Atlas, or Bella. I know Molly is struggling."

"So is Uncle Atlas," Fino said, with wisdom far beyond his years. He sighed and pushed his homework away from him. "I don't want to do this."

"Then you don't have to, honey."

Fino smiled at her, a soft, uncertain smile. "You're not going away, are you?"

Ebony shook her head. "No, darling, I promise."

Fino got up and came to her, crawling onto her lap and wrapping his small arms around her. Ebony hugged him tightly. Fino's little body was trembling. "I want to see Dada."

"I know, baby, we all do but...darling, you know we can watch old home movies, or look at photos."

"It's not the same. He would sing to me, or throw me in the air. Uncle Atlas...I wish he would do that."

"You can ask him, my love, I'm sure he'd love to, it's just he doesn't want to upset you. I think he thinks because he looks just like Dada, that it will upset you."

She felt Fino shake his head. "He doesn't look at me anymore. I think he doesn't like me."

Ebony's heart shattered. "Fino...Uncle Atlas is hurting, your Dada was his twin, and he feels...guilty that he is still here when your Dada isn't. But he likes you, honey. He *loves* you so much."

"It's not his fault a bad man hurt Dada," Fino whispered.

"I know that, but he feels responsible."

"I miss him. I miss Dada. And my Uncle Atlas."

Ebony's tears flowed unchecked then, and she buried her face in Fino's curls. "He loves you, baby, I swear he does. You haven't lost him too. Just give him some time. He's trying to make sure you stay with us for good now."

Fino looked up at her. "Like as a new daddy?"

"He'll never replace your father, sweetheart," she promised, feeling his body rigid with confusion. As she spoke, he relaxed slightly.

"He's my uncle. But will you be my momma?"

She smiled through her tears. "If you want me to be, then yes, darling."

He didn't say anything else, but his little arms tightened around her. Ebony looked up to see Atlas watching them from the doorway. His eyes were soft. "I love you," he mouthed, and she smiled at him.

LATER, after Fino was in bed and the house was quiet, Ebony and Atlas retired to their room, laying on the bed together and talking. Atlas, who had been meeting with his lawyer, stroked his thumb over her cheek. "Cormac doesn't have a case, that's the bottom line. I just don't understand why he thinks he does, why he feels he has to do this. He's always been an asshole, but I never thought he was this petty."

Ebony shook her head. "I can't tell you why," she said, "maybe it's just a reaction to Mateo dying. Maybe he feels guilty for treating him so poorly. Maybe he thinks by bringing Fino up, he can redress the balance."

Atlas smiled and kissed her. "I love the way you try and see the good in everybody, even in the worst situations."

"Atlas, you know you can tell me anything, right?"

"Of course."

"Then tell me...is there anything, anything Cormac could use against you? However small, however insignificant. Because if I know about it, we can get out in front of it."

Atlas sat up, studying her. "Ebony Verlaine...the fact you are so invested in this means more to me than you would ever know."

Ebony sat up, crossing her legs underneath her. "Thank you, but you avoided the question. We swore to each other we wouldn't hide anything."

Atlas sighed, hesitating. "The only thing, and I mean, the *only* thing he could even try to use was a bust for possession at college, and it was one joint, personal use. It didn't even go to court; I got a caution. But that's fifteen years ago, and no judge is going to hold that against me."

"Cormac must know all of this, so why the hell is he going through the motions?" Ebony sighed and wriggled closer to Atlas. "Darling, I can't see this going any other ways than yours."

He pressed his mouth against her forehead. "Me too, baby. You, I, Fino and the baby will be a family."

He pushed her onto her back and covered her body with his. Ebony, smiling up at him, wrapping her legs around his hips, sighing as he thrust his cock deep into her. "I love you."

Atlas' pace quickened as his arousal grew. "You're so beautiful, baby."

They made love until after midnight, then fell asleep.

Ebony's dreams that night turned into vicious, bloodthirsty nightmares, reliving Mateo's murder, then watching in horror as each of her friends, her brother, even Fino, was slaughtered by a faceless man. Finally, he turned to her, gun raised and shot her again and again until she woke with a cry.

Atlas sat up immediately, and she told him about the dreams. He took her in his arms. "No one is going to come near us again, I swear it."

But Ebony found she couldn't go back to sleep. Her stomach roiled with nausea, and finally, she slipped from the bed and went to sit in the bathroom, leaning her hot head against the cool tile. For once, her body didn't betray her, and she wasn't sick – maybe she was finally turning a corner.

At six a.m., the phone rang, and Blue told them that a different corner had also been turned at the hospital. Romy was waking up.

CHAPTER FIFTEEN

R omy wanted nothing more than to go back to sleep. Although she was delighted to see Blue, see the relief in his face as she woke from her coma, feel his kiss on her dry lips, the pain of her injuries was searing – and worse, she kept reliving the stabbing over and over again.

IT HAD HAPPENED SO QUICKLY, so utterly shockingly. One moment, she was walking down the corridor, charts in hand and the lights had gone out. One more step and she felt a crushing blow to her head and slumped to the ground. Then someone, a man, was flipping her onto her back and pushing her scrub top up. Dazed and disorientated, she heard him say, "I'm going to enjoy this."

Then the pain, *god,* the overwhelming, unimaginable *pain* as he drove the knife into her soft belly again and again. Her mind whirled...Dacre? Wasn't this what Dacre wanted to do to her? Had he come back from the dead? *No...*

He gripped the handle of the knife and stabbed her again, with more force this time. Romy could feel her spine scream with pain – he'd hit it. *Oh god...*she really was going to die here, wasn't she?

No more Blue. No more life. Just death. Her would-be-killer stabbed her again, clearly becoming aroused by her pain. *Someone...please help me...*she closed her eyes, not wanting to see the triumph on his face.

The shout. Closer this time. Now Dacre...no, *not* Dacre. Another man, another...Franks...Carson Franks...yes...that was him...cursed loudly and began to stab her with more urgency. She raised a hand, trying to stop him. Whoever it was coming would be too late.

God, a blow so hard that Franks had trouble wrenching the knife out of her. She could smell her blood, smell the rust and salt of it.

Her attacker bent down and whispered in her ear as she gave into unconsciousness. "I promised I'd gut you, pretty girl, and I have. You won't survive this...but if, by some miracle you do, I'll do it again, and again, and again until I know, once and for all, that you're dead." He gave a throaty chuckle. "And then I'll kill your husband and children..."

She had no time to scream before the emptiness came.

ROMY GROANED NOW, hearing the scraping of a chair. "Sweetheart?" Her mom. She felt Magda sweep a hand onto her burning forehead. It felt nice, cooling and soothing.

Momma? God, she hadn't called Magda that in years, but all she wanted to do now was cry. These last few years with Blue, the kids, dealing with Dacre and Gaius, and now this...everything had happened so quickly.

"Oh, sweetheart." Magda, tears swimming in her own eyes, dried her daughter's tears. "It's okay, we're all here, we all love you."

Blue. Romy's mouthed the words, her throat tinder-dry. Magda helped her sip some water.

"He's just getting some coffee, darling. He's been awake for twenty-four hours, hoping that since you woke up, he'd be able to talk to you."

Tired.

Magda nodded. "You will be honey, you've been through a tremendous trauma.

Gracie, the twins.

"Artemis has them at the moment. She and Juno have been taking turns looking after them. Romy, do you remember what happened?"

She nodded determinedly. *Carson Franks.* Magda frowned. "You're sure?"

Romy nodded again. She gazed at her mother. *Why?*

Magda sighed. "He says he has an alibi, but I believe you, darling. We'll inform the police. But don't you worry about anything...Blue has been working with them, as well as Atlas."

Atlas?

Romy saw her mother's eyes cloud over. "Atlas is fine, sweetie...but Mateo...Mateo was shot and killed. We think he was mistaken for Atlas."

Romy groaned silently, and began to sob, covering her face with her hands, inconsolable, and eventually Magda had to call one of the nurses. The nurses injected a sedative into Romy's i.v. drip. "You need to relax, Mrs. Allende. Your blood pressure is a little high for my liking."

Romy closed her eyes. Everything was such a mess. When she looked at her mother again, it was with anger. She managed to just croak, "Why isn't Franks in jail?"

"They're working on it, honey. Now that you're awake, it will be a big help and don't worry about security. There are two huge guards outside your door, and the kids have a protection detail like they're members of the Royal family. Which they are – to me, at least." Magda half-smiled and Romy squeezed her hand gratefully.

I love you, Momma.

Magda bent over and kissed her daughter's forehead. "Get some more sleep, baby. The more rest you get, the better you'll feel. I'm sure Blue will be glad you're lucid. He'll wait if you're asleep when you come back."

BLUE ALLENDE WALKED SLOWLY, heavily, up the stairs to Romy's floor. Since Romy's attack, he hadn't had more than a few hours' sleep, and it was taking its toll. *Now Romy was...not out of danger,* he thought, *she'll never be out of danger while Carson Franks is free.* No, Romy was beginning to recover, and now that she was, he could start to think straight again.

"Blue?"

He turned to see Atlas Tigri walking up the stairs behind him. "Hey, Atlas." His anger at the man was tempered now that Romy was awake – Blue had guessed that it had been Romy who asked Atlas to keep Carson Franks' threats quiet. It would be just like her, after all. Not wanting the fuss.

Besides, Atlas looked broken. Losing his twin brother, and worse, it being a case of mistaken identification...Blue didn't know how Atlas was still standing. "How are you doing?"

Atlas shrugged. "Like you, I suspect, some good days, most bad. If I didn't have Ebony and Fino..."

Blue clapped his shoulder gently. "I'm sorry, Atlas, about Mateo. I can't tell you how sorry I am."

Atlas ignored the mention of his twin, his eyes anguished. "How's Romy?"

"Still groggy. I'm just on my way to see if she's still awake. Come with me."

The two men made their way back to Romy's room, where Magda smiled at them both. "She's in and out of sleep and her voice isn't very strong, but she's lucid. She remembers what happened, and who did this to her."

"Franks?"

Magda nodded. "She seems angry."

"Wonder why. Hey, beautiful." Blue stroked Romy's cheek, and she opened her eyes and smiled at him. "Hey, sweet thing," Blue said tenderly, and bent down to brush his lips against hers. "I brought you a visitor."

He stepped aside so Atlas could see Romy, and she, him. Romy's eyes filled with tears and she reached for Atlas's hand. *So sorry.*

Atlas was visibly moved. "Thank you, Romy. Just keep getting stronger, will you? For all of us. Ebony sends her love. When you're stronger, she'd love to see you."

Romy nodded. She looked at her husband. *And the kids.* Blue hesitated, and she narrowed her eyes at him. He chuckled. "Fine, as long as they don't crawl all over you. You're still very sick, baby."

They'll make me... "...feel better." Romy croaked, motioning for more water.

Blue pulled up a chair next to her and helped her take a drink, then stroked her hair back from her face, his gaze intent on her.

"Don't worry, baby," she whispered, finding that speaking almost under her breath worked well. "I'm going to be okay."

Blue half-smiled. "You are in so much trouble, honey."

"I know, and I'm sorry I didn't tell you about Carson Franks. We get threats all of the time, so I wrote it off as another...it was my decision not to say anything so don't blame Atlas."

Atlas started to protest, but Romy stopped him. "Atlas... words cannot express how sorry I am about Mateo."

"Romy, please, don't. I should have made sure we were fully protected. I think, like you, I didn't take the threats seriously enough."

Blue was still studying his wife. "Romy...you sure it was Carson Franks who stabbed you?"

"Definitely. Mom tells me he says he has an alibi. Whoever is giving it to him is a liar. I saw him, I heard him, every second while he was attacking me." She swallowed hard, remembering. "He threatened to finish the job, should I survive, and then he told me he would go after you and the children."

"*Motherfucker!*" Blue hissed and got up, pacing. He yanked out his cellphone to call Det. Halsey. "Halsey?"

"Hey, Dr. Allende, I was just going to call you. Mateo Tigri's shooter just rolled on Carson Franks. We're going to his place to arrest and charge him now."

CHAPTER SIXTEEN

Ebony's shoulders slumped. "God, that's wonderful news, baby." She squeezed her eyes shut, grateful Atlas was at the other end of the phone and couldn't see her crying. "And you promise, Romy's okay?"

"She's getting there, it'll be a long road, but I think hearing Carson Franks will be put away for a long time is helping." She heard him sigh.

"Tired?"

"Exhausted, but I need to check in with my lawyer before I come home. I could bring take-out?"

"Good idea. Fino seems a little brighter, still clingy. Bella's taken him out for hot chocolate."

Atlas sighed again. "Good. You've been an angel with him, but I'm glad you have some time to yourself. I'll be home soon. I love you."

"I love you too, baby. Drive safe."

THE EMPTY HOUSE still echoed with grief. Ebony decided she would go to the kitchen, bake some cookies while she waited for the others to return. Stanley, who she had grown close to over the past couple of weeks, was in New York finalizing his retirement plans, and with Bella and Fino out of the house, she felt strange about being here alone.

Mateo's death had left a rip in their foundations, and Ebony didn't know how they would ever repair it. She tried to imagine if Obe died, how she would feel, but couldn't even bear to contemplate it.

Pushing the thought away, she settled into making some oatmeal raisin cookies, and when she slid them into the oven, the kitchen began to fill with the scent of cinnamon and nutmeg. Ebony rubbed her belly unconsciously, then startled as she heard a step behind her.

Cormac Duggan smiled at her, but his eyes were narrowed and cold. "Ah, Ms. Verlaine. I see you've made yourself at home."

Don't rise to it. "I think Atlas would rather you didn't come here at the moment, *Mr.* Duggan," she snapped back. "Not while you're waging this petty custody battle."

Cormac hooted. "Wow, he's really turned you into his Stepford Wife, hasn't he? Tell me, with your month-long experience of this family, what else Atlas would like?"

Ebony grimaced and turned away, but he grabbed her wrist. "I asked you a question."

Ebony wrenched her arm from his grip. "Don't you ever touch me again," she spat at him, then took a deep breath. "Look, I'm asking politely. Please leave."

At that moment, something in her stomach cramped violently, and with a gasp, she bent double.

Cormac's mood shifted immediately. "Are you alright? Here, sit down." He pulled a chair across and helped her into it. Ebony kept her head down, black dots appearing at the corners of her vision. She heard Cormac running the faucet then he was back with a damp cloth. "Here, put this on your head."

Ebony sucked in a couple of lungfuls of air and concentrated on figuring out what the pain was. Was she miscarrying? *Jesus, woman, don't be so dramatic, it's probably gas.* Another sharp twinge and she clenched her fists tightly. *Ouch.* A definite cramp, but she knew it could mean nothing.

"Are you okay, Ebony?" Cormac's voice was softer now. She nodded, but then an even harder cramp hit her.

"*Jesus, no*...I'm not okay. Pregnant," she hissed through gritted teeth. The next moment, Cormac had swept her into his arms, and before she knew it, she was in his car.

"What the hell are you doing?" She managed to choke out the question between doubling-up.

"Getting you to an E.R.," Cormac said. "Not only is it the responsible thing to do, and you do seem to be in considerable pain, but I can only imagine how Atlas would use the fact I was with you if you do miscarry."

Ebony looked at him. "Atlas isn't that petty, Cormac."

Cormac gave a short bark of laughter. "Ebony, don't be so naïve. I know you love him, but you're young, and you see him through rose-tinted glasses. Mateo wasn't mature enough to raise a child – what makes you think Atlas is?"

"Mateo was a wonderful father, and you damn well know it. *Oh...oh...*" The pain was getting worse, and she cried out as the car went over a pothole. Ebony felt Cormac's hand on her back, rubbing it. She didn't understand him; he seemed so kind, and yet he was set on making Atlas' – and by extension, Fino's – lives a living hell.

"Cormac, I'm asking you to please drop this lawsuit. When our baby is born, Fino will have his cousin and we're going to be a family. If you really love that little boy ... don't tear us apart."

Cormac didn't answer her but instead tapped on the phone on his dashboard. A second later, Ebony heard Atlas's voice.

"Atlas, I'm with Ebony...I'm driving her to the E.R. at Rainier

Hope. I think she's just experiencing cramping. I just want to get her checked out."

Atlas was silent for a second. "Can I speak to her?"

"You're on speaker phone. I'm driving."

"Atlas?"

Immediately Atlas's tone softened. "Are you okay, sweetheart? Has Cormac been bothering you?"

"No, not at all. I'm sure this is nothing, but it's best to get a doctor to say so."

"I'll meet you in the E.R., baby." There was a silence. "Thank you for bringing her to the hospital, Cormac."

"You're welcome. See you soon."

Ebony didn't have the chance to say goodbye before Cormac shut off the phone.

ATLAS WAS WAITING for them at the entrance, and he helped Ebony into the cubicle the receptionist directed them too. Cormac followed them, but as he stood by Ebony's bed, Atlas turned to him and offered him his hand. "Thanks for bringing her in," he said coolly, "But we can take it from here."

Cormac looked at Atlas's offered hand a long moment before shaking it. He gave Ebony a look she didn't understand, then nodded, once, briefly. "I'll let Bella know what's going on."

"Thank you."

As he turned to go, Ebony called out to him. "Thank you, Cormac...and please, consider my request. That's all I ask."

Cormac nodded again, holding Ebony's gaze a beat too long, then left them alone. Atlas pulled up a chair next to the bed. He brought her hand to his lips and kissed it. "How are you feeling?"

"Crampy," Ebony winced as another hit. "God, I know I said I didn't know what I wanted before, and when I found out I was pregnant, I didn't know what to do, but I hope to God that I don't lose her."

Atlas kissed her softly and said nothing, the pain of so much loss already etched deeply in his face.

In a few minutes, an OBGYN joined them. Dr. Melissa Fraser smiled at Ebony as she closed the curtains around them. "Hey there, I hear you've been having some pretty painful cramps?"

Ebony nodded, and Atlas, holding her hand, studied the doctor. "Is it usual to have these symptoms so early in the pregnancy? She's been having morning sickness too."

"How far along are you?"

"About six weeks or so."

"Well," the doctor was examining her stomach, "it's probably just cramping from the fetus attaching itself to your uterus. Are you spotting?"

"A little."

Dr. Fraser nodded. "Then I would be inclined to think that this is that. But we'll run a few tests and do some scans to make sure you're not experiencing anything like a tubular pregnancy. Is there anything in either of your medical histories I should know about?"

Ebony and Atlas looked at each other for a long moment then Atlas, clearing his throat, spoke. "Doctor...I'm not the biological father of this child, although I am hoping Ebony will let me be his or her father, to be sure."

"Ah, okay." The doctor's face wasn't judgmental in the least much to Ebony's relief. "So, do you know anything about the father?"

Ebony's face burned bright red. "I'm sorry, I don't."

"Well, not to worry, let's just concentrate on you, Mommy."

The doctor ran through some basic questions as she examined Ebony, then left them alone while she went to find an available scanner. Atlas kissed Ebony softly. "Are you okay, honey?"

Ebony nodded. "I feel a little foolish, but yes, I'm okay. It does make me realize how little I'm prepared to be a mother though if I don't even know the basics of pregnancy."

"Sweetheart, that's something we can do something about. Classes, online research, talking to Artemis, or Romy – when she's better, of course."

"Of course." Ebony leaned into Atlas's touch as he cupped her face in his palm. "Maybe after we're done here, we can go up and see her."

"I'll call Blue and see if she's up to it. *After* the scan," he added as Dr. Fraser returned. Ebony grinned at him, at the excitement in his eyes. She loved how the thought of being a father thrilled him. How Cormac could say he wasn't qualified...

Midway through the scan, the doctor smiled at her. "Well, all is well, Ebony. I think it's just the fetus implanting itself and causing you some pain. Obviously, if it continues or your bleeding gets worse, come back."

EBONY THANKED THE DOCTOR, and in a few minutes she was dressed and ready to go. Atlas was on the phone as she signed some paperwork and as she turned, she was surprised to see Cormac standing out in the corridor, staring at her. Ebony stepped toward him, then stopped as she registered the dislike on his face. It was so palpable it shocked her, and she gaped at his retreating back as he turned and stalked away from her. What had she done wrong?

Fuck. Her hormones were working against her now, and her eyes filled with easy tears. She quickly dashed them away before Atlas could see them. He wrapped his arms around her now. "Blue says Romy is sleeping at the moment but we can go sit with her for a while."

"Okay."

Atlas looked down at her. "You okay?"

Ebony nodded, and kissed him. "Always with you." And she took his hand and led him to the stairwell.

BLUE STEPPED out of Romy's room to take the call from Det. Halsey. "Did you arrest Franks?"

He heard the hesitation in John Halsey's voice. "He got away. He knew we were coming and disappeared."

Blue cussed loudly. "Jesus, Halsey! How did this happen? Who screwed us?"

"We're working on it, Doc, I promise. Until we get more answers, we're sending extra protection for your family, for Mr. Tigri's, for Haven. We will get our man, Dr. Allende, I promise you."

Blue ended the call and cursed under his breath. He hated the thought of Franks being out in the world, able to get to Romy. The day she'd been stabbed...it had been the worst day of his life, even worse than the day his step-brother had shot her. Would the woman he loved ever be safe?

"Hey, Blue."

He turned towards the sound of the soft voice and smiled at Ebony. "Hey, yourself, gorgeous. Everything okay?"

She smiled at him. "Yes, the baby is fine."

Blue smiled and kissed her cheek, shook Atlas's hand. "Congratulations to you both. And don't let anyone tell you it's too fast – I wanted to marry Romy and have kids with her the minute I met her."

Atlas nodded. "Thanks, man."

Blue looked at him. "Hey, while Ebony is in with Romy, can I grab a couple of words? No biggie."

"Of course."

. . .

WHEN THE TWO men were alone, Blue repeated what the detective had told him. Atlas' good mood disappeared. "Fuck."

"Yep. Look, it goes without saying, security is a priority."

Atlas nodded. "Considering our combined wealth, we can throw everything at it."

"Agreed. Look, I think the more we coordinate our plans, the better. Is your mansion secure?"

"It is *now*," Atlas said grimly. He sighed, rubbing his face. "Look, there's no way else to say it, but I'm sorry. I'm sorry I didn't say anything about the threats."

"Atlas, there's no use in brooding over that – at least that's what I'm telling myself now. Romy's alive...I'm sorry. I liked Mateo very much, he was a great man."

"He was. It's Fino who I'm scared for. Ebony has been so great with him, as has Molly. Now this thing with Cormac..."

"He's a jackass," Blue said, angrily. "Anyone who could do this..." He trailed off. "Cormac, we can handle. Atlas. You need testimonies, witnesses, we're there for you. But Franks is a different prospect entirely. He threatened to kill my kids. He threatened to kill them as he was butchering my wife. Franks doesn't get to buy his way out of this."

Atlas nodded slowly, holding Blue's gaze. "Agreed."

"I swear...Romy, my family, your family...I'll do whatever it takes to make them safe. Whatever it takes." Blue could see Atlas followed his deeper meaning as the other man, his eyes dangerous, nodded."

"Oh yes," Atlas said in a low voice. "*Whatever* it takes."

Ebony felt Atlas slip his arms around her waist as he got into bed beside her and she turned, smiling at him. "Strange day."

"Very." He pressed his lips against hers, kissing her tenderly, and then sighed, burying his face in her hair. "Today, I got so excited about the baby, and yet when we were looking at the scan, I thought – how can this baby *not* be mine? I feel like it is and yet I also feel strange saying that. I'm rambling, I have no idea what I'm talking about," he added with a laugh and Ebony chuckled.

"Yes, you are, but I get it. Atlas, I wish with every cell in my body that it was your child growing inside me. Today was a wake-up call. I really do know nothing about the child and maybe...maybe I should try and find the father." She looked at him with worried eyes and saw the slight hurt in them. "Atlas, I love you, as far as I'm concerned, you, me and the baby *are* a family. Don't you think though it would be better to know? Isn't that what Mateo discovered when he found out about Fino?"

Atlas sighed and closed his eyes, pain flashing across his face. "Of course, I know you're right. We should try to find out who the father is and give him the chance to be involved." He grinned at her sheepishly. "But I really hope he doesn't want you back."

"Ha, first, he never had me, so to speak, and secondly, no one could take me away from you, Mr. Tigri. Despite everything that's happened, loving you and this baby are the only things I know I'm sure of."

"Good." He took her hand and kissed the top of her fingers in turn. "So, if I asked you to marry me, that wouldn't be too fast?"

The breath caught in Ebony's throat. Marriage? Now? Soon she realized her hesitation had grown to more than was appropriate and that the hurt was back in Atlas's eyes.

"It's okay, you don't have to answer that question. Forget it."

Ebony crushed her lips against his. "Atlas, you are my everything. I just think we should slow down, take things one-by-one. You ask me that question a year from now? I promise I'll say yes."

Atlas half-smiled. "I told you, I'm impetuous. You're right, of course. Again."

She stroked his face, lightly scratching at his dark stubble and kissing him softly. "I love you so much."

Much as she would have loved to make love with him, she was as exhausted from the day's events as was he. They wrapped around one another and were soon fast asleep.

LATER, when Atlas was still asleep, Ebony woke with a dry throat and got up to get some water. As she padded down to the kitchen, she stopped and listened. She could hear crying. Worried in case it was Fino, she followed the sound of it until she heard a young woman's voice. Bella. Bella was crying as she talked to someone. Ebony inched closer to the door, raising her hand to knock when she heard Bella groan.

"No, you can't...no, that's not fair, it isn't right. But...I cannot believe you're going to do this. No...no...I won't. No, fuck you."

Ebony heard the splintering of glass against a wall and guessed Bella had hurled her phone across the room. She knocked tentatively. There was a hesitation then, "Come in."

Ebony pushed opened the door and smiled at Bella. The red-haired girl was sitting cross-legged on her bed, her face tear-stained. She wouldn't look Ebony in the eye.

"Are you okay, pumpkin?" Ebony went to sit by her and Bella shrugged.

"Just my mom being my mom."

Ebony peeked over at the smashed iPhone on the floor. "Being *extra*-Mom, I would say."

Bella half-smiled. "She just gets to me."

"Want to talk about it?"

Bella shook her head. "But thanks."

"Anytime." Ebony got up and went to the door before Bella called her back.

"Ebony...just...be careful. People sometimes aren't who they say they are."

Ebony frowned. "Who do you mean?"

"No one in particular. Just...be careful."

Ebony went back to bed after looking in on a sleeping Fino. The boy had lost weight and looked so tiny and vulnerable in his bed that Ebony wanted to cuddle him, wanted to promise him that nothing bad would ever happen again. Of course, she couldn't promise that, couldn't bring Mateo back for his son.

As she crawled back into the warmth of Atlas's arms, she couldn't help thinking about that terrible day. Mateo, his handsome face not comprehending at first what had happened, then understanding and grief for his son. His last thought had been for Fino, Ebony knew, and suddenly she was crying, trying not to wake Atlas, but she couldn't stop the tears. When she felt his lips against her forehead, and his arms tightened around her, she let go, sobbing out her grief.

As her sobs subsided, she looked up at Atlas, her eyes determined. "Atlas, ask me that question again. Ask me now."

Atlas looked confused. "Which one?"

Ebony smiled, but her face set with resolution. "Yes, Atlas Tigri, I will marry you. I will marry you because I love you now and one year from now nothing will have changed in that respect. I will marry you and and together we will fight for Fino, fight for our children. No one else is going to hurt this family again, do you understand me? *No one.*"

Gathering her into his arms, Atlas' kiss said everything his heart was too full to reply.

CHAPTER EIGHTEEN

Gracie Allende plucked her twin siblings away from their mother's abdomen. "What did I tell you?" She said to them primly, and Romy had to hide a smile. Gracie patted the twins on the head gently. "You can't crawl on Momma's tummy. It's sick, and we have to be careful."

Gracie looked at her mother with wide, green eyes. "That's right, isn't it, Momma?"

"It is petal, just for now. Just until I feel better. Then all five of us are going to go have fun. Daddy's already talking about going somewhere hot for a vacation...maybe somewhere you would like...maybe somewhere with a fairytale castle?"

Romy laughed as Gracie whooped. *All the money in the world,* Romy thought fondly, *and all my daughter wants to do is go visit Mickey Mouse.*

Gracie frowned at her. "Do you think the castle has a library?"

"A library?" Romy asked in confusion, aware her young daughter loved to read but still not connecting that with Disney.

"*Beauty and the Beast,*" Juno stuck her head around the door and grinned at her sister. "Come on, Romulus, keep up."

Gracie giggled at her mother's nickname, and Romy rolled her eyes. "Hey, twins, you can't crawl on Mommy, but Aunt Juno *loves* it." She grinned at her sister's expression as Gracie, taking her mother's joke and running with it, handed Juno the twins. Rosa immediately spit up on Juno's sweater, grinning widely afterward as if she'd achieved something spectacular.

Blue followed his sister-in-law into the room, and Romy saw in his eyes that he had something to talk to her about. "Hey, Gracie boo, why don't you go help Juno clean up, then she might take you all for some hot chocolate?"

Juno, taking the hint, nodded, and bore the children out of the room. Blue closed the door behind them then came to sit by Romy. He leaned over to kiss her. "Hey, *Piccolo*."

"Hey, gorgeous." She stroked his face. "You look tired."

"It seems to be my default position these days, so I'm used to it. Don't worry about me, Piccolo."

"Not an option," she said and pulled his face closer to kiss him. "I love you, big guy."

Blue sighed and leaned his head against hers. "I love you too, baby, which is going to make what I have to tell you harder."

Romy searched his eyes. "Franks?"

Blue nodded. "He's in the wind. Atlas and I have people searching for him, but for now, you'll notice extra security around."

"As long as the kids and you are safe, that's all I care about." Romy shifted and winced as her torn stomach muscles pulled painfully. Blue placed his hand gently on her belly.

"God, Romy...I swore I'd never let anyone hurt you again after Gaius..."

"This wasn't your fault. It was the act of a mad man, Blue, and that's all it was. Working at Haven, we've seen the results of a twisted mind so, so many times, Blue, we should have suspected something might happen like this."

Blue closed his eyes. "I know it's wrong, but the thought of you going back to work there…"

"But, don't you see, this is exactly why I have to go back to Haven. They don't get to win."

Blue stared at her with unhappy eyes but nodded. "You're my heroine."

"Ha," Romy grinned at her husband. "Well, the second I'm better, you can show me just how much you admire me, all night, every night."

Blue chuckled. "That, my love, is a guarantee. Sexy woman."

"Yeah, real sexy in my sweaty nightgown and with greasy hair. I would kill for a shower."

"Might be a little while before that happens, baby." He touched her thighs. "How are the pins-and-needles?"

"Still there but less, I think. At least I can move my legs. I got lucky." Romy regretted her words as soon as she saw the pain on Blue's face.

"*Lucky*," he choked out and struggled to contain his emotion. Romy tangled her fingers in his black curls and drew him down to her.

"I misspoke," she murmured, her lips against his, "I just mean…I'm still here. I'm still with you."

"You always will be," he rasped, framing her face with his hands. "I'll never let you out of my sight after this, my love, my life."

EBONY COULDN'T HELP but tremble as she held onto her brother's arm. Obe steadied her and made her look at him. "You don't have to do this, Ebs. We can go into that courtroom and tell Atlas it's too soon, or you're not ready. Just say the word."

They were standing out in the hallway at City Hall and, in a few moments, Ebony would join Atlas in front of the judge, and they would be married. She sucked in a deep breath and glared at her brother. "I am ready, *Mr-I-Got-Married-After-Three-Weeks*."

Obe grinned, shrugging good-naturedly. "Just checking, sis. I couldn't be happier for you, I just want to make sure you're doing this for the right reasons. Having a child out of wedlock is no problem in this day and age."

"It's not because of that," Ebony felt guilty that she and Atlas hadn't told anyone that the baby wasn't his, "it's because we love each other, and providing a solid family for Fino will help us in the court case. All the right reasons."

"Then all power to you both. You ready?"

Ebony nodded, and they walked together to the courtroom. Ebony smoothed her dress down over her knees, a simple but elegant cream tea-dress which brought out the gold tones in her skin. A single scarlet hibiscus was placed behind her ear, and she carried no bouquet.

Atlas, glorious in a dark blue tailored suit, smiled widely as he saw her walking to him. As she reached him, he shook Obe's hand and bent to kiss his fiancée's cheek. "You look sensational, baby."

The navy blue of the suit made his dark hair and light green eyes even more startling and Ebony sighed over his sheer physical beauty. This god-like man was about to be *her* husband, and she could barely believe it.

Fino, giving her a genuinely happy smile for the first time in weeks, stood next to Atlas as his best man. Ebony bent to kiss the boy's cheek. "Handsome boy."

The wedding vows were over in a flash it seemed to her, but she didn't care, Atlas was kissing her with so much adoration, and she knew without a shadow of a doubt that she'd made the right decision.

She gazed up at her new husband when they came up for air. "Our family," was all she said and Atlas, smiling, nodded.

"It's everything to me."

Juno, Obe, Bella, and Fino joined them for a celebratory lunch. Stanley, still in New York, had sent his best wishes, and Blue and Romy had called Ebony that morning.

Ebony sat next to Atlas, his arm locked around her, both unable to stop smiling at each other. "Atlas, Fino...I wanted to share this with you," she said, "but I thought I would wait until now, in case either of you found this upsetting."

She opened the locket on her necklace and showed them both the picture of Mateo she had placed in it. "I wanted your father, your brother to be a part of our day. He will always be with us, Fino, and if we are lucky enough to become your adoptive parents, we will never seek to replace him, but carry on the fantastic way he was bringing you up."

Fino nodded, his eyes filling with tears and he launched himself at Ebony and hugged her tightly. Atlas smiled at her, his gorgeous eyes shining at her. "Perfect, baby. Thank you."

"Oh!" Bella exclaimed loudly, making everyone start. "Sorry," she grinned sheepishly, "it's just I made some handmade confetti at home, and of course, I forgot it."

Ebony laughed. "We can use it for something else, don't worry."

A movement across the restaurant caught her eye. One of their huge security guys talking into his phone. Atlas's attention was caught too.

"Say, how about we take this party home?" He asked the question lightly, but they were all alerted to the fact that even on such a happy day, they were all still in danger.

As they got up to leave, a commotion began with one of the guards and a sharply-dressed man. "I have to bring this to Ms. Verlaine." He was waving an envelope, but the bodyguard wouldn't let him near her. He frisked the man then looked at Atlas who nodded. The newcomer, looking annoyed, walked over to them. "Miss Verlaine."

"Mrs. Tigri now," Ebony said coldly, "but yes, that's me."

The man handed her the envelope. "Congratulations, both on your marriage, and the fact that you've been served. Have a lovely day."

He left the party stunned and walked out of the restaurant, throwing a glare over to the bodyguard.

Ebony opened the envelope and read the letter. "What the hell?"

"What is it, baby?"

Ebony looked up at Atlas, confused. "It's Cormac. He's demanding a paternity test."

"For Fino?"

She shook her head. "No...for the baby. He thinks you're not the father."

Atlas stared at Ebony, and they shared the same sense of impending dread. How the hell did Cormac know...and what would he do when he found out he was right?

CHAPTER NINETEEN

"Can he make me do this?" Ebony asked her lawyer, her voice trembling.

"If he can prove to us that he has a good reason for thinking Atlas isn't the father. He may be attempting to prove that you are an opportunist, that you are claiming Mr. Tigri is the father to fool the court into thinking you are a family, that living with you would be the best for Fino."

"*Fuck.*" Atlas spat and stood, pacing behind Ebony's chair. "Ebony is no gold-digger, and as far as I'm concerned, that is our child growing inside her. How the *fuck* did Cormac even suspect?"

Ebony groaned. "He must have been listening when I had the scan at the hospital. Shit, why didn't that even cross my mind?"

"It's not your fault, darling. Damn it, he'll stoop to anything."

"Well, we have a preliminary hearing to ascertain whether he can force you to do this. I seriously doubt the judge will grant it, but we have to go through the motions. If you are willing to attend the hearing, it'll look good for you. Cooperating, showing you have nothing to hide. These things will strengthen our case."

THE DAY of the hearing was less than a week later. Ebony, hampered by morning sickness, held Atlas's hand as Cormac's lawyer outlined his request for Ebony to take a paternity test. Ebony was cheered by the skeptical look on the judge's face, and when he stopped the lawyer, her heart soared. *He's going to shut this down...*

"If I might ask Mr. Duggan directly," the judge said, his tone even, "Mr. Duggan, why on Earth would Mrs. Tigri's child have any bearing on this case? It seems to be a left-field attempt by you to embarrass a young mother-to-be for no other reason than spite. Could you clarify your reasons?"

Cormac stood. "Of course, Your Honor. I can assure you there is no malice on my part. I'm just seeking to find out the paternity of the child."

"For what reason?"

Atlas made a disgusted noise, but as Cormac turned to face them, Ebony saw something else in Cormac's eyes. Triumph.

"Because, Your Honor, I have very, *very* good reason to believe that the child Mrs. Tigri is carrying...is mine."

Ebony gasped, and Cormac smiled. "That's right, Ebony. Don't you remember our little tryst, almost two months ago now? In New Orleans? In that...specialist club, for want of a better description? You and I made love, and now I believe that is my child growing in your belly."

"You're lying," Ebony managed to gasp out as Atlas got to his feet, enraged.

"Oh, I think you know I'm telling the truth, Ebony. Atlas, you have to come to terms with the fact...you married a *whore*."

Cormac smiled, knowing exactly what Atlas would do next...

and Atlas didn't disappoint him, throwing himself at Cormac. The court was in an uproar, the security teams dragging Atlas off of Cormac. Ebony reached out for Atlas, but he wrenched himself from her grip.

"Don't touch me," he spat at her. "Don't ever come near me again...you just lost me, my nephew...*I never want to see you again...*" His eyes were wild, his face contorted with rage.

The shock was so powerful that she stopped still for a moment. Then Ebony reeled away and walked out of the court room, too numb to run, walked blindly through the halls, past curious onlookers, out of the building into the pouring rain. Deranged with grief and guilt, she kept walking through the downpour. And through it all, the realization replayed itself over and over in her mind.

Cormac Duggan was the father of her child, she knew it in her bones, and Atlas would never forgive her. She had lost everything...

STANLEY DUGGAN KISSED his step-daughter as he strode back into the mansion. "Where is he?"

"Upstairs. He's...broken, Dad. That's the only way I can describe it." Bella sighed and hugged her arms around her slender body. "We can't find Ebony anywhere. She gave her protection the slip and disappeared into the city. Juno and Obe are out looking for her."

"What about Fino? Is he here?"

"He is, but he knows something is wrong. He keeps asking for Ebony...I don't know what to tell him."

Stanley sighed. "Maybe you should take him out, distract him."

"I thought of that too. We could go to the Aquarium, I know he likes it there."

Stanley smiled at her. "Your mother decided to stay in New York for a while, Bella."

"Thank god."

Stan chuckled, hugging her. "Families are rarely, if ever, uncomplicated, Bella dear. Your mother loves you in the only way she knows how to."

Bella rolled her eyes. "Go see Atlas, Dad. I'll take Fino out."

"Good girl."

ATLAS WAS STARING out of the window in his bedroom as Stanley entered his room. "If you're here to lecture me about responsibilities, I wouldn't," Atlas warned as he saw Stanley.

Stanley sighed. "I'm not here to lecture anyone about anything, son." He sat on the end of Atlas's bed and ran a hand over his balding head. "But there's a young woman out there, scared, distressed, and pregnant."

"It's not my child."

"I understood you knew that from the beginning. So why does it make a difference that it's possibly Cormac's child?"

Atlas looked at Stanley for a long moment. "For the life of me, I will never understand how you could have produced a son like Cormac. He's petty, vindictive...and he's taken everything away from me. Do you think the courts will grant me custody now? He knew exactly what he was doing, he knew I'd attack him."

"I'll ask again...so it's his child. I take it Ebony didn't know?"

Atlas hesitated. "I don't know. I don't know who I can trust anymore."

"I do." Stanley stood and put his hand on his stepson's shoulder. "You can trust the woman who supported us all when your brother was murdered. The woman who sat up all night with Fino, holding him, talking to him, trying to help him process his father's death. The woman who changed her entire life to suit you. The woman who put up with your desperate *urges* when you were trying to bury your grief," Stanley said pointedly, making sure Atlas was clear on the fact that his behavior hadn't gone unnoticed. "The woman who wore a locket with your brother's photo to her wedding so he could be part of your day – yes, Bella told me."

Atlas's face set in a neutral expression and Stanley watched him, unable to read his mood. "Ebony Verlaine loves you, Atlas. She loves Fino, Bella, even me and Vida. She came into our lives when we didn't even know we needed her. Can you imagine our lives without her now?"

There was a long silence, then "No."

"Neither can I. Come on, let's go downstairs and discuss how we can find her. Because this behavior, son, is not a man's. And it is not yours."

BELLA PARKED the car in the parking lot of the diner and got out. Fino, tugging his coat over his head, looked confused. "This isn't our usual place."

Nervously, Bella pulled him toward her. "No. I thought we'd try somewhere new. It's okay," she said to the security guard with them, "you can wait here."

The bodyguard looked skeptical. "My orders were to…"

"And I'm telling you, you can wait here." Bella glared at him, then taking Fino's hand, they walked into the diner. Fino was immediately wowed by the retro look of the diner.

"This is so cool."

"Well, let's find a table, and we'll order some food, hey, sport?" Bella smiled at him, even though her heart was thumping wildly. This was the plan. *Get the boy to the diner, get him into the bathrooms…*

Bella swallowed hard. *Why am I doing this?* Her hands felt slippery with sweat, but then, as Fino cried out, she felt a jolt of shock.

"Ebony!"

Bella whirled around to see Fino run into Ebony's arms as the other woman slid from her seat, hidden in the corner, to greet the boy. Ebony looked tired and somewhat bedraggled, and Bella felt a pang of guilt, but then realized this was even better. She had a scapegoat.

She greeted Ebony with a hug. "Everyone's been looking for you."

Ebony seemed close to tears. "I didn't know where to go, what to do. He hates me, Atlas hates me."

"No." Bella made her sit down, an anxious Fino snuggled in next to Ebony. "Look, let me get you some hot coffee...Fino, do you need to use the bathroom?"

He nodded. Ebony took his hand. "I'll take him."

Good, this was good...except...

What would *he* do to Ebony? The man who wanted Fino, the man who was blackmailing her. Him. Would he kill Ebony?

Bella's hands bunched up into fists, but she made herself nod and turn away as the two of them went back toward the bathrooms. She leaned over to the waitress. "May we have two coffees, please?"

"Of course, coming right up."

Bella heard the door open and saw her bodyguard walking towards her. "Sorry, Miss, I just checked with Mr. Tigri. He doesn't want any of you alone." He looked around. "Where's Mr. Tigri Junior?"

"In the bathroom," she said casually. "We ran into Mrs. Tigri. They're both in there."

The waitress brought coffee, and with a shaking hand, Bella sipped it. There was no noise, no commotion from the bathrooms – but neither did either Ebony or Fino emerge. After a few minutes, the bodyguard stalked over to the doors. Bella stood, feigning surprise as he came out, barking instructions into his phone. "What is it? What's wrong?"

The bodyguard stared at her, his eyes trying to read hers. "There's blood in the bathroom, but no sign of Fino or Ebony. They've been taken. They're gone."

CHAPTER TWENTY

"What the fuck do you mean '*gone*'? How the hell did you let this happen?"

At some point, very long ago, it seemed, Atlas had been a gentle man. Now all he did was rage, and rage he was now, at the bodyguard, who glanced at Bella. She looked away from him. "I'm sorry, sir, I let them out of my sight for a few minutes."

Atlas rubbed his face and turned away, fists clenched. It was obvious to anyone present who knew him that he was angriest at himself for how he'd treated his brand-new wife.

How could I have treated her that way? What the fuck is wrong with me?

Terror clogged his chest as he avoided thinking that he might not get her back. That thought had to be avoided at all costs, or he wouldn't survive long enough to bring his wife home—his wife and nephew—and spend the rest of his life apologizing.

Stanley cleared his throat. "Look, the police are on their way...I think we know who's behind this."

"Carson Franks," Atlas said with a groan. "God, how? How

the hell did he know where they were? And how did Ebony come to be at the same diner? Jesus..."

Bella looked miserable. "I'm sorry, Atlas."

He didn't answer her. Stanley patted his daughter on the back. "Go make some coffee for us, would you, dear?"

Bella disappeared from the room. The bodyguard cleared his throat. "Sir, Mr. Duggan, I think you should both know that Miss Duggan insisted on going into the diner alone. This is not to tell tales or shift blame – it's entirely my responsibility, but she was quite insistent."

"Bella wouldn't have deliberately put them in harm's way," Stanley said, but Atlas could hear the doubt in his voice.

"Why would she do this? No, I don't believe Bella had anything to do with this, she adores Fino and Ebony."

Stanley's shoulders slumped. "Thank you, Atlas. Thank you for saying it. But it doesn't answer how the hell Franks knew they were there."

"Carson Franks has unlimited funds," Atlas pointed out tersely. "He's probably had us all followed. Maybe when Ebony took off from the courthouse, he saw his chance."

"What does he want with them? He can't be holding them for ransom."

"Not monetary, but he'll use them to leverage an escape route, passage out of the country. He knows he's finished here, that if he's caught, he'll spend the rest of his days on Death Row. Shit, I'd better call Blue, let him know what's happening."

"First," came an angry voice from the doorway, "you can tell me what the *fuck* is going on – and where my nephew and the mother of *my* child are."

Atlas looked at the anger, the fear on the face of his much-loathed stepbrother, and received the second shock of the day. This one was oddly more pleasant as he realized that, for once, he and his brother were united in wanting the same thing:

Ebony and Fino back home, safe and unharmed.

"*No. Oh, God.*" Romy looked shocked to the bone as Blue told her about the abduction. "Blue, he's a psycho, he likes to kill women. He'll murder Ebony whether she tells him she's pregnant or not. And Fino...god, that poor child."

She hugged Gracie to her harder, and her daughter clung to her. "Don't cry, Momma. The policemen will find Ebony and Fino."

Romy closed her eyes and sighed, leaning her face against her daughter's soft curls. "Of course they will, pumpkin. Thank you."

"I shouldn't have told you in front of..." Blue look apologetic, nodding at his daughter. "It was just such a shock. Look, you are safe here. The kids are safe. Your family is safe – Stuart's arranged for protection for everyone, and the hospital is on top alert." He sighed. "God, I just want this over, and I feel helpless to do anything."

"You're doing what you can, baby. I just pray the police find Ebony and Fino soon."

Blue leaned over to kiss her. "I'm going to call Atlas now. You're okay for now?"

"Perfectly," she smiled up at him. "I've got my little bodyguard here."

Gracie giggled as her mother tickled her and Blue smiled. "I'll be right back."

Blue heard the pain in Atlas's voice, and his heart went out to the other man, knowing how he would be kicking himself around the block endlessly. "Anything, anything I can do, just ask. No matter the cost, no matter what, remember?"

"Thanks, Blue." Atlas lowered his voice. "Cormac's here and I don't have the heart to throw him out. He's beside himself. I've never seen him so ... human."

"Maybe something like this puts it all into perspective."

"Maybe so. Blue—"

"Don't," Blue cut in. "What you did was unacceptable, yes, but not unforgivable. You'll find them both, Atlas, and you'll make it up to them. Especially to your wife."

"What was I thinking?" Atlas whispered. "That wasn't me in that courtyard. Blue, I would never—"

"You weren't thinking," Blue replied bluntly. "You've fallen down a rabbit hole of despair ever since Mateo's death and it's time to climb out, Atlas. Your living family needs you, my friend."

There was a long silence before Atlas cleared his throat. "I'm climbing," he rasped. "But I haven't heard from Franks yet...the police say I should expect a call from him. I just want him to give Ebony and Fino back, I don't care if he escapes."

"Yes, you do," Blue said, a little anger creeping into his voice. "Because this won't be the end of it. He stabbed my wife, threatened my kids and your family too. He murdered your brother. He doesn't get a free pass."

"I agree," Atlas sounded exhausted, "but I just don't know what to do. And there's something else...I think Bella might be involved."

That shocked Blue to his core. "No. *No way*, Atlas. Bella adores Fino; she'd never put him in danger."

"We'll see. Look, I have to go, wait for this call. Is Romy okay? Are your kids safe?"

"Yes, all good, don't worry about us. But you need anything, call me, man. I got your back."

"Thanks, brother. Talk to you later."

.   .   .

BLUE ENDED the call then leaned back against the wall, exhausted. One man, responsible for all of this horror. Blue knew that if Carson Franks stood before him now, he would have no problem ending the other man's life. He almost wanted Franks to show up to the hospital so that he, Blue, could punish him for what he'd done to Romy, to Mateo. And yet, he'd just cautioned Atlas from letting himself be consumed by anger, so he had to follow his own advice.

Blue sighed and pushed away from the wall, heading back into the room where his family was, thankfully, safe.

SHE WAS certain it was a dream...or a nightmare, to be perfectly correct. She was tied to a huge pipe, sitting on cold, hard concrete, her clothes soaking wet, her head pounding with agony. She opened her eyes and saw the giggling man, his face contorted by malevolence, a vicious looking knife in his hand. *Please don't kill me, don't kill my baby...*

Ebony fought the need to pass out again. She could feel a little body wedged next to hers, hear his soft cries.

"Shut up, kid, or I'll stick a knife in your momma."

Momma? Was he talking about her? "Ebony? Ebony?" She recognized that sweet voice...

"Fino?"

She heard his sigh of relief. "Ebony, are you okay?"

"I am, sport." At least her mouth still worked, even if her head felt split in half and her voice sounded funny. "Where are we?"

"I don't know."

She opened her eyes wider, fighting the dark spots at the corner of her eyes. Fino, his big eyes wide and frightened, was curled next to her, his arms locked around her waist. Their kidnapper, a blandly handsome man, was watching them.

Carson Franks. It had to be. He smiled at her. "Welcome back, Mrs. Tigri. It's nice to meet you at last."

"Let Fino go," Ebony said immediately. "Take me, but let him go."

Franks rolled his eyes. "Yeah, because *you're* the one in charge here, beautiful." He suddenly scooted down next to them. "Listen here. The brat's father is going to arrange a private plane for me, then I'll let him go. You, on the other hand...well, I need some sport. This," he showed them a knife, "hasn't had a workout since the pretty doctor. I'll leave your body on Tigri's plane to find."

"No!" Fino screamed at him. "No, don't hurt her. She's having a baby."

Franks smirked. "I really don't give a crap, boy. And scream at me like that again, and I'll cut your tongue out."

Fino cringed against Ebony, and she wrapped her arms around him. "You fuck," she snarled at Franks, "you pathetic little *fuck*. Spoilt little rich boy. You'll get yours, Franks, believe me."

Carson Franks' face contorted in rage, and he grabbed her face, his finger biting deep into her cheeks painfully. Ebony winced as Carson crushed his mouth against hers. She bit down on his bottom lip, then cried out in pain as he slashed at her side with the knife. Ebony felt the steel slice through her skin.

"Flesh wound, beautiful," he snarled, "next time it goes in your belly...the whole way."

He got up and left them in the small room, slamming the door behind him. Ebony tried not to whimper, and Fino, tugging off his sweater, pressed it again the flesh wound on her side. She smiled at him gratefully. "It's just a scratch, sweetheart."

He clung to her. "I love you, Ebony."

"I love you too, big guy. We're going to get out of here, I promise."

At least you are, my precious little one, she thought to herself. That's all she could worry about now – get Fino safely away from the psychotic Franks. The room they were in was small and damp, with a window high up on the wall. Standing on her shoulders, Fino could reach it, but even from here, she could see it was locked. Maybe if they could break the glass...

The door opened, and someone new came in: a young, nervous looking boy, carrying a tray of sandwiches and water bottles. He set the tray on the ground and slid it over to them. "Boss says eat and drink."

Ebony nodded, giving him a half-smile. "Thank you. Could you possibly open that window, let some air in? It's very dank in here."

Okay, so it was worth a shot, but the boy just shook his head. "Sorry."

He disappeared, and Ebony heard the door lock behind him. "Fino, eat a sandwich, please."

"Only if you will too."

"I'll try."

The truth was she felt sick to her stomach. Back at the diner, when they had been taken, a cloth with chemicals on had been placed over her face, and she'd blacked out. She could still taste the acrid flavor of them now, and her stomach roiled. That, and the pain of the small wound, was making her feel as if she would be sick. She took a couple of unenthusiastic bites of the sandwich and some of the water, then feeling a little better, finished the sandwich.

It became obvious all too soon that the food or water had been drugged as first Fino, then Ebony, passed out.

. . .

CARSON FRANKS LOOKED over the unconscious pair and grinned. "Time to call Tigri, I think, see how much he'll give me to get his wife and nephew back."

The other man, the young boy, Rex, nodded. "So, you are going to give them both back?"

Carson laughed. "Not a chance. Oh, the boy, I don't care about. We'll dump his body in the ocean, but the girl...she's all mine...and her body, we'll send back to Tigri just so he knows that you never ever mess with Carson Franks..."

CHAPTER TWENTY-ONE

John Halsey stood up from the chair in his office and looked at the three men. "You understand me, don't you? No heroics, no going off on vigilante missions. Let us handle this, or you risk everything."

The three men stared back at him. Atlas Tigri, Blue Allende – and their unlikely comrade in this, Cormac Duggan – all wore the same expression: Skepticism. John Halsey sighed.

"Look, I realize men in your position believe that money can solve all woes – it can't. You give Franks an inch, and you'll never see Fino or Ebony again."

"All we care about is getting Ebony and Fino back safely," Atlas said, but even to his ear, he knew it was more than that. All of them in this room wanted nothing more than to rip Carson Franks limb-from-limb with their bare hands, and Halsey could see he wasn't getting through to them.

"Alright, just promise me this...you won't impede our investigation, you tell me everything." He fixed them with a hard stare. "Regardless of circumstances, if you get in our way, I will arrest you for obstruction. No taking justice into your own hands."

"Detective, we are men of the world," Blue said, a little

testily, "and we have the resources to search every inch of it... which is what we are doing."

"And that's fine. Just don't take unnecessary risks, is all I ask."

"None of us are amateurs, Detective." Cormac Duggan was the most arrogant of the three, Halsey decided, and the most irritating. He could feel for Tigri and Allende; they'd been through hell. But this man...

"Mr. Duggan, I understand why Mr. Tigri and Dr. Allende are here – why are you?"

There was a long silence, Duggan glancing at Atlas, then Atlas sighed. "Because he's the father of Ebony's baby, and he's also suing me for custody of Fino." He recited all of this in a dead voice, and Cormac had the grace to look slightly ashamed.

"All I care about right now," he said softly, speaking directly to Atlas, "is that we get them back safe and well. Anything else... can wait. We can resume our usual feud when they're back safe and sound."

Atlas studied him for a long moment, then nodded curtly.

John Halsey sighed and nodded at the door, indicating the meeting was at an end. "I'll keep you informed, gentlemen. Remember what I said."

OUTSIDE THE OFFICE, Cormac turned to them. "I'll be in touch as soon as my men find anything. Can I ask you do the same?"

"Sure."

Atlas nodded. "Come by the house later if you can. We should all be together." Atlas couldn't quite believe he was saying it, but there it was. He wanted his brother desperately right now, wanted to feel that comfort, and in Mateo's absence, he would take even Cormac.

And he had to be fair – it was Cormac's child Ebony was carrying. After Atlas had lost it in the courtroom, he'd calmed down enough to hear Cormac's lawyer explain the circumstances of the conception and the dates, and facts, matched up. Stanley had talked to him when he'd gotten home after hours of searching Seattle's streets for his wife.

And now she's gone, and the last words I spoke to her were angry and insulting. God, Ebony, I'm so sorry. I'll make it up to you somehow, baby. I swear. Just be okay.

Atlas drove home now, to an empty house. He went to Bella's room but found no one. He sighed. Bella had fucked up for sure, but he couldn't believe she had done it out of malice.

His cell phone rang, and when he answered it, it was Carson Franks, telling him exactly what he would have to do to save the lives of the two people he loved most in the world.

EBONY, realizing that Carson was keeping them drugged to prevent them from escaping, figured it must mean they were still near civilization. Drugging them would keep them from screaming or figuring out an escape route. She began hiding her food, instructing Fino to only eat the sides of the sandwiches and take tiny sips of water.

"We have to pretend we're asleep, darling, so they think they're safe to talk about stuff we're not supposed to hear. Maybe they'll say something we can use to escape."

She couldn't think of any other way to explain what was happening to them. Luckily, the small bites they took didn't seem to be adulterated.

When Rex came in next, late at night, Ebony had her body curled around Fino's, protectively, as she always did, and pretended to be unconscious. She became aware that someone else was in the room with Rex when he said:

"We keep them warm and fed, don't worry."

"Are they hurt?"

A shock ran through Ebony, and she clamped her hand discreetly over Fino's mouth as she felt him jerk in surprise.

Bella. It was Bella's voice. She wanted to scream, to go for the girl, to beg her to tell her why she had betrayed them so utterly. A tear rolled down her cheek and Ebony struggled to keep up her façade of unconsciousness.

"They look cold." Bella's voice shook, and Rex sighed.

"I'll get them blankets, but look, come on, if Cormac knew you were back here, he'd kill me."

There was a silence and Ebony risked opening her eyes a crack. She saw Bella staring down at them, tears pouring down her face. "Look, Rex, let them go. I should never have agreed to do this. Take me instead."

"Ha." Rex gave a snort. "You did it to protect your own skin so they'd never find out it was you who let that shooter in."

"I didn't know what he was going to do! He killed Mateo..." Bella began to sob. "Please let them go. I'll get you money, enough to get away, live a life of luxury. Please, just, let's get them away from Carson."

"No. Come on, get out of here before I kill you myself. You did this. Bella, remember that."

"Wait. Just let me hug them one last time."

Before Rex could stop her, Bella dropped to her knees and put her arms around Ebony and Fino. "I'm sorry, I'm so sorry," she whispered.

Ebony, shielded from Rex's view, opened her eyes and met Bella's gaze. "Run," she whispered, "get help, Bella. If you want to make up for this, save us. Save Fino at least."

Bella squeezed her eyes shut, disguising her nod as a sob, then let them go. She stood, wiping her tears away, and Ebony watched as she and Rex left the room.

She let out a long breath and was about to tell Fino it was okay when she heard the gunshots. *Oh god, no...*

A second later, her worst fears were confirmed when Carson burst into the room, his face red and angry. "Fucking bitch!"

Ebony somehow knew he wasn't talking about her, but it didn't stop Carson from handling her roughly, cutting her ties and pulling her and Fino to their feet. The gun in his hand meant Ebony wasn't going to risk fighting him. If he had just killed Rex and, *oh god no,* Bella, then he would have no reluctance in killing both of them.

Carson pressed the gun against Ebony's neck and stared at Fino. "One false move, kid, and I kill her, understood?"

Fino, terrified, could only nod. Carson dragged Ebony out of the small cell and along a musty corridor. At the end, Ebony saw Rex's body, half of his head missing, and pulled Fino against her belly so he couldn't see. As Carson yanked her arm, she glanced to her left and saw Bella, laying on her back, her hands clamped over her stomach, coughing up blood. For a brief second, their eyes met, and Bella mouthed "I'm sorry" then went still, her eyes staring blankly. Ebony fought back a wave of nausea mixed with grief and terror.

As Carson pulled them out into the daylight, both Ebony and Fino cringed, their eyes stinging. "Get in the car. You, beautiful, in the front with me. The kid rides in the trunk."

"No, please, don't put him in the...please, he'll be scared."

"I don't give a fuck." Carson picked Fino up with one arm and popped the trunk, shoving the terrified boy and shutting him in. Ebony heard Fino screaming.

"Fino, baby, don't be scared," she shouted. " I'll be right here, right here..."

Carson smirked. "He won't be scared long."

He forced Ebony into the passenger seat and got in, not bothering to help buckle her in. Now that she was getting used to the light, she could see they were outside the city, a deserted farmhouse down a long dirt track. As Carson sped along the roadway, he was driving with one hand, the other aiming the gun at Ebony, she saw something out of the corner of her eye, and as the car hit the main highway, a dark sedan sideswiped them.

The last thing Ebony remembered was the car rolling, smashing into a tree, and then in the seconds before she passed out, she heard Fino screaming once more, this time in what sounded like agony ...

CHAPTER TWENTY-TWO

John Halsey delivered the news without sugarcoating. "They've been found. They were in a car accident and the driver who hit them called 911. It doesn't look good, gentlemen. You're gonna want to hurry to the hospital."

Atlas wanted to drive fast, he wanted to go 150 miles per hour. But getting himself killed wouldn't help Fino or Ebony, and he'd vowed to protect them from here on out.

I'm coming, he whispered as he fought the urge over and over to run red lights and stop signs, his knuckles the color of chalk on the steering wheel. *Wait for me. Don't give up, baby.*

Beside him, by the looks of things, Cormac was every bit as terrified and trying just as hard to hold it together.

As they rounded the corner to the hospital, he spoke suddenly.

"Atlas...you and I have never particularly seen eye-to-eye, and I think that's partially my fault. I don't give a lot of myself away, and I've made mistakes in our relationship...but god, man, I *love* that boy. I adore him, he's the son I've never had – and thought I never would have. Doctors told me there was very little chance I could conceive a child naturally." His half-smile was sad. "So, you can see why Ebony's pregnancy is a big deal for me." He rubbed his face and to Atlas' surprise, reached over to grip his shoulder. "Atlas...all I care about now is whether Ebony, Fino and the baby are okay. Everything else can wait until we know they're safe."

Atlas nodded, his heart in his mouth so he couldn't speak. They parked and ran into the building at a full sprint. As they waited, John Halsey, who met them in the lobby, told them what happened.

"We had our suspicions that Bella was involved, so we had her tailed. She led us right to where Ebony and Fino were being held, but before we could act, Carson shot his accomplice and Bella and took off. That's when the accident happened – one of our men side-swiped their vehicle by accident when Franks pulled out in front of him."

Atlas, almost demented with worry, struggled to control himself. "Ebony? Fino?"

"Ebony wasn't buckled in," Halsey said grimly. "She went through the windshield. We just don't know the extent of the injuries she received...or the baby. The doctors will be able to tell you more."

Cormac was suddenly there, holding Atlas up with a firm grip on his bicep. "And Fino?"

"He was in the trunk," Halsey replied, waiting until Cormac stopped cussing a blue streak. "He's shaken up and terrified, but the impact was far enough from him that the paramedics said they think he may only have a concussion."

It was Atlas' turn to support the man who he'd loathed up until this day. As they sank into nearby chairs, twin expressions of anguish on their faces, Blue jogged into the hospital.

He didn't stop as Atlas and Cormac jumped to their feet. "I'm on my way into surgery," he called as he shoved open the door to the stairs and vanished inside. His voice floated back before the door closed behind him. "Romy's there already. I'll come update you as soon as I can."

They were staring after him when Halsey appeared again. In the overall chaos, they hadn't even noticed he'd vanished.

"You can come see Fino. They have to do scans, but he checks out as okay enough for relatives."

TRAUMATIZED AS THE BOY WAS, his head swathed in a bulky bandage, he was admirably composed. Terrifyingly so, Atlas thought as he held Fino close before letting Cormac get in for his own hug. Who knew how many years of therapy it would take to help the kid stop having nightmares about the last month.

There were so many questions running through Atlas' head he didn't know where to start, afraid of overwhelming his already trembling nephew. So Cormac asked the hardest question.

"Did the man hurt you, Fino?" Cormac asked, sitting down on the edge of the hospital bed even though it wasn't allowed. "We know he put you in the trunk. But did he...touch you or talk to you in a way that made you uncomfortable?"

Fino shook his head, thankfully unaware of Cormac's subtext, and Atlas swallowed a sigh of relief. "He was scary, but he didn't hurt me. He hurt Ebony...he had a knife, and he cut her. Ebony said it was okay, but she was in pain. There was blood."

"God..." Atlas felt the blood drain from his face. He had no doubt that had they not found them, Ebony and Fino would be dead right now. Fino reached out his small hand and put it on Atlas's face.

"Don't cry, Uncle Atlas...Ebony said we were going to be family and I believe her. She'll be okay."

Even Cormac got teary then, much to Atlas' astonishment. He got up. "Look, I'm going to go talk to the detective...and then I'm going to call my lawyer. Drop the case. In the end, Fino's happiness is all I care about."

He turned on his heel and walked out of the cubicle, and Atlas could see the defeated slump of his shoulders. He looked at Fino. "Fino, would you be okay alone for two minutes? I have to ask Cormac something."

Fino looked like he was going to protest but then nodded, laying back on his pillows and closing his eyes. Atlas found a nurse to sit with him then went to find Cormac. Cormac was standing outside, out of the rain under the hospital's canopy.

"Cormac?"

Cormac turned to look at him. Atlas went up to him, then after a second, offered him his hand. Cormac shook it. "Whatever differences we have had in the past, and however strange this set up is...Fino loves you," Atlas said gruffly. "Ebony is carrying your child, whether I like it or not. So...we have to find a way of working this out."

Cormac nodded. "I agree. Look, here's the bottom line. A year ago, I was told it was unlikely I would ever have kids. My sperm count is low. I reacted by going a little crazy, going to sex clubs. Ebony...I could tell she was a newbie, so I took care of her in the club...and yes, we made love. I used a condom, but it broke. I swear, I did tell her, but the whole time, she never saw my face. I was wearing," and he laughed now, "one of those ridiculous masks...hey, I was trying something new, okay?" He added as Atlas smirked. "So, she really, truly never knew it was me. She told you the kid wasn't yours?"

"Yes."

"I respect her for that. Hell, I just respect Ebony – I'm sorry I called her a whore; she's anything but."

"Tell *her* that."

"I will, I promise." Cormac sighed. "So, bottom line, I just want to be involved with my kid's upbringing, as well as Fino's. I'll let you be a family, Atlas. Just allow me to be part of it. Please."

"No more shady tricks?"

"None."

Atlas regarded him for a long time. "When you told me you were the father of Ebony's child, I just flipped. I felt like everything, everything was being taken away from me. Mateo, Fino, Ebony, the baby...everything."

"I know. I'm sorry."

"I am too. We've both screwed up beyond belief, but at least you're making amends. I haven't even started yet."

"She'll forgive you," Cormac replied. "You were out of your mind for any number of reasons that day. Doesn't make what you said right, even if I pushed you over the edge. But she'll forgive you anyway, because she's that kind of person."

Atlas nodded, shrugging off more chaotic emotions. "And thank you for dropping the case. Fino does belong with Ebony and me - but he needs you too. As for the baby, really, that's up to Ebony now."

"Agreed." Cormac rubbed his face. "I wasted so many years hating you and Mateo for what now seems to be completely useless reasons."

"It's never too late."

"You're right." Cormac clapped Atlas on the back. "Come on, let's get back to Fino and wait for Blue to update us."

TWO HOURS LATER, Blue came to find them...and he was smiling.

CHAPTER TWENTY-THREE

ne year later...

ROMY GRINNED as she watched Ebony struggling with a very wriggly five-month-old. Even still tiny, Matilda knew how to twist her mother around her finger. Romy's own twins, now almost two, were chasing their big sister around with the help of Fino.

"Can you manage?" She finally asked Ebony, who rolled her eyes.

"Yeah, just about...she's a little monster." She blew a raspberry on her daughter's belly which made her giggle and chirrup. Ebony kissed her soft, downy cheek and hugged Matty to her. "But I do love you, squishy girl." She kissed her again, then handed her off, somewhat reluctantly to Cormac, who swung the child up in his arms, the usual look of elation all over his face. There was no question the man was totally besotted.

Atlas watched them, smiling. "What a weird family I have," he said, not for the first time, and laughed as they all groaned.

"Every time, you say that." Ebony touched his cheek, and he pulled her onto his lap, pressing his lips to hers.

Their extended family – Atlas and Ebony, Matty and Fino, Cormac and Lydia, Stanley and Vida, plus the Allende's – were enjoying a late summer barbeque together before Atlas and Ebony flew off for their long-awaited and well deserved honeymoon in the Seychelles.

"Two weeks of fucking you is all I want right now," Atlas murmured softly into Ebony's ear, and she shivered with excitement. "I'm going to have you as soon as we get to that villa on the beach, in every room, in every way, baby."

Ebony hid a groan of desire. "Well, you better keep that promise."

They both chuckled. Since Ebony had given birth to their daughter – Atlas still regarded Matty as his as well as Cormac's – they had grown even closer. When Ebony had woken after days of being in a post-surgery-induced coma, Atlas had spent hours apologizing to her until she stopped him and told him to kiss her instead. He happily obliged.

Ebony, in turn, was delighted that some good had come out of the horror of her and Fino's abduction. Cormac and Atlas were working on their relationship, Cormac dropping his custody suit. A devastated Stanley and Vida buried Bella – Ebony had defended the young woman and Stanley, in particular, had been grateful for that. "It's what Vida needs to hear now," he said softly, kissing Ebony's cheek. They found out from Mateo's murderer that he had tricked her into letting him into the grounds that day, and that the shame of it had led her to panic when Carson Franks began to blackmail her.

"Bella was simply too naïve," Stanley said, and Vida nodded. Vida herself had changed, become almost unrecognizable as the slightly annoying, vapid woman she had been. The loss of her only child had made her realize what she had with Stanley was precious, and as a result, they had never been closer.

Romy had recovered from her stabbing, although she still walked with a limp and used a cane. After months of rehabilitation, she was eager to get back to work at Haven. Knowing Blue was reticent, Atlas had made sure that Haven was a safe place to work for all of his staff as well as the residents. The move appeased Blue a little, but Romy was insistent on returning.

Carson Franks, knowing he was finished, made a plea-deal – he would plead guilty to avoid the death penalty and was sentenced to life imprisonment without the chance of parole. He would die behind bars. The relief they all felt that Romy, Atlas, Ebony and probably Fino would not need to testify was palpable.

LATER THAT NIGHT, Ebony kissed her daughter and held her tightly. "Are you sure you're going to be okay with her?"

Cormac rolled his eyes and Lydia – who, surprisingly, Ebony had become very close to over the months – smiled. "We can't wait, Ebs, don't worry. Matty is going to be spoiled rotten over the next two weeks."

Ebony grinned. "That's what I'm afraid of, Lyds."

Lydia laughed and took Matty from Ebony. "Look at this chubby face...adorable. Now, say goodbye to Mommy and Daddy, freckle."

Matty grinned and waved a hand at them, making them laugh. Matty was the happiest child Ebony had ever known – but then again, she was biased.

Atlas kissed his daughter. "Be good for Poppa and Lydia, little one. Love you." He turned and grabbed a passing Fino, swinging the laughing boy up into a hug. "And love you too, kiddo. Look after your sister for us."

"Will do, Pa." Fino kissed Atlas's cheek then went to hug Ebony. "Bye, Ma."

Ebony hugged him tightly. "Love you, pickle." She met Atlas's gaze over the top of Fino's head, both of them moved beyond words. It was the first time Fino had called them Ma and Pa.

THEY TALKED about it later on the plane, and then in the taxi as they travelled over the island. Outside, the ocean was a sparkling blue, the flora and fauna colorful, and the sun's heat soaked into their skins.

Atlas kept his promise. The moment the taxi driver had brought their bags into the villa and left with a generous tip, Atlas swung Ebony into his arms, making her giggle as he bore her off to the bedroom. It took two tries to find it, but as soon as she saw the huge bed, swathed in white mosquito netting, she grinned at him. Atlas dropped her onto the soft mattress and dropped between her legs, pushing up her dress and yanking her panties from her.

Ebony hardly had time to catch her breath before his mouth was on her, his tongue lashing around her clit, tasting and biting down on the sensitive bud until Ebony came, her body writhing beneath his as he moved to kiss her mouth. Atlas hitched her legs around his waist and thrust into her, making her moan with desire as he began to move, his rhythmic thrusts measured and deep. Ebony crushed her lips against his as they fucked hard, clawing at each other, the intensity increasing until they were both coming, moaning each other's name.

Making love late into the evening, they eventually collapsed from hunger and exhaustion, and enjoyed some food out on the veranda. Atlas stroked his hand through her hair and she leaned into his touch. "You know what's strange? I feel this is the first time we've really been alone since we met."

Ebony laughed. "Well, technically, we are. I had Matty in my belly the very first time we met so, yeah, you're right."

They both laughed. "You know what this means?"

"What?" Ebony was grinning, seeing the lascivious look in his eye, and knowing exactly what he was going to say.

"It means, my beautiful, sexy wife, that we can do very, very dirty stuff, all day, every day..."

Ebony leaned over and kissed him gently. "Just how dirty are we talking, Mr. Tigri?"

"Well," he said, pulling her onto his lap, "why don't we go back to bed and I'll show you exactly how dirty?"

Ebony giggled and stroked his face. "I love you so much, Atlas. So very much."

And he lifted her into his arms and took her back to bed.

IT WAS the middle of the night when she woke to a deep blue moonlight. Getting up, she went to the window and gazed out at the ocean, lapping at the little beach outside their villa. One year, six weeks, four days. Her life had completely changed in that time. Not only had she met Atlas, married him, and had her first child – *their* first child – she had become an adoptive mother and had survived kidnapping and injury.

All that...and now she was on the cusp of a major moment in her career. Over the last few months she had been working with Quartet record company and was about to release her first album. After this holiday, she would start to promote the record and then, in a few months' time, a tour. A tour of the best jazz clubs in America, starting with *Alley Cats* in Seattle down on 6th Avenue.

Ebony shivered in anticipation, then sighed happily as she felt Atlas's arms slide around her waist and he pressed his lips down on her shoulder.

"Bed got cold," he said and she chuckled.

"I doubt the temperature here drops below eighty degrees even at night."

Atlas laughed softly, "Okay, then, bed got empty."

Ebony turned in his arms and gazed up at him. He made her heart beat faster, just with that gorgeous green-eyed gaze. She smoothed her fingers over his features, drinking him in.

Atlas smiled down at her. "You're so beautiful. What were you thinking about?"

Ebony smiled, pressing her naked body against his and her lips against his mouth. "Tomorrow," she said, and led him back to bed.

THE END.

HER DARK MELODY EXTENDED EPILOGUE

September...

As they lazed about in their bed in their home in Seattle, Atlas Tigri chuckled and nudged his wife with his foot. "Hey, sleepyhead, here's a great one. *Verlaine's 'Angelheart' is a throwback to the sheer class and subtlety of Fitzgerald and Holiday, albeit, with a fiery sensuality which leave the listener's skin tingling—and perhaps in need of more than one post-coital cigarette.*"

Ebony sat up on their bed as Atlas skimmed through the reviews of her new album on his laptop. "It really says that?"

Atlas spun the computer around so she could read the review herself. "Wow." Ebony had been so nervous about releasing this album, her sophomore effort, because she had unleashed all her emotions on it; her love for Atlas, for her children, Matty and Fino, for her family. *Angelheart* was also a love letter to New Orleans, to the place where she had begun her musical career in clubs and cafés, and only the previous night, she had held her launch party at one of the first bars she'd ever sung, the *Hot Tin Roof*—which also happened to be the place where her boss' wife, Kym Clayton, had run away to before finding success with her own band. Roman Ford of the Quartet Record company had made sure the place was packed with both industry types, fans, and all of Ebony's family and friends.

They'd played a small set early in the afternoon so that Ebony and Atlas's children could help her celebrate. Ten-year-old Fino, her adoptive son, and three-year-old Matty, were, along with Atlas, her biggest cheerleaders and she'd wanted them to be part of the celebration. They'd had a riotous time, even the adults, who had stuck to soft drinks for this little party, enjoying the happy family vibe.

In the evening though, the atmosphere had changed, becoming adult and sensual. And when Ebony had performed some tracks from *Angelheart*, including the sexually-charged title track, she had seen Atlas, and only him, as he watched from the audience, his green eyes burning with desire for her. She had held his gaze throughout the song and later, when the children had been borne off by Ebony's brother and sister-in-law, Obe and Juno, for a weekend, Atlas and Ebony had returned to their hotel suite and made love for most of the night.

Now, she crawled over to him and kissed him. "Sorry, morning breath."

Atlas laughed. "You taste gorgeous, baby. Man, last night ..."

Ebony grinned and wriggled into his arms. Atlas pushed the computer aside and wrapped his arms around her. "I think it's safe to say, on this evidence, that your record is a critical success, baby. I'm so proud of you."

"Thank you for inspiring most of it," Ebony said, trailing her lips along his jawbone. "Scratchy."

Atlas grinned down at her. "I thought you liked me with a beard."

"I do. I like Scratchy." She nibbled at his chin and made him laugh.

"You've *named* my beard?"

"Not just your beard." They both started to laugh then, Atlas tickling her.

"You little nut job. Do I want to know what you've named my cock?"

"You might."

Atlas laughed loudly. "As long as it's not 'Tiny' or 'Floppy,' I don't care."

Ebony grinned. "It's definitely not either of those, big boy."

Atlas flipped her onto her back and hitched her legs around his waist. Ebony smiled up at him as she stroked his cock until it was ramrod hard and Atlas plunged it into her. Ebony moaned, the feel of him inside intoxicating, sending shivers through her body. As they moved together, they kissed, talking softly, murmuring each other's name.

Atlas increased his pace, slamming his hips as Ebony encouraged him deeper and deeper, then as he groaned and came, Ebony's body spasmed with her own release.

"God ..." She breathed as they recovered, "It just keeps getting better and better with you."

Atlas pressed his lips to hers. "Even after kids."

Ebony grinned. "Well, enjoy this weekend, baby; these moments we have to ourselves are rare."

"Which reminds me," Atlas said, looping his arm around her shoulders. "Your birthday in November ... I might have arranged for us to go away for another long weekend around then."

Ebony smiled. "You did?"

"Uh-huh. And, my love ... I thought we might try some new

things ... some new things that will involve you wearing little else but leather ..."

"Really?" Ebony chuckled, desire igniting in her eyes. "You do, do you?"

"Mm-hmm." He covered her body with his again. "What do you say, sweetheart? Wanna practice some mild BDSM?"

"With you, anything," she said and gasped as, grinning, Atlas thrust his cock back into her, and they made love again until dawn broke over the city.

November ...

"When you said a weekend break, silly me, I thought you meant a cabin down at Lake Tahoe," Ebony grinned as they looked out over the rooftops of Jaipur. "Not a freaking *palace* in India."

Atlas laughed. "Well, you never let me take you away or spend money on you, so I thought I would go way over the top."

They were standing on the rooftop terrace of the Maharajah's Pavilion at Raj Palace, enjoying the panoramic view of the lights as the day grew dark. Atlas had laughed when they had drawn up to the pavilion and Ebony's jaw had dropped. Inside, the four-floor apartment was sumptuous, and over the top in its decoration. Ebony had walked through each room slowly, drinking in every detail, every jeweled surface, every colorful decoration. In the bedroom, the huge gilded bed was comfortable, and no sooner had their busboy brought their luggage and left them alone, than Atlas had swept Ebony onto the bed.

"You like?"

"It's ... like some sort of fantasy world," Ebony was clearly shell-shocked. She grinned at him. "It's *so* different, Atlas, to anything I've ever experienced ... what a wonderful surprise."

"Well, that was the purpose of this vacation ... to try new

things." His gaze was intense on hers and she smiled, her own eyes sleepy with desire.

"Well, why don't you unwrap me and see what I have in store for you?"

His eyes lit up. "Oh, ho, ho, so I'm not the only one who's been keeping secrets?"

Ebony wriggled with pleasure and laughed. "Nope."

Atlas, grinning, slowly unbuttoned her lilac tea dress and then as he pulled the fabric apart, he drew in a sharp breath. "Jesus, Ebony ..."

A delicate gold chain crisscrossed her glorious body, making her dark skin glow, framing her breasts and her belly, sweeping between her legs. On her breasts were two gold nipple clamps. Atlas pressed his mouth to her throat, his hands running over her curves as Ebony stretched out, sighing happily. "Take your clothes off, Atlas; I want to see your body."

Atlas stripped, almost frenzied in his impatience to get back to her body. As he covered her body with his, Ebony ran her hands over his hard pecs, down his flat stomach, and took his cock in her hands. "I want to taste you."

"Together?"

She nodded and he moved so she could take his cock into her mouth while his own sought out her sex, lashing his tongue around her clit and dipping deep into her cunt. They brought each other to an exquisite orgasm, then Atlas hitched her legs around his waist and plunged his huge cock into her as she cried out his name. They fucked furiously, then as she came again, Atlas reached over and grabbed a thick dildo. "I'm going to fuck you with my dick in your cunt and this in your ass ... you ready?"

"Oh god, *yes* ..." Ebony was delirious with pleasure as Atlas hooked her ankles over his shoulder and slid the dildo into her ass as his cock ream her cunt mercilessly.

Ebony's brain whirled; her eyes rolled back as she was

fucked so expertly by her husband and when she came, she was astonished that it hit her so hard, her body jerked and she almost creamed the place down. She'd never let go as much as she did, and afterward, as she was catching her breath, she saw Atlas wasn't nearly done with her.

"Box of toys, little one," he said, and brought out a flat paddle. Ebony immediately rolled onto her stomach and squealed with pleasure as Atlas brought the paddle down hard on her buttocks. The quick, sharp pain, coupled with Atlas murmuring what he wanted to do to her made her cunt swell and dampen and she felt his hand snake between her legs, stroking her, sliding two fingers inside her, then three, then four as he stretched her out. His thumb stroked a gentle rhythm over her clit, juxtaposing the tenderness with the sting of the paddle.

"Your perfect little butt has goosebumps on it," Atlas said, and Ebony chuckled.

"Atlas ... fuck me. Fuck me until I pass out; fuck me until I scream and the whole of the city can hear me."

Atlas dropped the paddle and flipped her onto her back, his hard, throbbing cock straining to be inside her again and he thrust in hard, pinning her hands above her head, his green eyes dangerous and full of determination. It took Ebony's breath away when he was like this.

Atlas fucked her until she was, as promised, screaming, then finally let her recover. "We don't have do try everything tonight," he said, tender now, "but I have to say, the thought of having you in every way does turn me on."

Ebony trailed a finger down his chest, looking up at him from underneath her lashes. "As it does me ... I do have one favor to ask."

"What's that?"

Ebony grinned widely. "Do you mind if I take these nipple clamps off? They are *killing* me."

.   .   .

ATLAS HAD ARRANGED for them to go to dinner in an exclusive restaurant a little way out of the city center and as they ate, swooning over the food, Atlas stroked his finger down her cheek. "You know what I was thinking?"

"Usually sex, in your case," Ebony shot back with a grin. "But no, what?"

"One day, and I'm not saying soon, but one day, I'd like to have another child. *Our* child."

Ebony smiled. She knew what he meant even though they already considered Fino—who was Atlas's nephew in reality, and Matty, whose biological father wasn't Atlas—their children in every sense, making a baby that was truly their own was both of their dreams. "I know, darling. And if it wasn't for my career, I would have it tomorrow. But I do need to do this first."

"Oh, I know. Ebs, you can't imagine how proud I am. You're a superstar."

"Ha, not quite, but thank you, baby."

Atlas kissed her. "Mark my words ... this album is going to go global."

EBONY, skeptical, nevertheless appreciated his praise, but it wasn't until the following day when she even believed it a little. Roman Ford telephoned her, apologizing for interrupting her vacation. "Is Atlas with you at the moment? I think you should both hear this."

He sounded so excited that Ebony's heart began to thump harder as she switched the call to speakerphone. "Okay, Roman, go ahead."

"Ebony ... the Grammy nominations were announced this morning."

Ebony's heart leaped—but at the same time, she felt sick. Her first album had been roundly praised by critics but had failed to secure any Grammy love at all. Surely it would be the same this time ...?

"You've been nominated. Best Jazz Vocal Album for *Angelheart*."

Ebony let out her breath in a long whoosh. "Oh my God," she whispered as Atlas let out a whoop. Roman laughed.

"And ..."

Another Grammy nomination?? *Holy cr...* "And?"

"Album of the Year."

"*No.*" Ebony felt all the blood rush to her head and she sat down. Atlas wrapped his arms around her, his smile wide and triumphant.

"And ..." Roman was clearly having fun. "Song of the Year for the title track."

"No fucking *way* ..." Ebony rarely cursed, but her entire body was trembling. This couldn't be happening. "You're just teasing me now, Roman."

"*And ...*"

He surely wasn't going to say what she thought he was, was he? It was impossible.

"Record of the Year."

The big one. The Grammy *everybody* wanted. "You're making this up."

Both Roman and Atlas laughed. "I'm really not. Ebony, darling, congratulations. You deserve every moment of this. And, should you win, you'll be Quartet's second major Grammy winner. This is happening."

"God." Ebony put her face in her hands, overwhelmed. "This is just unbelievable."

"No, it isn't," Roman said cheerfully, "we all knew this was a special record. You let go on it and showed pure, unadulterated passion. By the way, I'll get in trouble if I don't pass on Kym's congratulations. She says she's just glad her band didn't release an album this year."

Ebony laughed. "Ha, lucky for me, rather. Thanks, Roman. I just need to absorb it, is all."

"Okay, honey, well, I'll leave you alone for the rest of your vacation. Come in to see me once you get back to Seattle."

"I promise. Bye, Roman."

AFTER SHE ENDED THE CALL, Ebony and Atlas stared at each other for a long moment, then erupted in a cacophony of cheering and whooping, hugging each other, rolling around on the floor like excited kids. Afterward they called Fino and Matty in the states and told them. Matty just gurgled happily down the phone, but Fino, who knew well what the Grammys meant, was excited and delighted. "Can I come? Can I come to the ceremony?"

"We'll see, champ," Atlas told his son, and laughed when he heard Fino's disgruntled sigh.

The rest of the vacation was a blur and as they left India for Seattle, Ebony sat back in her seat and smiled at her husband. "This has been the perfect break," she kissed him softly, "thank you. I'd love to bring the kids here one day. Perhaps not to a *palace*; we're not the Kardashians." She laughed as Atlas pulled a face.

"We could bring all three of our kids ... or four ... or five ..." He grinned as Ebony rolled her eyes, smiling.

"Slow your roll there, cowboy. Let's start with the third and see where we go."

Atlas brushed his lips against hers. "I love you, Grammy nominee Ebony Verlaine."

"As I love you, Grammy-nominee *seducer*, Atlas Tigri."

February ...

Ebony remembered that conversation now as she stood at the side of the stage at Madison Square Garden, waiting to go on to perform *Angelheart*. Swallowing down her nerves, which were made worse by the fact that she was opening the show, she took a deep breath in. The past three months had been a whirl of press, interviews, television performances and gigs, all orchestrated by Quartet to maximize her visibility and help her Grammy campaign.

Ebony had found it hard to go full-on with the self-promotion, but Atlas had told her, "All you have to do is show you believe in your work, show all that passion that went into making the record, and you'll be fine."

So, every time she went on a talk show, or did breakfast television, or talked to a hundred different journalists, not just from the music press, she tried to remember that and it got her through. This month, she was even schedule to do a photo shoot for *Cosmopolitan*.

"Me? A photoshoot?"

Emily Moore, her publicist, had rolled her eyes and grinned. "Ebony, you're stunning, and you have a unique look. *Of course,* the fashion magazines will want you."

Even now, as she was being announced, Ebony still felt like the newbie, even if she was wearing a skintight silver Versace dress and sky-high heels. Just don't fall over, she told herself, then felt her adrenaline spike as her introductory music began and she was waved out onto the stage.

Ebony couldn't remember much of the ceremony when she thought about it later. Her performance was greeted with wild and rapturous applause and when, forty-five minutes later, *Angelheart* was announced at the winner of the Best Jazz Vocal Album, she felt as if she were floating outside of her body. She was a freaking *Grammy* winner! *How the hell did that happen?* Atlas was beside himself with joy, picking her up and twirling her around before she made her way to the stage. Accepting her award, she thanked everybody who had been involved in making *Angelheart* happen—and then thanked Atlas and her children, a few tears escaping as she did.

Roman had told her that rarely did jazz albums or songs win the big awards, Album, Song, or Record of the Year, and so it proved with Album and Song which went to a pop act and a rap artist respectively. Ebony didn't care; the nominations were enough, and now she could enjoy the ceremony without nerves. She and Atlas snuck to the dressing rooms mid-ceremony and made love, giggling like teenagers afterward as they made their way back to their seats in the auditorium.

Madison Square Garden was packed, and when, as the final award, Record of the Year, was being announced, Ebony gazed around at the crowd, finally letting it sink in where she was. From tiny, sweaty clubs and bars to here. A sense of achievement and contentment settled over her.

Suddenly it seemed as if the noise of the place increased tenfold and every eye in the place turned on her. Beside her, Atlas and her friends were on their feet, roaring their approval. Ebony blinked and looked at Atlas in confusion. "What?"

His gorgeous face split with the widest smile, he pulled her to her feet and into his arms. "You won, baby, you won! Record of the Year."

Ebony felt all the blood drain from her face. "No way." But then she looked around and saw the entire place applauding at her and knew it was true. She had won the biggest award of the night.

. . .

"Did I actual sound coherent?" she asked Atlas in the cab back to their hotel, clutching her two gold Grammy awards.

Atlas laughed. "As coherent as I would sound in that situation. Baby, I cannot tell you how proud I am, and how much I love you. You made it, baby. You fucking *slayed* tonight."

Ebony giggled and kissed him. "Nothing without you, baby." She gazed at him. "I won everything I needed when I met you. But," she continued with a grin, hefting the awards in her hands, "these are pretty sweet too. And Fino and Matty can have one each in their rooms."

"They'll love it." Atlas pressed his mouth against hers then nuzzled her ear. "And when we get back to the hotel, baby, I'm going to give you something else heavy and hard."

Ebony burst out laughing and Atlas grinned. "You think I'm joking?"

"Oh, no, I'm just going to hold you to that ... all night long."

Ebony closed her eyes and shivered with pleasure. Atlas's huge, diamond-hard cock was buried deep in her cunt and his mouth was on her nipple, sucking and teasing it until it was unbearably sensitive. His hand stroked her clit and soon Ebony was gasping and coming hard as Atlas dominated her body. She felt his cock exploded inside her, filling her with his sweet, creamy cum. "Oh, how I love you, Atlas Tigri," she sighed as they caught their breath. "So, so much."

Atlas stroked her face. "As I love you."

"Maybe we should make another baby right now," Ebony said, her emotions in turmoil, a delirium of happiness.

Atlas smiled and kissed her. "How about we leave it to chance? I hate regimented things."

Ebony nodded. "Okay, I'll come off birth control and we'll roll the dice; what do you say?"

"I say, let's do it."

A FEW DAYS LATER, however, Ebony discovered that her burgeoning career was about to make being spontaneous a problem. At Quartet's offices, she met with Roman Ford and his business partner Dash Hamilton to talk about how to make the most of her Grammy win.

"We've already seen a three-hundred percent spike in sales," Dash grinned at her, "but what we want is longevity. Your genre has typically been based on album sales rather than singles, and if we play this right, *Angelheart* will still be selling thirty years from now. You have a once-in-a-lifetime talent, Ebony."

Ebony knew she shouldn't feel overwhelmed, but she still did. "So, what do we do next?"

Roman smiled. "Well, sadly, it will mean promotion, which means more interviews, performances ... and a tour. Here's the thing, Ebony. To really make the most of this situation, we're thinking a world tour. Which means time away from your family ... a lot of time."

Ebony was dismayed. "We can't do it in stages?"

"We could, and certainly there's scope for breaks between each country—to a certain extent. We are a business, after all, and we have to keep costs as low as we can to maximize profit. Which means, in effect, that when you go to Europe, you'll do two gigs in each capital where the biggest markets are, then move onto the next country. It'll be intense and exhausting ... but vital."

And there goes our plans for a baby, at least for a year or so. Ebony was surprised how much that upset her but she didn't feel she could say anything to Roman or Dash.

. . .

ATLAS LISTENED to what she had to say as they made dinner later that night. Ebony stirred the marinara sauce for the pasta, unable to look Atlas in the eye as she told him they would have to postpone their plans to have another baby for a year or so.

Atlas was quiet over dinner, but Fino and Matty kept up a steady conversation. They were both still enamored of their Grammy awards, sitting proudly on a bookshelf in each of their bedrooms. Ebony glanced over at Atlas, who was chewing his food, his eyes locked in the middle distance.

She was serving the children some fruit salad when he finally spoke. "Kids ... you know Momma is a superstar now? Well, she has to go away for a while and we may not see her much for the next year while she goes to sing around the world."

Matty looked wide-eyed. "A year?"

Ebony nodded, feeling wretched. Was there a hint of rancor in Atlas' words or was he merely being practical? Fino nodded sagely. "I knew you would have to go on tour, Ma. Can we come to some of the concerts?"

"Of course, Fino, baby ... but it might mean you won't see me for a long time. We can't interrupt our schooling, of course. Look," Ebony sighed. "I won't deny I hate the idea of being away from you all for so long. I *hate* it. But it *is* my job, and I owe it to Quartet. They have been so good to me."

Atlas reached over and took her hand. "I hate it too, but, yes. I think you have to do it."

LATER, in bed, Ebony snuggled up to him. "You can say what you really feel now, baby. It's going to mean we put off having our baby."

Atlas nodded. "And I won't pretend I'm not disappointed,

Ebony, and there's a part of me that wants to ask you to stay so badly, I could scream. But we're adults."

Ebony kissed his neck and stroked her hand down his body. "Show me how adult we are, baby."

Atlas smiled at her. "Actually, I'm kind of bushed."

The rejection stung a little but Ebony nodded. "Okay."

There was an awkward pause before Atlas tipped her chin up so he could meet her eyes. "I really am tired, baby; I'm not being ornery. I think I might have flu or something."

He pressed his lips against hers. "Hey, if I give you the flu, then you'll have to stay home." He grinned to show he was kidding and Ebony laughed.

"Would I get a note from my mom?"

"We could fake it."

Ebony giggled. "Silly man. I love you so much."

"And I, you, funny face. Listen, this tour ... we both know you have to do it. We can work it all out—I'll bring the kids out whenever I can ... and also arrange for us to have alone time as well. We can make this work."

"And then after the tour ... a baby." Ebony said determinedly. "Our baby. I want it so badly, baby."

"Me too, honey. We have all the time in the world."

A MONTH LATER, and Ebony stared out of the doctor's office, not believing what he was telling her and Atlas. Atlas didn't have the flu. He had cancer.

"The good news, if I can call it that, is we caught it early. We can operate to remove the rumor and if we get good margins, I don't even think you'll need chemo."

Atlas, as matter of fact as ever, nodded. "We need to get the surgery done before Ebony leaves for her tour, if that's possible, doc."

Ebony gaped at him. "Baby, there's no way I'm going on tour now. You need me."

"And I'll have you when I need you, but you're not canceling. Not for this. It's a blip, Ebony, is all."

"Cancer is not a *blip!*" Ebony, her nerves frayed and edgy, didn't mean to snap at her husband, especially not in front of the oncologist, but she was terrified. Her breath caught in her throat, and her voice broke. "This cannot be happening. Not you, Atlas, not you." Her tears began to fall and Atlas pulled her into his arms. The oncologist stood.

"I'll give you some privacy. Let me just say, Mrs. Tigri ... we caught it early. That's a huge advantage."

He nodded to Atlas who smiled at him. "Thanks, doc."

ALONE, Ebony let her terror out and sobbed. "I can't bear it, baby. Not you."

Atlas let her cry herself before he wiped her eyes. "Darling Ebony, my love, it's going to be okay. You saw the x-rays; it's a tiny tumor. The doc will cut it out and, boom, I'm back in business. No biggie."

Ebony leaned against him. "I'm staying with you."

"Nope." He smiled at her, his expression soft. "This is the oncology equivalent of having root canal is all. Done and done."

EBONY WAS FINALLY PERSUADED NOT to cancel the tour but, on the day of Atlas's surgery, she sat in the relatives' room, her arms tight around her body, worried sick. Juno and Obe were babysitting the kids, and Romy Allende was sitting with her. Romy's husband, Blue, was assisting the surgeon, using his privilege as Chief of Surgery to oversee his friend's case.

Romy hugged Ebony. "Blue says it'll be a breeze," she tried to reassure the terrified woman, but Ebony would not be comforted.

"If I lose him ..." She trailed off. Romy, who had been through two horrific attacks and had nearly died, smoothed Ebony's hair back from her face.

"I know, sweetheart, but he really is going to be okay. Blue told me there's no sign of it spreading and even if they have to take out one of his lungs—he still has another."

Ebony sighed. "He's never even smoked ... apart from a joint back in college."

"Which is probably why it's only a small tumor. Come on now, let's talk about something else. Your tour."

Ebony groaned. "God ... if you knew how little I wanted to do this tour ..."

"I do, but Atlas told me it's important and I agree. Ebony, you pressed pause for a while on your ambitions for yourself because of Fino and Matty and everything that went on. This is your reward, don't forget that. A career, something for you, outside of Atlas, and your life here. You are on the cusp of literally having it all. The Sisterhood says—don't you dare waste it."

Despite her nerves, Ebony had to laugh. "I know, you're right and I don't want to seem ungrateful, because I know how lucky I am. It's just ... Atlas and the kids mean everything to me."

"That's fair enough, but it's only one life we get, and you need to make sure you reach your potential."

"Yes, Mom."

Romy laughed. "Listen, I get it. But I also got shot *and* stabbed yet I'm *still* here. I'm grabbing everything because you never know when it's going to end."

AN HOUR LATER, Blue came to find them. As soon as Ebony saw his face, she began to smile. Blue sat down next to her. "Clean margins and the whole of the tumor excised. He's going to be fine, Ebony, just fine."

One year later ...

EBONY'S VOICE climbed to the final note and held it as the audience leaped to their feet, roaring their approval. The final night of her tour, back in her hometown of Seattle.

In the box, up and to the right of the stage, was her family. Atlas, his face reflecting the absolute love she felt for him, his body strong and healthy, held Matty in his arms as Fino jumped up and down in excitement. Her friends at Quartet were there, overjoyed at the tour's sellout success and the glowing reviews. Then there were Romy and Blue; Juno and Obe; Artemis and Dan; Magda and Stuart; Cormac and Lydia; Stanley and Vida. Her friends, her family, her life.

Ebony closed her eyes as she took the ovation and knew she had, as Romy predicted, managed to have it all. She blew kisses at her audience and waved at everyone she could see.

"Thank you, Seattle. I love you so much. Thank you, and see you again soon."

SHE APPLAUDED HER BAND, making sure she namechecked everyone and high-fived them all, then left the stage, her whole body electric with adrenaline. By the time she got back to her dressing room, having been stopped by well-wishers all the way, she smiled when she saw Atlas waiting for her.

"Hey, baby." She pressed her body against his as she kissed him. Atlas tangled his hand in her hair as his mouth moved against his.

"I told the kids," he said in a low, sensual voice, "that I was going to collect Mommy ... but we might be a little while."

Ebony grinned, reaching behind her to lock the door as Atlas slowly pulled the zipper on her dress down, then peeled it from her body. As he tugged the lacy cup of her bra down to take one dark red nipple into his mouth, Ebony sighed happily. "God, I love you, Atlas Tigri."

She smiled to herself as his mouth moved lower, his lips on the soft skin of her belly. Ebony hid a grin as he paused, and knew he was noticing the slight swell of her abdomen. He looked up her, his beautiful green eyes curious, and her own eyes filled with happy tears as she nodded.

"Yes," she whispered. "I completely lost track of my periods when I went on tour, but over the last few weeks, I'd been feeling odd. Not ill, exactly, but different. Because we had switched to condoms instead of the pill, I didn't think I could be pregnant yet. I wasn't sure at first, but I just did a test before I went on stage. We're having a baby, Atlas."

She laughed as his mouth formed a perfect 'O' of surprise, his face boyish, then he was gathering her up in his arms and showering her with kisses, making her giggle. Soon, though, they were naked and Atlas was thrusting his huge cock into her, and they fucked passionately, laughing and joking around the whole time.

As Ebony came, she clung to him, gazing into his eyes. "I love you so much, Atlas, and I can't wait for our child to be born."

"Me either, baby, me either."

SARAH CLELIA TIGRI was born five months later and as her parents gazed down at their first fully biological child, they knew their family was complete.

Three years later...

. . .

EBONY GATHERED ALL three of her children in her arms as they ran to her. Another long tour over, her third album, a huge success ... and now she was taking a well-deserved few months off with her family.

She and Atlas had bought a private villa in the Italian countryside, away from paparazzi, away from the bustle of the big cities. It had become their haven, and during the vacation months, they took their family to Italy, enjoying not only the summers but the winter holiday season too. It was Christmas again, and not only that, but Atlas's fortieth birthday celebrations.

For once, their villa was filled not just with their immediate family but all of their friends and family, and Ebony was throwing her husband a huge party.

As they changed for the party, Atlas tackled her to the floor and they made love, laughing and giggling. "Are we ever going to grow up?"

"God, I hope not." Atlas braced his arms as he thrust harder, making her moan with pleasure.

Ebony gazed up at him. "You're gorgeous."

He answered her with a grin and a final thrust of his hips before he came, Ebony reaching her own climax as she felt his seed filling her cunt. "God, I love you fucking me, Tigri."

"And we get to do it for the rest of our lives, baby." Atlas kissed her passionately and they smiled at each other as they caught their breaths. "You and I, we're for the long haul."

Ebony touched his face. "Happy birthday, baby."

Atlas smiled. "You're so beautiful, Ebony Tigri."

"Hold that thought, baby. We have a party to attend."

A few minutes later and they stood at the top of their staircase, looking down at the party in full flow beneath them. Ebony turned to her husband. "Before we go down, there's something I want to tell you."

"And what's that?"

She smiled. "I love you, is all."

Atlas smiled. "And that's all I'll ever need." And he led her down the stairs to greet their guests.

THE END.

ABOUT THE AUTHOR

Mrs. Love writes about smart, sexy women and the hot alpha billionaires who love them. She has found her own happily ever after with her dream husband and adorable 6 and 2 year old kids.

Currently, Michelle is hard at work on the next book in the series, and trying to stay off the Internet.

"Thank you for supporting an indie author. Anything you can do, whether it be writing a review, or even simply telling a fellow reader that you enjoyed this. Thanks

❀ Created with Vellum

CPSIA information can be obtained
at www.ICGtesting.com
Printed in the USA
BVHW041625011120
592283BV00011B/69